Advance Praise for *Storm*

"The best novels are not to be read but met. I have devoured many books on Luther, as well as his own writings. So I doubted Reg Grant's hero would rouse my interest. Then I picked up *Storm*. The cover swung open on a rich era. Germany was all about me, and I was lost for hours in an exciting world of faith and courage. Alas, the final page came. The back cover closed. I was instantly plunged into the world at hand—a drab planet by comparison."

—Dr. Calvin Miller, best-selling author

"*Storm* is sensational. Reg Grant did a masterful job making colorful Martin Luther come to life. I recommend this novel as a 'must read.'"

—Walt Kallestad, Senior Pastor, Community
Church of Joy, Evangelical Lutheran Church of
America

"Finally, a treatment of Luther that matches the charisma, power, and complexity of the man himself! From the fires of inspiration, Reg Grant the conjuror has called forth dramatic flare, amazing historical detail, and unmatched descriptive powers and forged them into a singularly classic work on one of Christianity's monolithic figures. Not since Umberto Eco's *The Name of the Rose* has a historical novel so enthralled me. *Storm* is a book for the ages. One of the best volumes I've ever read. From my favorite author."

—Jason Shepherd, Senior Writer, Insight for Living,
and coauthor of ten Bible-study books with
Charles R. Swindoll

STORM

REG GRANT

WATERBROOK
PRESS

STORM
PUBLISHED BY WATERBROOK PRESS
2375 Telstar Drive, Suite 160
Colorado Springs, Colorado 80920
A division of Random House, Inc.

Scripture quotations are drawn from the *New American Standard Bible* and the author's translation.
The *New American Standard Bible*® (NASB). © Copyright The Lockman Foundation 1960, 1962,
1963, 1968, 1971, 1972, 1973, 1975, 1977, 1995. Used by permission. (www.Lockman.org)

ISBN 1-57856-189-2

Published in association with the literary agency of Alive Communications, Inc.
7680 Goddard Street; Suite 200; Colorado Springs, CO 80920

Library of Congress Cataloging-in-Publication Data
Grant, Reg, 1954–
    Storm / Reg Grant.—1st ed.
        p. cm.
    ISBN 1-57856-189-2
        1. Luther, Martin, 1483–1546—Fiction. 2. Germany—History—1517–1648—Fiction.
    3. Germany—History—1273–1517—Fiction. 4. Reformation—Fiction. 5. Clergy—Fiction.
    I. Title.

PS3557.R2679 S76 2001
813'.54—dc21

                                                                    00-050975

Printed in the United States of America
2001—First Edition

10 9 8 7 6 5 4 3 2 1

To Lauren,
Castle Maker
Joy Pilot
Storm Chaser
My Heart's Delight

ACKNOWLEDGMENTS

Thanks, Lisa Bergren, for modeling patience. This "Storm" would have petered out years ago if you hadn't encouraged me to hang in there. Thanks, Traci DePree, for teaching me endurance and humility. Your edits were often better than my own drafts. Muchas gracias to my agent, Kathy Helmers, for continuing to believe in and encourage me. Blessings on Father David Balás for answering my questions regarding sixteenth-century Catholicism. Thanks to Ollie for showing me Jesus in your smile. Thanks to Gabe for being the rock that you are. Thanks and blessings on Nick for always asking, "How can I pray for you, Dad?" This book, Son, is the answer to many of your prayers. Keep praying. And a special thanks to Fred Holmes for your goodness and for all those "working" lunches at La Hacienda. Next time, I'm paying.

Cast of Characters

Albert		Archbishop of Mainz; opponent of Luther (historical)
Girolamo	Aleander	rector of the University of Paris; opponent of Luther (historical)
Katherine	von Bora	nun in the convent at Nimbschen; married to Luther in 1525 (historical)
Johann	Eck	Catholic theologian; debated Luther at Leipzig (historical)
John	Frederick	Luther's prince and protector (historical)
Elizabeth	von Gershom	daughter of Josel von Gershom (fictional)
Moira	Geyer	betrothed to Jaklein Rohrbach (fictional)
Thomas	Geyer	father of Moira; peasant working the land under Albert Toffler (fictional)
Charles V	Hapsburg	Holy Roman Emperor; violent opponent of Martin Luther (historical)
Ludwig	von Helfenstein	Catholic noble and a count; ruled Weinsburg; husband of Ingrid von Helfenstein (historical)
Ingrid	von Helfenstein	countess in Weinsburg; wife of Ludwig von Helfenstein (historical)
Zora "Black"	Hoffman	Gypsy witch in league with Rohrbach (historical)
Ulrich	von Hutten	Poet laureate of Germany and supporter of radical reform (historical)
Justus	Jonas	Luther's best friend (historical)
Martin	Luther	leader of the Reformation (historical)
Philip	Melanchthon	colleague and friend of Luther (historical)
Thomas	Munzer	radical reformer; enemy of Luther (historical)
Klaus	Reisner	miner; stepfather to Jacob Reuchlin; one of Luther's enemies (fictional)
Marta	Reisner	mother of Jonathan Reuchlin (fictional)
Jonathan	Reuchlin	one of Luther's students, then a colleague; a supporter of Luther (fictional)
Jacob "Jaklein"	Rohrbach	innkeeper and a leader of the peasant revolt (historical)
Maggie	Goetz/Schulz	adopted Elizabeth in Pforzheim (fictional)

Franz	von Sickingen	a knight and confidant of Ulrich von Hutten; proponent of radical reform (historical)
Elias	Sklaar	a Jewish doctor obsessed with Elizabeth von Gershom (fictional)
Georg	Spalatin	Luther's friend; chief advisor to Elector Frederick (historical)
Johannes	Staupitz	mentor to Luther who later became Vicar General; absolved Luther of his duties to the order to save his life (historical)
Albert	Toffler	most feared knight in Count Ludwig von Helfenstein's service (fictional)
Father	Winand	prior of Augustinian monastery in Erfurt where Luther became a priest; early instructor of Luther (historical)

POPES IN CHRONOLOGICAL ORDER

NAME	SERVICE
Alexander VI	(1492–1503)
Pius III	(1503-1503)
Julius II	(1503–1513)
Leo X	(1513–1521)
Adrian VI	(1522–1523)
Clement VII	(1523–1534)

Preface

In the sixteenth century a storm called the Reformation swept across Europe, ravaging as well as cleansing. The rumblings began in Rome, where the church was trying to figure out a way to finance an enormous new Saint Peter's Basilica. The corrupt leadership decided the fastest way to get the needed cash was to sell spiritual benefits called "indulgences" to parishioners. An indulgence was a paper signed by an emissary of the pope granting "early release" from purgatory—a spiritual place of suffering in Roman Catholic tradition, where the souls of the faithful have their sins burned away prior to entering heaven.

Sales were brisk. After all, what loving husband would be selfish enough to buy bread for his living children when the same money could purchase an indulgence that would relieve his dead wife of far greater suffering in the fires of purgatory? Surely, he must have reasoned, he and his family could sacrifice the few extra pennies Rome was requesting. But the Roman church's hunger for money had grown insatiable. It wasn't just the basilica that needed funding—there were wars to be fought; emperors to be crowned; influence, power, and glory to be gained. It all took money. And the demand for more of it charged the atmosphere.

Finally lightning struck in the person of a young cleric named Martin Luther. He condemned the abuse of indulgences and called for a return to the Scriptures, as opposed to the church Decretals or even the pope, as the supreme authority for the church. In that single demand, Luther stirred up the winds of radical change that produced a theological and political storm of epic proportions.

We follow in his footsteps as this sixteenth-century Odysseus strides across the years, exiting one adventure only to step into another with the turn of a page. He stood for grace in a graceless age. He admonished Christians to kiss the Son when they preferred to kiss bones dug from whited sepulchers. When deals were offered, when the siren song of compromise tempted him to turn aside, he lashed himself to the mast of the Scriptures and held his course. He never backed down. Never wavered. Martin Luther stood firm through the storm for what he believed to be just and true. He didn't tell us how to do it. He showed us how it should be done.

And we hear the rumble of thunder.

Chapter 1

A puff of wind kicked up the dust in the road. A killdeer cut across the late afternoon sky, an erratic check mark against blue-black clouds rolling in from the north. Lightning flashed briefly on the darkening horizon. A few seconds later thunder rumbled far across the summer fields.

Absently, Martin regarded his surroundings. He walked slowly, talking to himself, his eyes fixed now on the wagon rut in front of him, now on the windblown grass, now on the sky. His mood was as gray, his thoughts as confused, as the tumbling clouds. At least he didn't have to think about the road he was traveling. It was familiar, deeply grooved. Easy to follow. He had been praying for God to show him such a path for his life for months. He was twenty-one going on fifty, worried that his future was becoming his past without a present.

His parents were no help at all. Both of them, his father especially, insisted he finish his law degree in Erfurt. He could still hear his father's booming voice ringing off the rafters. "There's your path, Martin. There's your way," he had shouted. "God is guiding you, boy. But you're too dull to see it."

Martin's conscience gnawed at him. How many nights had his father, Hans, come home from the copper mines, dirty and tired and swearing he wouldn't spend his old age managing some shaft, scraping a living out of the mines he owned and operated. A good son, a dutiful

3

son, would save him from that. A lawyer could make enough to hire servants for his parents so his mother wouldn't have to haul wood for the fire. But Martin's studies had opened the Bible to him, and he was feeling the tug of something unfamiliar.

The reedy grass rippled in waves across the flat countryside. Most of the color had drained from the summer fields. It was as if a child had casually dipped a brush in dirty water and smeared the canvas, blurring the colors, leaving a confusion of lines, a lack of definition, an unimaginative sameness in its wake.

Then, suddenly, nothing. No wind. No sound. Martin stood still. Everything around him sharpened into hard-edged focus. The nearby trees, the unmoving grass, the gray clouds frozen on a cobalt blue background. He felt the hair rising on the back of his neck. He was aware of an odd metallic smell, a tingling in the air—then a violent burst of light and a crackling, sizzling sound and the boom of thunder. God's fire unleashed. He stood, staring, his eyes fixed above the road, gazing through what appeared to be a rip in an invisible curtain suspended between heaven and earth.

Through the gash in the celestial fabric he saw—sensed—a pulsing, divine presence, cloaked in glorious, multicolored light. All his senses ignited instantly, surged to full capacity and fused into a single responsive chord. Martin heard the colors, tasted the light, experienced a throbbing singularity that made him feel as if he were being consumed and filled all at the same time.

A movement caught his eye, and he dodged instinctively to his right, pulling away from the light. The rift began to close. Then more movement near the line of trees to his left—there, shadows hunching, lurching. His mind struggled to comprehend, to make sense of the darkling forms, bestial now, assuming greater definition each second…the clouds rolled. Clouds—yes, only the clouds casting shadows on the ground.

But there were too many—and too small for clouds and moving so fast, all toward him, so fast. Then he saw, in each shade, flashes of light, always in pairs as if they were eyes, glittering like silver-white points of fire wrapped in shadow. Demons. "Dark angels," his mother had called them. He recognized them from his nightmares, black obscenities loosed from the pit, skittering across the flat field toward him, hungry for his soul. He turned, stumbled.

Another lightning flash blinded him. He smelled burning hair. He fell. Blackness engulfed him.

He opened his eyes slowly. Something snuffled at his ear, then pulled away. He was off the road, lying in the ditch. He'd been there…how long? He felt something warm trickling down his cheek. He stared at his right hand. Blue fire arced off his fingertips. He closed his eyes. No pain. He drifted.

Rain, thunder, more lightning.

A dream lake boiled in front of him, boiled from the center outward. He woke, rolled over, and pushed himself out of the puddle that had formed beneath him. He crawled onto the rain-soaked earth and collapsed, rolling faceup to heaven. Cold shafts of stinging rain pierced him. He covered his face with his hands.

Flash!

Martin curled into a ball and felt the hot earth beneath him. He opened his eyes. A few feet in front of him, water in the ditch sizzled on an outcropping of rock. The thing snuffled his ear again. It was crawling over him. He tried to roll away, tried to push the shadow creature off, but he couldn't move. Something tugged at him, pulling him away. Voices called to him, but he couldn't speak, couldn't answer.

He looked again toward the light and saw…*Saint Anne! Patroness of miners, the one who helped in thunderstorms…*

Flash! *Flash!*

He screamed. "Help me, Saint Anne. I'll become a monk!"

A rush of flame.

Behind him.

Over him.

Wings of fire, hovering, arcing, blue.

Martin looked up. The shadow beast opened its jaws wide to devour him, to drag him into the burning abyss.

Martin screwed his eyes shut and screamed one last time.

Chapter 2

Seven-year-old Zora stumbled and fell, scraping her already bloody knees. Her mother, Sabine, and Marta, the townswoman who had come with them, jerked her to her feet and made her run on. She felt as if they had been running forever. She could still hear the dogs and the men on horses shouting after them, "Thieves! Witches! Over there! Over there!" Her legs ached, her lungs were burning. Zora hated those men. She wished them all dead.

In the moonlight, between the shadows, she could see the bulky sack her mother had slung over her back. Zora knew what was inside. Her mother had described it to her around the gypsy campfires. In the sack was a book of stars and spells, a book so filled with power that there was no other like it in all the world. One of the men back there in the dark—the one with the yellow eyes, her mother said—had stolen it from them years before. Sklaar was his name, and the book gave him great power and wisdom among the Jews. But this night, the gypsies had returned, and Zora's mother had taken back the book that was rightfully hers. Theirs. Zora had never seen the book, though she had imagined it often enough. Tonight, she would actually hold the prize in her own hands. Tonight she would look into the starbook and *see*.

Horses' hooves drummed through the streets, echoing off the buildings, a thudding rumble. The city gates were only a few blocks away. The riders passed them as they squatted behind a dung heap at the end of a dark alley. Zora saw the horses then, silhouetted against the moonwashed sky—their wide, black nostrils sucking in the night air, then blowing it out again in great huffs. One horse stopped. It reared, and the rider's wide eyes glinted yellow in the moonlight as they searched the stinking darkness at the end of the alley. Sklaar! He covered his nose, then spurred his mount on.

Each of the riders must have thought the others were watching the gates, because they had been left unguarded. The two women and the child slipped through the opening and across the road to the fields.

The night was still and warm as they ran across the rows of summer grain. The girl could hear the hunting hounds baying back along the streets and alleys of Anhalt-Dessau. The dogs were getting closer, would soon be through the city gates just ahead of their masters.

"The river! There!" Zora's mother whispered.

Fifty yards to their left, the western bank of the Mulde dropped off to a shallow crossing.

"Come on, come on! Stay off the rocks, or they'll pick up the scent. We can wade across here." Sabine plunged into the river and immediately sank to her waist but soon gained solid footing. She held the sack over her head and fought the current to the other side. Marta tried to pick up the little girl, but Zora shook her off and jumped into the river. Although Marta meant well, she was soft. She wasn't a gypsy. Zora was a good swimmer, and the current wasn't too strong. She saw Sabine clambering up the far bank. Zora was too old now to hope that her mother might look back.

Marta reached the bank at the same time as the girl. They climbed out of the river breathless, their hearts pounding, and clawed their way up the slippery bank, grabbing at roots to help them until they reached the top where Sabine was waiting. She heaved the sack over her shoulder again, and they began trotting upriver, keeping just inside the sparse tree line. The baying of the hounds was more distant now, muffled by the running river. As the women topped a small hill, then descended into a shallow valley, the distant barking faded completely.

"There's a barn close by," Sabine whispered.

"They'll find us," Marta said.

"No. It's an old hiding place for my people. We'll be safe there. Come on—across this field and through the woods on the other side." They ran, hunched over, thorns and nettles stinging and tearing their arms and bare legs. Zora bit her lip until it bled, but she kept quiet.

She strained to see the barn as she ran, but she could only make out a dark hulk back among the trees, obscured by a thorny tangle of vines and branches. When they reached the edge of the woods that bordered the field, they slowed to a fast walk. Sabine pulled Zora roughly through the outer branches and stopped in front of a high wall of bowed timber.

She moved a loose board. "Inside! Quick!" she said as she hurried the others into the darkness. The girl peered up and around, blinking, trying to see. Most of the high, broad roof had caved in, and one wall was missing. Thick roots and vines had erupted from the earth long years before like a misshapen hand grasping the old barn and holding it in place.

Sabine moved past her daughter and Marta, sliding through the darkness as quietly as a cat. A cloud passed, and moonlight streamed through the broken roof in slanting shafts. Zora could see her mother move in and out of the moonbeams, making her way to an empty stall. There she set the bag on a makeshift table—three dark planks balanced across two broken barrels. "Come!" she whispered as she reached into the bag and pulled out a flint and a lump of steel along with a deformed candle.

Their eyes had begun to adjust now to the deeper darkness of the barn's interior. Zora and Marta groped their way along, ducking under fallen rafters and rotting tree limbs until they reached the stall.

A spark from the flint startled them. Sabine tried it again, and a third time. Finally the tinder she had peeled from the rotting wood of the barn caught the flame. She lighted the candle and handed it to Marta. Then, reaching again into the bag with both hands, she pulled the ancient book out onto the table. She grabbed a handful of red-and-white speckled mushrooms from a pouch at her side and handed them to Zora and Marta. "Eat. Quick!"

Marta closed her eyes and squinted as she swallowed the first bite. "Not too much, is it?" she asked. "I threw up blood for days last time." Marta was soft. Not a gypsy.

"Just enough to open the gate," Sabine said, taking the last bite of her portion. Sabine chewed it into a mush and swallowed slowly. Zora watched, imagining the magic paste sliding down her mother's throat, making way for the change to come. Sabine closed her eyes and lifted her face to the moon. Zora lifted her face too, as she had so many times before, and together they inhaled the silvery light—that breath of moonlight that always changed her mother. Zora had been eating the mushrooms for months now, with little of the effect she desired. But tonight was special. Tonight there was a real chance she might see the things her mother saw.

"What is the book?" Zora asked quietly, eager to see inside its covers.

"Shh." Her mother breathed in deeply and let the air out in a whisper, her eyes still closed. "My book. My birthright. Mine. My mother…" She shook her head slightly and licked her lips. Zora felt it too. The mushrooms were already beginning to work. A numbness began creeping into her lips and along the edges of her tongue. The gate to the other side would begin to open soon. "We don't have much time." Sabine's voice was a raspy croak, and she no longer sounded like Zora's mother. Now she was something else. Something bigger. "Listen," Sabine rasped, and Zora strained to hear. "The stars are right. Nothing can stop us now."

"How long till the prophecy comes true?" Marta asked impatiently.

"The book will tell us." Zora glanced up through the hole in the roof and grinned. "The First Point of Aries," she whispered. "Tonight we will know." She opened the book and began leafing through its pages, muttering to herself. "Fat princes and pig kings. Not much time left for you, no. Not much time left at all for…"

"Shh!" Marta pressed her fingers to her lips. "Hear that? Listen!" Far away they could hear the baying of the hounds. "We shouldn't have stolen the book! I told you—"

Sabine whirled to face Marta, spitting out the words. "I took what's mine! He stole it from me, don't forget!"

"He is a powerful man—a doctor!"

"Don't be stupid. Of course he's powerful. He's had the book. Had it for years. And what's come of it? Him and his prince and all them with the power and the money have got rich and hid the truth from us, that's what. You want them to keep it? You want the time to pass? They know! Don't you see that? They know about the prophecy, and they want to hide it from us. Because they know if we find it, if we rise up at the appointed time, we'll strike them down and all their fine castles. And then their fisheries and their game and their lands will be ours."

The wind picked up. They could hear the hounds again.

Marta held the candle and peered through the cracks in the side-wall, straining to see. "Those dogs," she whispered, her pale face still pressed against the rough timber. "They tear you to bits. I've seen it. Nothin' left. That, or burn us for witches…"

"Quiet!" Sabine grabbed Marta by the sleeve. "They can't burn what they can't find," she whispered through clenched teeth. "Those hounds are still on the other side of the river. I heard 'em before from here. I know. Running water don't carry scent. Besides, it's got to be tonight, or the stars won't be right for another year, and by then it'll be too late. It's gotta be now, this night!"

She released Marta's sleeve, shoving her back. "Keep quiet and let me think." She turned to the book and began to leaf through the pages slowly, looking for something.

Marta leaned against a post and waited. Zora stood, gazing at the tattered book, scanning the pages as her mother carefully separated each one before turning it. She could *feel* her senses sharpen as she focused on the small world of that room, that hour. The musty odor of the crackling parchment, the dampness of the old barn, the flickering candlelight that cast otherworldly shadows on the walls of this place.

And the curious black and red marks on the paper itself—large runes etched along the borders of the pages. Some of them had been torn or burned. Scores of maps and charts filled the book's interior. The inky scratches flickered past Zora's eyes as the pages turned, the contours of the marks glimmering for an instant in the brief light as if each held a small fire of its own. Then, two blackened pages. Sabine reached into the sash at her waist and withdrew a short, sharp knife. She ran the tip along the seam between the pages, separating them carefully, revealing a solitary sheet folded into quarters.

"Ah, here we are," she sighed. She pushed the great book aside, then unfolded the sheet and laid it on the makeshift table. Long, stiff fingers smoothed the creases.

The yellowed parchment cracked as the woman pressed it flat against the wood. The three held their breath. Unfolded, the paper covered all but the outer edges of the table. Marta lowered the candle, and holding a small swatch of cloth beneath it to catch any hot wax, Zora could see that it was a map.

"What's this?" Marta whispered. "There's nothing on it."

They began to breathe again, slowly.

"Douse the candle," Sabine said, her eyes still fixed on the blank parchment.

Marta blew out the candle. Zora looked up, following her mother's gaze through the gaping hole in the roof. The crescent moon shone brightly, lighting that small circle of the barn's interior in a soft glow. Her mother turned the paper until it received the full light of the moon. At first nothing happened. Then, slowly, marks began to emerge—gold and silver, crimson, blue, sapphire and emerald letters and drawings. Zora had seen maps before but none like this. The lines on this map crisscrossed each other in a crazy arcing pattern. And she could see that the dots on the chart weren't towns and villages and forests.

"What are they?" she whispered.

"Stars, child," her mother murmured. "Now hush." The lines connecting the stars made pictures of animals, all named and numbered, with the larger stars colored in fiery paint. Small, spidery print—words, numbers, symbols—in a confusion of scripts and what the girl supposed must be languages filled the page edge to edge. Her eyes began to close. A heaviness pulled her down, closer to the map.

Suddenly the page was no longer flat. The lines disappeared as the map became an open window through which they could see the glowing script and figures floating on a coal black sea. Stars burned and tilted slowly as if suspended in oil. The words hovered now, above and around the star pictures, shimmering.

Sabine extended a bony finger and traced the outline of a star cluster that formed the constellation of the great fish. The letters glowed, sparkled along their edges.

"What is it?" Zora whispered.

Her mother continued to read the small print as she spoke absently, trying to maintain her concentration. "The twelfth sign. It's what we've needed—to know the time for war."

A night wind rattled the boards, whined through the cracks. Marta shook her head and looked around nervously. "Hurry," she said.

Sabine hissed and raised her hand. "Quiet, and light the candle."

The flint sparked, the tinder caught, and the candle lit the room. Instantly the page reverted to an empty piece of parchment. Sabine moved the map and pulled the old book back to the center of the table, opening it near the middle, just past the blackened pages. She turned the leaves of the book carefully, stopping in the middle of a page filled with columns of numbers and words. She began whispering, closed her eyes and breathed deeply, then opened them and looked down at the page, frowning. She spoke clearly, interpreting what she had read.

"One must come first. Son of a magic woman. Cloud chaser. Storm maker. Liar, hater, lover, fool. The prophecy follows him. Or is wound about him. I can't tell." She started to fold the star chart.

"When?" Marta whispered.

"Soon. He was baptized on Saint Martin's Day; that much is sure." She tucked the page inside the great book and closed it gently.

"What? He's a child, then?"

"No. He's grown. His turning is soon. On the wings of a storm."

"What kind of turning? To us? To the way?"

"Perhaps. We have to wait."

"It's the fish's gut, isn't it?" Marta asked. "The prophecy?"

"Yes. It starts with the one who is coming. The storm will break with him."

Zora stepped far back into the shadows, away from the others, and clung to one of the splintered posts that had once supported the roof. She had eaten the mushrooms on an empty stomach. Her tongue was burning now. Dizziness and nausea swept over her. She knelt beside the beam, then curled around it, grasping it, trying to hold on. But she felt herself being sucked into the darkness.

Zora sighed, moaned, then, with a jerk, went rigid. Her arms and fingers strained to break free of the limitations imposed by flesh. She could see her mother looking at her, could hear whispering from far, far away. She watched her mother take the candle from Marta and hold the flame near her face. They all were drifting now, floating farther out of reach, until they flickered…and died. Then she heard her mother's voice, still far away, though strong and clear, speak down the dark well. "You're to the other side, child. Shh. Look about. What do you see? Girl?"

Zora looked around at her black world and saw nothing. But she heard another voice whispering to her out of the darkness, then near her, then inside her. She began to murmur. She could hear her own voice, though it didn't sound like her voice at all but like a stranger's, speaking *for* her from the bottom of a deep, dry well. It spoke, and the voice came out of her mouth, low and guttural. "We will rise," she rasped. "On a high hill we will cut them down. Kill them all."

"Kill them?" her mother said. "Kill who, girl? Talk."

"The evil. The golden people. Kill them all."

"You see it? You see it, girl?"

"When? When will it be?" It was Marta's voice coming to her out of the darkness.

Zora started shaking, sweating. She felt herself falling, falling into herself, farther and farther into the void. She heard dogs in the darkness, chasing her. She could feel the black forms leaping at her, could feel them dragging her down, tearing at her, eating her alive. She saw their eyes only inches from her face, blacker than the night and burning wider and deeper than any fire. And the burning onyx eyes became an open door. She stepped across the threshold of the door, and the man with the moon-yellow eyes, Sklaar, was waiting there. He stepped aside, and the girl looked and saw, and smiled. And the breathless word formed on her lips. "Fire."

Then something struck her, and suddenly the room and the night came rushing back. She was in the old barn again, her cheek stinging, her mother shaking her. But she could still hear the baying of the hounds.

"Come on!" Marta whispered frantically.

Sabine blew out the candle, threw the book and the map in the sack, and jerked Zora to her feet.

Together, the three stumbled to the far wall of the great barn, climbed through a broken board, and ran into the forest. Zora could hear the men shouting as she ran. She could hear the horses drumming the earth on the far side of the great barn. Then it was all a jumble—a flash of black on black as the snarling dogs rushed in from the side. Marta grabbing at the bag, tearing it away as she ran beyond Zora's line of vision. Then—the dogs lunging at Zora, barking, tearing at her skin with their teeth before they turned back to her mother. Her mother's scream as the dogs dragged her down, ripping at her throat and legs. Zora turned and stumbled through the close tangle of trees, then through bushes and on and on until she fell, exhausted and alone.

Chapter 3

Jonathan Reuchlin curled up into a tight ball and tried to disappear into the darkest corner of the one-room hovel that was his home. He cupped a tiny sparrow in his hand, stroking its breast. It was dead. He had found it earlier in the day, hopping beside the path, its wing broken. As usual, Jonathan brought it home to feed it and to help it heal until it could fly again. He really thought this one would live, it was doing so well. Then his stepfather came home, drunk again and in a sour mood. He had heard the bird cheep, walked over to Jonathan, and without a word had crushed the little bird as Jonathan held it in his hands. Then he slapped him for good measure.

Jonathan looked at the man now as he sat hunched over a rough wooden table near the fireplace. He was wet head to foot, having just come in from the summer storm howling outside. Rain dripped in a steady stream through the cracked roof onto the floor, the table, and one corner of the large family bed in the center of the room.

Jonathan wiped away the tears from his stinging cheek as he watched the old brute lift his empty tankard again, looking for the last few drops. The boy's gaze shifted to the man's twisted shadow on the wall behind him, and he took in a short breath. He had suspected for weeks, but now he was sure. *"Yes,"* he thought. *"He's just been hiding in skin. He's really a troll."*

"By Saint Anne and the Virgin," the crumpled fellow sputtered, fixing a dull gaze on Jonathan's mother. "The boy's six. That's old enough, Marta. There's other wet-noses work the mines littler than him—bring in one, two pieces of silver a week. What does this lout bring in but half-dead birds? He ain't no better just because he's yours."

Jonathan turned to look at his mother and found that she was looking at him. Suddenly she rose from the bench and stood rigid.

What was she going to do? Talk to the troll? She had told Jonathan she was going to say something. But not now. No. She had to stop before the troll—did what? He wouldn't just hit her anymore. Not now that Jonathan knew he was a troll. Trolls ate people.

That was what happened to Jonathan's real father, they said, though his mother insisted that it was the mines and not trolls that had swallowed him in a cave-in five years before. One thing was sure. Whatever it was down there deep in the belly of the earth that had gobbled up his father and the other miners, it had spit up Klaus Reisner. They never found Jonathan's father or any of the other miners. Klaus was the only one who came out alive. Now Jonathan knew why. *Trolls don't eat other trolls.*

A few weeks later Klaus married Jonathan's mother. She had married the man to save them—her and Jonathan—she used to say. But it sounded to Jonathan as if she was apologizing for something bad she had done, especially when she talked about being confused and wishing she had taken more time to think before marrying again.

Still, she had said only a few days before, she was thinking straight now, and that was why she could finally say something to the animal squatting at her table. Because soon everything would be made right. Soon the prophecy upon which she hung all her hopes would begin to unfold, and this man wouldn't be able to hurt either of them anymore. She stole a glance at the bundle tucked back on the high shelf above the door, and Jonathan noticed she stood a bit straighter.

He stayed perfectly still as he heard her speak, her voice stronger than he had ever heard it before. "He's a child, Herr Reisner," she said, addressing her husband by his surname as he required. "Look at him. Johnny, stand," she whispered, motioning to her son.

The boy laid the dead sparrow in the straw, rose from the corner, and stood, shaking. His mother reached out and pulled him to her. She stood by his side, her hand around one shoulder.

Jonathan stared at the man. His long hair hung in filthy yellow strands that hid his face and almost touched the table. Jonathan's stomach turned, and he clenched his fists and held his breath, trying not to throw up. He felt his mother's hand trembling on his shoulder. "He's so young," she said. "It's your stories, sir, your stories about the mines that scare him to where he can't sleep nights."

Just the mention of the tales made the boy's skin crawl. Late at night, when he was half asleep, and the three of them were tumbled into the great bed together, his stepfather would whisper to him that the mines were really deep graves waiting to be filled. The thunder was God moving the great stones of heaven, and someday the sky would crack and the stones would fall, crushing everyone, and there would be nowhere, *nowhere*, to hide.

After she'd spoken, Klaus didn't move.

Marta's fingers dug into Jonathan's skin, but he didn't squirm. "The mines would take him, Herr Reisner," she said. "The mines would swallow him up like they did Robert." She caught her breath. Once, five years before, she had mentioned her first husband's name. Klaus had broken three of her ribs and knocked out two of her teeth. It was one of Jonathan's earliest memories. Since then, his mother hadn't dared whisper his real father's name to anyone but God and her son.

The boy glanced out a window, wishing himself away from this place, pretending not to hear.

The summer storm was growing. Wind and rain blew hard against the limestone walls of the house. Lightning cracked, thunder rolled. The sky was ready to split wide open. A gust of wind rushed down the chimney. A small cloud of smoke and ash billowed from the hearth in the center of the great room. Then the ash settled on the straw-covered floor like dirty snow as smoke curled around the lintel and up to the rafters, looking for a way out. Jonathan watched a mouse skitter along the floor, hugging the wall and disappearing under a small mound of moldy hay. He wondered if it knew a secret way to the outside.

Klaus tipped his empty tankard toward his gaping mouth and shook out a final drop of beer. Then he set the mug down gently. Jonathan took in a short breath and grasped his mother's hand more tightly. A slow grin creased one corner of his stepfather's overlarge mouth, then faded quickly. "Here, boy," he said.

She pushed him gently forward. He stood looking down at the floor, his hands behind his back, twisting his fingers.

Klaus sniffed loudly, then coughed and spat on the floor. "You remember how the thunders come?"

"Herr Reisner, please," Marta said in a tone Jonathan had never heard her use before.

Her husband shot up from the table. Jonathan was shocked that a man so fat could move so quickly. He lunged for his wife and had her hair in his hand before she could move. Jonathan closed his eyes. There were no words. Just the thump of the bench hitting the earthen floor, a sudden breath, and the muffled sound of hair being torn—it reminded Jonathan of weeds being ripped from the earth. And yet his mother hadn't screamed. She never did. The man dragged her across the room, opened the door, and threw her out into the muck in front of the house.

A rush of wind and rain blew in before he slammed the door with a bang and slid the bar in place. Klaus turned back into the room, righted the bench, and sat on it again as casually as if he had merely flicked away a flea. Jonathan was shaking, trying to stifle his sobs, certain the troll-man was about to eat him. His mother would be at the door, he knew, listening and praying for him. There was some comfort in that at least. Maybe it wouldn't hurt so much, with her praying.

Klaus cocked his head to one side, looking at the boy's small figure in front of him. The old man rubbed his bulbous red nose vigorously, then squinched it tightly between his thumb and forefinger. Jonathan lifted his eyes briefly and stole a glance at his stepfather. He was struck by the lines in his face. Most miners, his mother had told him, were dead by forty. Klaus Reisner was past forty-two. Only trolls lived to be that old.

A blast of thunder shook the house. Jonathan could feel it in the earth beneath his feet. He hunched his shoulders. Klaus grinned again and picked at his teeth with a splinter he peeled from the table. He leaned back and let out a tremendous belch.

Then, in a guttural whisper, "That's right. You know, don't you, scab? And here me thinkin' you was stupid! Naw, you remember how it is when the roof of the world comes down and it goes all black as the shaft on number three. You bein' so smart, you remember the time the sky almost cracked and split and we heard the great rocks move an' all. It's a wonder they didn't come tumblin' down that night—right through the cracks in the sky to land on us just like on those poor devils in number three. 'Course, you bein' so smart an' all, you know why they died." Of course Jonathan knew. The trolls had eaten them all. But he wasn't about to say, because then the need for pretending would be over and his stepfather would just eat him on the spot.

"Your ma says you're not the age for the mines yet. I say different. Any boy old enough to carry water's old enough to carry ore's what I say, and that's the God's truth." He spat out the last words loud enough for Marta to hear outside the door. "There's other boys workin' the mines younger'n you. You spent five years livin' off my hard work. Look here to me! If you want to stay you'll earn your keep, and then some. I want silver in my hand, boy, and you're gonna get it for me. Otherwise, there's the road. Now what'll it be?"

Jonathan could only stand and sob. He couldn't imagine living on the muddy streets of Stotternheim, and as far as he knew the only other towns in the world were the ghost villages in his stepfather's stories. He wanted desperately to ask his mother what he should do. He wished he were older. If he were only ten, he thought, then he would know the answer, then he would know what to do.

"Well?" the old man demanded. Lightning ripped the sky so close that the air crackled as the thunder slammed into the sides of the house. Marta screamed outside, and Jonathan broke for the door. The blast of thunder and the boy's quick movement caught Klaus off guard. Jonathan slid the bar out of its latch just as Klaus caught him and yanked him back into the room. Jonathan tripped and fell, cutting his head on the sharp corner of the bench.

The door flew open. There, leaning heavily against the frame, his head bowed and one arm around Marta for support, stood a young man. His nice clothes were muddy and torn, and Jonathan could tell he was hurt. Reisner, still red-faced and furious, kicked the boy on the floor, twice in the stomach and once, hard, in the head, sending him flying into the corner. "Johnny!" Marta screamed and rushed to him, bending to cradle her son's bleeding head in her arms. Jonathan wiped the blood and tears from his eyes and clung to his mother.

Klaus turned on the stranger. "You got no business here! Out! Get out!" He made a clumsy grab for the man's cloak and missed. With his hand to his head, the stranger stumbled back against the open door.

Klaus wheeled on his wife and tried to jerk her away, but Jonathan held on. Klaus struck her hard with his fist. She lost her hold on her son as Klaus grabbed her by the hair and threw her back across the room where she bounced off the wall next to the door. Before Klaus could move toward her again, the young man lunged at him. He jerked the miner around and pinned him to the wall, his forearm pressing firmly into the fat beneath his chin. "Leave them alone!" he shouted into Klaus's shocked face.

The young man blinked hard and shook his head. "You touch this woman or the boy again and I'll...I'll..." He put his left hand to his brow. His grip loosened and his knees buckled as he fell back, landing with a thud on the long bench by the table.

With the young man in a faint, Klaus suddenly found his courage again. He grabbed a heavy walking stick away from the wall and raised it high to smash in the intruder's head.

"No!" Jonathan heard his mother scream, saw a fast-moving shadow behind Klaus, then a sickening *crack*. Klaus dropped the stick and fell, unconscious and bleeding from the back of his skull. Standing behind him and slightly to the left, Jonathan saw his mother. The iron poker fell from her hand with a dull, metallic thump.

"I'm sorry," she offered to no one in particular as she moved back to care for her son. The young man had revived slightly. He sat up on the bench and stared at the man on the floor. "It'll take more than a knock to do him in," Marta said. "He'll come to in the morning and won't remember a thing. Help me move him." She grabbed Klaus's muddy boots while the young man took his wrists, and together they dragged him to the far corner of the hut where they deposited him in a heap of straw.

The stranger closed the door and sat on the edge of the table. "Sorry for the trouble," he said. Marta glanced at him as she knelt beside her boy. "I should introduce myself. My name is Martin. Martin Luther. Thank you for helping me."

"Marta Reisner, and it's me should be thanking you," she said as she lifted Jonathan and carried him to the great bed in the center of the room.

"How is the boy?"

"This boy? Oh, this boy's going to be fine as a new penny!" she said, smiling at her son. She found a jar of salve and began gently pressing the ointment into the gash on Jonathan's head. He cried out and turned his head away. "Shh, shh," she whispered, and then she sang a child's lullaby as she wrapped the wound with some narrow strips of cloth she had pulled from a bag beside the hearth.

Jonathan was feeling sick to his stomach, but he felt a little better if he turned on his side toward the fire. "You try to sleep some," his mother said, throwing a rough blanket over him and kissing him on the forehead. He closed his eyes but opened them again when she rose from the bed. He watched as she brought the medicine to Herr Luther at the table.

"Are you always this kind to strangers?" he asked, as she laid out the strips on the table.

"You saved my boy and me, Herr Luther," she said. "Are *you* always this kind to strangers?" She dipped two fingers into the ointment. "Now let me see that cut."

Jonathan had drifted off to sleep, but he opened his eyes at the sound of a particularly loud snort from his stepfather, still asleep in the corner. His mother was sitting on the bench beside Herr Luther. He had a bandage tied around his head, and she was tending to the large cut above his eye.

"The boy's too curious by a stretch," Jonathan heard his mother say quietly. "He thinks. Wants to know reading. Herr Reisner don't like it— wants him down the mines. Now," she continued before Herr Luther had a chance to respond. "What's this about lightning?"

Jonathan turned his head on the bed so that he could hear better. "Beg pardon?"

"Outside. You said something about lightning while I was helping you up."

"Oh, sorry. Still in a fog a bit. I was on the road to Erfurt when the storm hit," he said. "A bolt of lightning struck me down."

Jonathan could see his mother turn her head to look at her guest. "Never met a man struck by God's fire and lived to tell it," she said. "My father knew a man, though. Father said lightning goes to the blood and the brains—makes a man boil inside, so he's not right in the head no more. Father said it's the judgment of God or the blessing of the devil."

Jonathan could see Herr Luther's eyes. They looked like shiny black stones. "I heard God speak," he said. "Saint Anne spared me."

"Well, somebody was watching over you, that's sure," Marta said. She tilted his head back slightly to work the salve into another scrape. Jonathan could see him looking at something above the door. There, on a high shelf, was a cloth sack. Jonathan could see it himself without turning. Its neck had fallen open to reveal the yellowed pages of a book. Jonathan's mother had brought it home the night before, but she hadn't let him see it or even touch it. It had powers, she said.

"I see you're a scholar too," Herr Luther said.

"Hmm?" She continued to clean his wounds.

"The book."

She glanced up. "My first husband taught me to read," she said plainly.

Martin Luther sat up a bit straighter, cocked his head to the side, and raised his eyebrows. "Really? And what have you learned from your reading?"

"Secrets," she said, one corner of her mouth lifting in a half grin. "It's a book of charts, that's all. Charts and maps."

Herr Luther nodded. "Could I see it?"

Her smile faded. She lowered her head and focused on scraping the excess ointment off her fingers along the inside edge of the jar. "It ain't no Bible, sir," she said.

"I was just interested."

"Mmm." Marta laughed softly to herself and coughed. She glanced up at the book, then back to her guest. "There's a trouble comin', Herr Luther. Not now, not right away, but there's trouble comin' sure, on all them that's done wrong, on all them that takes things that ain't theirs." Her voice had an edge to it now, and her face had grown stern.

Herr Luther spoke softly. "There's always trouble. Nothing unusual in that," he said, leaning forward and resting his elbows on the table. "But I don't think it's coming. I think it's here all around us and we find it. We walk right into the middle of a storm just like I did this afternoon, but God protects us…"

She lifted her hand, enough to halt the young man in his speech. She extended her hand slowly and touched his cheek. "Cloud chaser…," she whispered so quietly Jonathan could barely hear her. He saw Herr Luther frown as if he didn't understand her.

Marta leaned in closer to him. "You're a baptized Christian, then?"

He hesitated. "I am, yes."

"What day?" she asked.

"Saint Martin's Day. Why?"

She stared at him without speaking and rubbed her brow. "Very well, then," she said quickly. "I'll show you some of what's in the book. But you be warned, sir. There'll be a price to pay for knowing, a price to pay, mark you," she said, rising suddenly and helping him up off the seat. She dragged the bench to a spot under the door and mounted it. "It's comin' soon," she said as she reached up to the shelf above the door. "That's what the stars say."

She removed the book carefully from the tattered sack. Deep, rust-colored stains streaked its torn sides. The old leather binding crumbled at Marta's touch, revealing the board covers beneath. She sat at the table and opened the book to a marked page. Jonathan could see the pages clearly, though at an angle. There was a picture, a woodcut of a fish with something spilling out of its belly.

"What's this, Frau Reisner?" Herr Luther wanted to know.

"It's the prophecy. A day's comin'. The day of the fish when all's goin' to be made right." She looked at her guest. "And you are part of it, Herr Luther."

"What?"

"You're part of the prophecy. I just learned it tonight, this very night. Like it or not. You will start this," she said, pointing to the wood-cut. "The stars say so."

"The stars have no voice, Frau Reisner, and I am not out to start a war."

Jonathan saw his mother close the book and push away from the table. "I see. God can speak in the lightning, but he can't speak in the stars." Herr Luther started to say something, then stopped. Jonathan's mother rose slowly and returned the volume to the sack, then to its place on the shelf above the door. Martin sat still, saying nothing as Marta sealed the medicine jar and returned it to its place and then lifted a shawl from a nail by the door.

"You need a bit more mending, and we're out of cloth for bandages." She wrapped the shawl around her shoulders. "The rain's let up some. I'm going to run over to Clara's house." Jonathan wanted to call out to her not to go, but she was out the door before he could say anything. His eyes went to Herr Luther, who sat still for a moment, staring at the closed door.

Jonathan tucked his hands in close to his chest. Martin lifted his eyes to the shelf above the door. He rose slowly from the bench and started to move.

"Hey!" Jonathan called out, sitting up in the middle of the bed.

Herr Luther turned sharply toward him. "Your mother's gone to get some bandages. She'll be right back."

"My head hurts," Jonathan said.

"I know," Herr Luther said softly as he crossed to the boy. "But do you know the best thing for a sore head? It's to lie still in bed. Come on, lie back down now."

"Don't talk to me like a little kid. I'm six years old after today."

"Sorry. I didn't mean…"

"Your name's Martin Luther. I heard Mama say," Jonathan said as he lay back in the straw.

"That's right," the man said, pausing slightly. "And you can call me Martin, Jonathan."

"You know my name," Jonathan said matter-of-factly.

"I know many secrets." Martin glanced over to where Jonathan's stepfather was snoring loudly. He looked at him for a moment, then back to Jonathan. "Jonathan," he said, assuming an air of great dignity and lowering his voice, "I must speak with you man to man. Now, as you know, the age of six is the age of promises."

"Mmm-hmm," Jonathan nodded.

"Therefore," Herr Luther continued, pressing his lips together and clearing his throat in an official-sounding way before continuing, "I, Martin Luther, scholar, commission you, Jonathan…"

"Reuchlin."

"Jonathan Reuchlin, to keep the following promise: to be obedient and kind to your mother tomorrow and every day after until the Lord comes back. Agreed?"

The boy pulled the blanket up under his chin. "Yes sir," Jonathan said. "Are you a conjurer, sir?"

"A conjurer? My that's a big word for such a little man. No." Martin smiled. "But soon I'm to be a monk, God willing."

"Do monks know secrets?" Jonathan asked.

"Oh yes. Now go to sleep." Martin tucked the blanket around the boy's shoulders.

"Can you tell me some?"

"Maybe someday. But first I have to learn them myself. Good night, Jonathan."

"Martin?"

"Yes?"

"Why are you going to be a monk?"

Martin tied his cloak under his chin. "Because I need to keep a promise too. Now, good night. And don't forget that promise."

"I won't."

As Martin crossed to the door, he pulled two coins from the purse at his belt and left them on the table. Then, closing the door gently behind him, he walked out into the now light rain on his way to Erfurt.

Chapter 4

Pope Julius II was in no mood for delays. The highly respected bishop of Fiesole, Father Amadori, and his assistant weren't actually due to arrive until the bells struck the noon hour, but Julius had been waiting, pacing for half the morning. The table for lunch had been prepared well in advance. The pope had ordered the wine poured and the cold lamb sliced, so as not to waste any time when the men arrived.

He wanted a good report on the projected expenses for the new basilica, and he wanted it quickly. Building delays on his papal palace and endless postponements on the plans for the basilica kept him constantly irritable. Julius had the power to keep a soul in purgatory for a million years, but the Vicar of Christ himself couldn't hurry the architects, the painters, or the stonemasons by so much as a month. He stood now, chafing under the layers of his semiformal robes, mopping his forehead with a cloth he would later dispense as a blessing.

He peered through a crack in one of the nine windows that lined the sidewall of the chamber. The fractured pane of heavily pebbled amber allowed him to see just enough of the outside world to discern the distorted movements of two men approaching the eastern entrance of the papal palace. Julius drew in a deep breath, returned to his chair, and sat, arranging his garments to drape just so, as if he lived in a perpetual state of studied casualness, awaiting his portrait.

The men entered the dining room silently. Alessandro stopped suddenly and stared slack-jawed at the pontiff sitting immobile as stone.

"Holiness," he stammered, "are we late? I was sure…"

"*We* are nothing. You, however…" He let his voice trail off as he pulled distractedly at his snow white beard. He would control the time now. He lifted his eyes heavenward with a look of long-suffering and exquisite humility. "But my time, whatever is left of it, shouldn't concern a young man such as yourself, busy as you are. Come, my son."

Alessandro hesitated, and Julius cast his eyes on him. "Come, come."

Alessandro, followed by his young colleague, walked around the end of the table and knelt before the pope. Then the bishop rose and spoke quietly. "Your Eminence, allow me to introduce the young man who has been so faithful in your service these last weeks. This is Father Giuliano D'Espino, an architect from Milan."

"An honor, Your Eminence—," Father D'Espino began, but the pope cut him off.

"Yes, well, in view of the lateness of the hour, gentlemen," he sighed, "please, sit and we will conduct business as we eat." They moved quickly, but the pope was already swallowing his second piece of lamb before they had pulled their chairs up to the table. Julius saw Giuliano look to Alessandro for direction. The senior priest closed his eyes for a moment, then began to eat. Giuliano said a hasty, silent prayer and crossed himself inconspicuously before picking up a bit of cold lamb.

Julius kept his eyes on his food. "You bring me good news," he said between sips of wine. It was a statement of fact, not a question. Julius was uncompromising in his desire for the best, the most expensive of everything. The basilica would be no different.

"I bring that which I know Your Eminence to value above all," he said, smiling slightly. "I bring you the truth."

"Don't be coy with me, Amadori. How much to build the new basilica?" The pope glared at Alessandro.

Alessandro sighed. "More than we have in the coffers of Rome," he said flatly.

Julius blinked once, picked at his teeth with the little finger of his right hand, then resumed chewing slowly. "You haven't answered my question, priest. How much?"

Julius could see the tendons in Alessandro's neck tighten. "I'm sure Your Eminence would prefer to preserve the beauty of a thousand years of our heritage…"

"What?"

"I've…worked out a compromise, a solution, Holiness, that we could afford. Of course the idea isn't all mine. I believe Pope Pius thought of it first. We could renovate—"

"Amadori, have you—?" Julius sputtered, turning in exasperation to Giuliano. "Has he lost his mind?" Alessandro pushed his chair back from the table and grasped nervously for the leather-bound case at his feet.

"If Your Holiness would consider…"

"I would consider finding a new bishop in Fiesole if I don't get some answers!" Julius exploded, suddenly rising from the table, upending his massive chair and spilling the red wine across the white brocade table-cloth. Both men sat frozen in place, not daring to move. Julius sneered as he noted the beads of perspiration dotting Alessandro's brow. Now he was getting their attention.

The Holy Father took several short steps, then turned to face Alessandro. The words slipped out in razor-thin sheets. "Pius. Pius wouldn't know the difference between a basilica and a privy. And besides that, he's dead."

"I meant no disrespect, Eminence," Alessandro said softly.

Julius grunted. He bent slightly and pushed his forefinger across the bottom of a dish, burrowing through a slick of strawberry sauce. He straightened slowly and considered the red stain running down his erect finger before stuffing it in his mouth. He turned and stared at a nearby window as if he could see through it to the small stone courtyard outside. He withdrew his finger and licked it. Then, with his gaze still fixed on the window frame, he extended his soiled hand toward Alessandro.

Julius knew the father to be a proud man. Now he would see if he was equally foolish. Father Amadori reached for a napkin and crawled forward to wipe the excess spittle from the pontiff's hand. Penance.

Without turning, Julius spoke, his voice a bit softer now. "What I'm trying to tell you, Father Alessandro, is that the basilica *will* be restored. The cost is irrelevant. I will have a decent resting place, is that understood?"

Alessandro responded immediately. "We understand, Holiness."

The pope caught a glimpse of Giuliano out of the corner of his eye. He was staring dumbly, his mouth slightly open. Alessandro cleared his throat and Giuliano picked up the cue. "Yes, Holiness," he said quickly.

Julius turned toward them. "You come here, waste my time. And what have you brought me? Nothing but whining! Nothing but excuses, Amadori. Your incompetence is insufferable." He paused to catch his breath, then let out a long, tired sigh. "I've decided to use Donato Bramante," he said, shaking his head sadly as if he had been sorely disappointed by one in whom he had high hopes. Alessandro's mouth fell open as the words found their mark. "Oh, I interviewed Sangallo and Giocondo. I looked at their plans." He spoke quickly, casually, as if he were slitting the throat of a pet lamb. He made a dismissive gesture and a hissing noise between his teeth before continuing, his voice smooth as oil. "I'm sure you will agree Donato's skill as an architect is unmatched."

Alessandro took an involuntary, shuddering breath. Julius despised his weakness. *You should have seen this coming,* Julius thought. "Come, come. You were aware, were you not, that I had employed Donato from the first day of my papacy. What, then? Did you hope the great architect would be too busy on the courtyard of the Belvedere to take on the basilica? I assure you, Donato is the greatest architect in Rome."

"Bramante is a great architect, Your Eminence, no doubt."

"Mmm? You know of one greater, my son?" Julius kept his tone pathetically condescending.

Alessandro stared at the floor, as if only half hearing the words.

"Come, come, Father Amadori, if you have information let's have it. You've made me late enough as it is."

Alessandro looked up slowly. "Perhaps Your Eminence knows of the artist Leonardo—"

"Of Vinci, yes," the pope interrupted. "Who hasn't heard of him? A cousin of yours, I believe."

"He's my nephew, Eminence, by my older brother's first wife." Alessandro's voice carried an edge of frustration. "But that's not why I—"

"Oh, of course not," Julius said, his words colorless, his sarcasm thick and bitter. "I'm sure he is wonderful, though I've heard he's as much the spendthrift as you are the pincher."

"Your Holiness would know spendthrifts best, I'm sure." Alessandro's eyes grew wide as if he'd realized what he'd just said. The pope stared at him icily.

"You and your associate may return to Fiesole, Father Amadori. I'm sure they are missing your thrift there.

"Oh, and I'm sure you will make a fine bishop, Father Giuliano," he continued, turning to the younger man.

Giuliano looked up, obviously surprised that Julius still knew he was in the room. "Bishop, Your Eminence?"

"Certainly." The pope glanced over his shoulder at Alessandro and smiled benignly. "Father Amadori will be much too busy managing all the moneys for the church in Fiesole. You are the new bishop there, Father Giuliano, effective immediately. That will be all."

Giuliano looked at Alessandro. His face was hard as stone, his eyes cold. Giuliano bowed hesitantly, and the two men started to withdraw. Nearly to the door, Giuliano turned back. "Holiness," he began, then he felt a strong hand on his shoulder.

"Don't," Amadori whispered. "Leave it. It's God's will."

"Wise counsel," Julius said as he reached for a piece of cheese and popped it into his mouth. "Your audience is ended. Good day." He rose to exit the room, making the priests wait until he reached the far end of the hall. He placed his hand on the door, then turned back. "Oh, and Godspeed, Amadori."

He made the sign of the cross, mopped his brow again, and walked out, smiling.

Chapter 5

Martin sat facing his mother, Margaret. She perched on the kitchen bench, straight and still as a stick—her characteristic pose when tension filled the house. Martin had come to regard her as rather a sun-bleached soul who had reduced life to achromatic duty, to gristle and sinew. She was someone he knew but with whom he had virtually nothing in common. He was also aware, even at the tender age of twenty-one, that change had always bullied itself into his mother's life. He could understand her wondering why any sane person would actively pursue the unknown as he was doing.

Martin's father, Hans, paced back and forth, pausing occasionally to stand in front of the empty hearth. His jowly face reddened as he stared into the blackened firepit.

"Ungrateful prig...," Hans muttered. Martin had made up his mind before setting foot in the door—he would not yield to this bullish man. And he *would* control his temper, even if his father didn't.

"I made a vow...," Martin began calmly.

Hans whirled on his son, pointing his finger. "By Saint Anne, don't talk to me about vows!"

"It's for Saint Anne I made the vow, Father," Martin said simply.

"You watch your lip, boy."

"I meant no disrespect, Father."

"I'll cut you off without a penny, Martin."

"As you wish, Father," Martin said. "Any money I receive as a monk would go to the church anyway."

"Shut up! That's what I wish." His father began pacing again. "It's a boy's dream, that's all."

"I said the words, Father."

"Words! Words mean nothing."

"Father—"

"Who are you," Han's interrupted, "that God should listen to you? God didn't hear you, Martin."

"How do you know?"

Hans looked at his wife. "That lightning's cooked his brains, that's what," Hans shouted. Margaret didn't respond. "Martin, listen to me." Hans took a deep breath before continuing, his voice more conciliatory. "The facts are you were struck by lightning and survived, thank God."

"Father, we've been through this—"

"Let me finish!" Hans thundered, losing control again. "The facts are also that I have paid good money to educate you, boy. All to make you a lawyer. And now you want to throw it all away because of a stupid vow. It's not right."

"It wasn't just the vow, Father," Martin said as calmly as he could. He knew his father and mother were counting on his work as a lawyer to support them in their old age. Entering the monastery would benefit them spiritually, but it would also mean his father would have to work for the rest of his life. Martin continued delicately. "You know I've been thinking about this for months now. Remember the afternoon before the storm I was here in this house asking your counsel."

"So? You think I've changed?" Hans roared. "Has my counsel changed? No! I don't allow my passions to blow me about like some piece of straw in the wind, boy. You will not leave your learning. You will stay in school. You will complete your law studies." Martin shook his head and looked down at the floor.

Hans walked over to his son and stood looking down at him. His voice shook as he spoke. "I promise you, Martin, you give up law, you give me up in the bargain."

Martin looked up. "Father—"

"That's it. That's my word on it."

Martin rose to his feet slowly and faced his father. "You taught me that a man's word is sacred. You said that the man who keeps his word keeps his honor."

"Aha! Good then! I have you there, Martin! You swore to me. You gave your word to me that you would finish school!"

"Father, put yourself in my place. If you had to choose, which vow would you break? One made to men or to God?"

"You made no vow to God."

"To Saint Anne, then. There's no difference."

"Don't sass me, boy! I will not stand here—"

"Would you have me break my vow to the saint of all miners? The saint who saved your life and the lives of your workmen a hundred times? You said so yourself. Should I break my vow to Saint Anne?"

Hans Luther stood, chewing on his lower lip, glaring at his son.

Martin knew he was right. But he also knew that he had pushed too far. He could see it in his father's eyes. He had just declared his allegiance to God over his father, and he wondered even then if he would ever be able to win back his father's love. Still, there was no taking the words back. He must leave.

Martin picked up the bag at his feet and crossed to the door. He hesitated, trying to think of a way to make the parting easier.

"Perhaps Jacob could take over," he began, referring to his brother, but his father turned away from him and held up his hand.

Martin looked at his mother. She stared vacantly at the empty space where Martin had been sitting. "I will write," he said, barely loud enough to be heard. "Please forgive me." He opened the door, then walked out, on his way to live a life of solitude and quiet reflection in the Augustinian order in Erfurt.

"I'll hold on to this," Father Basil said, indicating the sack in Martin's hand. Basil grasped the neck of the bag in his skeletal fingers and held it away from his side as if afraid it would touch him. "If Father Winand grants your request to join the order, you won't be needing it." The two men completed their short walk down the hallway to the cell occupied by the Prior of the Augustinian monastery in Erfurt.

"What should I say?" Martin asked, looking at the closed door.

"That's a question for God, my son. Not for a humble priest such as myself." As Basil turned to go, he said, "Don't dally. The Prior is a busy man." Then he disappeared into the shadows of the long hall.

"Well, Martin," he whispered to himself. "If you're going to live a life of prayer, I suppose this is a good place to start." He bowed his head and crossed himself quickly. "Father, give me the words. Please. Amen."

"Amen," said a second voice.

Martin looked up, surprised to see a tall, smiling priest standing in the archway of the open door.

"Oh, Father, I didn't hear the door—forgive me."

"Forgive you for what? Praying? There's plenty to forgive, Martin, but prayer isn't on the list." The white-haired priest was dressed in a coarse brown robe, tied at the waist with a small rope belt. He wore no shoes. "I'm Father Winand. Come in, please." He stepped aside to allow Martin to precede him into the small room. It felt like a cave hewn out of stone.

"What should I...?" Martin began.

"You are Martin Luther, son of Hans, the miner." Father Winand crossed behind his desk to sit on his stool. He rested his elbows on the desk, his chin on his folded hands, and looked directly at Martin with the bluest eyes Martin had ever seen.

"I knew your father too many years ago to count," Winand continued. He was a good farmer, as I recall. But I've heard he owns what, two copper mines now?"

"Three, Father," Martin whispered, embarrassed at his father's success.

"Mmm." Father Winand sat straight as an arrow on his stool. Martin noticed he hadn't blinked once since sitting down. "If you become a priest, will your parents be cared for?"

"I believe so, yes, Father. But he won't be able to run the mines forever, and he had set his heart on my becoming a lawyer and supporting him in his old age."

"I see. And am I to understand you wish to abandon your law studies and devote your life to the Augustinian way of life?"

"God desires it, Father."

"How do you know?"

"Two weeks ago I was caught in a terrible storm. A lightning bolt nearly killed me. I made a vow to Saint Anne that I would become a monk if she would save me. She did, and I intend to keep my promise. If not here, then in Eisleben or Weimar or Leipzig or Wittenberg. But this is my first choice."

"We are honored, I'm sure." Martin felt himself redden at the gentle sarcasm. "You are aware there is a fraternity of Saint Anne here at Erfurt?"

"I am aware, Father."

"Sounds like you've called yourself into God's service, Martin. It usually works the other way around."

"I've listened to my own voice for too long, Father. Now I hear the voice of God. This is his will."

The prior nodded and rested his hand on his cheek. "You may come to find, Martin, that God's will is clearer at twenty than at sixty. Do your parents know of your choice?"

Martin hesitated, not sure how much he should reveal. "They know I was thinking of it. I have brothers to provide for the worldly cares of my parents. I will provide for their spiritual well-being." Martin felt he was losing the advantage. He leaned forward, placing his hands on the edge of the desk. "Please, Father. Accept me. Accept my service."

The prior took a deep breath and let it out slowly. "There will be a year's probationary service as a novice—you understand this?"

Luther nodded.

"You will present yourself tomorrow morning."

"Thank you, Father."

"Come in, Basil," Father Winand called out to the closed door. Martin turned to look. He hadn't heard a knock. The door opened slowly, and Basil stuck his head in sheepishly.

"I was just passing by, and—"

"Basil," the prior interrupted, "Martin will be needing a place to sleep this evening. Will you see to it?"

"Of course, Father," the monk said, bowing, then turning to Martin. "Follow me."

The two men rose, and Martin trailed Basil. At the end of the hall, Basil paused before the closed door of his own cell. "Wait here," he said, then went inside. He returned quickly. In his hand was a small book.

"Do you know the liturgy for reception?" he whispered.

Martin shook his head. It hadn't occurred to him that he would have to memorize anything before he was accepted. Basil clucked like an old hen and stiffened a bit.

"Martin. It is Martin, isn't it?" His voice was as cold as the stone corridor, and had the inflated ring of a man who wanted more authority than he would ever deserve. "You say you want to present yourself as a novice and you haven't even read the liturgy? How will you know the answers when Father Winand asks you?"

Martin lowered his head. He didn't much care one way or the other what Basil thought, but he was ashamed to admit that the man was right on this point. Martin had always been one to leap before looking. "I thought to answer with my heart, Father."

Basil sighed pontifically. "Here, take this," he said impatiently, handing the book to Martin. Its edges were frayed and some of the pages torn.

"I can't take your own liturgy, Father," Martin said.

"Oh, for heaven's sake, it isn't mine. We have no property here, or don't you remember my telling you that when we talked earlier? Now take it."

"I'm sorry, I forgot. Thank you."

"You need to learn to listen, my young friend."

Martin glanced at him quickly. "I'm sure I will learn much of listening from you, Father," he said without a hint of a smile.

Basil looked at him through narrowed eyes for a moment, sniffed and tapped the book with his forefinger. "Page twenty-three. It's simple, really. Read it and memorize your part. This isn't the time or the place to trust your heart, Martin. Come." He turned and walked away with the young scholar following slowly behind.

Martin lay facedown in front of the altar. The early morning light filtered in through the eastern windows, washing the small chancel in a soft-waking glow. The choir stood to the right of the altar, ready to begin chanting the prescribed hymns. Martin felt the stones, cool and immutable against his hands and face. Father Winand stood on the steps of the altar and intoned the ancient Latin liturgy, "What seekest thou?"

Martin spoke the words into the stone pavement, to Saint Peter himself, and to Saint Anne. "God's grace and thy mercy."

Father Winand knelt and took Martin by the shoulders and helped him up. "Art thou married?"

Martin glanced behind the priest to the altar. Answering "no" was the same as vowing never to marry. He might perform weddings himself in the future, but he would never know the joys of a wife and children. He hoped the desire for women would pass with the promise. "No, Father."

"A bondsman?"

"No, Father"

"Art thou afflicted with any secret disease?"

"No, Father."

"Those entering the order of Augustinian Hermits renounce self-will. They content themselves with the daily bread, which the Lord provides. They wear the coarse cloth of the poor. They keep watch by night and labor by day, and in all things mortify the flesh. They embrace the reproach of poverty, the shame of begging, and the life of the cloister. Art thou prepared to take these burdens upon thyself?"

"Yes, with God's help," Martin replied, "and insofar as human frailty allows."

Father Winand nodded and smiled as the choir began its chant. One of the monks moved forward with a razor and bowl. He stood on a small stool behind Martin and began shaving the crown of his head. The tonsure left only a ring of hair, reminiscent of Christ's crown of thorns. Another monk stepped up with the habit of the novice and handed it to Martin. The novice knelt before his prior.

"Bless thou thy servant," Father Winand continued. "Hear, O Lord, our heartfelt pleas, and deign to confer thy blessing on this thy servant, whom in thy holy name we have clad in the habit of a monk, that he may continue with thy help faithful in thy church and merit eternal life through Jesus Christ our Lord. Amen."

As the last hymn began, Martin prostrated himself, his arms extended in the form of a cross. With the final strains, the brothers of the convent surrounded Martin and welcomed him with the kiss of peace. Father Winand held up his hand, and everyone grew still.

"Not he that hath begun but he that endureth to the end shall be saved." Then he smiled and embraced the novice. "Welcome, Brother Martin."

Chapter 6

"Martin, they're waiting." Martin could sense his friend Father Justus standing over him. He sounded almost as nervous at Martin felt. He knew they were waiting. But he couldn't move. Martin remained on the low stool, his head in his hands, rocking back and forth.

He heard Justus walk to the other side of the room and open the door just a bit, enough to look through the crack, Martin thought. The small sacristy room where Martin and Justus were waiting was located just off the south transept, at the far end of the church, near the altar. It was so situated that a peek through the door provided a full view of the congregation and the nave leading to the narthex and the central portal of the church. Justus whispered back into the room what he was seeing out in the chapel. "Father Winand just came in. Then Basil and some of the other deacons. Looks like they chose Malcolm to be your thurifer. I think he polished the incense bowl again last night."

"The choir?" Martin asked, his head still in his hands.

"They're all in place. The rest of the parishioners are pretty much in."

"Do you see—are there any guests yet?"

"Lots of people I don't recognize. I'm sure your father and mother are out there somewhere."

Martin moaned. "You're not helping," he said.

Justus sighed, then spoke again without glancing back at his friend. His voice was cool and matter-of-fact. "Bullheaded pride, is all it is. You think it's humility, but it's pride." Votive candles flickered on a low table just inside the narthex, casting soft shadows on the whitewashed walls.

Martin didn't move. "You know that's not it," he said, looking up. His voice was hoarse.

"I know you're afraid," Justus said. "But it isn't worth throwing the last two years down the drain. Martin, come here and look."

He rose slowly and crossed to the door. Justus moved so Martin could see through the opening. His mother and father were kneeling at the head of the aisle. Hans had just finished crossing himself and was helping Margaret to her feet. Behind them a cortege of twenty knights entered. They knelt one by one at the table, crossed themselves, and took their places near the rear of the chapel. Hans had brought an honor guard to celebrate the day. Martin leaned back against the wall, and Justus closed the door gently.

"What more do you want?" he asked. "This is a sign. It's God's blessing to have your father come—and like this!"

"Justus," Martin said quietly. "First you condemn me for being a prideful man, then you appeal to my pride. Make up your mind!"

"Martin, remember what Father Winand told you after you passed all the rest of us in Latin."

"You've reminded me often enough, Justus," Martin said, but Justus had already begun to repeat from memory Winand's admonition. "Pride," he said, "stands alongside Wisdom at the portal of the priesthood. Both are lovely at a distance. Both call out in the sweetest voices for men to enter. Be careful, Martin. Wisdom will exalt Christ in you. But Pride will exalt you in Christ."

Martin grunted.

"Look, if Father Winand didn't think you were ready to say Mass, do you think he would let you? And your mother and father—"

"Father Winand," Martin interrupted, smiling slightly at his friend, "has always had a misplaced confidence in my abilities. And as for my parents…"

Someone knocked at the door, and a muffled voice came from the other side. "Father Martin? Are you ready?" It was Basil, impatient as always.

"We'll be right there," Justus answered. They heard a "humph" and the sound of bare feet padding away on the cold stone.

A minute later the cloister bells began to chime, signaling the start of the Mass. The choir began to chant the psalm "O Sing unto the Lord a New Song."

Martin knew if he didn't go now, he would disappoint Father Winand, not to mention disgracing his father, and to top it all off, he might actually be guilty of pride, as Justus had suggested. He nodded to himself, and stood away from the wall. "O Mother of God, give me strength now," he said as he put his hand on the knob. "Thanks, Justus."

"You'll do fine," Justus whispered. "Now go."

Martin opened the door a bit too fast. It creaked loudly on its hinges and scraped the floor. All eyes turned to him, and he felt suddenly like a bride on her wedding day. Now the realization slammed into him. This was a marriage. A holy rite of divine matrimony. This day he would wed the Christ in the presence of witnesses. He would say the words that would transform the Host into the body and the wine into the blood of Christ, and grace would flow. Not even the angels had this privilege. Or this power.

Time and movement thickened all around him. He felt as though he were moving through waist-deep sand. He could feel his own heart beating against his ribs—could sense his blood rushing as a river through his veins.

It wasn't the order of the Mass that terrified him, or the fact that he was the designated celebrant. If anyone was prepared to celebrate his first Mass, it was Martin Luther. He had memorized the breviary so that he could have chanted the hymns and prayers for the canonical hours in his sleep. He knew the five "ordinaries"—the choral pieces—by heart. He had sung the Kyrie, the Gloria, the Credo, the Sanctus, and Agnus Dei every day for nearly two years. He had checked and rechecked his vestments. As far as he could tell they were properly arranged, though he still trembled over their placement. The more rigorous among the church hierarchy regarded a mistake here as worse than any one of the seven deadly sins. It was horrifying for Martin to think that he could actually wind up in hell over a misplaced piece of fabric.

He took some comfort in the knowledge that even if he made a mistake he wouldn't necessarily lose all hope of heaven since the virtue of the sacrament depended only on the motive of the celebrant's heart. He could always ask forgiveness for any error after the Mass. His motives, as far as he could tell, were pure. At least for the moment. Intellectually, he was ready.

But the thought of holding in his hands the broken body and the blood that had spilled from the veins of his Savior paralyzed him emotionally. He couldn't bring himself to look at anyone in the room. He stared transfixed at the wooden image of Christ hanging on the cross over the altar, stared into his hollowed eyes, and longed for him to speak.

Instead, Martin knew *he* must speak. Now. He made a rough start but began to feel a bit more confident midway through the Mass. Then he stood before the altar and gazed down at the bread and the wine. His legs began to tremble. He grasped the rim of the paten too tightly. It shook as he elevated the Host and mumbled the words, "We offer unto Thee, the living, the true, the eternal God."

With those words, the transformation of the bread and the wine was complete. He now held the blood and the flesh of the Savior of the world, and he was speaking directly to the living God, the One before whom angels in all their glory trembled at that moment. There he stood as Aaron the High Priest had stood before the Ark of the Covenant, as Israel had stood before the thundering God of Sinai, and he wondered that the Lord hadn't already reduced him to ash.

He glanced down and became aware at once of his father. Hans was sitting with his eyes closed. He opened them and looked back at Martin as if he sensed his son's gaze. Martin thought he detected a small nod, but he couldn't be sure. Then he ate the bread and drank the wine on behalf of the congregation. Having finished the Mass, he walked down from the altar, exhausted and limp, and embraced Father Winand.

"How was it, Father? Not too wide of the mark, I hope." His voice sounded high and a bit strained even to his own ears.

Father Winand smiled. "You didn't do this for me, my son. But I think the Lord would approve." He smiled again and patted Martin on the shoulder. "Now go enjoy your friends and family. This is a day to celebrate."

Martin turned and moved through the congratulatory line of his fellow monks and out to the fellowship hall. A table filled with food stretched the length of the room. All the brothers sat together on the far side of the table, while Martin's family and his father's guard took the seats of honor on the side nearest the chapel. Martin took his place quickly, with his father on his left, and his mother on his right. Winand began the meal with the traditional blessing. But following the "amen," he remained standing and addressed the group.

"God has twice blessed us this day," he began. Martin noticed his father lean back in his chair as if he were anticipating a fine dessert. "And we have Hans Luther to thank for both." A murmur circled the table as Father Winand paused dramatically. "First of all, Herr Luther has provided us a fine priest in Father Martin." Here everyone applauded politely. Martin blushed. "And," the priest continued slowly, drawing out the tension, "he has donated…twenty gulden to the work of the monastery!"

Applause erupted around the table, accompanied by audible gasps. Martin sat stunned, gaping open-mouthed at his father. Twenty gulden! Apparently his father had gotten along quite well without him. Martin recovered himself sufficiently to join in the applause just as it was dying down.

"God's blessings on you, Herr Luther!" Father Winand was beaming. He spread his arms and nodded toward the guests, and all began to enjoy the meal and quiet conversation. Hans said nothing but began eating hungrily. He still hadn't spoken to his son.

Martin turned to his father as he had a thousand times before, looking for a word of approval or of praise. He wasn't sure what to say. The words came out halting and unsure.

"Father, thank you for coming." Herr Luther looked at him between bites of chicken as if he weren't quite sure what Martin had said. Martin decided to risk another attempt. "I said—"

"You're welcome, Mr. Scholar," Hans said, grunting and glancing across Martin to his wife. "Oh, excuse me. *Father,*" he said, looking down into his plate, the last word dripping like acid from his tongue.

"I've often wondered," Martin said evenly, "why you objected so to my becoming a priest." Hans stopped eating and looked up at him as Martin continued, "And now, even now after all this, you're still not satisfied, are you?" By now others near them had stopped talking. Martin's mother looked up sharply at her son, catching his eye, but he ignored her. The room grew quiet. Hans clenched his hands. "Life here is so quiet and godly. I—"

Glaring at Martin, Hans banged the table with the flat of his hand and shot up out of his chair. "You, learned scholar!" he spat the words out, pointing a trembling finger at his son. "Have you never read in your Bible to honor your father and your mother?" Martin sat, stunned and speechless. Hans blustered on, oblivious to the gaping crowd of doctors and priests and honored guests. "Here you abandoned me and your mother, and you have the gall to ask me if I disapprove?"

Martin simply stared at him. Martin had obeyed the call of the Lord. He had forsaken father and mother and the allurements of this world for the sake of the gospel. And for the greater rewards that would come through his obedience. How could he make his father understand? He wasn't being selfish; he was serving an eternal good. "Father," he said firmly, "I labor for you in my prayers. I'll do you more good by my prayers than by my labor in the world."

Hans let out a deep sigh. The fire had spent itself, and now he was smoldering.

Martin continued, a bit more gently, "A voice from heaven called me, Father. He spoke to me from the thundercloud and called me to this office."

Hans glared at his son, obviously tired, bitter, and unconvinced. "God grant," he said loud enough for others to hear, "that it wasn't the voice of the devil."

APRIL 18, 1507
THE PAPAL PALACE, ROME

"Donato, you bring good news." Pope Julius forced a smile through yellowed and graying teeth.

"I bring news, Your Eminence. The simple fact is we need more money."

"If I get you your money, Donato, will it be finished in time?"

"Your Eminence has many years left, I'm sure."

Julius shot him a look that suggested he was in no mood for flattery.

"It's difficult to say just when it will be finished, Holiness. There are so many variables. The availability of the stone, the health of the masons, the weather. It's a miracle anything gets built when you think of the number of things that could go wrong."

Julius rubbed the weariness from his eyes and sighed. "You had little trouble demolishing the work of Constantine, *Maestro Ruinante*," he said tiredly. Bramante had garnered the nickname "Master Wrecker" for the zeal with which he had razed the thousand-year-old wooden basilica.

"Would that we could create as easily as we destroy, Your Eminence. Then we would be more gods than devils."

Julius considered the man before him. Donato Bramante was the fastest-working master architect in Rome. He built quickly, and yet his designs conveyed patient study and nuance. Five years before, Julius had fallen in love with Bramante's Tempietto in the courtyard of San Pietro in Montorio, the place of Saint Peter's crucifixion. It was a simple building, round, domed, and unadorned. Still, it was one of the most exquisite architectural pieces in all of Rome. It inspired Julius to plan something on a much larger scale.

"We're about a great work here, my friend," Julius said quietly. "You and I are rebuilding the Rome of the Caesars. We mustn't let it fade before it has begun."

"I'm afraid the accounts are quite low, Eminence," Bramante whispered apologetically. "My men are yet to be paid for last month's work."

Julius straightened himself in his chair, pressed his fingers together, and closed his eyes. He had been mulling over the money problem for some time and had come up with a solution weeks before.

He opened his eyes slowly and smiled, keeping his fingertips pressed together. He spoke as if he had just received a vision and was relaying it, unedited, to those who had ears to hear. "The Holy See will be pleased to grant certain spiritual *benefits* to those who wish to contribute to the great work of God in the rebuilding of Saint Peter's."

Donato's jaw went slack. His voice came out in a thin whisper. "An indulgence, Your Eminence?"

"Oh, it will take more than one, I'm sure," the pontiff said, rasping out a laugh. "We should see a tidy sum before long."

"This is genius, Holiness," Bramante said, bowing his head.

"God in his mercy has spoken to my heart, Donato. Imagine. For a modest investment we offer an indulgence that allows even the peasant in the street the chance to avoid suffering for his sins. Yes," he sighed, sitting back on his throne. "It's a lovely thought. Lovely."

Chapter 7

"And what will you be havin' today, your royal highness?" Thomas Geyer bowed deeply and doffed his cap. His three-year-old daughter, Moira, sitting on a blanket beside a cart full of freshly picked corn, squealed and clapped her hands.

"Milk, please, and cheese, please, Papa!" she said, collapsing into a fit of giggles. The soft sunlight danced on her golden curls.

"Cheese! Cheese, please?" Thomas exclaimed as if it were the most outlandish request ever made. Then he turned to a tall cornstalk and addressed it in a formal voice. "The princess would have some cheese, if you please!" He turned back to Moira and with a low, rumbly voice said, "Why we have the best, yes the very best green cheese straight from—where?" he asked, looking up.

"The moon!" Moira shouted, pointing up to the blue and crimson sky.

"Yes, the moon," Thomas said, pulling out the piece of cheese his wife had wrapped in a napkin. "And here it is just for you and your papa." He broke off a piece and handed it to Moira, who took it and started to wolf it down.

Thomas looked up to find the sun. It was closer to setting than he had realized, and the sky was painted orange and purple now. "Oh, goodness, Moira, we'd better get you home, or Mama will skin me standin'. Come on, girl, up we go." And with that he hoisted his little girl along with the blanket onto the back of the small, corn-filled cart, picked up the long pole handles, and started pulling the cart toward home.

"You there! Stop!" the horseman shouted as he trotted across the field. Five others followed on horses behind.

Thomas Geyer stopped and looked back over his shoulder. The men were riding toward him with their backs to the setting sun. Thomas shielded his eyes, but he still couldn't see their faces. He lowered the handles of the small wagon he had been pulling and lifted Moira out of the cart to stand beside him. The little wagon was top-heavy with corn, and a few ears spilled to the ground when Thomas lifted her. He had started to pick them up as the lead horseman reached him.

"Leave it!" the man ordered. He sat tall in his saddle, and Thomas could see he was outfitted as a nobleman. He carried a sword at his side, long and shining. His hair blew in long, thin wisps around his face.

Thomas took his daughter's hand, but he kept his eyes on the man on the horse. "Stay behind me, Moira," he whispered.

"You're trespassing. Get off this land now," the man said in a calm, even voice.

"This here is my corn, sir," Thomas said, glancing at the man's sword, then at the men behind him. "I growed it on my land for me and my wife and child, and to sell some." Little Moira began to cry. Instinctively, he picked her up. "Shh, shh, Moira."

"I'll say it once more," the nobleman said. "You are trespassing. On *my* land."

Thomas squinted up at him, then at the men behind him, then back again. "You're Toffler," he said. "I heard of you."

The group of horsemen laughed among themselves.

Thomas continued, "You take what don't belong to you."

"Oh, it belongs to me. His Holiness granted this land to His Majesty, and His Majesty granted it to me for fighting in the crusade—

along with everything on it, including that hut over there," he said, pointing to Thomas's home on the far side of the field. "And any pigs and chickens I happen to find in it. You do keep pigs in your home, don't you, peasant?" he asked, and all his men laughed again.

"I worked this land all my life, sir," Thomas said with all the courage he could garner. "And my father before me, and his father before him. It's my land by right."

"By right?" Toffler said, laughing. "You have no right to anything, you stupid pig!" He spat on the ground at Thomas's feet.

Thomas was beginning to shake. He felt Moira's arms around his neck and he held her tightly. He'd heard what these men did to anyone who crossed them. To their daughters. "You can't come here and—"

"I *can*, and you shut your mouth, or I'll kill you and the brat where you stand!" Toffler shouted. "Then I'll see to your wife."

Thomas stood still, holding Moira, saying nothing.

"You know, I'm in a good mood today, Kremler," Toffler said loudly, looking back to one of the rangers mounted behind him. The man to whom he was speaking nodded. Toffler turned back to address Thomas. "So I'll tell you what I'm going to do for you, peasant," he said. The men behind him snorted. "I'm going to let you work for me. You get to stay in your mudhole over there, and I'm only going to charge you, oh, let's say, all the corn you can grow. And I'll require more variety next planting season. After all, I've got men to feed, and they all have discerning tastes. You'll grow some vegetables here and strawberries. A patch over there closer to the river. Yes."

"And if I do these things, sir?" Thomas asked.

"You see these men behind me, peasant? These are my rangers. If you obey me, you will probably never see them again. And your little mud hen there," he said pointing at Moira, "gets to grow up and breed more little mud hens." Then he spurred his horse forward a couple of steps and pointed at Thomas. His voice was as cold and hard as ice. "But if you ever disobey me—if you try to steal any of my crops, rest assured, peasant, my rangers will find out. And you *will* see them again. And you will wish I had killed you this day." He turned his horse and spoke over his shoulder. "Leave the corn. My men will be back for it tomorrow. You get to keep what they leave behind." He rode away slowly, his men following.

Thomas could hear them laughing all the way to the tree line and then into the woods that led to the river road. When he couldn't hear them anymore, he bent down and picked up a mud-spattered ear of corn off the ground and looked at it. He felt Moira's grip tighten around his neck. He kissed her shoulder and dropped the corn back to the ground as he turned and walked slowly toward his home.

AUGUST 1509
ERFURT

It was Father Johannes Staupitz's turn to take confession, but it had been a long day, and he hoped he might use the time to catch a quick nap before evening prayers. He had barely settled onto the short bench and found a comfortable spot leaning back into the narrow corner of the confessional when he heard the familiar *pat, pat, pat* of bare feet on stone. Perhaps this would be an easy one.

The supplicant entered the booth, knelt before the lattice which divided the confessional in half, crossed himself, and bowed his head. "Father, forgive me for I have sinned," he moaned.

"Martin? Is that you?" Father Staupitz asked.

"Will you hear my confession, Father?"

"Martin, this is the fifth time this week."

Luther was silent for a moment. "I know, Father. Perhaps I should begin by confessing my own lack of compassion for your well-being. You have been most patient. But my heart condemns me, and I don't know where else to turn."

"Very well. Go on."

"I have fallen into the sin of pride again."

"How so this time?" Father Staupitz asked, fighting a yawn.

"My Greek classes. I did well on my exams this afternoon."

"And?"

"I…felt as if I had earned the honor on my own merits."

"Martin—"

"As if this mind, this flesh"—here he plucked hard at his rough cowl—"had produced something worthy of honor."

"This is no serious sin, my son," Father Staupitz said softly.

"Oh, Father, that is my problem. The smaller I regard my sins, the greater they become in God's sight. Why has he made me so weak?" he asked hotly. Father Staupitz could see his hands folded into a hard fist. "I know," he continued with a shuddering breath, "I know in my heart that he is angry with me."

Father Staupitz prayed a silent prayer, asking the Lord for wisdom in how to help bind up the wounds of this young cleric. Martin's guilt over the slightest imperfection in his conduct or thought was consuming him, transforming what should have been a life of peace and joy into an extended death sentence full of self-loathing. Then an idea flashed through his mind. "Martin, listen to me. I am your confessor, true?"

"Yes, Father."

"And I am your friend, also true?"

"By God's grace, Father."

"Then you can trust me when I tell you this." Father Staupitz leaned in close to the lattice that separated him from his oversensitive son in the faith and whispered through the curved pieces of wood, "Martin, God is not angry with you. You are angry with God."

NOVEMBER 1510
ERFURT

Martin stood at the foot of his bed, staring down at his half-packed bag. The same one he had brought with him from home five years before. He breathed in the cold air and exhaled a frosty cloud. He was grateful for the cold. He had fewer stomach problems in the winter months, but this morning his belly had started churning again. He rubbed the rope that cinched his habit.

He took little notice of Justus standing at the head of the bed with his arms folded, trying to keep warm. "I can't believe you get to go," Justus said for the fiftieth time.

"I'm sure I've forgotten something," Martin said, ignoring the comment. He stood shaking his head and rubbing the back of his neck. Justus laughed and crossed the room.

"Martin," he said, slapping him on the shoulder, "you could put everything you own in that old sack and still have room left over."

Martin smiled. "I almost have," he said. The journey to Rome would take several weeks and, as usual, he wanted to be thorough. He had been appointed to represent the Augustinians before the pope in Rome over the role of the monasteries in church reform. It was an honor to be chosen, but the trip would be hard.

"Here," Justus said, offering a small, bulging sack to Martin. "It's just a few onions. You'll need them to spice up that bland Roman food."

Martin chuckled as he took the smaller sack and stuffed it into the larger one. "Onion breath. That should impress His Holiness."

There was a light knock at the door. "Father Martin?" It was Basil.

Justus flattened his back against the wall and mouthed the words, "I'm not here."

Martin frowned in mock severity as he moved to the door.

"Father Mar—"

"Yes, Father?" Martin answered, opening the door with a suppressed grin.

Basil entered and stopped suddenly, placing his hand a bit too dramatically over his heart. "Why, Father Justus," he said. *He isn't much of an actor,* Martin thought. Martin detested his prissy correctness and constant suspicion, but Basil appealed to Martin's sometimes twisted sense of humor. "I thought you would be tending garden by this hour."

"Is there something we can do for you, Father Basil?" Martin asked quickly. "I'm afraid I'm a bit preoccupied with preparations for the trip and all."

Basil turned to Martin with a sneer. "As a matter of fact, there isn't. Father Winand has called for Father Justus." Martin and Justus exchanged a quick, wondering glance as Justus walked out into the corridor. Basil closed the door behind him, avoiding Martin's gaze.

Father Winand looked up at the gentle knock at his cell door.

"Enter," he said, pushing his stool back and rising to greet his visitors.

Basil and Justus stepped inside. "Good to see you, Justus. Thank you, Basil, that will be all for now." Basil bowed stiffly and started to leave.

"Oh, Basil," Winand interrupted, "Father Justus will be occupied with extra duties for the next few weeks. I've asked Father Jonathan and Father Charles to share the kitchen and chapel cleaning duties for Justus in his absence."

"I shall be glad to supervise—," Basil began, but Winand cut him off.

"And I know how you love the garden, so I saved its tending for you."

Justus stifled a laugh with a cough and covered his mouth quickly.

"Father, I…I don't know what to say," Basil stammered, sounding even more wounded than he looked. "I know Father Richard would…," he stuttered.

"Nonsense. You've earned it," Winand said strongly, smiling as warmly as ever.

As soon as Basil had closed the door behind him, Father Winand smiled at Justus and resumed his place on the stool behind the table. "Justus," he said slowly. "I'll keep this short. I've been praying about this for weeks. I should have spoken to you earlier, but I wasn't sure." He eyed Justus carefully. "I know Father Martin is capable in debate."

"He's the best I've ever seen, Father," he said honestly.

"Still," Winand continued, "he is, at times, a bit headstrong. He could make more enemies than friends."

"A strong personality, Father—"

"Martin can be insufferable, and you know it as well as I. He doesn't—*sometimes* he doesn't know when to stop arguing."

Justus made no reply.

Winand took a deep breath and let it out slowly. He stared at Justus, measuring him. "You know why I'm sending Martin to Rome."

"To argue our case before the Holy Father."

"He will appeal the decision of the vicar general to open our monasteries to the world. I have no doubt Martin will represent our cause well," he said rather stiffly. "Still, I believe it wise to send someone with him. To calm him when he gets too hot in debate. A friend he can lean on for strength. You know his health hasn't been the best these last few months. Fasting is good for the soul, but God made the body to survive on food, not just prayers. Martin needs a traveling companion, and I can't think of a wiser choice than you. There now." He exhaled, as if a great weight had been lifted from his shoulders. He noticed that Justus did the same. "I know it's short notice, so I'm not going to order you to go. I'm asking you as a favor to me and to the order. Will you…?"

"Yes, Father. It would be an honor. Thank you for considering me."

Winand leaned over and shook Justus's hand. "You're welcome, my son. Now I believe you have some packing to do. Don't forget an extra cloak. Rome's as cold as we are this time of year." Justus stood to walk out of the room. "Oh, Justus," Winand said as he opened the door. "Make sure Martin takes his cloak as well. Just between us, his penchant for mortifying the flesh needs a bit of balance."

"Certainly, Father." Justus nodded and was gone. Winand smiled as he heard the sound of bare feet running down the corridor.

Chapter 8

Six weeks of hard travel brought Martin and Justus in view of the Tiber River. They had celebrated Christmas Mass on the northeastern branch of the Via Aemelia and had spent the last few days traveling southwest on the relatively safe Via Flaminia. It would carry them all the way to Rome.

Martin marveled at the straightness of the ancient Roman roads compared to the serpentine paths of Germany. He had studied them before they left and now provided a running commentary for Justus. "Do you realize," he said one cold and rain-soaked day, "that this road has been in place since the beginning of the second century before Christ? More than fifteen hundred years. Look at it. To this day it still drains efficiently, the sand is still tightly packed between the stones, the foundations are as strong as ever."

Justus looked at him without comment and continued to walk, drawing his hood tighter about his head.

"And imagine what they used for mortar?" Martin continued. "A mixture of volcanic ash called 'pozzolana' and lime. Strong enough to last forever. It's a fine highway for the gospel of Christ, Justus!" Martin laughed out loud, but Justus trudged on in silence. Martin lifted his face and shouted into the rain, "And a fine day for a walk, Old Devil! A beautiful day for a stroll on the King's Road."

Justus smiled in spite of himself and shook his head. "Saint

58

Christopher protect us," he said, loudly enough for Martin to hear. "The man'll debate the devil himself to gain some conversation!"

Day after cold, dreary day passed one step at a time. The early January wind sliced through the coarse cloth of the priests' habits, chilling their flesh and thickening their blood. Justus hunched against the wind, shivering badly as the two men crossed the bridge that spanned the Tiber.

The dark river churned beneath them, sluggish and weary. Martin tried to stand straight into the wind, tried to maintain the stoic air that was supposed to distinguish a member of the Augustinian Eremites. But ice crystals stung his face, forcing him to lift his arm in self-defense. He smiled to himself. The mortification of the flesh. It was all part of the price of salvation. He had longed to come to Rome ever since he had entered the monastery five years before. Where else in the world but in Rome could he make sure of his salvation?

The merits of the saints were relatively inexpensive to obtain here. By simply viewing the relics of the saints, one could gain an indulgence, relief for himself or a loved one from at least some of the fires of purgatory— sometimes thousands of years per holy relic. Martin had studied about the relics, but he still wasn't sure if the smaller bones—of the foot, for example—would be as efficacious as, say, a femur. Perhaps he would ask.

His pulse quickened at the thought of how much there was to see. The single crypt of Saint Callistus alone held forty popes and seventy-six thousand martyrs. Here he could view part of Moses' burning bush. Here he could receive an indulgence of fourteen hundred years just by viewing one of the coins paid to Judas for betraying his Lord. He would be sure to make his way to the south side of the city to view the Appian gate. There pilgrims could still see white spots on the walls—the places where stones had turned to snowballs when the mob had tried to kill Saint Peter. Along the way he would try to take in the portrait of the Blessed Virgin which Saint Luke had painted with his own hand.

The two men made their way through the Flaminian gate and onto the Via Corso that would carry them into the heart of Rome. A narrow street off the Corso led them to the edge of the winding Tiber, which they had to cross once more before making the short walk to the Vatican. A few minutes later Justus paused before the Sistine Chapel, the crowning achievement of the papal palace.

Martin continued to walk toward the chapel. Justus could have all the art in Rome for all he cared.

The two turned and walked quickly along the southern perimeter. Martin and Justus picked their way through the excavation for the new basilica of Saint Peter, skirted the edges of the deep-set piers, and made their way across the courtyard toward the old palace.

"Excuse me," Martin said to one of the monks as he was passing in the great hall. "I'm Father Martin and this is Father Justus. We just arrived from Erfurt..."

"Erfurt!" He leaned in close to the two priests, his voice dropping to a conspiratorial whisper. "You Augustinians! You've come to appeal, am I right?"

"Yes, we—," Justus began.

The monk interrupted with a guttural laugh. "You can forget it," he said, his voice back to full volume.

"What?" Martin asked, trying to keep his voice level.

"You'll never get in the door. I came from Nuremberg weeks ago, and there have been a few others. They won't even hear an appeal. The Holy Father considers the case closed."

"But it's our right to appeal," Martin objected. "We've traveled six weeks. They can't just lock us out without a hearing!"

The short man rolled his eyes. "Maybe you haven't heard, brother, but the Holy Father has been given the keys to more than an appeals court."

"This has nothing to do with apostolic succession," Martin said, barely controlling his anger.

Justus stepped in. "Father Martin—"

The monk cut him off. "It has everything to do with it if you are on the side opposite His Holiness," he said. "Listen, my friends, my advice is to forget all this and invest your time in, uh, the more pleasurable pursuits Rome has to offer." He winked and patted Martin on the shoulder, then walked away without looking back. "There's a great deal here to enjoy," he said too loudly, "if you have the money." His laughter echoed off the massive stone walls. None of the other passing monks took any notice.

Martin and Justus watched him go, too stunned and too angry to speak. They walked outside to a small fountain, dropped their sacks at their feet, and sat on the wide stone ledge. "What now?" Justus asked after a few minutes.

Martin didn't answer at first. Then he straightened suddenly and smiled at his friend. "What do we normally do when we run across an ass braying in the street?"

Justus laughed. "We ignore him for the stupid beast he is and get on with our business." They picked up their sacks and started back across the courtyard to the hall.

Martin glanced back over his shoulder and then to Justus. "This priest was a good reminder to us, Justus. I was beginning to think how nice it would be to return to the applause of Erfurt after I'd won the appeal here in Rome. Luther, the great debater! But he reminded me that if God gives us victory, it's his victory to give, not mine to take. And if he gives the other side victory, then so be it."

Justus sighed and shook his head. "It's hard for me to believe that God really wants the world to invade the monasteries."

Martin stopped walking and looked at his friend. "Maybe that isn't it," he said. "What if we have it backward? Maybe the way to real, lasting reform is for the monasteries to invade the world."

Martin was fuming. Justus sat beside him with his hands folded. The man who stood between Luther and an audience with the pope,

General Giles of Viterbo, sat on the opposite side of the desk and placed his head in his hands, as if trying to calm himself. He had allowed Martin and Justus a brief audience—not to present an appeal, they had realized, but as a professional courtesy in view of their long trip. He took a deep breath and began to straighten the papers on his desk as if the interview was nearing its end and he was ready to tidy up and go home.

"I don't understand, Father," Martin said, the urgency in his voice giving an edge to his words. "We have the right to appeal. The monasteries of Saxony simply wish to be left alone in this. God called us out of the world, and now we are being forced to invite the world inside our walls."

"Father Martin!" Giles interrupted, holding up his hand to halt Luther, his voice hard and flat. "How can I make this clear to you? I have tried to be patient, but you won't listen to reason."

"Reason?" Luther exclaimed. "What reason can there—"

"No, no!" Giles shot up from his chair and pointed at Luther. "Stop right there! I've heard enough. Now I've told you—I've shown you, here." He reached down and lifted several of the official documents from the desk and waved them in front of Luther's face. "On the twenty-fourth of March 1506, His Holiness issued a bull declaring that the Saxon congregation was obligated to obey the general. You know this!" He slammed the papers down on the desk. "The decision has been made, and you must abide by the decision of the Holy See."

"And I will, Father," Luther said, his coal black eyes boring through the general. "But obedience to the general does not expressly deny our right to appeal!"

"It's implied in the bull, Father!"

"Show me!" Luther shouted, slamming his fist into the table.

Justus reached out and touched Luther's arm, trying to quiet him before he got them both thrown into the papal dungeon. "Martin, enough!" he whispered, but Luther pulled away.

"That's all I ask!" he said, still glaring at the general. "Show me the words on the page that deny Saxony the right to appeal!"

"Very well then!" Giles grabbed a long white quill from the stand beside his desk and jabbed it into the inkpot, while he grabbed his register with his other hand and opened it to the current date. He scribbled out a rough line and shoved the book across the table to Luther. "There!" he said.

Luther turned the book and read the words, "According to the laws, the Germans are forbidden to appeal."

Martin approached the Scala Sancta with tears in his eyes. The twenty-eight steps that had once stood in front of the palace of Pontius Pilate rose before him, the top lost in heaven, as far as Martin was concerned. All the other merits he had earned while in Rome paled in comparison to the benefit of climbing these steps on hands and knees, repeating the "Our Father" at each step. Here he would be able to set his beloved grandfather Heine Luther free from the flames of purgatory. At the twenty-eighth step, with the last "amen," angels would bring Heine into the very presence of God.

But there would be a benefit for Martin, too. For on the twenty-eighth step, he was sure he would find the peace of God that had been eluding him for so many years. He hadn't found it in his law studies, or in Erfurt, and to his surprise, he hadn't yet found it in Rome. Martin reasoned it was because all his other pursuits had been tainted with selfish desires. Even here, he prayed that his longing for God's peace wouldn't disqualify his service.

He knelt and began his prayers quietly, his head bowed, his hands resting on each step. He didn't open his eyes until he reached the top, until he said his last "amen" and crossed himself. Justus was standing there, waiting for him when he rose to his feet. Tears streamed down Martin's face.

Justus smiled and put his hand on his friend's shoulder. "God bless you, Martin. You've done a wonderful thing."

Martin took in a deep breath and shook his head. "Who knows?" he said, staring back down the steps at the long line of pilgrims climbing their way to the top. "Who knows if it's true?"

SEPTEMBER 1511
ERFURT

"Sit down, Martin," Father Winand motioned to the stool opposite his desk. He sat hunched over a sheaf of papers with his head on his fist. He didn't look up as Martin took his seat. "I'm afraid I have some bad news."

"I think I know, Father," Martin said quietly.

Father Winand sat up straight and looked Martin in the eye. "I have to transfer you. You leave me no choice, Martin."

"There's always a choice, Father," Martin said simply. But his eyes were burning.

"No," Winand insisted. "Not this time. Not unless you think I should keep you and lose the rest of the faculty here at Erfurt?"

Martin shrugged. "What I think doesn't really matter here."

"It did matter, Martin."

"Only as long as I voted with the majority of my colleagues."

"Your opinion," Winand pressed, "mattered as long as you supported the cause of our order. You cut your own throat, and you know it. Once you sided with Staupitz and his concessions, you set yourself up for a fall. There was nothing I could do. "

"Father Staupitz's concessions were honorable, Father. He called on both sides to compromise to achieve the reform we all want. We might have lost the battle, but we would have won the war."

"So you say," Winand said, bitterness and disappointment creasing his voice. "But that's not the way the rest see it, Martin. That's not the way I see it. If you had only had the courage to stand fast with the rest of us." Winand waved his hand dismissively, as if he were clearing the air of a bad smell. "At any rate, I have to let you go if I'm to have any peace around here."

Martin nodded, and smiled slightly to himself. "It wasn't just the concessions, was it, Father?"

Winand looked away and took in a deep breath, then let it out slowly.

Martin waited.

"There were some," Winand began, still looking at some speck on the wall, "who said you were beginning to question the efficacy of certain, uh—"

"Indulgences, Father."

"It's true then?" Winand asked.

"The word I believe you used was 'question.' Yes, I admit I question, not to disprove or deny but to find the truth. I'm searching for the truth, Father, that's all. Surely that's what we all want. How can we find it if we quit looking?"

"Martin, Martin. There's no need to look any further. The answers have all been found. Long ago. By men far wiser than you. That's your failing, my son. Pride. Thinking you're going to find something new and then make something of it."

Martin considered a rejoinder but decided to let it rest. He folded his hands in his lap and asked, "Where are you sending me?"

Father Winand stared at him for a moment without speaking. A great sadness shone in his eyes. He was saying good-bye to one he had come to love as a son, and Martin knew he would probably never see him again after this night. "I'm sending you to Wittenberg."

Chapter 9

Johannes Reuchlin leaned out the window of the carriage and swore at the coachman. Seventeen-year-old Jonathan suppressed a smile as his uncle pulled his head inside and settled back onto his hard board seat. Johannes Reuchlin, philologist and traveling professor of Hebrew studies, delighted in taking his nephew on annual outings. Jonathan enjoyed the trips as well. Through his famous uncle he was being given the chance to see the would outside Stotternheim. This year they were going to Rosheim, a city with a large concentration of Jews from whom Johannes hoped to extract considerable information on the Talmud.

"Well," he huffed, adjusting his spectacles, "he's managed to hit every pothole and rock in the last sixty miles. I may as well give this up altogether," and with a few clumsy movements he gathered the leaves of the Hebrew manuscripts he had been studying and stuffed them into a black leather valise.

"Oh, good heavens, I'm getting too old for this," he said, mopping his brow. "Now, Jonathan, if God spares us and we arrive in one piece, I'm going straight up to the room and lie down. You can have a look around town as long as you're back by dinner. Agreed?"

"How much farther is it, Uncle?" Jonathan asked.

"Oh," his uncle said, looking back out the window, "another three

66

or four miles is all. Back by supper then," he said, returning to his original statement.

"By supper, yes sir."

The sun was halfway down the sky when the coachman pulled up in front of the Red Feather Inn. Jonathan helped carry the trunk that contained their clothes upstairs, then he was off to find adventure.

Adventure in Rosheim, however, was slow in coming. After walking the streets for an hour, Jonathan found himself on the outskirts of the city, near a stream which ran inside steep banks. An arched rock bridge spanned the water and opened onto a winding road that led away into a copse of trees and then out into a broad meadow. Jonathan crossed halfway over, where he stopped and rested his elbows on the low rock wall and gazed down into the clear water about ten feet below. The shadows of small fish darted back and forth against the current.

Something plopped into the water, scattering the fish. At first, Jonathan thought he must have kicked a pebble into the current, but he looked down and noticed the rock wall was solid.

Plop!

This time he saw what had made the noise. A small stone had come from—

Plunk!

There—someone under the bridge, tossing rocks into the water. Jonathan leaned out over the wall but couldn't see far enough to make out who was throwing the rocks. He walked down, around the low wall, and to the edge of the bank. Just as he was about to look again, his feet slipped on the wet grass and he tumbled headfirst down the steep bank and landed rear end first in the middle of the stream, soaking himself from head to foot.

Somewhere between the slip and the splash he was dully aware of a short scream, and then, as he was shaking the water out of his ears in the streambed, laughter. He looked around, wiping the water from his eyes as he stood, and saw a girl about his own age sitting on a rock on the bank under the bridge. One hand covered her mouth, the other was slapping her knee, and she was laughing so hard she couldn't catch her breath.

"Oh, oh, oh," she said, standing weakly, and trying to compose herself. "I'm sorry. Are you hurt?"

Jonathan said nothing but stood, dripping wet, in the middle of the stream. The girl arched her eyebrows and bit her lip but finally gave in to another fit of laughter.

Jonathan thought it was the most beautiful sound he had ever heard, so clear and high and sweet. Her auburn hair was gathered in a scarf and pulled back, but he could tell it was a mass of curls. Her dark eyes sparkled, and she had a smile that would wake the morning. She wore a simple dress, buttoned to the throat with a narrow white collar and, he noticed, boots that were caked with mud.

Suddenly she snorted, then let out a little embarrassed scream, then dissolved into another fit of giggles. Jonathan laughed himself, and shook his head as he trudged through the water to the girl's side of the stream.

"My name is Jonathan Reuchlin," he said, extending his hand.

The girl wiped the tears away from her eyes and held out her hand to his. "I'm Elizabeth," she said, smiling again. They shook hands.

"Oh. Sorry," Jonathan said, realizing that his hand was still dripping wet.

"No need. I won't melt," she said.

Jonathan laughed again, this time self-consciously, and wondered what humans were supposed to say to angels.

DECEMBER 21, 1516
ROSHEIM

"Elias! Welcome! *Boquer tob!*" Esther von Gershom grasped the arm of the darkly clad man and pulled him inside. "Come in, come in out of the cold and make yourself at home. I just have to get something off the fire," she said as she hurried into the kitchen. "You might enjoy looking at the sketch of Elizabeth we're having done."

Dr. Elias Sklaar placed his doctor's bag at his feet, then methodically removed his hat, and then his gloves, one finger at a time. He had visited this home on many occasions, and he knew every room intimately. It was comfortably furnished, though Sklaar suspected that Josel could have afforded better—could have, at least, up until a month before, when someone had broken in and stolen most of his fortune. It was enough to crush most families. But not the von Gershoms. Josel went right on working, and Esther continued to keep her home clean, kosher, and always presentable, even at this hour of the morning.

She needed to, Sklaar thought. Half the Jewish population of Alsace frequented this home, dropping in for surprise visits or legal counsel from Josel. He was their *shtadlan*, their emissary and legal representative to the Gentiles. Elias had passed Josel's carriage in front of the court-house on his way out of town. He was, undoubtedly, arbitrating another case this morning between one of his Jewish kinsmen and a disgruntled Gentile. More and more were coming all the way to Rosheim from Germany these days. Amazing.

Sklaar glanced around the familiar interior. The place had a feminine touch—not one that Elias particularly appreciated. His own tastes were decidedly more Spartan. He had lived most of his thirty-five years in tight, windowless apartments. Most of his patients still paid him in chickens and eggs, and occasionally a knitted scarf or gloves. What money he got, he squirreled away in a variety of hideaways: some under his mattress, some in old teapots buried in the woods. Dr. Sklaar couldn't abide waste.

Unfortunately, Josel's daughter Elizabeth tended to embrace her father's spendthrift ways—nice dresses, jewelry, at least two pairs of shoes. *"A slight character flaw but correctable,"* he had noted in his ledger. Sklaar would raise the issue once they were married. The house once divested of its excessive accouterment would prove an efficient domicile. The land and her dowry, assuming Josel restored it, would establish

Elias as a powerful and prosperous tradesman. He was sure it would all add up to a significant amount of money. Elizabeth would be a profitable investment indeed.

He walked casually into the parlor, but he stopped immediately after crossing the threshold. On the wall to his right hung the most incredible image he had ever seen—a simple, rough drawing of Elizabeth. He held his breath. There was something about the drawing that wouldn't allow him the luxury of looking at anything else. Her eyes...

"Beautiful, isn't she?" Esther said, walking in from the kitchen. "Josel and I think we may not have the painting done after all, we enjoy the sketch so much." She laughed softly. But the portrait had captivated Sklaar—his eyes were transfixed. "Now then," she said, touching the sleeve of his coat to get his attention, "to what do we owe the honor of this visit?"

Finally pulling his gaze away, the doctor took off his broad-brimmed hat. "A social call, Esther," he said, turning to her with a thin smile. "Is Elizabeth home?"

"Actually," Esther said, "she's been ill. Nothing to worry over. She's sleeping right now."

"I'll come right to the point. You have told Elizabeth, haven't you?"

"Told her? About what?" she asked too innocently.

Elias coughed and tugged at his collar. "We have an agreement," he said.

Esther smiled and folded her arms. "Elias, it isn't a business deal," she said. "It's a marriage."

Elias ignored the rebuke. He was angry now. Unable to control his tone. "Has Josel prepared the girl for our marriage or not?"

Esther's smile faded quickly. "He's been gone so much lately, Elias. You know he's had to take more cases since our money was stolen..."

"Which reminds me," Sklaar interrupted. "I'm sure Josel is taking the necessary steps to restore Elizabeth's dowry."

Esther sighed and folded her arms. "Elias, strangers broke into our home and stole nearly all our savings. That included Elizabeth's dowry. I wish we could bring it all back with a wave of the hand, but we can't. It takes time and a lot of hard work."

Sklaar held up his index finger to stop her. "I'm a patient man, Esther, but I have to think of Elizabeth. I'm not wealthy."

"Elias, you know Josel is an honorable man. He's doing everything in his power to save enough for all of us…"

"And Elizabeth's dowry," Sklaar said.

"*And* Elizabeth's dowry. You won't be disappointed, Elias. You have Josel's word on it."

"Then he has spoken to Elizabeth."

Esther swallowed and averted her eyes momentarily. "As I said, there just hasn't been time."

"Esther!" he interrupted. The word came out louder than he had intended. He took a deep breath then continued. "Esther, Rebbe Zimmler has agreed. It's a good match. You said so yourself." He removed his small oval-shaped glasses, pinched the bridge of his nose, and closed his eyes. It was another of his terrible headaches. This one had been building all morning. An uncomfortable silence passed between them.

Esther finally spoke, "Elias, you are a worthy suitor, but—"

"But what?" he asked evenly, without opening his eyes.

"But you can't rush this," she said, and Elias knew she had intended to say something else entirely. They were considering canceling the whole betrothal. He could see it in her eyes, the way she wouldn't look at him. The liars! "You must give us time. We—"

"Time?" he demanded, opening his eyes and staring straight at her. "It's been three months since Josel agreed. Since you agreed. You, both of you, talked with my uncle. All of you said yes, this is a good match, a fine match." The pain in his head streaked through his eyes, making him blink repeatedly. "But now it's 'Keep quiet, Elias,'" he said, his voice trembling. "'*We* will tell Elizabeth,' 'Be *patient*, Elias,' 'Just a little while *longer*, Elias.'"

"Josel and I think we should—"

"No! I will not be humiliated like this. All Rosheim knows that Elizabeth and I are to be married."

"We said nothing, Elias," Esther said, emphasizing the "we" pointedly.

Sklaar stiffened. She was accusing *him* of spreading the news. After *their* betrayal of trust? He could have killed her where she stood. "No more talk. No more waiting. You tell her today. This day. This night." He pulled on his gloves roughly and picked up his doctor's bag with a grunt. "I'll come back tomorrow. If you haven't told her by then, I'll tell her myself." He turned without another word, walked out the door, and mounted his horse.

Esther followed him out. She put her hand on the horse's withers. "Elias, listen to me." Her voice was strong. "I wanted Josel to tell you himself. But I can't let this go on."

Elias held the reins tightly in his left hand as he looked straight ahead, his jaw clenched. Esther took a deep breath and spoke.

"Elias, please don't be angry at this. The fact is, Josel and I did tell Elizabeth."

Elias didn't move.

"And she's…resistant, for now. I'm sorry. It isn't you. I mean, she's just a headstrong girl. I'm sure she'll come around."

Without warning, Sklaar jerked on the reins. Esther stumbled backward as the animal whinnied and broke into a fast trot.

"Elias, wait, please!"

He spurred his horse on toward Rosheim. He would deal with the matter himself. Headstrong girls were like iron—they could be molded. It was only a question of how many blows.

DECEMBER 21, 1516
WITTENBERG

In the five years since his transfer to Wittenberg, Martin had earned his doctorate and immersed himself in the Scriptures and in teaching. But the peace he had failed to find in Rome still eluded him in Wittenberg. The more deeply he studied, the more learned he became, the more ill at ease he grew.

Black smoke curled up from the dimly burning lamp in Martin's cell and was lost in the darkness above. He had been at work now for over two hours—picking up his pen to jot a few notes in his text on Romans, then kneeling, praying for greater insight, rising moments later, pacing, arguing with himself, reasoning his way through his discoveries.

He noticed a piece of folded paper on the floor, one corner of it still under the door. Martin opened the door quickly and peered outside, but the corridor was empty. He picked up the note and walked slowly back to his desk. This was the third note in two weeks. The handwriting was the same: a careful Latin script, even margins, and, of course, no signature. "You put more than the bridge at risk. Think! Think of your own monastery!" The next words were inked out. Then, "Frederick is displeased. Others also. The Holy Father himself issues indulgences. Stop and think."

The "bridge" referred to the rotting hulk that spanned the river Elbe. Prince Frederick, the elector of Saxony, where Martin lived, and a loyal follower of the pope, intended to raise the necessary revenues for the bridge's repairs by granting indulgences to those who would pay to view his thousands of relics. The questions Martin had raised years before regarding the value of indulgences had flowered into full-blown disdain. His open opposition to the flagrant commercialization of indulgences was creating tension with Frederick, which in turn put the repair of the bridge at risk. And more, according to the note. He crumpled the paper and tossed it. His thoughts were back on his text before the paper hit the floor.

Before launching into the study of Romans, Martin had spent three years plowing through Psalms. He was convinced from his New Testament studies that the Holy Spirit had given the church the gift of distinguishing between the spirit and the letter of the law. What he had uncovered in the psalms was not, he knew, the product of human discernment alone—God was illuminating his word. Martin was merely the witness to the light.

The Scriptures had revealed that the Church of Jesus Christ was the battleground for the great conflict between Satan and God. The psalms in particular clearly pointed to the soon return of Christ for his people, and so Martin had encouraged those in his congregations to work hard in light of Christ's imminent return. The Bride must be ready when her Bridegroom appeared. Ready with enough good works to save them, to justify them before a wrathful God.

But now, searching through the epistle to the Romans, Martin had discovered a truth that had set his soul on fire. He walked slowly back to the desk. He turned the pages back to the first chapter. His fingers traced the last words of the seventeenth verse: "The just shall live by faith." He read the words repeatedly, the verses before and the ones that followed. He had been wrestling with this for months now. Something was missing. Where did works fit in if faith was all that was required for the just to live? How were sinners justified if not by works? This night he had, he believed, found the answer at last. And it was only two chapters away: "…we are justified freely by his grace." By his *grace*. Martin recalled Ephesians 2:8 and 9: "By *grace* you have been saved through faith, and that not of yourselves—it is the gift of God, not of works, lest any man should boast." But if this was the answer, if Martin was right, it meant salvation itself was a free gift. All of his efforts to earn it had been in vain. And everything he had been taught concerning it had been wrong. He began to tremble. It wasn't the midwinter cold of his cell or the fatigue that dogged his waking hours. It was the fear of God. The realization that the truth of God's grace would, *must* change everything.

He turned to the small altar against the wall, knelt, and crossed himself. He stared hard at the wooden crucifix hanging there, stared at the face, and into the carved eyes of Jesus. Martin longed to hear a voice. He needed a sign, some assurance that what he had found in the text of Romans chapter 3 was true. The road he walked now was just as lonely, just as desolate as the road where God had struck him to the ground with his call to the monastic life years before. He listened for thunder, hoped for lightning, there in his cell, but the only words that filled his mind were the words of the scriptures he had been reading minutes before.

The Scriptures. Of course. Martin had his answer. God had spoken. Not mystically through dreams or in a clap of thunder but clearly, in his word. In the Bible. There, Martin sensed, he would find the peace he had been looking for. There, in God's word, he would find the truth.

He bowed his head, closed his eyes, and asked for strength to pray longer. "Father, my Lord Jesus denied himself food at the well in Samaria. He denied himself rest, and fed five thousand men instead. Fill me, Lord, with the bread of heaven, that I might not long for the bread of earth. Grant me your peace, your rest, that I might not long so for the sleep of men. Father," he said, struggling to focus his mind, "your word is my guide as well as my fortress. A lamp unto my feet. And your name is a strong tower. O Lord God, eternal Father, light my way with your word. Guard me, Father, against error, seal my lips against heresy. Let me speak only your truth, your grace, and only in the power of your Spirit. In the name of our blessed Savior, amen."

He rose slowly and rubbed his face vigorously with both hands before returning to sit at his desk. He turned the pages of his Bible to the third chapter of Romans. Then, picking up his quill, he made one last note, the end of a sentence he had begun before his last interruption: *ergo sola gratia justificat.* Justified by grace alone.

ROSHEIM

Midnight. Moonlight clear. Trees, grass, hills awash in cold, airy silver. Two shadowy riders, Jonathan Reuchlin and the auburn-haired beauty named Elizabeth he had met at the stream several weeks ago, galloped across an open field and slipped into the shelter of the tall trees. A stream glittered and gurgled in its course along the footpath. The two stopped by a glade they had discovered nights before. From the edge of the trees, they peered out into the open space, watching, listening. They dismounted, tied their reins to a limb and entered the moonlit ring slowly, holding hands.

At the center of the glade, they looked up beyond the encircling treetops to see the twinkling stars. They turned to each other. He saw the starlight dancing in her eyes. Then slipping his hand in his pocket, he withdrew the gift he'd been waiting to give her. "Close your eyes," he said.

She looked at him quizzically, a smile at the corners of her lips. "What's this about?"

"Just close them!"

She did as he requested, her long lashes touching the tops of her moonlit cheeks. Jonathan resisted the urge to kiss her right then, as he lifted the necklace with an amethyst pendant—it draped from his fingers, catching the light in a sparkling line.

"Now open them."

When she did, her eyes lit up and her hand went to her mouth. "Oh, Jonathan, you shouldn't—"

"I had to, for you. I'd do anything for you, Elizabeth. Let me meet your father and ask for your hand."

"Oh, I wish," she began softly. "Tomorrow." Her eyes held him. He couldn't think of what to say. Or do. He moved in back of her and placed the chain around her throat, adjusting it so the amethyst lay just right.

"There," he said and kissed her temple. A soft breeze riffled the grass in waves around them. One of the horses nickered.

"Tomorrow I leave," Jonathan reminded her.

She said nothing but turned toward him and slipped her arms around his waist. He looked at her and saw the tears.

"What is it? Why can't you tell me now?" he asked.

"Shh," she whispered and kissed him softly on the lips—a sweet, tender kiss.

They walked hand in hand through the shadows of the tall, slender trees to a waterfall. The stream cascaded down the black, shining rock, a silver ribbon in the moonlight. They said nothing but drank in the night together, standing at the water's edge, holding each other, feeling the cool spray on their faces. He placed his hands on her shoulders and turned her to face him.

He whispered, soft as the night, "Elizabeth, I love you."

She stared up at him, then down at her hands. "Jonathan—"

"Elizabeth," he interrupted, "I tell you now with all my heart, that it doesn't matter who you are or who your family is, I will love you forever. Look, I've told *you* about *my* family."

"Jonathan..."

"I've told you about how I worked the copper mines, and cave-ins, and about my mother, and...I even told you about the troll!" he said, smiling. Elizabeth laughed. "So whatever it is you can't tell me about your family, it can't be as bad as having a troll for a stepfather." She laughed again and then turned her face away, embarrassed at her tears.

Jonathan couldn't bear to see her cry. He reached out and took her hand. "This is our last night together," he said softly. "Won't you tell me?"

"I can't. They don't even know I'm gone—I told my mother I was ill, going to lie down..." She took in a short breath and nodded to herself as if she had just made up her mind about something. "There's something I must do before I tell them about you. Come on," she said, smiling now as she wiped away the tears. They held hands as they walked back to their horses, then rode through the night, to the borders of the lighted town.

Some of the alehouses were still open, but the streets were mostly empty. Horses and a few empty carriages stood along the side streets and alleyways. Rough laughter rose and fell from deep within the lantern-lit taverns. Shadowy figures stood just inside the open doors. A few men leaned against nearby posts, silhouetted against the yellow-stained interiors, soaking up the night. Jonathan angled his horse away from the tavern and stopped in front of a store on the other side of the muddy street. Elizabeth rode up beside him and put her hand on his arm. "Jonathan," she began, but something distracted her. She looked back over his shoulder into the shadows.

"What?" he asked.

"Nothing," she said, barely above a whisper. "I thought I saw some-one. I was sure—"

Jonathan looked back. The men who had been standing there when they rode up had disappeared, either back into the tavern or out into the night, he guessed. "There's no one there," he said before turning back to Elizabeth. She was still staring into the darkness. Even in the moonlight Jonathan could tell her face was pale. "You're frightened," he said, taking her hand.

She looked back to him, as if embarrassed, and smiled briefly. "Sorry. It's nothing, Just scared of the shadows." She placed her other hand on top of his. "Jonathan. You must promise you won't follow me," she said.

"Elizabeth, please. Let me talk to your father. I can make him understand."

She leaned over and put her fingers to his lips.

"Promise," she insisted gently.

"I promise. I won't follow."

She kissed him quickly. "Tomorrow you will know. Wait by the rock bridge at midmorning." She kicked her horse, prodding it into a slow trot, and disappeared down the street and into the night.

Jonathan turned to leave, struggling to keep his promise, trying to understand why she wouldn't allow him to meet her family. *What secret could be dark enough to keep us apart?* As Jonathan spurred his horse, one of the men exited the alley beside the tavern and stepped out into the street, directly into the path of Jonathan's horse. "Whoa, watch out there!" Jonathan shouted as he reined his horse out of the way, just in time to avoid hitting the man.

But the fellow didn't flinch. He kept walking as if Jonathan and his horse didn't exist. He stumbled, almost losing his broad-brimmed hat in the process and dropping a small, black bag into the muddy street. Jonathan shook his head at the rail-thin figure, as he righted himself unsteadily. The man stood there for a moment, looking at his bag in the muck. And then up at Jonathan—staring at him, Jonathan felt, as if he were somehow responsible for his misfortune. The man bent low to pick up the bag, his eyes still on Jonathan. He curled his long fingers slowly around the handle and jerked it up. It made a sucking sound. And, Jonathan noticed before spurring his horse away, it clinked.

A key scraped in the lock. Dr. Elias Sklaar placed the filthy bag at his feet, then put his shoulder to the door and pushed it open. He grasped the small silver bell above the door to silence its jingling. "Mustn't waken anyone," he whispered to the empty room. "Mustn't call attention."

He picked up his bag, entered, and closed the door quietly behind him. Leaning back, he took off his glasses and rubbed his eyes. It had been a long night. First the news of Elizabeth's rejection, then a patient died in childbirth. Then he'd seen Elizabeth with that boy. The tavern had helped him there. But no matter how much he drank, he couldn't wash away the ghosts, couldn't drown the screams that haunted him.

"Please," he whispered to the darkness, as if the shadows might pity him and restore the source of his powers, the book of spells that had been stolen ten years past. If the witches hadn't taken his book, he would have had Elizabeth long ago, and her young lover would be dead by now. He took a deep, shuddering breath, and then he could smell something in the air…an aroma at first weak, then stronger. So strong he could almost taste it. The book. It might be gone, but its power lingered. At least what he could remember of it—a pulsing power that lived and breathed inside him. He smiled. He could sense it, smell it, feel it reaching out to him to calm him, to speak to him. To remind him of why he had come back to his office so late. "Get to work. Yes, we remember the formula. The book's not all gone, is it, Elias?"

He made his way across the small room slowly, feeling ahead with his hands, until he touched the counter. The effects of the wine unsteadied him only slightly. He moved to the end and around behind to a small drawer where he pulled out a penny candle and lit it. The shades were drawn. The bright candle's glow hurt his eyes, and he fumbled for the brass holder.

"Foolish girl," he mumbled to himself as he held the candle up to a large case filled with row upon row of small, long wooden boxes. The labels had faded, but Dr. Sklaar remembered what he had put in them for the most part—an assortment of leaves, grasses, herbs, and powders. His fingers tugged at the brass pulls on each box, and he sniffed the contents until he found the one he was looking for: belladonna.

He took three leaves and turned to get a mortar and pestle from under the counter. Blowing the dust from the bowl, he placed the leaves in the bowl and began to grind slowly, thoroughly crushing the leaves into a fine powder. Then he spread the powder on a metal tray and heaped it into a brownish mound. He pulled a vial from the shelf behind him and scraped the tiny mound of powder into it, then reached for a wine bottle he kept on the shelf under the counter, uncorked it, and filled the vessel half full. He replaced the cork and shook the container vigorously for about a minute. Sklaar held the ruby-colored liquid between his eye and the candle. He couldn't detect a single floating grain of undissolved powder. Wine was an effective solvent and would enhance the sedative effect of the belladonna. He uncorked the vial again, topped it off with wine, and resealed it.

Sklaar smiled to himself. The next morning Elizabeth would be sleeping soundly while her young lover waited, wondering where she could be, his stupid heart breaking. Then he would return to his home far away in the south, and they would never see each other again. And Elizabeth would belong to him. He filled a beaker with three fingers of the wine, emptying the bottle, and sat back in his armchair and stared at the crimson-filled vial, then lifted the makeshift goblet in a toast. "He would have bored you, my love. To us." He drained the beaker, removed his glasses, and closed his eyes. Slumping down into the chair, he let his head rest against the wall of boxes behind him. Comfortable now, he conjured an image of Elizabeth dressed in a gossamer gown and drifted off into thick dreams.

The early morning sun hurt Sklaar's eyes as he rode his horse through the town. He pulled on the reins to keep the animal from cantering. The last thing he wanted was excessive movement. His head was about to split open from the previous night's drinking.

He arrived at the Gershom home about a mile and a half from the outer edge of Rosheim at half past seven. Dismounting slowly, he walked to the door. Elias took a deep breath and knocked. This wasn't going to be easy.

The door opened quickly. It was Esther. Sklaar was hoping to find Josel home for once. "Why, Elias, I…good morning," she said, her manner uneasy. She kept one hand on the half-closed door.

"May I come in?" he asked. His voice sounded splendidly remorseful, he thought. At once she opened the door fully, as if embarrassed that she had kept him waiting in the morning chill.

"Of course, please," she said graciously, and Sklaar stepped across the threshold. She closed the door softly behind him.

He stood ramrod straight with his eyes closed, trying to shut out the pain that was pounding behind his eyes.

"Is Josel home, Esther?" he asked in a hushed voice.

"No. He should be back tomorrow or the next day. Why, is something wrong?"

Elias cleared his throat and looked away momentarily. "Two things. First, I owe you an apology."

"Elias, please don't. You were upset—"

"No. There's no excuse for that kind of behavior. God is teaching me patience, and if there was ever a prize worthy of infinite patience, it's your daughter. I ask you to forgive me."

"All is forgiven and forgotten," she said, smiling.

"Thank you," Elias said, relieved that his "confession" was over. "Now, you said Elizabeth wasn't feeling well."

"Oh, I'm sure it will pass. She said her head was hurting and—"

"Yes, yes," he interrupted as he reached inside his cloak and pulled out the small glass vial, "Well, we can't be too careful. I've brought some medicine to help her rest. She'll be back on her feet in no time."

"You're a good man, Elias," Esther said, extending her hand. "It's so generous of you to—"

Sklaar pulled the vial back. "That will be three marks, Esther," he said. "You can pay…whenever. Tomorrow's fine, or if you're going into town this afternoon."

"I'm afraid Josel has the purse."

"I see," Elias said, barely able to mask his disgust. All of them, even the rich ones, found excuses not to pay. "Well, if you can't trust your future mother-in-law, then who?" he said with a starchy laugh. "I'll just see to Elizabeth." He brushed past Esther and started to climb the stairs to Elizabeth's room.

"She's still asleep," Esther whispered.

"I'll wake her gently." Sklaar was at the top of the stairs, opening Elizabeth's door. He could see Elizabeth's auburn hair cascading across the thick pillow. He gazed at her lovely form, desiring her more with each breath. Her lips were full and parted. An amethyst pendant hung on a chain around her slender neck. Another sign of excess, Sklaar thought. Shameful waste.

"Elias," Esther whispered, now at his side.

"Esther," Sklaar protested, "I'm her doctor, for heaven's sake."

"And you are also to be her husband. But I'm still her mother," she said, forcing a smile as she pulled him back out the door and down the stairs. "That's two arguments to one. I win."

"Esther, really," Sklaar began.

"I'll give her the medicine, Doctor. Now you trot along to your other patients. Go on, shoo!"

"Listen," he said, pulling away. "Make sure she takes this as soon as I leave."

"I'll be faithful, Doctor," Esther said, pushing him toward the door. Sklaar tensed. He reached out and put his hand on the door, keeping it shut. Wheeling around, he looked down on her. It took every ounce of his strength to control his voice.

"It's important that she take this medicine immediately."

"I understand," Esther said. "I'll take care of it right away. Good day to you, Elias." Sklaar found himself outside the house, his back to the closed door. He heard her latch it quietly as he was mounting his horse, then he jerked the reins roughly, a smile creasing his thin face as he rode away.

Elizabeth was dressed and ready to leave to meet Jonathan when Sklaar entered the house and interrupted her escape. His plan to take her as his wife sickened her. She had tried to object, but her father wouldn't listen. He had arranged the marriage with Sklaar months before. Josel von Gershom was a hard man. Once he had given his word, there was no taking it back. Ever. Prominent doctors married the daughters of prominent lawyers. It was the way things were done. The matter was closed.

But that didn't change the way Elizabeth felt about Jonathan. She loved him, and she knew that he loved her. She couldn't put it off any longer—loving him meant she had to be honest. It meant she would have to tell him she was a Jew. That she was betrothed. If he hated her for it, then better to know now than later. But if he still loved her—even if it meant running away together, then so be it. She had thought it all through. Her father would almost certainly disown her. Her mother would try to reason with him, but it would do no good. If she ran away with a Gentile, then she wouldn't exist as his daughter anymore. There would be no coming home, because she wouldn't have a home.

Jonathan would be at the bridge soon, waiting for her. She had to find a way of getting out of the house quickly, of getting to him at the bridge without raising suspicions. Then Sklaar had come. She undressed quickly, and kicked her clothes and the small bundle she had packed under the bed. She put on her nightgown, lay back down, and waited.

Soon after Sklaar left, Esther came to her daughter's room and tried to coax her into drinking the medicine.

"Mother, I'm not sick," Elizabeth protested.

"You were in bed all last night," Esther said. "Come on, now. Elias says it will be good for you, and it won't be too bad if you swallow quickly." She uncorked the vial and handed it to Elizabeth.

Elizabeth grimaced as the bitter liquid slid down her throat. "Oh, that's awful!" she coughed.

"There," Esther said. "All done. Now I have to go into town to pick up a few things. I'll be back by dinner." She leaned over and kissed Elizabeth, then rose quickly to leave the room. Elizabeth waited until she heard the front door open and close again. She threw off the covers and went to the window where she saw her mother walking away in the direction of Rosheim. She turned quickly back toward the bed, took two steps, and the room started to tilt and swim. She barely reached the bed before she collapsed into a dreamless sleep.

On the other side of the town, Jonathan left his uncle's guesthouse and rode at a fast trot through town to the swollen stream on the south-eastern edge of Rosheim. He and Elizabeth had first met on this bridge. Here he would again ask her to be his bride.

A small cloud of dust far down the twisting, tree-lined road marked the approach of a horse and rider, coming at a gallop. Jonathan smiled. It was midmorning. Surely it was Elizabeth.

The rider slowed to a trot and then to a walk, just fifty yards away around a bend in the road and behind a clump of trees. Jonathan stood quickly and started to mount his horse. Then he saw the rider. A man with a wide-brimmed black hat. The stranger approached the bridge slowly and crossed without a word. He looked vaguely familiar.

Jonathan's eyes were already scanning the far turns in the road. He paid no attention to the *clip-clop* of the hooves on the stone bridge or the muffled jangle of metal on metal from the black bag that was tied across the back of the saddle. Jonathan sat down to wait.

"She will come," Jonathan said to himself. He heard something behind him and turned to look. The horseman had dismounted and stood peering over the edge of the bridge into the water. He didn't turn his head toward Jonathan but spoke out across the water.

"She won't, you know," he said in a dry voice.

"What?" Jonathan turned to face the man, who continued to stare out over the stream. Then he recognized him. This was the man he had seen in the street the night before.

"Elizabeth. She won't be coming. In fact, she asked me to speak to you."

"I don't understand. How do you—?"

"It's really quite simple. Elizabeth and I are to be married next week. Her father and I agreed long ago that we were well suited for each other, and—"

"No," Jonathan interrupted. "Elizabeth and I—"

"Elizabeth and *you?* You, my boy, were a momentary amusement. A distraction, nothing more. Elizabeth didn't want to embarrass you, so she asked me to convey her best wishes for your future happiness. How would I have known to come here to meet you? She was trying to spare you. Now, if you will excuse me, I have business to attend." He turned and mounted his horse, without ever looking Jonathan in the eye.

Jonathan stood unable to move or to speak, staring at the back of the man in the black longcoat as he rode casually across the rock bridge and off in the direction of Rosheim.

As he disappeared around a bend in the road, the rider seemed to pull the rest of the world after him, leaving Jonathan alone and empty. He turned his eyes back to the long line of trees and the winding trail. Only now he wasn't waiting for Elizabeth to come to him. He was mourning the fact that she never would.

Chapter 10

Elizabeth awakened to the sight of her mother sitting on the bed beside her, holding her hand. Her eyes fluttered open and she moaned, still groggy from the drug her mother had given her. A candle burned on the table beside her bed, filling the room with shadows.

"Well, finally you've decided to come back to us then," her mother said. She bent over her and kissed her.

"Mmm?" Elizabeth murmured.

"I was beginning to get worried," Esther whispered. "You've been asleep for two days. Elias is downstairs. I'll get him."

Two days? Elizabeth realized, suddenly more awake. *Jonathan...* "Mother, don't!" Elizabeth tried to say, but her speech was slurred and muffled. Esther was already gone. Elizabeth slipped off to sleep again, and dreamed briefly that Jonathan had found her and had come to take her away. She could hear him saying her name.

"Elizabeth," the voice said. But then she knew it wasn't Jonathan's voice at all. She felt someone come near the bedside. Felt a cold finger pulling her eyelid open, forcing her to look into the amber eyes of Elias Sklaar.

"Elizabeth." He spoke in a voice that reminded her of ashes—dry and lifeless. She didn't move, tried to feign sleep.

"You're awake, my dear," Sklaar whispered close enough that only she could hear. "I can tell by your breathing. Why do you test me so, Elizabeth?" He stood and addressed Josel and Esther. "She's fine. Just as I told you she would be."

Josel moved to sit beside his daughter. "You gave your old father a scare, Elizabeth," he said. "It was a good thing Elias was here. If you'd gotten that medicine later who knows what would've happened. He's a good man—you've misjudged him." Elizabeth looked to her mother, who said nothing but stared straight ahead.

Esther shook her head slightly as if to say, "Let it be," then glanced at her husband as she moved to the side of the bed. "We're going to let you get some rest now, sweetheart. Is there anything I can get you?"

Elizabeth was dying for a drink of water, but she shook her head no.

"All right then," Esther said, moving toward the door. "There's apples and figs and a jar of well water there for you if you get hungry or thirsty, dear. You just rest as long as you need, and I'll check in on you later."

Elizabeth glanced at the food on the table beside her bed, nodded, and closed her eyes as if she were already half-asleep again. As soon as the door shut, she sat up slowly and tried to shake off the fog. She reached over for the jar of water and drained it quickly, its coolness clearing her head a bit, though she still felt sluggish, as though she were trying to move through a river of thick syrup. She climbed unsteadily out of the bed and padded over to the door. She could hear her father and Sklaar talking downstairs. Her father was speaking.

"I'll tell her tomorrow, Elias. She needs to have her wits about her. It's no small thing."

"She's a strong girl, Josel. Stronger than you think, believe me. As her husband I think I know best what—"

"You aren't her husband yet, Elias, and Elizabeth is still living under my roof."

Elizabeth could hear Sklaar take in a sharp breath through his nose. "We have an agreement," he muttered.

"Oh, for heaven's sake, Elias, calm down. I'm a man of my word, you know that. You will take Elizabeth to wife next Wednesday. Nothing will change that. But I will tell her in my own way, in my own time. Call it a father's prerogative." Elizabeth could hear the lawyer's smile in his voice.

"Tomorrow," Sklaar said, and she heard the familiar *clink* as he picked up his doctor's bag. "First light, Josel."

"I'll come get you," Josel said, opening the door. "And I'll bring Elizabeth with me. Good day, Elias."

Sklaar mumbled something that Elizabeth couldn't hear, and she heard the door close.

"Well," her father said, Elizabeth assumed to her mother. "He's intense, we can say that." Elizabeth didn't hear her mother respond. Her father continued, "He'll mellow after they're married, Esther, I'm sure of it."

Elizabeth heard her mother say something as they walked away from the stairs. Shaking off the remainder of her drug-induced lethargy, she turned back to her bed. She knelt and reached for the bundle of clothes where she had kicked them under the bed two days before. She grabbed them, pulled off her nightgown, and threw on the clothes she had discarded earlier.

While she was getting dressed, she was trying to think of Jonathan, desperately trying to remember if he had said where he would be going when he returned with his uncle. But all she could think of was Sklaar, and the fact that he had forced open her eye with his thumb and made her look at him. He had haunted her dreams too during her long sleep. Even then she felt him near, as though he had found the key to her mind and could enter at will. To watch her sleeping. To take her.

She would die first.

She had to run. Run as far as she could. If her father wouldn't save her, she would save herself. She took a large handkerchief from one of her drawers and spread it out on the bed. Then she took the plate of apples and figs on the bedside table, dumped them into the handkerchief, tied the corners together and put it into the sack. She opened her window and climbed out onto the roof, then threw her bag down to the ground and climbed down the rose lattice on the back side of the house. She knew her father and mother would start looking for her at her friends' homes, then in the near village to the north where they had relatives. Jonathan had told her he lived somewhere to the south. She would search for him. It was her only choice. She fingered the amethyst still at her neck, a reminder of his love.

She peeked around the corner of the house to make sure her mother hadn't gone outside. The way was clear. She darted across the small, open field behind the house and into the shelter of the nearby forest. She took a minute to catch her breath and orient herself. She had always been good at finding her way home. Now she prayed she would be able to find her way to Jonathan.

Esther carried the candle up the dark stairs and down the hall to Elizabeth's room. She opened the door quietly so as not to disturb her, and peeked inside. A cool breeze blew in through the open window. Moonlight spilled onto the empty bed.

"Elizabeth?" Esther entered the room, holding the candle high. She went to the window and peered out into the night, searching. "Elizabeth!" she called out.

Silence.

Quickly, Esther descended the stairs and went outside. No need to panic. She was probably in the privy. She walked quickly to the far side of the yard. A sudden, cold gust of wind blew out the candle. The small hut was empty.

She ran to the barn, then the well, thinking some terrible accident might have happened. Nothing.

Esther sat on the well, taking in short, sharp breaths. She could feel the panic tightening around her throat. Calm. Stay calm. But the tears started to come. "Elizabeth!" she cried out. *Oh, Josel, I need you.* She had to get to him, but Josel had taken the carriage and their only horse into Rosheim and wouldn't be back for hours. She had no choice but to start to walk as quickly as she could the mile and a half into town. Her long dress slowed her, as well as the lack of sure footing on the dark path. Along the way, she called out for Elizabeth every few seconds. But heard nothing in return.

Esther entered Rosheim and walked straight to the home of one of Josel's clients. The man informed her that he and Josel had concluded their meeting early and that he had said something about having a drink before returning home. She might still find him at the tavern.

She found the tavern quickly and almost ran into Josel and another man just coming out. The other man was Elias Sklaar. At the sight of her husband, Esther burst into tears and fell into his arms, exhausted.

"Esther!" he said. "What are you doing here? What's wrong?"

"It's Elizabeth! She's gone!" Esther sobbed. "Oh, Josel, I looked everywhere. She's gone!"

"What? Did someone take her? Esther, look at me. Look at me." Josel gripped her shoulders and held her away from him, trying to calm her with a soft, measured tone. "Esther, did you see anyone?"

"No, nothing, nothing."

"Now think. Did you hear anything? The sound of a horse outside or a carriage passing on the road, or—"

"No one took her, Josel," Sklaar said.

"What?" Josel said, turning to the doctor. "What do you mean? How…"

"Elizabeth ran. She ran away. I'm sure of it."

Josel held Esther close and looked hard at Sklaar.

"What do you know? Why would Elizabeth run, Elias?"

Sklaar took in a deep breath and folded his hands in front of him. "I didn't want to tell you," he said gravely, "but…I've heard rumors—"

"Rumors?" Josel interrupted.

"People have been talking for weeks. I won't say who." Sklaar cleared his throat and glanced around as if to make sure no one else was listening. Then in a low voice he said, "There was a boy, a stranger. A *Gentile*, Josel."

Esther drew in a sharp breath and covered her mouth with her hands. Tears filled her eyes.

"I don't believe it," Josel protested. "Elizabeth would never—"

"You're wrong, my friend," Sklaar said quietly. "Apparently they have been seeing each other secretly for weeks now. Anything could have happened, Josel. Anything. He was the reason she didn't want me."

"No, I…," Josel stammered weakly.

Sklaar put his hand on Josel's shoulder. "Now do you see why I was pressing so for our marriage?" Sklaar asked, his voice sounding pathetic and thin. "Oh, Josel, I wanted to spare you this, this humiliation."

Esther pulled away from Josel's embrace. "You're wrong, Elias. You're wrong. You don't know."

"Esther, hush," Josel said. "Hush." He turned back to Sklaar, his face hard, his voice low and angry. "You're sure of this? You know this? A Gentile boy?"

Sklaar nodded.

Josel nodded in return and held Esther close. When he spoke, it was in a half whisper, as if he were talking to himself. "I spend my life defending my people against these Gentile…*pigs!*" He spat out the word and took a trembling breath as he looked at Sklaar. "And you tell me my own flesh and blood has…has…" But his voice trailed off. A bitter slice of wind whipped down the street as Josel turned and started to walk away, his head bowed in shame, his arm still around his wife. She wept softly into his shoulder as they made their way down the dark street toward the carriage.

"Josel," Sklaar called. Josel stopped and looked back. Sklaar stood perfectly still, his lean form backlit by the yellow light that spilled out of the tavern. His hands hung limp at his sides. His voice was calm. "I'll find her," he said. "No matter how long it takes. I'll find your daughter."

Josel shook his head slowly. Tears were streaming down his own cheeks now as he turned to walk away. "You're wasting your time, Elias," he said over the wind. "I have no daughter."

Elizabeth managed to stretch what food she'd brought over two days. At the end of the second day, she approached a small village and was about to go up to a house and ask for something to eat when she spotted Sklaar on the edge of town. She was certain he was following her, looking for her, but she was equally confident that she had seen him first. She decided to forgo the chance for food and keep to the woods.

The third day she had nothing but water and a few berries she picked from bushes near the road. Just after sunset, the clouds swept in and with them a heavy, wet snow. It had been warm in Rosheim the day she left, so she hadn't thought to bring a coat. The temperature was dropping fast. She had to find shelter quickly, but there was only the dark, empty road before her. Shivering and hopeless, she began to cry but stopped herself. This was not the time to lose control. This was the time to think, explore her options. Do something.

But there was nothing left to do. So she prayed. It was the first spontaneous prayer she had ever uttered. Her father or the other men in synagogue had always prayed. It was their job. But theirs were all memorized bits and pieces of Torah. She tried to remember some of the prayers of her father, but she was so cold she couldn't recall any of the words. So she bowed her head, closed her eyes, and simply said, "Almighty God, help me, please. Help me find a safe place."

It felt so strange, speaking to God alone. There had always been other voices speaking with her, or for her. She hoped it was acceptable to do that—hoped she hadn't offended God by speaking to him in such a personal way. She kept her eyes closed, not knowing what to expect—a voice? Some kind of direction? An idea? Nothing. But perhaps she was being impatient. She stood still for as long as she could, the snow piling up around her, the dark clouds closing in. Finally, when it grew apparent that she wasn't going to get an answer from the Lord, she opened her eyes and started to walk again.

In the few minutes she had had her eyes closed, the dark gray of the evening sky had yielded to the blackest night she could remember. The snow clouds shut off any hint of moonlight. And yet as her eyes adjusted to the darkness, she thought she could detect a faint glow off to her left. Maybe God was answering her prayer after all. It just had to get dark enough for her to see the light.

Two hours later, hungry, exhausted, and bitterly cold, she entered a town and saw candles burning in the windows of a large building. A synagogue! God *had* answered her prayer! She would be warm; she wouldn't freeze to death, and there would be food. They always had food at synagogue.

The door was ajar. She pushed it open and stumbled across the threshold and into the soft light of a hundred candles. People crowded the place. More than she had expected—row after row of worshipers, all with their heads bowed, praying. Something was different here. A man stood near the front, talking, but he didn't look or sound like any rabbi she had ever—then it hit her. She was standing inside a Christian church!

She couldn't move. Mustn't move or they might notice her. If the Christians discovered she was a Jew, they would kill her on the spot— stone her as they always stoned the Jews in her grandfather's stories.

She felt as if she were wearing a sign with the word "Jew" around her neck. Perhaps if she didn't move too quickly…she mustn't run, mustn't call attention. *Oh, why did she ever pray? Stupid, stupid. God was punishing her, sending her to this evil place.* She pressed her thumb into her clenched fist so hard the nail cut into the flesh of her forefinger.

She took a deep breath and turned, as calmly as she could, to leave. Then the remembrance of who was lurking outside froze her. Sklaar was out there somewhere in the darkness. He might be riding into town right now. She knew he was determined, but she seriously doubted he would ever enter a Christian church. She would stay right where she was. She walked along the sidewall and took a place on the back bench where she tried to sit still enough to disappear. There was something soothing in the chanting of the choir and the priest's voice. Something vaguely like the synagogue she had attended all her life, and yet unlike anything she had ever experienced there.

She stayed in her seat after the service, her eyes downcast. Finally, when only a few parishioners remained visiting with one another near the front of the chapel, she edged out of her seat and made her way toward the door. She wasn't sure what she would do once she was outside, but she simply couldn't risk what might happen if she stayed. With just a little luck she could find a nice Jewish family who would take her in. She thought of Sklaar again, but only briefly. She passed the table filled with glowing candles. The night air blew in through the open door, and she was thanking God for sparing her when someone touched her on her shoulder. Elizabeth gasped and turned to see a woman of about fifty staring down at her.

The woman smiled. She had a kind face. "Merry Christmas, dear," she said, and started to pass by. Three simple words. But they were the first kind words anyone had said to her since she left home, and they almost broke Elizabeth's heart. She burst into immediate, uncontrollable sobs. The woman was shocked at first, then she wrapped Elizabeth in her shawl and walked her outside, away from the staring crowd. And then to her home.

MARCH 28, 1517
THE BANKS OF THE SAALE RIVER NEAR PFORZHEIM

The chill spring wind soughed through the trees along the banks of the Saale, sending a few leaves spinning down to settle like discarded thoughts on the slow moving water. Jonathan Reuchlin sat near the river, tossing small pebbles at the floating targets. His mother, Marta, sat higher up on the bank, her eyes closed, breathing in the crisp, clean air. The sun was setting, and the temperature was dropping fast.

Jonathan picked up a rock and skipped it across the water. "I was going to ask her to marry me."

"Well." His mother took a deep breath. "I was wondering when you were going to get around to talking about that. It's been over three months. So why now?"

"Uncle Johannes. I heard you talking last night about our trip."

"Ah. Yes. He filled me in a bit."

Jonathan said nothing. "Why didn't he say anything when he brought me back in December?"

"I don't know," Marta said. "I think maybe he wanted to give you a chance to tell me first. He's leaving tomorrow morning for Erfurt. Then to Paris. I'm sure he'll have some stories to tell next time we see him, can you imagine?"

Jonathan shrugged.

They were both silent for a few minutes.

"You waited for her," his mother said softly. "But she never came to the bridge."

Jonathan shook his head slightly. "She was going to marry someone else. That's why she would never give me a straight answer—there was always something there, some reason she wouldn't tell me about her family."

"I'm sorry, son," Marta said. "But honesty's an important thing for a marriage. Besides, jumping into something so quickly isn't always the best. I think we learned that with Herr Reisner. Johannes said you were getting serious much too quickly."

"Uncle Johannes talks too much."

"He wouldn't have to if I had a son who would talk to me instead!" she said, jabbing his shoulder. She stood up then, brushing the grass from her dress. "Your uncle would skin you alive if he knew you were talking of getting married. He's got other plans for you…"

Jonathan turned to face her.

She took a deep breath. "I know you aren't made for the mines, Jonathan. I know that, and so does your uncle. Anyway, that's what I talked to him about last night—to see if he thought you might have a future for learning."

"And?"

A smile broke across Marta's face. "He wants you to go to with him to Erfurt. Tomorrow."

Jonathan's mouth dropped open. "Erfurt? That must be two hundred miles or more…"

"Jonathan, it means not having to work the mines. Not as long as you make your marks. That's part of the deal."

"And he wants me to go with him *tomorrow?*"

"He has other business there at University."

Jonathan turned back to face the river again. He picked up a green leaf and twirled it between his hands. The wind blew sharply and the river carved its way around the rocks.

"There's something else," she said quietly. "He wants you to study for the priesthood."

Jonathan laughed and shook his head but said nothing.

"Your Uncle Johannes, he's a very religious man, and he wants a priest in the family," she said in her most reasonable tone. "There are advantages, he says. And the stars say it's a good time. A good thing."

The stars. How many times had he heard that from his mother? Jonathan nodded slowly. When he spoke, his voice was just above a whisper. "But who will take care of you?" he said. "What if Reisner comes back? I can't protect you if I'm in Erfurt."

"There's nothing keeping you here, son. Johannes is my brother— he'll look after me. You can't spend your whole life worrying about your mother."

"But Reisner—"

"Jonathan, don't," she said quietly,

"We don't know he's dead," he interrupted. "He could still be alive out there. He could still come back."

His mother moved down the bank so that she could look him in the eye. "Son," she said, "Klaus Reisner was a drunk. He could barely find his way home from the mines every night. Even if he *was* alive, do you really think he would be able to track us here to Pforzheim after all this time? He's gone, and he isn't coming back."

No one had seen Reisner since his last day at the mines near Stotternheim, nearly three years before. He had finished his day's work and had said he was going to the tavern. He came home first, though, looking for liquor money he had stashed in a box near the bed. When he couldn't find it, he accused Marta of stealing it and beat her nearly senseless. Then he took her book down from the shelf over the door and left with the bag slung over his back. He wasn't going to sell it, he'd said. He simply wanted to punish his wife. So he took her only worldly possession and walked out. That was the last anyone had seen of him.

The next day the town constable launched a halfhearted effort to find him but came up with nothing. Most folks figured he was robbed and killed and his body thrown in the river. A few days after Klaus's disappearance, the carcasses of about twenty scavenger fish had washed up on the banks of the Saale. The local joke was that the fish must have found Klaus first.

Marta took a deep breath. "Jonathan, I've never had money. Never. This is a real opportunity for you."

For the next minute only the brittle wind and the icy liquid *shush* of the Saale passed between them. Jonathan had fixed his gaze on a point down the river, wondering whether Elizabeth was thinking of him at that moment. If he became a priest, he would never marry.

And yet, he realized, he would never love another woman as he had loved Elizabeth. Memories and dreams of what might have been haunted him now. Perhaps the priesthood would help him forget.

In the days that followed Elizabeth's arrival in Maggie's home on the north side of Pforzheim, Elizabeth came to appreciate her benefactress as the most loving, the most giving person she had ever known. She learned quickly that Maggie was an excellent seamstress and a compassionate midwife. She said that each birth made up for a little bit of all she had lost along the way. Her own children had died—a daughter in infancy and her son in his fourteenth year. God had taken him, the priest said.

Her husband had killed him with his cane.

A few months later a stranger killed her husband in a drunken brawl. She had been without him now for the better part of four years. They had been the best years of her life. If she could have had her son or her infant daughter back it would have been perfect.

But now God had given her Elizabeth. Miraculously. Wonderfully. Mercifully.

Elizabeth told Maggie nothing of her past. Not even that she was a Jew. Only that she had been running from an evil man. Maggie could understand that, she said. They would talk for hours about Maggie's son, and her vile husband, and how most men weren't worth the trouble it took to darn their socks. During the long winter nights, Maggie would tell Elizabeth stories she recalled from the Bible. Elizabeth loved hearing the tale of the midwives over and again, and how brave they had been to preserve Moses.

"You know, dear," Maggie said one night, "who deserves the real credit for saving the children of Israel, don't you? Everyone says, 'Moses was the great deliverer of Israel.' 'Moses was the one who led them through the Red Sea!' Well, there wouldn't have been a Moses if it hadn't been for the midwives. The midwives and Moses' mother, Jochebed, worked to keep him hidden away."

"Then, why doesn't the story talk about that?" Elizabeth asked.

"Elizabeth dear," Maggie said, tilting her head to the side. "Who wrote the first five books of the Bible?"

"Oh, of course. Moses."

"Of course. Typical man. Taking the credit and giving the midwives short shrift. Not that Moses didn't do his part, mind you, but it was the women who did the real work. That's the way it's always been, dear. It's a man's world, but it's a woman's work that makes it."

Maggie's admiration for those underappreciated women inspired her own work as a midwife. She taught Elizabeth midwifery as well, and with it the joy of bringing new life into the world. The parallels to the biblical story weren't lost on Elizabeth. Just as the Egyptian midwives had saved the Hebrew babies, so Maggie was saving a Hebrew child. She had pulled Elizabeth from the reeds, had rescued her, and given her a home.

At night Elizabeth would dream of her father back in Rosheim. She could see him searching desperately for her, through woods, across rivers and empty plains, but he could never find her. She was invisible to him, remaining at arm's length, always wanting to call out to him. But as soon as she started to speak, Sklaar would appear beside him, holding a knife and looking for her, and she would run.

In another dream she could hear her father, but she could not see him. He was praying that God would let him find her by Rosh Hashanah; otherwise, Josel would take it as a sign that Elizabeth was dead. In her dream, a menorah rose out of the ashes of her synagogue, each candle burning brilliantly. Suddenly a breath from heaven blew out all the candles, leaving a smoky ribbon curling up from each blackened wick. Then her father would appear, walking away from the smoldering stubs toward Rosheim. But Sklaar would stay.

She dreamed of Jonathan and what he must have thought of her when she failed to meet him at the bridge. She dreamed of her mother, her friends in Rosheim, her family, and her father's business associates— all of them looking for her. But she was invisible. And she never told Maggie.

As the months ran together, her memories, at first sharply defined, gradually faded into soft-edged shadowy images. Elizabeth filled her days with hard labor. She took on responsibilities she had never known in the house of her well-to-do father. The daylight hours were busy, learning the art of the loom and of the kitchen. Her hands gradually became tough and strong. As Maggie's business grew, Elizabeth began to develop a keen eye for style and the quality of different fabrics. It was a good life, and she had come to love Maggie nearly as much as she had loved her own mother.

But there were windswept days when she would ride alone to a hill on the far side of town. There she would sit and stare away to the south, and wonder what road Jonathan had taken, and if he still thought of her at all.

Chapter 11

OCTOBER 31, 1517
WITTENBERG

"Martin? Come on, I know you're in there." Martin pushed back from his small table and marched impatiently to the door of his cell. He opened the door quickly. Justus was just turning to leave.

"Come in, sit down, and be quiet. I've got to finish this," Martin said absently.

"Good afternoon to you, too," Justus said, closing the door behind him. "How's your stomach?"

"The same, thank you." Martin continued to write.

Justus sat on the end of the bed. "The way you left nones in such a rush, I thought it must have turned sour again..." Justus noticed Martin's left hand was clenched in a fist. He was writing furiously. "What are you working on?"

Martin held up his left hand, a request for silence. A minute or so later he laid down his quill and picked up the long sheet to examine it.

"What's this?" Justus asked. He moved to his friend's side and read over his shoulder.

"Just a few points I'd like to discuss with our friend Tetzel." Johannes Tetzel was one of the most successful—and unscrupulous—indulgence peddlers in that part of Europe.

"You're raising questions about indulgences?" Justus said flatly. He was not smiling. "And this?" he asked, pointing to a sealed letter on the desk.

"I'm sure the bishop doesn't know about Tetzel," Martin said, glancing over to the letter. "I'm simply writing to encourage him to rein the old boy in before he can do any more damage." Tetzel had been raising a great deal of money for the building of the new basilica in Rome through the sale of indulgences. But in the process, he had stripped thousands of peasants of what little they had to live on. And other indulgence sellers were following his example.

"You can't be serious," Justus said.

Martin didn't reply. He dusted the ink to keep it from smudging and stood to leave.

Justus put his hand on his friend's shoulder. "Martin, you're my friend. Just hear me out."

"I know what you think already."

"Any day but this day, Martin. Please."

"Today is the best day, and you know it."

"Just stop and think for a minute. What is Frederick going to say? Tomorrow is All Saints."

"I know it's All Saints, Justus," Martin said, imitating Justus's whiny tone. "I know that Frederick is the elector of all of Saxony. I also know that he paid seventeen gulden to keep me on faculty here at Wittenberg. He will not take offense." With that, Martin opened the door and walked out.

Justus followed quickly, speaking under his breath. "Not take offense? Martin, most of Saxony is going to be here tomorrow, and all of them are coming to view Frederick's relics."

"To buy God's forgiveness," Martin said disdainfully, without breaking stride.

"To make their contributions, Martin. We all have to put in something, after all…"

At Justus's words, Martin turned on his friend. "Really?" he demanded. "Show me in God's Word where it says we must 'put in' something to be forgiven. Show me where in Scriptures it says that God's forgiveness is for sale."

"Lower your voice. You're angry because of Tetzel. I agree he's gone too far. Germans shouldn't have to pay for a Roman basilica, even if Saint Peter *is* buried there. But Martin, Tetzel hasn't set foot in Wittenberg, and neither have any of the other indulgence peddlers."

"They didn't have to," Martin shot back. "Tetzel's voice carries like an old cow on a hillside. Only instead of wanting to be milked he milks others with his infernal indulgences." Martin wheeled around and continued to walk down the hall, still speaking at full volume, daring someone to shush him. "You look, Justus. Look in the pockets of our fine Wittenberg citizens, and you will find indulgences from Magdeburg and Halberstadt."

"Frederick has already objected to some of your sermons," Justus said. "And you know why."

"He misunderstands. He simply doesn't see the harm Tetzel and the other peddlers are doing, but I will not stand for this abuse. To sell forgiveness just so they can pay for their bridges and basilicas... I'm just turning over the moneychangers' tables in the temple. If Frederick is one of them, then so be it!"

Justus stopped several feet behind Martin as he was about to open the heavy door.

"Fine. You want the primate of Germany on your back, calling for your head, fine. But don't be so naive to think that if Frederick 'misunderstands' your charges he won't..." Justus stopped and took a deep breath. "Martin, tomorrow Frederick will offer his own indulgences. Thousands of people will be here. They'll read your charges, and then what? What good will they do? Shake the people's faith, that's what. Cause them to doubt, cause them not to contribute."

"Ah, at last we get to it!"

"It's not about money, Martin!" Justus said, exasperated.

"Of course it is, Justus. It's all about money," Martin said, stepping closer to his friend. "If the people don't buy the indulgences from

Frederick, the castle church doesn't get any money. If the castle church doesn't get any money, the Augustinian Hermits might actually have to fulfill our vows of poverty. Oh, it's about money, believe me. I was just wondering how long it would take you to get to it." He turned away and started to open the door.

"Martin, we all have to live with Frederick."

Martin paused, his hand on the iron ring. He turned only slightly, enough for Justus to see the side of his face. The muscles in his jaw were tight. "What is the elector's title, Justus?"

"Martin, this isn't about words. This won't be just another debate."

"Just tell me his title."

Justus sighed and folded his arms. "I'm not going to tell you his title."

Martin started to laugh. He turned to face his friend and leaned with his back against the heavy wooden door.

"Because," Justus continued, "if I say, 'He's known as Frederick the Wise,' then you'll turn it inside out. You'll say, 'Then he's wise enough to know the difference between right and wrong,' and you'll go out there and post your ninety-five indictments and stir up a rumpus that will come down on all our heads."

"Are you finished?" Martin asked, still smiling.

"What? You aren't going to berate me for overreacting?"

"Why should I, when you obviously are quite capable of anticipating everything I will say anyway? Now, if you'll excuse me, I'll get on with my business and leave you to continue to fret over nothing."

Martin opened the door and started to go out but stopped at the last minute. "If you noticed, Justus, I wrote it in Latin. It's a call for scholarly debate, that's all. Even if they could read it, the people wouldn't bother." Martin closed the door behind him, but he heard Justus open it and run to catch up. They walked together in silence. People had begun arriving for the All Saints festival the day before. Now there was a steady stream of pilgrims jostling their way in and out of the town market, clogging the narrow streets, and milling about the church precinct.

Martin left Justus on the edge of the crowd and made his way to the door of the church. The remnants of an old posting still clung to the small nails. The wood in the door was as hard as iron, but it was cracked and worn so that Martin could easily pull the nails out with his fingers. He pierced the paper with the nails and wedged them back into the cracks. He stepped back to survey the work, then turned and walked briskly away, stopping next to Justus on the other side of the street.

"Better not get too close, Justus. You might get trampled," he said jokingly as he put his hand on his friend's shoulder. Justus harrumphed and stood beside Martin, staring at the door with the long sheet of paper fixed firmly to it. Several citizens did stop to have a look, but when they saw it was in Latin they moved on.

"See," Martin said. "You get so worked up! Come on, let's get something to eat."

"Wait," Justus said. "Look." Out of the swirling mass of people, several young men paused in front of the castle door and studied the piece of paper. They weren't simply gazing at it as the uneducated did, fascinated with the mysterious marks that somehow made words. They were reading.

Justus looked at Martin. "Humph," he grunted triumphantly.

Martin patted his shoulder. "Reading isn't a sign of intelligence, Justus. It's merely a sign of learning."

"That's what I'm afraid of," Justus countered. "It's as you said, Martin. 'A little learning can be a dangerous thing.'"

Chapter 12

Luther stood pale and thin before Cardinal Cajetan. His monk's frock was in fair shape but only because he had borrowed one from a friend when he passed through Nuremberg on his way to the hearing. Because of his anxiety over the coming interrogation concerning his ninety-five theses and over the shame he would bring on his parents if he was condemned to the stake, he suffered such severe stomach cramps he had to ride the last few miles to Augsburg in a wagon.

Luther had wanted to submit to the interview as soon as possible, but friends had convinced him to wait for a letter of safe conduct from Emperor Maximilian, which would guarantee his safety. It had taken four days to obtain the letter, even though the emperor happened to be hunting near the site of the inquisition in Augsburg. Still, the four days had allowed Luther some rest, and a chance to regain a measure of his strength.

The interrogation began October 12, with Martin observing the finest details of protocol. At his first meeting with Cajetan, Martin prostrated himself at the cardinal's feet. Cajetan gestured for him to stand, but Luther rose only to his knees and stood only after Cajetan had gestured a second time.

By the fifteenth, Martin was worn down physically, but he had taken his stand for Scripture, and he would not back down. Cajetan had been unable to cajole, threaten, or in any other way pressure Luther into recanting on a single issue. He was making one final, emotional plea for Martin to revoke his charges. "One word," the cardinal whispered, his face only inches from Luther's. "That's all I ask. One word: 'revoco.' It can't be that difficult. You can whisper it if you like."

Luther suppressed a smile and remained standing with his hands folded in front of him. As they had been for the past five hours.

"All I require, Your Eminence, is proof from the—"

"I know what you require, Father Martin, but you're not going to get it." Cajetan's voice was trembling. "I will not prove my argument from Scripture. Not to you or to anyone else."

"My point exactly," Luther said.

"What?" Cajetan almost shouted. "Don't be insolent."

"I was merely saying that you just proved my point," Martin said. "You will not prove your argument from Scripture because you cannot. And the reason you cannot is because it isn't there. It doesn't exist. Also, since the councils themselves have supported the Scriptures as the sole binding authority in matters of faith and obedience, I must submit to the higher authority of God's Word."

Cajetan pinched the bridge of his nose and closed his eyes. He rose from his chair and paced back and forth in front of Martin, who stood perfectly still. He circled Luther slowly, then stopped and faced him. "Before I pronounce judgment, I want to make sure of something," he said.

The two men stood staring at each other. The cardinal's expression wasn't malignant but resigned. "I like you, Martin. I do. But you leave no room for grace, my son."

"Eminence—," Martin started to interject.

"Silence! Listen. Listen. I want to be merciful, Martin, but your ideas—these foolish theses of yours—they fly in the face of two hundred years of official church theology. And that, my son, is heresy. You know this."

Luther knew very well. More than one hundred and fifty years before, Pope Clement VI had issued an official document called "Unigenitus" which claimed that the spiritual treasures of the Church were at the disposal of the pope for the purpose of issuing indulgences. Those indulgences, duly authorized and signed by a papal representative, guaranteed the remission of punishment for sins. If Luther rejected the "Unigenitus" of Pope Clement, then he was effectively rejecting the pope's claim to absolute authority.

"You reject the supreme authority of the Holy Father then?" Cajetan asked. His voice was even now, and measured.

"That is not quite true," Luther said. "How can I reject something I don't believe exists? You might as well ask, Your Eminence, whether I reject the elephant sitting on that chair over there. There is no elephant, and so there is nothing to reject."

"Then you don't believe in the authority of the pope?" The cardinal was incredulous.

"That's not what you asked before," Luther replied.

"It's precisely what I asked," Cajetan said, his voice rising. "And I warned you about being insolent."

"Forgive me, Eminence. But I recall your asking if I rejected the *supreme* authority of the Holy Father. Of course, I do not deny his authority, but the Scriptures do not support the *supreme* authority of any single man save our Lord."

"But our Lord isn't here, Martin," Cajetan countered.

"His Word is here. And his Holy Spirit is given as our guide."

"You hold to the supreme authority of the Holy Scriptures then?" Cajetan asked.

"I do."

"And from whom do the Scriptures derive their authority?" Cajetan asked.

Martin knew his ecclesiastical history as well as the cardinal. For hundreds of years ecclesiastics had taught that the Bible received its authenticity and authority from the church. It was a doctrine Martin found reprehensible.

"The Scriptures are not subject to the authority of the Church and never have been. We may recognize the breath of God in his word, but we do not invest God's word with anything but our obedience to his commands."

Luther took a deep breath. He knew they were at an impasse, but he would make one last attempt. "Eminence, I don't claim to be infallible. I know I can be wrong. I have offered to submit to the decision of a council of the church. I would welcome the judgments of the learned doctors of Basel, Louvain, Freiburg, and Paris. A chance for dialogue and discussion of my theses is all I ask." Then he was quiet.

"Paris." Cajetan smiled slightly. "Indeed. You know very well Paris rejects the authority of the Holy Father."

"The *absolute* authority, Eminence," Martin said.

The papal legate looked at Luther without speaking for a few moments. He shook his head slowly from side to side and, without taking his eyes off Luther, said, "You're insane." His tone was flat, but his eyes were burning now. "You've lost what little brain you had. You stand here in a coarse habit, and you reject hundreds of years of wisdom in the blink of an eye."

The cardinal's voice started to rise. "You claim to be wiser than Saint Anselm? Than Saint Thomas? Wiser than all the popes who have gone before? I have tried, Martin. I have tried for four days to speak to you as I would to a son, but you will not listen to reason. What choice do you leave me? You are a Hussite, Martin. A heretic. And your opinions carry no more weight than those of a honking goose."

Martin felt the blood drain from his face. Hus, whose name meant "goose," had died a martyr a little over one hundred years before because he had dared to accuse the pope of dissipation. It wasn't the prospect of death at the stake that shook Martin. He had come prepared to die for what he believed.

Excommunication, however, which Hus also suffered, was another matter, and one that he had not stopped to consider fully. Growing up,

Martin had been taught that the pains of excommunication extended far beyond the grave—a terrifying thought not easily dismissed.

Martin cleared his throat. "I beg you," he said, "to intercede on my behalf with the Holy Father not to thrust my soul out into the darkness when I seek only the light, only the truth, Eminence. Show me from the Scriptures where I am wrong, and I will gladly—"

"Revoke!" Cajetan spoke through clenched teeth.

"Show me—"

"Revoke," he said under his breath again, moving so close to Luther that his lips were nearly touching Martin's ear. "Or on the authority of the pope I will excommunicate you and all your friends. Do you honestly think that piece of paper from the emperor will protect you after you leave here? There isn't a place in all Germany where you will find shelter. I will place an interdict on every town, every village, every stable where you try to lay your head."

"I must obey my conscience, Eminence," Luther said quietly.

"Revoke, Martin, or don't come into my presence again!" Cajetan said, as he turned away. He would hear no more.

Martin bowed, turned, and walked out of the hall.

Martin waited two days without hearing from the assembly. He sought counsel from his old friend and spiritual advisor, Staupitz. Staupitz hadn't always agreed with Martin on the way to achieve reform in the church, but Martin knew he could count on him to give an honest opinion. And he could respect that opinion, even if it ran counter to his own, because he loved and respected Staupitz so much. He entered Johannes's room where he found him alone and agitated.

"Cajetan is hatching some kind of plot. I can smell it," Staupitz said.

"I have the emperor's letter…," Martin began.

"Cajetan's a lawyer at heart, Martin. He'll find a way around it, and he won't hesitate to take you by force. My advice is to try another letter—an apology. If he doesn't respond, we know what we have to do. But, Martin, don't give up too much."

"Sir?" Martin asked. "I thought you wanted me to recant."

"I did, it's true. But I've been thinking. Even old men can still think, you know," he said, smiling. "Martin, I'm faithful to the church, you know that. But I have to confess—I listened in there, and I believe your arguments for the supremacy of the Scriptures are sound. Still, this goes far beyond indulgences. Far beyond, and you know that." He paused and took a deep breath. "All I'm saying is—and this is only my opinion, mind you—you make a good case, but at times you sound very much like John Hus."

"Hus!" Luther said dismissively.

"You heard Cajetan in there, calling you a Hussite, and I can see his point. If you want them to hear you, Martin, if you want them to *listen,* then you must be careful with your words, son. Especially when the argument gets hot. And," he added cautiously, "you…well, you were a bit coarse from time to time."

"*He* was a bit coarse!" Martin said.

"All I'm saying…"

"Peace, peace! You win, Father. I'll apologize—if you promise to receive my confession for lying afterward."

After sending the apology, Martin waited three more days. Nothing. Late the night of the eighteenth, a knock came at his door.

He rose from his prayers and opened it to find Staupitz, accompanied by several of Martin's supporters.

"May we come in?" Staupitz asked.

"Why, why certainly. Please," Martin said stepping aside as the men entered. He could see the strain in Johannes's face. His old friend had been appointed vicar general—second in rank within Martin's order, making Martin subject to his authority. But Staupitz was under the authority of Rome—and Rome wanted Martin dead. Martin closed the door quietly behind him. "Sit down, please, Father," he said, offering a chair.

"No," Staupitz said. "This is difficult for me, but I must do it, Martin, for your own sake. You know if Cajetan has decided to take you into custody, it will fall to me as vicar general to see to your arrest. This, I will never do." He placed his hands on Martin's shoulders. "You have a lonely journey ahead of you, my son. There is little I can do to help you now. I do think we can buy some time for you, though, if I relieve you of your duties to the order. And to me."

"Father I...I will not forsake you," Luther said, fighting the emotion that choked his voice.

"Of course not," Staupitz said, smiling. "But this legally separates us. Old Cajetan will have to find someone else to put the shackles on you! So! Here in the presence of these witnesses, I, Johannes Staupitz, vicar general, absolve you, Martin Luther, of obedience to me and commend you to the Lord God. Done."

Luther embraced his mentor. "Thank you, Father," he said. "Thank all of you."

"No, Martin. It's I who thank you." Staupitz slapped him on the back and raised his voice to those standing around. "Besides, I'm too old to try to rein you in!" They all laughed. "Now, my brother," he continued more soberly, "from this day forth, all that you do in service to the order and to me will have to be done out of love or not at all."

OCTOBER 20, 1518
AUGSBURG

The hooded escort, hired to provide Martin safe passage to Wittenberg, ducked under the low arch in the city wall and cantered out onto the path that led away to the little village of Monheim. Luther rode the second horse bareback, a hard-trotting nag that made him pay for rousting her so late at night. He wore a borrowed frock as well as a pair of knee britches but without spurs, boots, or weapons.

Back through that small gate, down the streets of Augsburg, and into the interrogation room, Martin left his last hope for peace with the head of the Roman church. He knew it would define him from that moment on.

He and his companion camped that night on the road, then rose the next day to travel the eight miles into Monheim.

The town was a welcome sight to Martin. The last few days had left him so exhausted he was about to fall off his horse. The two men rode up to a stable near an inn where Luther dismounted and collapsed immediately into the straw.

In the ten days it took Martin and his guide to get back to Wittenberg, they passed scores of peasants beside the road and on the city streets, carrying their possessions on their backs, begging for money. All of them complained that they had lost all they had to their landlords and princes—they had no choice but to leave their farms and beg. Martin and his companion entered Leipzig late one evening and found a tavern still open. After buying a beer and some cheese, Martin approached a knight drinking alone at a table. He introduced himself and asked if he knew why so many of the peasants were out begging.

"Another tax, Emperor Maximilian handing out more land to idiot crusaders, priests like you buying church office. Take your pick," the man said, staring at Luther through red-rimmed eyes. "One more article for the Gravamina, for all the good it does." He took another sip of ale.

Luther had heard of the Gravamina, a collection of complaints and demands of the German ruling class against the Holy See in Rome, but he knew few of the specific articles.

"Rome is bleeding us dry," the knight said. "They keep demanding more, more, more money. I can't ask my tenants for any more money. They don't have anything as it is."

"What's the tax for?" Luther asked.

The man snorted into his mug of ale. "You're the priest, you tell me," he said bitterly, then he continued, his speech slurred. "What's the tax for? Huh. The war on the Turks, which doesn't even exist. Who knows where all the money goes? Into that sinkhole of a church, most likely. The new basilica for the pope. You add up all the taxes and all the indulgences and what do you see? You see Germans starving and the pope getting fat—that's what you see, Father." He rose unsteadily, belched, and put his mug down on the table with a thump. He mumbled something incoherent and stumbled out of the tavern.

Two days later they arrived in Wittenberg, tired but glad to be home. "Justus! I can't believe it!" Martin reached down from his mount to take the hand of his old friend.

"Good to see you, Martin," Justus said, catching one of the bags Martin had thrown. "What can't you believe?"

"I've been gone for three weeks, and the castle church is still standing!" He dismounted, laughing. Justus smiled but said nothing.

"Martin, I'm afraid there's some bad news."

"What? What is it?" His smile faded quickly.

"It's the cardinal. He's ordered you back to Augsburg."

"What?"

"Cajetan's asked Frederick either to banish you from Saxony or send you to Rome for trial."

Chapter 13

Frederick did neither. Instead, Luther reached an agreement with the papal mediator several weeks after the Augsburg trial: He would keep silent as long as his opponents kept silent. The verbal truce was short-lived. Johann Eck, the greatest debater of the age, and one of Luther's strongest adversaries, had issued a series of notes called the *Obelisks* in which he presented his objections to Luther's theses. Luther responded with his own set of notes called the *Asterisks,* in which he defended his position but also expressed his desire to keep their debate out of the public eye. It might have died right there had not Luther's colleague at Wittenberg, Andreas Karlstadt, obtained a copy of Eck's notes and defended Luther publicly with 380 theses of his own.

The argument escalated first between Eck and Karlstadt. Luther tried to serve as peacemaker between the two, but when Eck introduced the question of the superiority of the Roman church over all other churches, Luther himself joined in the war of words. At that point, a public debate became inevitable. Eck decided on the city of Leipzig, and obtained permission to hold the debate at the university there; however, it soon became obvious that the university couldn't accommodate the crowds that jammed the streets trying to get a glimpse of the two great men. So the city officials decided to move the proceedings to the Pleissenburg Castle, the largest public room in Leipzig.

Seventy-six armed citizens guarded the debate hall. Inside, special tapestries lined the packed law court. The tall and powerfully built Eck stood at a lectern decorated with a picture of Saint George. Luther, gaunt and exhausted, faced him, supporting himself behind a rostrum emblazoned with a picture of Saint Martin. It was July 7, the fourth day of Luther's turn at debating Eck. The issue had come down to the primacy of the pope—his supreme authority in all matters of faith and practice.

"Allow me to understand, good Doctor," Eck said, his voice frayed but still loud enough to fill the large hall. "You claim that the Holy Father is capable of error, correct?"

"I do not dispute the supremacy of the holy Roman church, nor have I ever," Luther answered evasively.

"Of course you don't," Eck croaked. "Because that would clearly place you in the camp of the detestable Hussites, wouldn't it? No, you are too subtle for that, too gifted an orator or should I say 'magician'? On the one hand you affirm the supremacy of the Holy See, but on the other you deny the infallibility of the Holy Father. It's a fine sleight of hand, Doctor, but it won't work here."

"It's you who are playing tricks with words, sir," Luther said. "May I not affirm the excellency of the ship and maintain the frailty of her captain? His Holiness stands at the helm of the church, but he must read God's map with the eyes God gave him, and those eyes can fail him as they can fail any man."

"He is not pope then, by divine right? Did not God Almighty establish this holy office?"

Luther took a deep breath and gripped the edge of the lectern. "Prove it from Scripture. If you prove it from Scripture… I have said this enough. I don't know how to make it any plainer. I don't know how to make it simple enough for you to understand. Prove to me from Scripture the divine right of the pope, and I will recant."

"You reject the councils! You reject the fathers! You reject the authority of His Holiness! For only you, sir, are wise! Only you have interpreted the Scriptures rightly, and all the combined wisdom of Constance and Chalcedon and Ephesus are only smoke in your nostrils… Is that what you would have us believe, sir?"

"What I would have you believe, Dr. Eck, is the truth of God's Word. I would also have you believe the truth that I wish to be an obedient son of the church—the church under the authority of God's Word. The Scriptures must have supreme authority in the church, and no man, not even the pope himself has the right to exalt his authority over the Word of God."

A dark murmur swept through the crowd. Even the Wittenbergers on Luther's side of the great hall shifted uncomfortably.

"Oh yes, of course," Eck said, turning to the crowd. "Doesn't this sound familiar? I hear the voice of John Hus calling to us from the flames but hissing through the lips of Martin Luther. 'Only the Scriptures are authoritative!' But what he means is, 'Only the Scriptures as *I* interpret them!' All the heretics say the same thing, Doctor. Only *they* are right! Only *they* are to be believed! That is precisely what Hus said. And that is precisely why he was burned as a heretic!"

Luther's voice rose to match volume with Eck. "If I am burned, sir, you will have to use the Bible as kindling. I do not reject the authority of the church, Doctor Eck. Nor do I reject your argument—"

"Ah, there it is!" Eck thundered, pointing at Luther. "At last you admit that I am—"

"You have failed utterly," Luther continued, "to provide one shred of legitimate evidence from the Bible for the primacy of the pope! The grass of Rome will wither and the flower of Rome with fade, but the Word of God will stand forever. And so will Luther!" At that the Wittenbergers roared their approval and stomped their feet.

ERFURT

Jonathan Reuchlin bowed his head and prayed fervently for the third time that day. He had missed matins three times that week and was preparing himself for confession. He knelt on the stone floor and tried to concentrate on the last prayer of his rosary. "Hail Mary," he whispered, his lips barely moving.

He prayed that he might find some peace in this, the fifteenth and final bead of the rosary. He always opened his eyes during his last prayer and gazed at it. He thought of his mother as he touched the delicate globe, so different from the blue and red paste beads that garnished the rest of his string. It was a small pearl Marta had pressed into his palm the night before he had left.

She'd said, looking at the pearl, "I know it's a material possession and all, but surely they'll let you keep it on your rosary. A reminder to pray for your old mother." She smiled at him then, the pride shining in her eyes. Jonathan kissed her forehead.

"You're a good boy, Jonathan," Marta had continued, her voice halting. "A priest with a real education... I couldn't have asked more for you."

"I won't be gone forever, Mother. I'll visit—"

"I know." She'd patted his hand. "But things are never the same when a child grows up."

Kneeling before the altar, Jonathan remembered the mixture of joy and sadness in her face, and he vowed he would be the best priest he could be. For her.

She had died several weeks before. The guilt of his not being there for her was only now beginning to fade. But it wasn't his mother's death that was haunting him now.

He had other reasons for feeling guilty.

He whispered the doxology, "Glory be to the God and Father of our Lord Jesus Christ..." *Glory to God,* he thought to himself. *Not glory to Jonathan.* "Father, take this prideful ambition from my heart, and grant me your peace," he whispered, departing from the rosary formula. "Father, you've given me a heart for the poor, for the little ones with broken wings. But now I want to fly, and I don't know how to help them. I'm not even sure I want to help them anymore, and I know that's wrong. I long for the praise of the world. I want to walk with powerful men. O God, why have you put this desire in my heart if it is so hateful to you? Dear Lord, purify me and grant me, I pray, your mercy in confession now. Let me be honest with Prior Winand. Thank you, Father, for your—" He jumped as a hand gripped his shoulder.

"Well, Father Jonathan," Basil said in a loud whisper. "How nice of you to visit us. Father Winand wants to hear your confession. That is, if you're not too busy," he added sarcastically.

"Yes, Father." Jonathan was staring at the floor, too ashamed to speak. He felt Basil turn and walk away. When he couldn't hear the footsteps anymore, he left the chapel without looking around at his fellow monks. Prime was over.

"Enter." Father Winand's voice sounded stern and cold. Jonathan walked into the cell with his head bowed. "Here," Father Winand said, rising from his stool and crossing in front of his small desk. He pointed to the floor in front of him.

Jonathan lay in front of the prior of the monastery and spread his hands out to the side. "Forgive me, Father, for I have sinned."

"I will hear your confession, my son," Father Winand said without any trace of emotion in his voice.

"I missed matins three times this week and prime this morning."

"Why did you miss, my son?" a bit of warmth in his voice now. Jonathan paused.

"Jonathan, why did you miss the hours?"

"I was thinking, Father," Jonathan managed.

"Thinking. About your mother? It's understandable if you're still upset over her death. I know you wish you could have been there."

"I think of her often, yes, but I'm at peace with her passing, Father. At least it's getting a little easier."

Father Winand sighed and looked at the younger priest with kind eyes. "Something is bothering you, Jonathan," he said quietly. "Impure thoughts, perhaps?"

"I've been…," he paused. "Father, may I ask you a question?"

"Certainly."

"Did you ever long for higher office? Did you ever want to be a bishop? A cardinal? When you were young, I mean?" Jonathan watched him closely for his reaction.

Father Winand frowned a bit, but he didn't seem to be angry. He returned to his stool behind the desk and sat, folding his arms in front of him. "When I was young?" he asked. "Father Jonathan, we old codgers can lust after glory just as readily as you or any other young buck you could name."

"It is a sin, though, to lust for high office?"

"Lust is always a sin, Jonathan, no matter what the object of desire is. But there is a difference between lust and righteous desire. Lust is always selfish and prideful. Remember James and John. They asked the Lord Jesus to place them on his right and his left, the positions of highest honor in his Kingdom, and the Lord rebuked them for it because their motives were selfish. If you desire high office to make you feel important so that others will admire you and bow to you, then yes, no doubt, it's a sin. If, however, you are that rare man who desires high office so that he might serve more of God's children and serve them better, then it's a righteous desire."

"I do want to serve, Father, especially the poor. But I also know that I love the applause of men."

Father Winand smiled. "An honest answer. Now here's an honest piece of advice. Don't seek the office. Seek to serve instead, and let God open the office ahead of you. 'Humble yourself under the mighty hand of God, and he will exalt you,'" he said, quoting James 4:10. "Now is that all?" he asked.

"By Saint Augustine," Jonathan said solemnly.

"Jonathan, let's stop before you add another sin to the list," Father Winand said, lifting the young priest from the floor. "Your penance will be fifteen Aves, five for each of the matins, and five Paters for missing prime this morning, and don't let it happen again.

"Now," Father Winand continued, his fatherly tone restored, "I think you need some time away, and I've got an assignment for you. It isn't a particularly pleasant assignment, but given your current struggle with ambition, this may be a divine appointment." He said the last word with a noticeable smile as he looked at the papers on the table that served as his desk. "Sit, sit," he said, and Jonathan lowered himself into a chair in front of the desk. "You've heard of Luther, I imagine?" Winand asked.

Jonathan didn't know how to respond. He wondered for a moment if someone might have told the prior what he had been reading. He had gotten his hands on some of Luther's books and had been reading and rereading them for weeks. It was Luther's words that had awakened a renewed sense of sin and of God's grace in Jonathan's soul.

"I've heard of him, Father," he said. It wasn't a lie but close enough to make him nervous.

"He was a student here, you know," Father Winand continued. "Not that long ago. He teaches over in Wittenberg."

"Yes, Father."

"He is a thinker," he continued. "I'll give him that. But his ideas—some of them—deny the authority of the church. He could have repented in Augsburg—he had the chance. He refused, of course." Father Winand looked down, cleared his throat, and shuffled papers on his desk.

"You disagree with Luther's views, then," Jonathan said, trying to conceal his disappointment.

"His view was subversive," Father Winand said. "But that's not the same as being wrong, at least not to my way of thinking. Luther wouldn't budge at Augsburg or Leipzig. He wouldn't take anything but Scripture as absolutely authoritative. You should have heard him. He dismissed the councils, the apocryphal writings, all the decretals of canon law. Phew!" He raised his hand in a sweeping gesture.

"He denied the authority of the councils?" Jonathan asked, incredulous that Luther's stance was so extreme. To Jonathan, questioning the council was the same as questioning God himself.

Father Winand nodded. "He said they could make mistakes. Straight out. Said it to Johann Eck's face in front of the whole assembly at Leipzig. So, of course, Eck accused Luther of being a Hussite, and Luther thundered back that he was no Bohemian. Oh, it was incredible."

Jonathan swallowed hard. Father Winand continued, "Then, the last couple of days, Eck brought up purgatory, and you can imagine what Luther did with that."

"Refused to accept Second Maccabees?" Jonathan asked.

"It isn't Scripture!" Father Winand said, imitating Luther's voice. "Of course he rejected it. Eck knew he would reject it, but he made him say so publicly. They talked about penance, they talked about indulgences, on and on—for *seventeen days,* believe it or not. They'd still be going if Duke George hadn't stepped in."

Winand's tone became more serious. "What happened at Leipzig makes it impossible for Rome to ignore Luther. He embarrassed Eck, and if you embarrass Eck, you embarrass Rome. Luther should have known that, but then I doubt it would have made any difference to him what Rome thinks. At any rate, the Holy See is concerned, to say the least. A representative came to see me the other day."

"Really?" Jonathan asked, more excitedly than he intended. Father Winand looked up at him, measuring his response quickly.

"It was a private meeting," he explained with a hint of warning in his voice. "I can only say that we have been ordered to investigate certain charges against Luther. He's supposed to have written in his own hand that he is a son of the devil, or some such nonsense. I've known Martin for many years—I've never met a more sincere, devoted man of God."

Winand smiled slightly. He spoke again, his voice barely above a whisper. "But for Rome, the truth is whatever condemns Luther as a heretic. They're grasping at straws, but if they can make these accusations stick, it may be enough to force Prince Frederick to turn Martin over to the authorities."

"And they want us to investigate?" Jonathan asked.

Winand shrugged. "Could be any number of reasons: Luther taught here recently, I know him better than anyone in Wittenberg except Staupitz, and Rome would never ask him since he and Luther are such close friends. Who knows? Maybe they think I would be more willing to find what they are looking for. There's a comforting thought." He lowered his eyes slightly. "At any rate, we *will* investigate. Fairly. Impartially. Understood?"

Jonathan's heart was pounding. "Understood, Father. But you do understand that I tend to favor—"

Winand raised his hand. "We *all* tend to favor the truth, don't we my son? The truth, am I right?"

"Of course, Father."

"Good." Winand relaxed and leaned back against the wall. "I'm sending you to Grimma. You know the place?"

"I think so. About half a day's ride east of Leipzig. Isn't there a convent down that way?"

"Nimbschen, yes. A stone's throw from Grimma. You'll find a man at the Broken Bow Tavern there in Grimma. You are to ask for Herr Schwartz. He's the one with the charges against Father Martin. Tall fellow. Over six feet, I understand. Black hair, fiftyish. Here, I've written it all down for you." He took one of the pieces of paper from the desk, folded it, and handed it to Jonathan.

"Write down what he says carefully. Bring back a detailed report. I want to look into his claims myself before we send them on to Rome. Godspeed on your journey," he said, rising from the stool and crossing to the door.

"When am I to go, Father?" Jonathan asked.

"Can you be ready tomorrow?"

"Certainly." Jonathan rose, bowed, and turned.

"Oh, I almost forgot," Father Winand said, crossing to his bed. He knelt and dug a pouch from under his bedding. "The…powers that be…agreed to pay him fifteen silver pieces." He jingled the coins in the cloth bag as he stood. "I hate asking you to do this," he said, still looking at the pouch. "Jonathan, please, you must, you *must* be careful." He handed the pouch to the young priest quickly.

"I will, Father," Jonathan said, crossing the room. He closed the door softly behind him and walked quietly down the shadowed halls, wondering what kind of information would be worth this much money.

Chapter 14

1519

GRIMMA

The Broken Bow wasn't hard to find. As Jonathan approached the building, his eyes were drawn to the sagging second story. The spine of the roof had buckled into a broad V, forcing the eaves at both ends of the tavern to strain back toward the center of the roof at an awkward angle. Rough lumber covered several of the windows. The whitewash had long since darkled into brown and moldy green splotches. Overall, the structure resembled a bloated toad with a bad back squatting in the mud.

Jonathan pushed open the door. It scraped along the packed earth floor, resisting his entry until it finally stopped, allowing him just enough room to squeeze through with the board he used as a portable desk tucked under his arm. He took out the note Father Winand had given him and strained to read it again. His eyes adjusted slowly to the thick darkness inside the tavern. Candles burned at several of the low tables. There were few patrons at this hour of the morning and no one behind the bar. The two men slouching at the tables looked as if they had spent the night in those same positions. They were arguing loudly.

"What?" a voice boomed behind Jonathan.

"Ah!"

"Who are you? What do you want here?"

Jonathan turned to face a tall man with coarse black hair that hung in thick strands from his balding head and reached almost to his shoulders. "Good grief, man, you scared me half out of my wits!" Jonathan said, as he caught a whiff of the man's scent. His breath was fouled from bad beer and rotting teeth. The stink almost made him gag. "I'm Father Jonathan Reuchlin. I'm looking for a man named Schwartz," he said.

"You come from Erfurt," the man said impatiently.

"I did. Are you Schwartz?" he asked.

"I'm his business partner, you might say." The man squinted his eyes and cocked his head. He was a big man and burly, and was apparently more accustomed to asking rather than answering questions.

"Why didn't he come himself?" Jonathan asked.

"That ain't your business, priest." He took a step toward Jonathan and lowered his head. "Now you listen up, bright boy. This Luther is in with witches. I got proof. But it's gonna cost."

"You show me your proof. If I like what I see, then you get the money," Jonathan said. "Otherwise I go back to Erfurt."

The man cursed. "I could kill you where you stand and take it right now in a twinklin'," he muttered. He pulled a rusty knife from a sheath behind his back.

"You won't kill a priest," Jonathan said, trying to sound confident and at the same time calculating the distance to the door. "Where would you find forgiveness then? You'd burn in the fires of hell. No purgatory. No heaven. Hell. Forever." The man didn't move. His face fell. He might be a stupid bully, but he was scared when confronted with the threat of eternal pain. "Now show me your proof," Jonathan said. "Or I'm leaving."

"Here," the man said, lifting a bag containing something heavy onto the bench that served as a bar. "Make it quick."

Jonathan reached into the sack and pulled out a large old book.

"What's this?" he asked, holding the text up to the candlelight. The book was falling apart in Jonathan's hands. String was laced through the binding to hold the pages in place. Then, in a flash, he recognized it. He had grown up looking at that book. He opened it quickly to the marked page where he saw the woodcut of a great fish. He remembered it well.

Remembered seeing it first on the stormy night Martin Luther had come to his house when he was a child. Jonathan felt his stomach tighten. Memories rushed back over him, flew at him like thin shards of glass: memories of his stepfather beating him, cutting him, ripping his mother's hair out. And of the book. This book that had meant so much to her.

He closed the volume and looked up at the man. "Where did you get this?" he asked, his voice hard.

Jonathan's sudden anger caught the man off guard. He didn't answer.

Jonathan slid the book back in the sack and tied the neck of the sack in a knot.

"I said, where did you *get* this?" Jonathan turned to face the man.

The man crouched slightly. "Don't matter. I got it, that's all."

"Luther's name isn't in this book, you idiot," Jonathan said, as he took a step closer.

"It is so," the man said quickly. "There's a prophecy—"

"Yes, but Luther isn't named."

"What?" The man was confused. He was backing up now, his eyes, darting right and left.

Jonathan took another step forward. He knew now who was behind all this. "Your partner—what's his name? I'll wager it isn't 'Schwartz.'" His eyes bored into the man.

"I didn't steal nothin'," the man said, his voice rising.

"His name is Reisner, isn't it? Klaus Reisner!"

The man's eyes focused on something behind Jonathan, and he stopped his retreat. "That name ain't nothin' to me," he said angrily, taking a step forward. "Give me the money, priest!" He glanced quickly over Jonathan's right shoulder.

At the same time, Jonathan saw a shadow pass over the man's face. Someone was coming up fast behind him. Over his shoulder Jonathan caught a glimpse of a trollish lump of a man swinging at his head. Jonathan ducked, and the chair slammed into the chest of the man in front of him, sending him sprawling across the floor.

Jonathan came up swinging the sack containing the heavy book and caught the short man behind him squarely on the side of the head, knocking him back into the shadows.

The first man scooped a fistful of dirt and threw it in Jonathan's face. He stumbled backward, dropping the sack, trying to wipe the sand from his eyes. Both his attackers were on their feet in a flash, one beating him in the ribs from behind, the other slamming his fist into Jonathan's face. He slipped and fell. Reaching out with his hand, desperately searching for anything to defend himself, his hand found the knotted sack on the floor. He lurched to his feet again, swinging wildly, but missing. The two men dodged the first and second swings, then caught him and launched him out the door and into the street where he landed on top of the book, winded and dazed.

"The purse! Get his money purse, and cut his throat!" one of them shouted.

But Jonathan was too weak to resist. He was on the verge of passing out when he felt one of the men ripping his money pouch free from his belt.

"Hey! Hey there!" It was a different voice and sounded far away and hollow.

He heard the men curse him, then heard their footsteps running away as his rescuer approached. He felt an arm around him. A woman's voice was suddenly close. "Father, Father, are you hurt?" she asked.

Jonathan was still too winded to speak. He braced himself against the strong arm and pulled himself up to his knees. Then he glanced up to see the one who had saved him. Before him stood a young nun of no more than twenty years. "Ohh…" He lowered his head and moaned as he rocked back on his heels.

"Here," she said, "let me help you." Sudden dizziness swept over him, and he had to lower his head to regain his balance. The young woman knelt beside him in the street, placing her small basket by his side as she grasped his hands to steady him.

"Thank you," he said weakly. "You probably saved my life there."

He looked at her again, and what he saw froze him. Her mouth was perfectly formed and small, her skin fair and smooth as ivory. But it was
her eyes—dark, wide-set, full of mystery and strength—that most
reminded him of Elizabeth. For a split second he hoped…but it wasn't
her. He shook his head, trying to clear his thoughts.

"Do you think you can stand?" she asked. She helped him to his
feet, then picked up the basket.

"Thank you. I'll be fine. I'll be fine," he said, finally standing erect
but with his hand to his forehead. He bent over again, trying to get his
wind and shake off the dizziness. He felt the back of his scalp. He had
a growing knot at the base of his skull and a nasty cut. He looked
around and found the sack containing the starbook. He picked it up
and struggled to stand up straight.

"What happened?" she asked. "I saw those men…"

"The tavern keeper. He and another man robbed me."

"I know the tavern keeper here in Grimma, Father. I've never seen
those two in my life."

"I should've expected as much."

"They knew you had money?"

"Oh. Yes, I'm sorry. I'm here on church business, about Martin
Luther—oh!" He put his hand to his head again and took a step back
to regain his balance. "Forgive me, Sister. I haven't eaten in almost two
days. You wouldn't have any bread in that basket, would you?"

The girl smiled. "I've just come from the market. Here." She pulled
back the plain white cloth, broke off a piece of bread, and handed it to
him. "And if you feel you're up to a short walk, we can get some cold
water from the well at the convent."

"Thank you. You're very kind, Sister…?"

"Katherine. Katherine von Bora."

"Sister Katherine. I'm Father Jonathan. You don't happen…?" he
said, returning her smile. She looked at him expectantly, but he said
nothing more. He was still looking at her. The resemblance to Elizabeth
was striking. Katherine cleared her throat.

"Father?" she asked.

"Yes, yes," Jonathan said, shaking his head and smiling. "I'm sorry. It's just that you remind me of someone I knew years ago."

A few miles away in the forest on the outskirts of Grimma, two men sat huddled over a low-burning fire. A jug and a money pouch lay to one side. Two short stacks of silver coins graced the flat rock that served as a rickety table between them, a single stack in front of each man.

"There. That's it then," said the one with the purple-and-black bruise on the side of his face. "Ten and two for you. Ten and two for me."

"All those years, think on it...," the other reminisced. "That old book was nothing but a doorstop! And now it's made us rich."

"You gotta put books to practical use, that's what I say. It made a fine doorstop too. Where'm I gonna get another as good, is what I'd like to know."

"Yeah, well you can buy yourself a doorstop now with that coin, my friend. Thanks to Mr. Luther."

"Here's to Mr. Luther then," the other said, lifting the jug in a toast. "And here's to the old cow I married and left to rot."

"What you want to waste good liquor for, drinking to her?"

"Because she's the one kept harpin' on Luther bein' in the book, that's why! Day in, day out, 'Luther's the storm chaser! Luther's the one that's in the prophecy! Luther's goin' to give us poor folk our freedom!' Bah! The only thing Luther give me is this scar, see?" He pointed to a gash on the back of his head, then took another pull from the jug. "So anyways I figure if a priest as high powered as Luther is in that book of witchin', it ought to be worth somethin' to them as wants his head on a pike. And was I right?'

"You was."

"'Course I was." The little hump of a man with the filthy yellow hair grunted as he picked up the stack of coins in front of him, and dropped them, clinking, into his palm one by one. A thin line creased his face. He loved the heft of silver in his hand.

Jonathan and Sister Katherine hadn't gone far beyond the western out-skirts of Grimma when they found themselves standing beside a wall, perhaps seven feet tall, that stretched for a good two hundred feet, and then turned to the left. They followed the wall around the bend until they came to a high iron gate. A carved sign affixed to the wall read "Order of the Sacred Heart, Nimbschen."

"Wait here," Katherine whispered as she moved toward the entrance. She rang a small bell, and soon another sister approached. She unlatched the gate and pulled it open to allow the young woman entrance. As soon as she was inside, the other nun closed the gate with a clang and slid the bolt into place. Then they turned and walked away. Sister Katherine moved quickly around the corner and disappeared, leaving Jonathan standing and munching on his third piece of bread. Then, quite unexpectedly, an idea broke upon him.

"Oh, Lord," he said. "You led me to this place, this blessing, with nothing in my hand. Perhaps I could lead others here who need help, who have nothing…" But before he had time to think further, the sis-ter returned, carrying a large cup of cool well water.

"Sister, thank you——," he started, but she put a finger to her lips then slid the bolt back to open the gate. She slipped outside, glancing back through the bars to see if anyone was watching.

"Come, we can't talk here. Follow me." They walked about thirty yards, then around the corner of the convent wall. There they stood in the shade of a large maple, nestled in a quiet, out-of-the-way nook on the back side of the convent.

"I come here often to pray. And to think," she said, gazing up at the tree. Her eyes refocused on him quickly. "Father, you mentioned you are acquainted with Dr. Martin Luther. Do you have any of his pamphlets?"

Her eagerness surprised him. "No. I really don't know him. When I was a boy…but I'm afraid not," he said. "You know how to read?"

"Of course I know how to read, Father," she said with a hint of impatience. "Tell me—do you know him?"

"I know *of* him. A lot of people think he's dangerous, but I've read him, and I find his views—how should I say?—interesting," he said with a smile.

Sister Katherine stiffened a bit. "Father, please. Don't patronize me. Luther's views are—"

Clang! Clang! Clang! The bell pealed out sharply. "Sister Katherine!" a woman's voice bellowed from the other side of the wall.

"Coming!" she answered quickly. "I must go," Katherine said, taking the cup from Jonathan.

"Sister Katherine, one last favor…"

"Yes?"

"Do you take in the poor, the homeless?"

"At times. For a few days. Now I must go. Good-bye, Father." She ran from the small grove before he could say a word, then slowed to a more dignified walk as she rounded the corner and disappeared.

Jonathan made the trip back to Erfurt in just under two days. He had received what he had come for, the "evidence" against Luther, which he promptly handed over to Father Winand, who knew precisely what to do with it. He wouldn't destroy it—in case the Holy See later decided to review the contents. Instead, he would place the starbook in a safe place, away from prying eyes. Then he would compose a letter to his superiors expressing his surprise at not having found one shred of evidence against Luther in the book. He could "hardly contain himself," he would write, upon discovering that Luther was innocent of the charges against him. And that was the absolute truth.

Chapter 15

Pope Julius had died, leaving the new basilica in Rome unfinished. The new Pope Leo had taken up the cause with gusto, adding his own considerable aesthetic influence through the artists he had commissioned to complete the project. Progress had been good, but tragedy had struck in the death of Leo's favorite painter in April. Raphael, only thirty-seven when he died, was the most beloved artist in Italy. His death had depressed Leo for weeks, forcing him into seclusion in the country. Here in the sylvan setting of his hunting lodge in Magliana, Leo tried but failed to rid himself of his personal darkness.

Raphael's vivid style provoked mere curiosity in the culturally unlettered, but in a man like Leo, who not only appreciated great art but understood it, Raphael's untimely death was at best careless of God and at worst capricious. The artist's unexcused absence left Leo drained and bitter, and caustic to the lesser lights of the Italian court.

One of those smoldering wicks was Archbishop Gabriel Merino, the man chosen to wait on Leo this morning. Leo had initially elevated Merino to an archbishopric because of his beautiful singing voice, but he had noted early on that Merino also happened to be a decent social secretary. Most of his duties here in Magliana involved scheduling the pontiff's daily hunt, various games of cards and dice, musicians, and of course the clowns, whom Leo would engage in debating the immortality of the soul at the dinner table.

But Leo despised Merino's thin skin. Like all artists, his sensitive nature was too easily bruised. He needed toughening, and Leo would see to it. So, even though Merino was not much of a sportsman, Leo insisted that he serve as his whipper, the man responsible for driving errant hounds back into the pack on the hunt. He knew that Merino loathed the assignment, but he could hardly decline his duties. Besides, it would serve to run some of the softness out of him.

Along that line, Leo made a mental note to restrict some of Merino's meals. One of the archbishop's more delightful duties was to eat for Leo. The pope's doctors had placed him on a restricted diet for his failing health, but he had been such a voracious eater for so many years that he couldn't bear the thought of totally abandoning his delight in food. So he would enjoy his Lucullan feasts vicariously, watching as Merino and other courtiers consumed vast quantities of food in his presence. There was a certain tepid pleasure in it, but Merino was growing too fat to chase the hounds effectively. It would do Merino's soul good to suffer some deprivation as well. It would help him appreciate the agonies of his pontiff.

"Good morning, Holiness," Merino said as cheerily as he could, knowing what was coming. "I pray you had a fine—"

"Merino, it's bad enough I have to put up with stale bread, rotten fruit, and weak wine for my breakfast. I shouldn't have to listen to your tripe as well."

"Apologies, Holiness," Merino said, bowing.

"The cardinal told you about the English King Henry, I suppose?" Leo said as he mounted the small platform, then tried to squeeze his bulk between the arms of the minithrone.

"No, Your Holiness."

"The man's attending a Bacchanalia—gorging himself on the finest wine, the most exquisite food in the world."

"Surely these are rumors, Your Holiness—"

"Imagine," Leo said, ignoring his archbishop. "England and France, the festival of the century, and they didn't have the common courtesy to invite the Vicar of Christ. Cajetan says they are meeting just outside Calais on the Field of the Cloth of Gold. Ten thousand courtiers at least—*ten thousand!* And the banquets—ah, Merino, and the tournaments and the spectacles—it's supposed to last for the better part of a month." He leaned back and closed his eyes and lifted his hand in a slow circle as if to circumscribe the circus in the air. Then he opened his eyes and pointed a stubby finger at the underling. "Now you tell me where France is getting the money for this? Hmm? Where?"

Merino could only shake his head.

"I'll tell you where! He's borrowing it—putting France in a hole she will never be able to climb out of." He took a deep breath and wiped the sweat from his face with his handkerchief, then folded it into a neat square. He muttered, "He should be sending his money to help rebuild the great basilica for Saint Peter instead of digging a grave for France!"

"I'm sure Your Holiness is—," Merino started, but Leo cut him off again.

"Bring me the papers," Leo mumbled just loud enough for his archbishop to hear.

"At once." Merino backed away quickly, then turned toward the doors. Ten minutes later he reentered with a stack of loose documents of varying size.

"What's this?" the pontiff asked stiffly, as he shuffled through the pile. He hadn't moved from the corner of the chair, nor had his expression changed in the least. "Well?"

"The papers you asked for, Holiness," Merino offered apologetically. "Here is your recent correspondence with the emperor. This one is the encyclical you've been composing for the last two weeks. Here is your defense on papal infallibility. And I believe this one—"

"I can read," Leo said, spitting the words out. "I'm not that old, am I? Not that blind! These have all been signed, or have *you* forgotten how to read?" Leo threw the pile at the confused bishop. The papers fluttered across the floor. Merino stooped immediately to pick them up. "And why haven't they been posted?"

"I beg your pardon, Holiness. Please, I thought—"

"You thought! You...you need a brain to think, Merino. Why in the name of Saint Peter I ever made you archbishop, I..." Leo put his face into his hand and rubbed his pounding forehead. "Just bring me the bull against Luther," Leo added.

"At once, Your Holiness," Merino said, withdrawing. He returned in less than two minutes with the papal condemnation. "You wish to sign it, Father?" he asked slightly out of breath. He had brought his small writing desk, a quill, and some ink.

"Read it to me," the pope said without looking up.

Merino cleared his throat and began to read as smoothly as his rapid breathing would allow.

"Arise, O Lord, and judge thy cause. A wild boar has invaded thy vineyard."

Hearing his own words read back to him was one of the few worldly pleasures in which Leo could still indulge without suffering immediate consequences. He often tried to incorporate his surroundings in his writings. Eck, the theologian who'd had a decidedly poor showing in his debate against Luther at Leipzig, had written the rough draft, but the final touches were distinctively Leo's. He lifted his eyes to examine the stone and raw wood of his surroundings as Merino read. His writing worked on an aesthetic as well as a theological level. The allusions to the boar and other beasts in this bull were thoroughly apropos to the ambiance of the hunting lodge—even though few if any would know that the bull had been composed "in the wild," so to speak. The archbishop continued to read.

"We can scarcely express our grief over the ancient heresies that have been revived in Germany. We are the more disheartened because the office can no longer tolerate the pestilent virus of the following forty-one errors. Number one—"

"No, no," Leo interrupted. "I know the list. Go on with the letter."

"Yes, Holiness. Let me see, yes, here… 'We can no longer suffer the serpent to creep through the field of the Lord. The books of Martin Luther that contain these errors are to be thoroughly examined. As for Martin—'"

"Wait. Change that last line. Make it read, 'The books of Martin Luther which contain these errors are to be examined and burned.' Write it down."

Merino fumbled a bit with the quill and the small ink glass, then scribbled a note to himself in the margin. "As you wish, Holiness."

"Go on."

"As for Martin himself, good God, what office of fatherly love have we omitted in order to recall him from his errors? Have we not offered him a safe conduct and money for the journey? And he has had the temerity to appeal to a future council although our predecessors, Pius III and Julius II, subjected such appeals to the penalties of heresy. Now therefore, we give Martin sixty days in which to submit, dating from the time of the publication of this bull in his district. Anyone who stands in our way places himself under the wrath of Almighty God."

Merino was an excellent reader, having built to an understated climax on the word "wrath." He placed the manuscript in Leo's lap with a small flourish and awaited his good pleasure.

"Add 'and of the apostles Peter and Paul,' and this date, et cetera, to the last line," Leo said offhandedly.

Merino made the necessary notations. "Will that be all, Holiness?" he asked, his voice betraying a hint of disappointment. He placed the manuscript in the small desk and closed the lid.

"Make the changes quickly and bring it to me to sign." He rubbed his face again then glanced up sharply. "Go! What are you standing around for?"

The archbishop turned and was leaving when Leo spoke again,

"Oh, Merino…" The door opened, and he stepped half back inside. "Today's hunt? You'll be my whipper."

"Of course, Holiness."

MAINZ

It was a cold, sullen day when Dr. Girolamo Aleander, rector of the University of Paris, dismounted from a tired black mare in the center of town and stood beside a low pile of sodden pamphlets and books. He carried a flaming torch in one hand and hoped the slow falling rain wouldn't douse it before he could perform his task. The wetness dripped off the brim of his hat, and a cold trickle sneaked behind his collar and slipped like a sliver of ice down the middle of his back. He sneezed twice, then sniffed and straightened himself. He cleared his raw throat, hoarse from so many cities and villages. His station in life should have afforded him the privilege of having his message read by a city official. But few in the small villages could read at all, and when he found someone who could read, it took forever. So he soon gave up and submitted to the indignity of reading himself. As he coughed again, he could see his breath, a light gray cloud hanging then dissipating in the darker air. "Hear ye, good citizens of Mainz," he called out in a rasping voice.

A few of those who had already stopped to see what was going on drew closer.

"I am Dr. Girolamo Aleander, rector of the University of Paris," he said, holding the torch high. "I, along with my colleague Dr. John Eck—perhaps you've heard of him…" Aleander peered into their eyes but found the same suspicion he had encountered in every other German hamlet he had visited over the last three weeks. None of them was even close to being adequately impressed with his credentials. And every one of them, so far, held sympathies for Luther. He turned, reaching into his saddlebag with his free hand, and withdrew the papal bull. "I have been commissioned by His Holiness Pope Leo to publish this papal bull condemning the heretic Martin Luther and his works. In order to do that—are you following me?—in order to do that, I will first read the bull—this piece of paper here." And he lifted it high for all to see, though he immediately felt foolish since there were only six or seven stragglers present. He continued, "Then I will set fire to the books of the damnable Hussite. God's will be done."

He took a step forward and, holding the bull in his left hand and the torch in his right, read the condemnation as loudly as his inflamed vocal cords would allow, though he had to pause often to cough. Three of those gathered left halfway through the reading. Near the end of his recitation, a few women who were herding a flock of geese to market paused to investigate. The geese were honking so loudly, Aleander had to strain his voice even more to be heard. The largest of the matrons folded her arms and listened, a furrow deepening between her eyes.

"Agnes, you hear?" she said. "It's Dr. Luther he's talkin' about." She turned to face Aleander. "Say, your lordship, those Dr. Luther's books there?" she asked, pointing to the small stack.

Aleander finished the last sentence, folded the bull with a practiced motion of one hand, and stepped forward. "They are Luther's works, madam, and they are to be burned." The "works" consisted of two of Luther's pamphlets to which Aleander had added a few nondescript manuscripts to increase the heft of the pile.

"Burned?" Agnes shouted. "How could you do such a thing? And Dr. Luther not even here to defend himself!"

Aleander tossed back his cape with a flair. "The monk has had time enough and more to recant his heresies. I know for a fact he received a copy of this bull over a month ago, and still he's made no reply. His Holiness has graciously given him sixty days, but Luther will never do it. Never. The judgment of the Holy See is final and irrevocable. Luther's books shall be burned. Now!"

He stepped back dramatically, intending to put the torch to the small pile of soggy manuscripts. But in stepping back so quickly, he failed to see a goose that had wandered behind him and tripped over it, sending him sprawling into the street, dropping the bull and the torch onto the sodden pile of papers.

The bull provided sufficient tinder as it caught immediately and burned weakly on top of Luther's waterlogged and now thoroughly flame-retardant manuscripts. The women, however, were red hot. They picked up some loose stones and began to pelt the dismal rector of the University of Paris, even as he lay prone in the mud. He struggled to his feet and tried to grab at his horse's reins, but the beast broke and galloped off down the street. The geese had simply gone mad and were running around in all directions, honking, flapping their great wings, and nipping sharply at whoever got in their way, including the esteemed doctor.

"Burn the good Doctor Luther, will ya?" one of the women shouted as she picked up another rock. "Take these stones back to Rome for your cathedral! You'll not get a penny from us!"

"Aye, bless Dr. Luther we say, and Rome can burn!" another added, throwing a rock that caught Aleander in the ribs. The rest of the women joined in and sent Aleander scurrying down the street to a chorus of honking geese and a hail of stones. If the local abbot hadn't taken pity on him and given him shelter, Aleander might not have made it out of Mainz in one piece.

Chapter 16

The road from Erfurt north to Wittenberg cut through over one hundred fifty miles of forest and farmland, hills and lowlands. But winter had left the countryside barren, and this had been a snowless December. All the land whistled with the sameness of an icy north wind, and the roads had all turned to hard-packed earth and rock.

Jonathan sat in the back of the slow-moving oxcart, his knees drawn up to keep him warm and to make a knobby shelf for his folded arms and his chin. It wasn't quite daylight yet and it was bitterly cold.

Justus Jonas, Martin Luther's dear friend, pulled his cloak tighter about him. "It's a wicked wind this morning," he said.

Jonathan said nothing.

Justus shook his head, then looked at Jonathan. "It's time to count your blessings, Jonathan." Justus held up his hand and marked off the blessings on his fingers. "In the last six weeks you got ordained, Father Winand recommended you for a teaching post, then Staupitz himself sends me to fetch you to Wittenberg to teach at university. Three major blessings in less than two months, and yet here you sit, sullen as a lump on a log. Wittenberg, Jonathan. Martin Luther. Reform. Think!"

Jonathan hadn't told Justus, or anyone else for that matter, about Luther's late-night visit to his home when he was a child.

Justus sighed. "It's time to put the past behind you, Jon."

142

Jonathan shook his head and said nothing. The two men stared out at the barren countryside. Justus studied the younger priest for a few moments, then lowered his voice and leaned in closer so that the driver of the cart might not hear. "You have to forsake your desire for that woman."

Jonathan lifted his head and his mouth dropped open. "What woman?"

"Jonathan…"

"What? Father Justus, there is no—" He caught himself before he got too loud, then continued in a lower voice, "There is no woman."

"Lying's still a sin, Jon."

Jonathan started to say something, then stopped himself.

Justus leaned back and picked up his traveling bag from the front of the cart. "The one you met on the trip to Grimma," he said.

"That was a year and a half ago!"

Justus jumped off the cart and began to walk. "Thanks, friend," he said to the driver as he passed him on the road. "I think we'll walk for a while." The old man waved and nodded as Jonathan grabbed his bag and joined Justus. They were both walking fast and soon left the oxcart behind.

"Father Basil took me aside last evening and shared his heart," Justus said.

Jonathan stopped in the middle of the road. "Basil? Basil talked to you about…oh, this is too much," he said, putting his hands on his hips.

Justus turned back to face him and spoke calmly. "He believes it may be love for some woman that's been eating at you these months."

"All due respect to Basil, but he has no idea of what's going on in my heart." Jonathan turned to walk at an angry pace. "It isn't what you think, Father," he said.

Justus was silent. They walked on without saying a word for another mile. Then Jonathan spoke.

"I did meet a woman there. Her name is Katherine."

"Ah," Justus whispered as if determined to keep any trace of victory out of his voice.

"*Sister* Katherine," Jonathan continued. "She's in the Nimbschen Convent."

Now it was Justus's turn to stop and stare at Jonathan. "A nun? You fell in love with a *nun?*"

"No," Jonathan said. "But she reminded me of someone—a girl I knew years ago."

"I see," Justus said. They started to walk again. "Well," he continued, clearing his throat. "A new start in Wittenberg. It's just the thing— a new life, really. That's the way to look at it. God has blessed you, Jonathan. He's opened this door for you, and now it's time to leave the past behind and walk into a new beginning."

Jonathan reached out and put his hand on Justus's arm. "What did you say?" he asked.

"I said that it's time to leave the past ."

"No, before that."

"That God has opened a door for you?"

"Yes. God *has* opened this door hasn't he, Father? *He* has done it. I haven't sought it."

Justus smiled briefly and glanced over at Jonathan.

"What?" Jonathan asked.

"Sometimes," Justus said, "God gives us what we want, to show us what we need."

Jonathan thought about it, and asked, "Then how should I pray?"

Justus kept his eyes on the road. "Pray that he will give you what you need before you get too much of what you want."

PFORZHEIM

"Maggie!" Elizabeth shouted. "Maggie, please!"

The baby was crowning, and Elizabeth was starting to panic.

Maggie had stepped out for a moment to get some fresh towels, but the baby had decided to enter the world in that brief span. Maggie ran back into the room and stood beside Elizabeth, putting her hand on her shoulder.

"You're doing fine, sweetheart," Maggie said. Her calm voice soothed Elizabeth. She took a deep breath and let it out in a shuddering sigh.

"What do I do? What do I…?" Elizabeth whispered.

"Shh. Get ready now, this contraction should do it. Here it comes. Ready, push! Push! That's right, Sarah. You're doing wonderfully!"

Elizabeth gasped as the child slipped into her waiting hands, slick with blood and quivering with life.

"It's a boy!" she said, tears streaming down her face.

"You did it, Sarah!" Maggie said quietly. "You have a fine new son." Even as she spoke, she bent down to take the newborn from Elizabeth and showed her again how to clean the baby's nose and then to cut and tie off the umbilical cord. "Now turn him over and give him a good whack on the bottom," Maggie said, handing him back to Elizabeth. She had done it once before, but she was still tense. She turned the baby over and spanked him. Nothing. She swatted him again, and this time the child let out a tremulous cry, then a cough, then another wailing cry.

"Well, we know this one's blessed with a good, strong voice," Maggie said, smiling. She came back to take the child. "Elizabeth, why don't you go tell the new father that he has a son, but tell him to give us another few minutes. I'll rinse him off and give him to Sarah. He'll be wanting his first meal before long."

"Yes," Elizabeth said, her eyes welling with tears at the beautiful sight. It was Elizabeth's first baby too. She had assisted Maggie as second midwife on a number of births, but this was the first she had delivered almost entirely on her own. Maggie had told her it would be different than merely watching, but Elizabeth was unprepared for the intense joy of ushering a new life into the world. And being the first to hold that life in her arms. "Oh, Sarah, I'm so happy for you." Sarah was leaning back on the pillows, exhausted. But she managed to mouth the words, "Thank you, Elizabeth."

Elizabeth smiled as she rinsed her hands in one of the basins, then dried them quickly on a towel as she ran out of the room to tell Sarah's husband that his firstborn son was hale and hearty.

COURT OF CHARLES V, HOLY ROMAN EMPEROR
AACHEN, WESTERN GERMANY

Aleander was livid. Emperor Charles had actually invited Luther to attend the general assembly of German princes in the city of Worms the following year. After having Aleander traipsing across the countryside denouncing the heretic, the emperor was turning the tables! It was hard enough for Aleander to accept the fact that Charles, barely twenty, had recently been crowned Holy Roman Emperor. Apart from the pope, this boy-king was the most powerful man on earth. And now he had summoned Aleander to Aachen to ask his opinion regarding this absurd invitation to Luther. Very well. If the emperor wanted his opinion, Aleander was ready to provide it. He stood before Charles in private session and argued his case against Luther's attending the diet, the general assembly of princes.

"Never, Your Majesty!" Aleander said. "Dr. Eck and I suffered greatly at the hands of men and the fangs of wild beasts to burn the books of this heretic Luther. And now Your Majesty wishes to invite him to a dialogue at a national assembly in a prominent city? The man will turn it into a pulpit for his heresies, Your Majesty."

"I never said a 'dialogue,' Father Aleander. I conferred with his protector prince—what's his name?—ah, yes, Frederick. I spoke to him in Cologne, and expressly requested that he bring Luther to the diet to be investigated."

"By whom, Your Majesty?" Aleander was taking a chance here. He had virtually cut off Charles in midsentence, but he felt he must impress on the young emperor the foolishness of allowing Luther to argue his case before a secular assembly. "Does Your Majesty feel that any in the imperial court are qualified to judge the case?"

Silence.

"Is Your Majesty qualified?"

Silence.

Aleander lowered his voice and softened it. "If the Holy Roman Emperor himself feels that he is unqualified," he said, referring to Charles by his Catholic title, "then who else among the Christian laity would dare presume the office of judge in a case such as this?"

He took a step closer to the throne. "I would gladly confront this Satan myself, Your Majesty, but I beg you, don't compromise the authority of the Holy See by subjecting this judgment to the laity at Worms. The Holy Father himself has condemned Luther. It is the common German peasants, and a few of the subversive free knights who embrace this devil. Surely, it would be in Your Majesty's best interests to keep this case out of their unschooled hands. All due honor to Your Majesty, the only competent judge in this case is the Vicar of Christ. How can the Church be called the ship of Peter if Peter is not at the helm?"

Charles rested his chin in his hand and studied Aleander.

"If Luther wants an audience," Aleander continued, "he can have safe conduct to Rome. Or to Spain," he said with a hint of a smile.

Charles picked up on the small joke—granting Luther safe conduct to Spain would be tantamount to promising no one would kill him on the way to the stake. Aleander took two casual steps forward. He spread his arms slowly, magnificently, and made his final calculated statement.

"Has the Catholic Church been dead for a thousand years to be resurrected by Martin Luther? Has the whole world gone blind and Luther alone has eyes to see?"

His words hit home. The emperor sat immobile, staring at the priest. "Thank you, Father," he said at last. "I will weigh the matter carefully. You have been of inestimable value."

"Your Majesty." Aleander bowed and made his exit gracefully.

WITTENBERG

The morning of December 10 broke over the spires of Wittenberg—a clear sky, brittle with cold and sharp with light. It was nearly nine o'clock when the two young theologians came in view of the spires of Wittenberg.

A crowd of citizens, faculty, and students of the university were pushing through the Elster gate and out past a line of trees and into the meadow that lay between the wall of the city and the river Elbe. Justus and Jonathan had just arrived, and they ran ahead and joined the crowd.

Justus stopped suddenly and caught Jonathan by the sleeve. "Oh, wait, wait, maybe we can catch him," he said. "Martin! Martin! Here, I want you to meet our newest faculty member." A stocky man of medium height stopped in midstride, halting the crowd following in his wake, and looked at Justus impatiently. His eyes shone like two black coals. "This is Father Jonathan Reuchlin. Jonathan, meet Dr. Martin Luther."

Jonathan extended his hand which Luther took in a strong grip. "A pleasure, Dr. Luther."

"Reuchlin. Father Staupitz sent for you, I believe."

"Yes sir."

"Well, Father Jonathan, welcome to Wittenberg. You're just in time to help us burn the canon law. Should give you something to discuss with your students tomorrow, eh?" Luther slapped him on the shoulder, and with that, he was off, the crowd following behind.

"I...I beg your pardon?" Jonathan stammered. But Luther was already halfway down the slope. The procession following him was noisy until it reached the meadow, where it grew solemn and quiet and formed a circle around its leader.

Justus put his hand on Jonathan's shoulder to get his attention. "And that, my friend, is Martin Luther," he said.

Jonathan stared, open-mouthed. Was this the man of the prophecy? The man his mother believed would deliver the German nation and lead the poor and the oppressed to victory? It was difficult to imagine. "He's smaller than I remember," Jonathan whispered back.

"What? I thought you'd never seen him before."

"Oh, well," Jonathan stuttered, remembering that Justus knew nothing of Luther's visit to his home. "I had a picture in my mind, you know, from the time I first heard of him. He's smaller than I thought he would be is what I meant."

Justus laughed. "Most people make that mistake," he said. "Look. There's Philip Melanchthon," Justus said, pointing at the thin man standing on the inner rim of the growing circle near Luther. "Incredible scholar. Martin's right-hand man, really."

"Melanchthon's a reformer, then?" Jonathan asked.

Justus laughed. "If anyone here is more of a reformer than Martin Luther, it's Philip Melanchthon."

"So he's always been? A reformer, I mean."

"Oh, I think most of us knew the church needed to change. We just weren't willing to do anything about it until Martin came along."

"What did he mean about burning the canon law?" Jonathan asked.

Justus smiled. "Just watch."

At a signal from Luther, Melanchthon and some students carried a stack of books and documents to the center of the ring. Several of the faculty, obvious from their regalia, began whispering to one another. Jonathan couldn't hear what was being said, but they were obviously disturbed over what was about to happen.

Luther pointed to the pile of paper in front of him. He raised his voice and all the whispering ceased. "The papal decretals and all the canon law," he said in a clear voice that echoed off the near city walls. "Here is the word of a man—words not infallible but flammable!" He held out his hand, and one of the students handed him a burning torch.

Luther touched it to the edge of the pile, and the paper caught immediately. Soon the flames were shooting into the air.

"Since they burn my books, I burn theirs. And I burn this." Here he pulled from his cloak a short, rolled scroll. He held it high for everyone to see. "This bull condemns not Luther but Christ himself. The canon law has never been worth anything more than what you see now—smoke and ash! For it makes the pope to be a god on earth, and the pope is not God. With this burning, I purge Germany of the execrable bull of the Roman monster once and for all!" And with that he cast the paper into the flames. A brief updraft caught it for a moment and held it suspended in the tower of fire where it ignited in a flash and crumpled into a blackened lump on the pyre. Luther stood silently with the large crowd and watched the rest of the papers burn, then he and his colleagues and many of the townsfolk walked back into Wittenberg.

A large crowd of students stayed, solemn and thoughtful. Justus and Jonathan, too, stood at a distance and watched.

"He actually did it—he burned the canon law." Jonathan whispered.

"Oh yes," Justus said. "They burned his books at Cologne and Mainz. This is no surprise."

"No, no surprise," Jonathan said. "It's just I didn't expect him to be so...so..."

A voice near the fire interrupted Jonathan's thought. Someone had started singing a hymn of praise to God. Soon others joined in the *Te Deum,* and the voices drifted up with the sparks into the night. As soon as it was over, one of the students began shouting jests at Rome. Then another sang a dirge for the death of the canon law.

"I wonder if Dr. Luther knows...if he really understands what's happening here," Jonathan said quietly.

"They're just students, Jon. Blowing off some steam."

Jonathan continued staring at them, singing around the fire. He spoke quietly. "No, Father. They are Germans. The rebellion is coming, don't you see? It isn't just the peasants anymore."

"Dr. Luther isn't fighting a military battle, Jonathan."

"Father, I've been in the south. Thomas Munzer is getting a peasant army together now. Luther is so popular there he could call up a hundred knights tomorrow if he wanted. Some say more. These students know that."

"Jon, think. If there really are a hundred knights spoiling for a fight against Rome, then why are they waiting for Luther to call them? Some in the south have already declared against Rome. Why don't the knights join them and the peasant army now? I'll tell you why. It's because most of the knights want to hold on to their land and their power. If they side with Luther against Rome, they're cutting their own throats."

The two men turned toward a sound on their left.

Some of the students who had left earlier came running out the Elster Gate dressed in weird costumes—baggy trousers, clowns' hats, and the like—carrying an enormous parchment, a mock bull, fastened to a pole. They waved their compatriots back up the hill and into the streets of Wittenberg where some others had formed an impromptu brass band. Justus and Jonathan followed them through the Elster Gate and then left to make their way to Jonathan's new home at the university.

In his room Jonathan lay on his bed with his head near the window and listened. He could still hear them—the students playing their horns and banging their drums in the streets, banging on shop doors and the doors of home after home. Occasionally he heard the breaking of glass.

He tried to unravel the tangle of feelings that kept him awake. He had known before leaving Erfurt that Wittenberg was promoting more profound reforms for the church. But Jonathan hadn't been prepared for the burning of the canon law, a flagrant challenge to the supreme authority of the pope himself.

He rose from his bed and wandered toward the edge of the city and back out through the Elster Gate. He wrapped himself in a blanket he had brought from his bed and sat in the shadows with his back to the wall.

An hour or so later the band finally dispersed and a smaller crowd of students exited the gate to Jonathan's left and walked back down the slope where they started a new bonfire. They had several scrolls that looked like the one Luther had burned—mock bulls, Jonathan imagined. They threw the scrolls on the fire along with all the other writings they had collected during their march through the city. Jonathan closed his eyes and listened as the students chanted another *Te Deum*. Then, after they had left, he watched the fire die as the winter wind scattered the ashes across the meadow and into the icy river.

Chapter 17

The snow fell softly onto the streets and housetops of Aachen, lending the city of Charlemagne a veil of peace that was fragile and as transitory as the moonlit snow itself. Emperor Charles was on business in the city when word came of Luther's burning of the canon law and the papal bull. One more crisis to add to the growing pile of political problems. Since leaving his native Spain to take up residence in Germany, the young emperor had received nothing but bad news from back home.

A group of cities called the "communeros" had organized a Santa Junta, a Holy League, at Avila in July. The sole purpose of the Junta was to protest the king's leaving the country for Germany even as he continued to enlist Spanish men and money for imperial purposes. Now radicals had replaced the existing leadership, and Spain was on the verge of chaos. All this and the Roman curia continued to insist that he deal with Luther. The twenty-year-old monarch had quite a full plate and little appetite for what had been served him.

Charles sat before the great fireplace in his private chambers, leaning back against the hard leather of the ancient chair. Charlemagne himself had sat in this very chair, staring into the fire, and experienced the same loneliness that Charles felt so deeply now. His thoughts drifted back to Spain, and he found himself trying to recall his father, who had died when he was only five. Charles wondered if he celebrated

Christmas in heaven with the angels. Someone knocked at the door.

"Yes?"

"Begging Your Majesty's pardon," came the muffled voice from the other side. "Father Glapion requests an audience."

"At this hour?"

"He says it's urgent, sire."

Charles sighed as he rose from his chair. Glapion was one of the leaders of the Catholic moderates and the emperor's loquacious confessor, but he didn't know when to rest content. His late-night intrusions were far too frequent for the emperor's tastes. "Show him in," Charles said as he crossed to his desk and sat heavily in the uncomfortable wooden chair. The door opened almost immediately, and Father Glapion entered as energetically as if it were ten in the morning.

"Forgive the lateness of the hour, Your Majesty, but I think we may have an answer to the Luther problem, if you would permit me?"

"Father, if this is about trying to get me to retract my invitation to Luther, you're wasting your time. Aleander has already tried and failed. My mind is set. We must settle this matter once and for all."

"I agree, Your Majesty, We must deal with Luther. But not in public. Let me go to Frederick. I can make a case for settling this whole matter privately and without giving the devil a foothold."

"How?"

"I would suggest a compromise. Your Majesty has been far too busy to read some of Luther's earlier writings. They are actually quite good, some of them. I would remind Frederick that there was what I would be so bold as to call a wonderful Christian spirit in many of them.

"Then there appeared this abominable little tract called *The Babylonian Captivity*, which lacked any blush of irenic spirit. Frederick can't possibly support Luther's views there. His attack on the sacraments was shocking, to say the least. I find it difficult to believe that the words of that pamphlet came from the same pen that produced such gracious words before. If Luther did write it, it had to have been in a fit of passion."

"Your point being, Father?" Charles asked impatiently.

"Consider the situation, sire. Frederick is a powerful prince. He controls a large part of Saxony. He commands hundreds of soldiers and a number of knights, all of whom have sworn allegiance to him and to you. Part of their oath requires that they protect the priests who serve them. So Frederick is legally bound to protect even insubordinate priests like Luther. But Frederick is also a rational man. He has to acknowledge that Luther simply wasn't himself when he wrote *The Babylonian Captivity*. By all accounts, Luther is a rational man as well, and if his earlier tracts are any indication, he's also a man of peace. Any rational, peaceful man should be willing to modify, perhaps even retract, something as hateful as *The Babylonian Captivity*."

"Do you think Frederick would require Luther to publish a retraction?"

"I do, Your Grace. It would be a significant concession to Rome, and it would put Your Majesty at a decided political advantage as well, I might add. Once Frederick convinces Luther to retract *The Babylonian Captivity*, Your Majesty gains an ally in Frederick, Luther becomes inconsequential, and the free knights who are following Luther lose their political advantage. As soon as they see Luther *and* Frederick negotiating with the true church, they'll run home with their tails between their legs."

Charles leaned forward and rested his chin on his fist. "Let's say Luther accepts our conditions—what does he get out of it? Do you think His Holiness might rescind the bull against him?"

Glapion lowered his head for a moment before speaking. "Of course I can't speak for the pope," he said. "But I know for a fact that Pope Leo is ready to put this matter behind him. If Luther accepts the compromise, well—let's just say arrangements can be made to have the entire incident disappear. I'm sure of it."

Charles glanced up at him with a bemused smile. "You're sure of it?"

Glapion nodded. "It's our chance to hobble the devil, Your Majesty." Charles wasn't sure if he meant Luther or the Prince of Darkness, but it didn't really matter. The result would be the same.

"What if your plan fails, Father?"

Glapion shrugged. "Then we treat Luther as any other heretic. But we do it discreetly," he said matter-of-factly.

Charles laughed quietly and shook his head. "And tell me why we don't treat this Hussite as a heretic right now? Why not lead him to the stake, make a public example of him, and be done with all this trouble?"

"Because, Your Majesty," Glapion said slowly. "Public examples tend to become public martyrs. And *that* is when the real trouble starts."

Charles sat for a moment, weighing his confessor's advice. Then he stood slowly. "Frederick will already have my invitation for Luther to attend the council in Worms. A reversal would be embarrassing."

Glapion put his fingers to his lips thoughtfully. "Your Majesty may recall that Luther burned the canon law and the bull condemning him only a few days ago."

"Yes," Charles said, picking up a paper from his desk and unfolding it. "I received a letter from Frederick this morning. Here," he said, tossing the page across his desk to Glapion. "It seems some churchmen burned a few of Luther's books in Cologne and Mainz. Luther was responding in kind."

"It's different," Glapion said. "Those churchmen burned the words of an insubordinate priest. Luther burned the words of the Holy Father."

Charles smiled as Glapion's argument dawned on him. "And it simply wouldn't be appropriate to invite such a man to a hearing. He has already made his statement by burning the papal bull, wouldn't you say, Father?"

"I would, Your Majesty," Glapion said, nodding.

"Well, then," Charles said, walking around the desk. "I'll rescind the invitation tomorrow, first thing. Luther will not be coming to Worms!" He opened the door for his confessor and placed his hand gratefully on Glapion's shoulder. "Thank you, Father. You just gave me my first good night's sleep in a fortnight!"

JANUARY 1, 1521
WITTENBERG

Jonathan stood beside Martin on the bridge overlooking the Elbe. He had a handful of small rocks, which he was tossing one by one into the slow-moving stream. Martin leaned against the railing and spat into the current.

"There," he said. "That's how much I care for the royal invitation to Worms."

Jonathan laughed and threw another pebble into the water.

Martin looked at him. "What? You don't believe me? You think I disparage it because I can't have it? And now that they've rescinded their invitation, I'm free to despise it, is that it?"

The question startled Jonathan. Since he had arrived a few weeks before, he had made it a point to spend as much time in Martin's company as the professor would allow. To his delight, Martin not only allowed his company but sought it out. Their long "talking walks" around the city and out into the fields and forests were refreshing to Jonathan. He had never heard the Bible discussed in such an open, real way. It drew him.

Now, Jonathan feared, he had overstepped the bounds of familiarity and had offended the good doctor with a careless laugh.

"I'm sorry, Herr Luther. I didn't mean—," he stammered.

"Didn't mean? Didn't mean what?" Luther interrupted.

"To give offense. Please forgive me."

"All right, I forgive you," Luther said dismissively. "Now answer the question. Do you believe that I despise the royal invitation to Worms or not?"

"I'm surprised by it," Jonathan admitted, though he felt his stomach tightening.

"Oh, now there's a good answer. You're 'surprised' by it, which admits neither belief nor disbelief. Perhaps you should consider becoming a lawyer rather than a priest, Father."

Jonathan could feel his face redden.

"Jonathan, I'm not angry with you," Luther said, taking the pebbles from the younger priest's hand, his voice gentler now. He turned back to the railing and started dropping them one by one into the water below. "It's fine to question," he continued. "The trick, though, is to question the right thing. Instead of questioning my integrity, you might ask why I hold the invitation in contempt. Assume a man is telling the truth, Jon, until you catch him in a lie."

Jonathan was silent for a moment before he spoke, choosing his words carefully. "It...it just seems that the emperor himself was allowing you—no, asking you—to come to the general assembly to defend your position. Isn't that what we've wanted? What *you* have wanted?"

Luther kept looking down into the water as he spoke. "Jonathan, listen to me. Listen carefully. First," here he dropped a pebble. "What you or I want means less than the ripples I made when that small stone hit the water. You see? They are already gone as if they never existed. The only thing that is important is what God wants. Second," he dropped another pebble. "You assume the invitation came from the emperor himself. I am certain it did not, it was only offered on his behalf. I know nothing of the men who offered the invitation, nor do I owe them any allegiance. They could sink me without Charles ever knowing, as surely and as easily as that stone sank to the bottom of the Elbe, never to be seen again. If I disappear, that means nothing, but I will not allow the message of God's grace to be so carelessly dismissed, as though it were nothing but a pebble in the hand of a fool."

"What if the emperor asked you himself? Would you go then?"

"Ah, a wise question!" Luther laughed and turned to face his young colleague. "You are learning, Jon!" Then, in a more serious tone he added, "If Charles asked me himself, I would take it as a request from the Lord since the Lord has established Charles as emperor. I would go if I were too sick to stand. Even if I suspected betrayal at his hands, I would not hesitate," he said. "I will not allow the gospel to suffer because of my own unwillingness to suffer for the sake of my Savior and to seal that testimony with my blood."

FEBRUARY 10, 1521
THE RED WHEEL INN, BOCKINGEN

"Ale if you please, sir," the man at the bar shouted above the noise. Jaklein Rohrbach, proprietor of the Red Wheel Inn in Bockingen, turned at the far end of the bar to see his customer. He didn't know the man or the young woman wrapped in a cloak standing beside him.

He held a tall stein under a spout and filled it to within an inch of the brim. As he placed the mug on the countertop, the man pulled out a small purse to pay.

"First time in the Red Wheel?" Jaklein asked.

"The Red Wheel?" the man asked.

Jaklein pointed up toward the ceiling. The man and the girl at his side looked up at the enormous iron wheel painted bright red and suspended nearly eight feet above their heads. More than a hundred candles burned in the wheel's rim. "The name of my inn," Jaklein said.

"Well sir, ain't that fancy?" the man said appreciatively, still gazing at the wheel. He looked back at Jaklein. "We're new to your town, sir, here on business. My daughter and me live on some land close by Weinsburg." He opened his purse. "How much, then, for the ale?"

"Your first drink in the Red Wheel is free of charge, friend," Jaklein said.

"Free of charge?" the man said. "Well, then, look at this, Moira. Ain't it good of this fella? The name's Geyer. Thomas Geyer," he said, extending his hand.

"Jaklein Rohrbach." Jaklein shook his hand but pulled it away before

Thomas had a chance to break it in his enthusiasm. "Could I get you something, miss?" Jaklein asked the young woman at Thomas's side.

She shook her head.

"Oh," Thomas said, "and this here is my daughter, Moira Geyer."

Jaklein bowed. "Miss Geyer," he said.

"Sir," Moira said, inclining her head and smiling. Then she looked directly at him, looked right into his eyes.

That was when it happened. Instantly. Irreversibly. It was as though Jaklein hadn't seen her until that moment. She couldn't have been more than sixteen, but Jaklein thought she was more beautiful than any woman he had ever seen. Her skin was tanned from years of working in the sun. Her golden hair, a mass of curls just visible inside the hood of her cloak, shone softly in the candlelight. And her eyes were the blue of a bright summer sky. A thousand candles on a thousand wheels would have dimmed in the light of those eyes, that smile. Jaklein suddenly became aware that her father was speaking to him.

"...owns the place, then?" were the only words he heard.

"Oh," Jaklein said. "Sorry. What was that?"

"Your father, he owns the place?" Thomas asked, and took a long drink from his stein. Jaklein noticed that he kept his eyes on him even as he drank. And was looking at him now as a father looking at a young man who had just seen his beautiful daughter for the first time.

"My father was killed last year, Mr. Geyer. He got into a fight with some of Toffler's rangers. You're from Weinsburg. I'm sure you've run into..."

At the mention of Toffler's name, Thomas set his stein on the counter and wiped his mouth with the back of his sleeve. "I know Toffler," he said, his eyes darkening. "It's a no-good lot. I'm sorry for your loss, sir. Come on, Moira, we'd best get on." Moira gave Jaklein a quick look, as if to apologize, then took her father's arm and they turned to go.

"But, Mr. Geyer...," Jaklein called out.

"Good night to you, sir, and thank you for the ale," Thomas said without looking back.

Once outside the inn, Moira pulled away.

"What was that all about, Papa? What did he do?" she asked angrily.

"First, the way he looked at you…"

"Papa !"

"First," Thomas repeated, raising his voice a notch. "The way he *looked* at you. And then, he's on Toffler's bad side, and I won't traffic with nobody who—"

"It was his father, Papa. Not him. His father."

"You don't know Toffler, little girl. You've never even seen him since you're old enough to remember. It don't matter who it is gets on his bad side, the whole family's gonna pay, and that's a fact. Besides, that young fella in there has a darkness in him. I seen it in his eyes."

"Oh, Papa, he's—"

"That's all!" Thomas said and made a characteristic chopping motion with his hand that meant all conversation was at an end.

But Moira had made up her mind. She would come back to the Red Wheel Inn. She would see Jaklein Rohrbach again. With or without her father's permission.

ALEANDER'S APARTMENT, WORMS

The wind whistled shrill and cold outside the second-story apartment where Father Girolamo Aleander sat at his table, writing.

12 February, 1521

Father Karl, my dear friend,

My extended absence from civilization makes this infernal tooth hurt worse than ever. I can't sleep, so thought I would write a letter to you to take my mind off the throbbing. Don't bother writing me back to suggest I should go to a dentist. I refuse to open my mouth before one of these German barbarians unless it's to condemn Luther.

I wish I had better news. I am afraid I lost a golden opportunity, and may not be able to make up for it. Shortly after the new year I approached the emperor with an edict against the Satan, Luther. My suggestion at the time was that His Majesty issue the edict independently of the diet. This, he said he couldn't do in light of the fact that neither Albert, Archbishop of Mainz, nor Frederick, Elector of Saxony—and now Luther's champion, I might add—were present.

Then, for some reason that escapes me completely, the archbishop objected to the edict, even though he authorized me to burn Luther's works in his own city of Mainz not a month before! At any rate, when Frederick did arrive—on Epiphany, no less—he cajoled the emperor into taking personal responsibility for Luther's case. At first I was wary, mainly due to the emperor's youth and inexperience.

But he soon asked me to address a committee he had appointed to handle the case, and I thought all would be well. This is where I made my great error. Not that my argument was bad in itself but ineffective because my tactics were out of place. In addressing the committee I argued against Luther as a heretic and for the primacy of the papacy. Such an argument might have won a hearing with Cajetan in Augsburg or with Eck in Leipzig but not here. Not now.

I should have pressed for the church to decide the case. I should have argued that the secular committee I was addressing had no jurisdiction in this matter. But I didn't, and the opportunity slipped through my fingers, and now things are infinitely worse. What work the devil can do in a month!

And the blasphemous pamphlets! One of your large carts couldn't hold the vile tracts that flood this city. The commoners have made up pictures of Luther with a halo and a dove above his head. And, Karl, the people kiss these pictures—as if Luther were the Holy Father! One picture has Luther with a book in his hand, a knight at his side dressed out in his armor with a sword under the caption, "Champions of Christian Liberty."

Pray for me, my friend. I need God's wisdom for the days ahead. The emperor has asked me to address the plenary session of the assembly tomorrow. I will present a new version of the edict that allows for their consent to the ban against Luther. I have three hours, and think I can make a convincing case. Certainly more effective than the last outing, let us hope.

There is a sticking point, however. Yesterday I received the bull from the Holy Father excommunicating Luther. If I produce it at tomorrow's session I would overcome their objection that I can't outlaw a man the Church has not yet banned. The problem is, the bull also names Hutten, one of the knights who has taken Luther's message as a call to arms, and I am not sure the assembly would agree to condemn both men in the same measure. Nothing is simple, is it? Whether it's the extraction of a tooth or a heretic, nothing is simple.

I cannot go into the streets without the Germans putting their hands to their swords and gnashing their teeth at me. Nine-tenths of them cry, "Luther, Luther!" and the other tenth shout, "Death to the pope!" I pray His Holiness will give me a plenary indulgence and look after my brothers and sisters if anything happens to me.

Yours for the True Faith,
Aleander

The General Assembly, Worms

Aleander stepped confidently to the rostrum. There was already a tempest brewing in the committee, and Aleander was determined to meet it head on.

"Luther," he said, "is nothing but a heretic who brought up John Hus from hell and endorsed not some but all of his articles." Out of the corner of his eye, he noticed Frederick shifting in his seat. Aleander continued, "One must assume that he also endorses Wycliffe's denial of the presence of Christ in the elements of the Eucharist!"

"That's a lie," Frederick rumbled loudly enough for others to hear. "He never—"

"He rejects monastic vows. He rejects ceremonies. He appeals to councils, and in the next breath he rejects the authority of councils. Like all heretics, he appeals to Scripture and yet rejects Scripture when it does not support him! He is an obstinate, stiff-necked heretic. He asks for a hearing, but how can a hearing be given to one who will not listen to an angel from heaven? Tell me, why should we hear this revolutionary? He encourages Germans to wash their hands in the blood of the papists!"

Frederick shot up from his chair. "Sir, you know very well that Prierias goaded him into saying it!" Aleander suppressed a smile. Years before, Sylvester Prierias, an influential and highly respected Catholic theologian, had insisted that the pope's authority was superior to the authority of the holy Scriptures, and that he was, in fact, infallible. That letter, coming from a high church official, was in Luther's mind an affront to Christ himself. Now Frederick was visibly angry, and the rhetorical advantage shifted to Aleander.

The Elector of Brandenburg, sitting opposite Frederick across the hall raised his hand slightly and mumbled in a condescending voice, "Control, Frederick, control."

Aleander forged ahead.

"This Satan will soon be formally excommunicated by the pope!"

The bull of excommunication was in his pocket as he spoke. "Unless he is absolved, he should be imprisoned and his books burned."

"Yes," said the Elector of Brandenburg, loudly enough for all to hear.

Aleander, thus strengthened, continued, "Anyone who doesn't support this edict," here he glanced at Frederick and paused, "would be guilty of lese majesty, and our sovereign, Emperor Charles V, would take the insult as a personal affront and a crime against the crown."

Frederick, along with the Elector of Brandenburg and the Elector Palatinate all exploded out of their seats at once and rushed toward each other on the floor of the assembly, swinging fists, canes, and anything else they could lay their hands on. Cardinal Lang leapt into the fray, prying Frederick's fingers away from the fur-lined collar of the Elector of Brandenburg.

"We will not...," Frederick shouted as he twisted free from Lang and the others trying to restrain him, "we will *not* dignify this *ad hominem,* this calumny, with an answer. Blast you, sir, for your ungracious spirit. Blast you and your elector for your empty charges against a man who has yet to be condemned, a man whose shoes you aren't worthy to scrape clean." He whirled around and with a majority of the other estates in tow, swept from the room, leaving Aleander with his heart pounding and the Elector of Brandenburg rubbing his neck.

APARTMENTS OF EMPEROR CHARLES V, WORMS

Aleander put his fingers to his lips and closed his eyes. His emperor was pacing the room furiously.

"Stupid, stupid, stupid!" Charles shouted. "I have to reinvite Luther now, or I'll have a full-scale rebellion on my hands among my own electors!"

"We have support, Your Maj—"

"Support!" Charles stormed. "Support from the Elector of Brandenburg, you mean—you two almost caused a riot!"

"If I could prepare a—"

"No, Father, you may not. This is the second time in two weeks I've given you the opportunity to make a case against Luther."

"And we have, Your Grace," Aleander interrupted again.

"And nearly lost the war in doing so! You are the one, you who so desperately wanted to keep Luther away from this secular assembly, and now you play right into Frederick's hand. You had Luther's excommunication in your hand! Why didn't you use it?"

"Because Hutten is named as well, and I didn't think the diet would support the bull if it had to condemn both men.".

"Don't you see, Father?" Charles asked. "It wasn't the assembly's decision to make. The Holy Father has already pronounced the excommunication. It was only up to the diet to carry it out. You are the one responsible for turning this assembly into a church council, not me."

"We could always go back, Your Grace, and—"

"No! I will not go back. I will not make another retraction! Luther is coming to the diet, and that's the end of it. Under safe conduct, too. Frederick will insist on it, I'm sure."

"The edict, Your Grace, we could—," Aleander began, but the emperor cut him off again.

"You have it with you?"

"The original, yes, sire."

"Give it to me."

He withdrew it from his cloak and handed it over reluctantly. The emperor tore it to shreds.

"Now," he said catching his breath. "I will compose a new version. We will do away with the penalties for lese majesty, and we will address Luther with the dignity of a doctor of the University of Wittenberg. I shall have it delivered by our imperial herald."

"His books, Your Majesty, please."

"I will allow his books to be sequestered but under a separate edict not to be published until he has had a chance to respond to our invitation. Under no circumstances is Luther to know of this. It could influence him to reject the invitation. Understood?"

"Of course, Your Majesty."

ERFURT LECTURE HALL

"And so," Martin said in conclusion, "I learned from a friend that they plan a separate edict that calls for the sequestration of my books."

A murmur rippled through the packed crowd of students and the faculty in the Erfurt lecture hall. "Perhaps they were afraid that if I knew they were going to burn my books, I wouldn't come!" This drew hearty laughter and some relieved applause. "No, I have decided to go to Worms. And…" Here he paused to let them quiet down a bit. "I have decided to recant!"

At first there was a hush, and then a defiant "No!" from several in the audience. Luther plowed ahead over their protestations.

"And this shall be my recantation. Before, I said the pope is the Vicar of Christ. I recant. Now I say the pope is the adversary of Christ and the apostle of the devil!" The audience burst into laughter and applause. "Unless I am held back forcibly, or Caesar revokes his invitation, I will enter the city of Worms under the banner of Christ against the gates of hell!" He gathered his robes about him and left the podium to the thunderous applause and shouts of the audience.

Justus Jonas and Jonathan stood near the podium as Luther came down. "Well," Martin said, looking out at the cheering crowd, "I've had my Palm Sunday. I wonder whether this pomp is merely a temptation or whether it might also be the sign of my impending passion."

Chapter 18

Father Glapion knocked lightly on the door to the emperor's apartments.

"Enter," Charles answered from the other side.

Glapion opened the door slowly.

"Father, I've been expecting you."

The priest closed the door behind him and took his place in a small chair beside the fire. He had spent the last few days trying to convince the knights Ulrich von Hutten and Franz von Sickingen to lay down their arms. His argument had been practical in content, unemotional in delivery. The simple fact of the matter was, he had argued, that their resistance was hopeless. Why should these two and a handful of free knights, all of whom professed to follow Luther, insist on raising a peasant army when Luther himself had refused to resist by force of arms? And what kind of army could they sustain, at any rate? Undisciplined peasants with sticks and pitchforks would be no match for the tens of thousands of trained soldiers who had remained loyal to the emperor and to Rome. Reasonable men would, he thought, see the logic of his argument. But he had underestimated their resolve, and now he had to face Charles with the news.

"I'm afraid I bring a disheartening report, Your Majesty," he began darkly.

"What? That Sickingen and Hutten wouldn't bite?"

"Why, yes, sire. That's…but how did you know?"

"Father, you underestimate me. I've been emperor of Germany now for two years and King of Spain for three. One thing I've learned is that I can't allow my hopes to become expectations. I did hope that we could avoid bringing Luther to Worms, but I never really expected Hutten and Sickingen to back down from a fight. Sickingen is a warrior and Hutten is a poet. The one loves battle and the other loves the idea of battle. 'Compromise' isn't in the vocabulary of a warrior. No, I appreciate your effort, Father, but it is no surprise to me that you failed, and I certainly don't hold it against you. You served me well, you served Germany faithfully, and for that we are thankful."

Glapion recovered sufficiently to stutter out a response. "Your Majesty is too gracious."

Charles turned away to gaze at the fire. "Luther will not think me so when he arrives," he said. "I assure you."

THE ROOMS OF GIROLAMO ALEANDER, WORMS

Jonathan tried to catch his breath before knocking on the door of Dr. Girolamo Aleander. He had been called only three weeks before to attend Aleander as his official aide during Luther's audience before the emperor at Worms.

He didn't like the idea of helping those in opposition to his new-found friend, but he simply could not refuse a direct order from an authority as powerful as Aleander.

Jonathan had eaten little and slept less on a trip that spanned every kind of countryside over more than three hundred miles, most of which he covered on foot. He had literally run the last mile in order to reach Aleander before he retired for the night. He set his traveling bag on the floor and braced himself against the doorframe. He was still breathing hard and bent over at the waist when Aleander opened the door suddenly.

"Father Jonathan, I take it?" he said flatly.

Jonathan stood straight and tried to control his breathing. "Yes, Your Eminence. I came as quickly as I could, but I had no horse, and—"

"You are late. You will find that I don't tolerate excuses, and I certainly don't tolerate slovenliness," Aleander said, looking Jonathan up and down and sniffing the air. "Good heavens, man, don't you know how to clean yourself?" He reached into a pocket of his robe, withdrew a handkerchief and covered his nose and mouth.

"Sir, I…"

"I've reserved a room for you at the end of the hall. Here," he said, speaking through the handkerchief. He reached inside a small purse at his waist and extracted a silver coin. "Give this to the innkeeper and tell him I said to give you a bath immediately. You have a change of clothing?"

"Yes, Your Eminence. In the bag here."

"Then change and be back here after you've washed off that stink. I have questions for you." Aleander pulled back inside his apartment and closed the door sharply.

An hour later Jonathan, washed and in a fresh habit, once again knocked softly at the door. No answer. He knocked again, this time a bit harder. Nothing. He put his ear to the door to listen. Suddenly the door flew open.

"Close it behind you," Aleander said, as he retreated to his chair. "Well, I must say, this is an improvement. It was a long trip then?" he asked, staring at the papers on his desk.

"The Lord watched over me, Your Eminence."

Aleander looked up with half of an oily smile. "Of course. I sent for you for two reasons, Father. First, you are supposed to be something of an expert on Luther."

"I have studied him quite a bit, Eminence. I find him—"

"I wasn't finished," Aleander said dryly.

Jonathan felt his face flush.

Aleander continued, "I don't want to know what he has written, Father. I've read more than you on that count, I'm sure. I want to know *Luther*. You've been with him. I want to know his cracks. His weak points. Which brings me to the second reason I sent for you. I want Luther to see you standing by my side tomorrow at the hearing. Perhaps it will puncture his overinflated pride to know that one of his own colleagues is actually standing for the truth in all this."

"Excuse me, Your Eminence, but did you say, a 'hearing'? Isn't this supposed to be a debate?"

"Don't be ridiculous. Of course not. The emperor isn't going to all this trouble just to hear more of Luther's blasphemy. Now sit down, and don't waste my time. I want to know everything about the man." Aleander leaned back in his chair and pressed his fingertips together, waiting.

Jonathan hesitated. He hadn't known quite what to expect from Aleander, but he hadn't been prepared for this. Aleander was asking him to betray a man he had come to respect and admire. "I…I haven't really known him very long, Father," Jonathan started, trying to buy time.

Aleander said nothing for a moment as he stared at Jonathan, measuring him. "I see," he said through his fingers. He lowered his hands slowly and let his eyes drift up to the ceiling. "You know, my son, the world is a much larger place than your little village of Wittenberg. The world outside is full of palaces. And position. And power…" Aleander looked directly at Jonathan. "You are being given a rare opportunity, Father Jonathan—a chance to walk with great men. You can have a part in purifying the church, to help rid her of a pestilence." He leaned forward and placed his long fingers on Jonathan's hand. His voice was low and secretive. "God rewards those who help the church, my son."

Jonathan's mouth was so dry he couldn't speak. He tried to clear his throat, and coughed instead. Aleander settled back in his chair, and Jonathan noticed just the hint of a smile at the corners of his mouth.

"Well?" Aleander asked.

The door behind Jonathan opened suddenly, and someone walked in unannounced. Aleander looked up, then stood immediately and motioned Jonathan to do the same. "Johann," Aleander said, addressing the man in the doorway, "I trust you had a profitable audience with His Majesty."

The middle-aged man closed the door softly behind him. He looked first at Aleander, then at Jonathan. "It was, thank you, Doctor," he said distractedly, as he eyed Jonathan. "I think we have a good case."

Aleander crossed to the man from behind his desk. "Allow me to introduce my assistant. This is Father Jonathan."

"Ah, yes," the man said, lowering his heavy eyelids as he arched his brows. "The priest from Wittenberg you told me about."

Aleander turned to Jonathan. "Father Jonathan, this is Johann von der Ecken, chancellor to the archbishop of Trier, and Herr Luther's inquisitor. I have the honor of sharing these quarters with Herr Ecken."

Ecken ignored the compliment. "So," he said, acknowledging Jonathan with a nod. "You're supposed to know all about our friend, Dr. Luther, hmm?"

"Yes," Aleander said before Jonathan could respond. "We were just about to get to that when you came in. Father Jonathan just arrived." He gave Jonathan a withering look as if he blamed him for not *flying* all the way from Wittenberg to Worms.

"Yes, well, too late to do us much good, I'm afraid," Ecken mumbled. "The emperor wants us both in his quarters now, Girolamo."

"Now?" Aleander asked. "At this hour?"

"How much sleep did we need when we were twenty-one?" Ecken asked. "Come on."

The two men turned to go, but Aleander spoke back over his shoulder to Jonathan as he opened the door. "Good night, Father. So glad you arrived in time to be of service."

It was ten o'clock the next morning when Martin and his retinue neared the city of Worms.

"Martin, look," Justus said as he spurred his horse to the side of Luther's cart. The citizens of Worms were rushing toward them through the city gates.

"There must be five hundred of them," Justus said.

"God be praised," Martin said, his voiced tinged with sarcasm. He had been feeling miserable for the last few days after contracting a high fever early in their journey. "If they've come to kill us, at least we won't have to ride any farther in this contraption." Martin and his three companions rumbled along in the primitive Saxon two-wheeled cart, surrounded by one hundred mounted soldiers, dedicated to making the promised "safe conduct" sure. But the people weren't attacking. They were shouting words of greeting and encouragement as they ran across the fields and crowded around, trying to touch Martin.

By the time they reached the city gate, hundreds more, trying to get a glimpse of the man who had caused all the fuss, jammed the narrow streets. The soldiers surrendered Luther to the care of eight of their best horsemen, who escorted him to his lodgings in the Johanniter Inn. It was a convenient location, not far from the quarters of his own Prince Frederick, and just down the Kämmererstrasse from the episcopal palace where the emperor was staying, and where the diet was to convene the next day. When the cart stopped, the crowd pressed around him right up to the door. Luther stumbled a bit, still weak from his fever.

One priest ran up to him and embraced him, touching his habit three times and shouting for joy. Martin looked at the shouting crowd in disbelief. He had never anticipated such public support. He shook his head, then said just loudly enough for Justus to hear, "God will be with me." Justus turned to him once they had made their way inside. "It seems the people have made up their minds," he said jokingly.

"Then let the people stand before the emperor," Martin said. He was sweating, and his gut was on fire. He leaned against the closed door and let his stomach settle. "It's one thing to stand for what you believe in the presence of a thousand friends," he said. "It's quite another to stand against a thousand years of bad tradition. And," he added as he turned to go to his room, "before the most powerful man on earth."

Martin spent the day in conversation with a number of men and had a good dinner with ten or twelve of the church leaders who had gathered for the general assembly. After another extended visit he retired for the night but awoke long before the bells summoned the other monks to the daybreak services. He rose quietly from his pallet so as not to waken Justus and edged toward the door.

The floorboards in the hall were like ice, and Martin thought of how warm the bed had been and how he longed to be back…but he stopped himself angrily.

That was precisely the reason he should have denied himself covers. The more comfortable a man made himself—especially the comfort of rest—the harder it became to rise to duty, and the more difficult to sustain himself in the disciplines of self-denial, particularly of prayer. He kicked himself for accepting the blanket when his well-intentioned host insisted.

Martin forced himself to think on the suffering of Christ on Calvary, of his wounded head and pierced hands and side—how he had nowhere, nowhere at all to lay his head. He thought of Christ in the Garden of Gethsemane and how in his passion he had prayed so fervently that he sweat drops of blood. He prayed now, even as he made his way to the house altar, that God would grant him that kind of fervency in his own prayer, though he knew that his trial paled in comparison to that of his Lord. Jesus had faced the hellish prospect of actually becoming sin and being cut off from fellowship with God the Father. Martin merely faced losing his life, which he knew would mean finally getting to enter perfect and unbroken fellowship with his Savior.

Suddenly he found himself kneeling at the bench before the modest house altar. The room was small, cold, and empty. Above the altar a small iron crucifix hung like a black shadow emerging from the white rock wall. Martin stared at the icon, trying to make out detail in the iron sculpture. He looked for several minutes, but his eyes failed to adjust to the high contrast of black metal Jesus on black metal cross against a moonlit white wall. He could only discern the image of the cross itself. The harder he looked the more the thin black lump in the center melded into the cross on which it was suspended. The crucifix seemed to move out, away from the wall slowly, floating. It was empty.

Something whispered to his heart. "Whom do you seek, Martin? Whom do you seek here on this cross? You won't find the one you are looking for here."

"Oh, God, help me see him," Martin whispered. "Oh, Father, strengthen me, give me faith to see." Then a terrifying thought ripped through his consciousness. "Am I blind? Or deaf? Is that what you're telling me, Father?" His earthly father's voice echoed back across the years, reawakening doubts and fears Martin had long tried to suppress. "How do you know, Martin, that you heard the voice of God in the lightning?" Perhaps he'd been listening to the voices of demons all along—so that now, when he longed to hear the voice of his heavenly Father, he could not. Perhaps hell had stopped his ears to the voice of heaven. He strained to hear. Desperately wanted to hear.

Nothing.

Finally Martin himself broke the silence.

"Father, guard your honor, I pray. Silence me. Slay me before I speak a lie in your name. I ask these things in the matchless name of my risen Lord, Jesus Christ. Amen."

Martin crossed himself and rose, shaking, to his feet. He made his way back to his quarters where he ripped the coverlet off the bed and threw it on the floor. He lay shivering on the thin pallet, staring at the ceiling until the first light turned the sky from inky black to gray and the bell tolled for lauds.

APRIL 17
THE GENERAL ASSEMBLY, WORMS

Martin stood, palms sweating, stomach rumbling, outside the doors of the "Bishop's Court," waiting to be summoned by the emperor to appear before the diet. He had been called at four in the afternoon, but nearly two hours had passed since he arrived at the episcopal palace, the ancient fortress of the kings of Burgundy.

Martin had time to think, to recall the history of this storied palace, and he felt a strange connection to it. Here, a thousand years before, the vassal Hagan, a grizzled and loyal warrior, had achieved immortal fame by being the last to stand strong for the rightful king, Gunther. *If he could draw his sword now,* Luther thought, *old Hagan would cut me down where I stand for daring to oppose the king.* He paced, trying to shake off the feeling that he was being judged not only by the living but by the dead. Another voice intruded into his thoughts—his father, whispering, *Even the ghosts condemn you, Martin. What are you doing? Stupid! Listen! Listen to the voices, you thankless son!*

Martin shuddered. The muffled voices from the other side of the door stopped abruptly. The sound of footsteps on paving stones approached. The doors opened, and Martin walked through. He stood for a moment and took in the room.

Electors and princes from every state in the empire lined the walls, occupying every available space. Justus Jonas had managed to slip in earlier and stood near the back right corner. At the end of the room, one man sat—Charles V, the twenty-one-year-old emperor of the holy Roman empire. To Charles's right stood Johann von der Ecken. In front of Ecken was a pile of books—Luther's works.

All were silent as Martin approached the emperor. He felt as though he were walking through waist-high sand. Then, halfway down the aisle, he began to smile as he looked each member in the eye. It wasn't a smile of confidence. How could he speak before such a group? The idea was laughable. The situation was so far beyond Martin's natural ability he simply gave it up to the Lord's care. And he smiled.

Martin noticed Jonathan standing with his eyes averted near the famous Girolamo Aleander. Justus had informed him earlier that Aleander himself had called Jonathan up from Wittenberg to attend him at council. The appointment wasn't surprising. Jonathan's intellectual skills and natural teaching ability had made him a quick favorite among students and faculty alike in Wittenberg. But it was an obvious slap at Luther to call one of his own colleagues, and especially one as close as Jonathan, into the service of one of the men who would be condemning him. Jonathan had no choice in the matter. He had to follow the directive of Rome or risk banishment himself.

Luther stopped in front of the table full of books and bowed before the emperor, but before he had straightened, he heard the emperor say to Aleander, "This man will never make a heretic out of me." It was just loud enough for those close by to hear. Aleander chuckled. It spread into a low ripple of laughter that circled the room. Ecken waited for the laughter to subside, then he asked two questions in quick succession.

"Martin Luther, do you acknowledge these books published under your name as your own? Are you prepared to recant what you have written in these books?"

The question took him completely off guard. Then the awful truth came crashing in on him. This wasn't to be a debate at all. They wanted a yes or a no so that they could decide whether to accept his recantation or burn him as a heretic. Martin's legal counsel stood nearby and was quick to respond to the first question.

"The titles of the books must be named!" he said forcefully.

Ecken rolled his eyes and called on a subordinate to read all the titles. It gave Martin a few moments to consider how he might respond. But what could he say to a question so obviously designed to reduce his theological arguments, some of them colorful, some subtly shaded, to an inadequate black or white?

He needed time to think.

When the last title had been read, Martin cleared his throat and mumbled, "They are mine. The books are all mine. And I have written more."

One question down. Ecken glanced over at the emperor who was sitting perfectly still, his chin in his hand, staring at Luther as a hunter would stare at a stag just before loosing a deadly arrow. Aleander, standing closest to the emperor, arched one brow and smiled arrogantly.

The papal legate narrowed his eyes and looked hard at Martin. He asked the second question again. "Do you defend all of them, or will you reject a part?"

Martin stared at the pile of paper. Slowly, he shook his head and spoke in a low voice, as if to himself. "This business touches on God and his word and the salvation of souls. I dare not say too much or too little. It would be too dangerous, for Christ himself said, 'He who denies me before men, him I will deny before my Father.'"

Martin felt as he had elevating the Host at his first Mass. He could feel his legs shaking and the eyes of the court boring through him. But it wasn't the powerful men who intimidated him most. It was the fact that they all stood accountable before God for the decisions they would make here—decisions that would affect the eternal destinies of every man in this room and of every family in the empire.

"I beg you," Martin said, looking at the emperor, "give me time to think it over."

Ecken and the emperor exchanged surprised glances. A low rumble of shock and disapproval broke the silence. Charles whispered something to Ecken who then turned to Luther.

"You will wait outside, Herr Luther," he said. Then he turned his back on Martin and spoke to Aleander.

Martin bowed and he and his lawyer took their leave. Justus was right behind them with a few of Martin's other supporters.

Once outside the doors, Justus approached his friend. "They aren't going to let you defend yourself, Martin. The best we can hope for is that the emperor won't rescind his promise of safe conduct back to Wittenberg." Martin was silent, thoughtful. "Of course," Justus continued, "you always have the option of trying to escape tonight if they decide to grant your request."

Martin smiled. "No. I'll give them an answer. But I need a few days to think of how to answer. They tried to trick me, to pressure me into recanting or at least changing my views. If there's an ounce of fairness in the emperor he will allow me time to reconsider my defense."

Suddenly the door swung open, and they were ushered back inside.

Ecken was standing red-faced and ramrod straight. Aleander wouldn't even look at Luther, and the emperor was obviously angry. Ecken spoke. "His Majesty finds it incredible that you aren't prepared to answer such a simple question. You are a seminary professor, Herr Luther, and yet you waste the time of His Majesty and this honorable court with your request. His Majesty has, however, decided to grant you time to consider your response."

Luther bowed, acknowledging the beneficence.

"One day," Ecken continued. "That's all. We will reconvene tomorrow afternoon at four o'clock in plenary session of the diet. You are dismissed."

"Thank you, Your Majesty," Luther began. "I realize—"

"I said," Ecken interrupted loudly, then lowered his voice to a tense growl, "you are dismissed. If I were you, sir, tomorrow I would come prepared."

Chapter 19

Ecken summoned Luther the next day as promised, at four o'clock in the afternoon. The emperor had moved the meeting to a larger hall to accommodate the crowds—and to intimidate Luther, no doubt. So many had packed the hall that the emperor himself barely had room to sit.

For his part, Luther was a different man. He had considered once more the evidence in favor of his argument. In particular he recalled a discovery he had made only a few months before.

Martin's political and military ally Ulrich von Hutten had translated Lorenzo Valla's 1457 treatise, which proved the famous *Donation of Constantine* to be a forgery. Supposedly, back in the fourth century, Pope Sylvester I had miraculously healed the Roman Emperor Constantine of his leprosy and subsequently led him to faith in Christ. To show his gratitude, Constantine had transferred sovereignty over the Western world to the pope and his successors, or so went the story.

For hundreds of years, Rome had appealed to this document, called the *Donation of Constantine,* as proof of that transfer of power—but it had never happened. It was all a lie, and Rome had covered it up for centuries in order to keep the upper hand of power in the West. When Martin discovered the truth, he was first shocked, then outraged.

As if that weren't bad enough, the Dominican and highest-ranking curial theologian, Sylvester Prierias, had refuted Luther in a tract that upheld the pope as the head of the only true church, and that church was based in Rome. The pope, he said, was infallible, incapable of error when he spoke ex cathedra, and was thus more authoritative than the church councils and even the Scriptures themselves. Prierias summed up by claiming that there was no authority higher than the pope and that the pontiff could not be deposed. Here Prierias quoted canon law: "…even if he were to give so much offense as to cause people in multitudes to go to the devil in hell."

Martin had never been surer of anything in his life. The church had to purge itself of the evil influence of Rome. "So," Martin had written soon after discovering Rome's complicity in the affair, "farewell, unblessed, doomed, blasphemous Rome; the wrath of God has come over you." The time for silence was past. He had spoken on paper. Now if the diet would open the doors, he would roar.

The business of the day took two hours longer than planned, so that it was six o'clock before Martin walked slowly into the hall. Hundreds of candles burned brightly in their sconces. Soldiers stood at attention in gleaming armor. It felt to Martin as if the whole German nation had somehow squeezed itself into that room. Every eye was on him as he approached the emperor and Ecken. The pile of Martin's books lay sprawled on the table, looking exactly as it had on the previous day. Nothing had changed except the location and the man in the brown monk's habit—today he knew what he had to say.

Luther bowed before the emperor. Ecken lifted his voice in a thin and condescending tone. "Are these writings yours, and will you recant?"

Martin took a small step forward and addressed the emperor, Ecken, and the assembled diet in a voice that rang. "Most serene emperor, most noble princes, most merciful lords, if I have not given some of you your proper titles I beg you to forgive me. I am not a courtier but a monk.

"Yesterday you asked me if these books were mine and if I would repudiate them. They are indeed mine." A murmur rippled through the crowd. "But," he continued, "to answer your second question, they are not all of the same kind."

King Charles frowned. Aleander rubbed his eyes and pinched his nose in frustration. "Some of my books deal with faith and life so simply and in such a Christian spirit that even my enemies read them," he said. "Even the pope's bull doesn't denounce all my books. If I were to do as you say, if I were to renounce these books, I would be the only man on earth to deny the truth we all agree on."

Martin took a deep breath. He knew that what he was about to say would set him apart for the rest of his life from the Roman Church and possibly from the monarch who held his life in his hands.

"Another group of my writings reviles the evil lives and teaching of the papists for the desolation they have brought on the Christian world." The emperor leaned forward in his seat. Aleander's eyes stared unblinkingly, and Ecken's mouth actually fell open. Martin continued before they could collect themselves enough to say anything. "Who can deny this when all the world screams on the rack of papal law?"

"No!" the emperor shouted, pounding his fist on the arm of his chair.

Martin continued coolly. "Rome is a beast. Germany is its prey, and our people are being devoured! This tyranny, this mad-dog tyranny threatens every German. If I were to recant now, I would unlock the door to still more tyranny. And how much worse if I did so at the insistence of the Holy Roman Empire?"

Several of the electors—including Duke George, who had sided with Eck at Leipzig—grunted their approval. Unscrupulous legates and greedy popes had abused Germany long enough. Martin sensed the shift in mood. They were quiet still but not sullen.

"A third group," Martin continued, "contains attacks on private individuals. I confess I've been more caustic than my profession would seem to allow, but that is not the issue here. Whether or not I am abrasive or smooth is beside the point. The question is what I teach concerning Christ; therefore, I cannot renounce these books either without increasing tyranny and impiety.

"If our Lord demanded that Annas produce witnesses against him, why may not a worm like me ask to be convicted of error from the prophets and the Gospels?"

Aleander snorted out loud.

"Show me my error," Luther said, "and I will be the first to throw my books into the fire. My teaching creates dissensions, I know. I can answer only in the words of the Lord, 'I came not to bring peace but a sword.'

"Take warning from the examples of Pharaoh, the king of Babylon, and the kings of Israel. God confounds the wise. I must walk in the fear of the Lord. I don't say this to scold but because I can't escape my duty to my Germans. I commend myself to Your Majesty. I pray you would not allow my enemies to blacken my reputation without cause. I have spoken."

Ecken obviously wasn't satisfied. "Herr Luther, you neglected the greater distinction in your works." He gestured casually to the pile of books. "The earlier were bad and the latter worse!"

"All I ask is to be heard from Scripture—," Martin began, but Ecken waved his hand defiantly.

"Every heretic wants to be heard from Scripture. Look behind you, Martin. It isn't your shadow there but the shadow of Wycliffe. Listen to the voice coming out of your mouth and you will hear the rasping heresies of John Hus. But I hear other voices too—the voices of Jews and Turks singing in the streets, rejoicing to hear that Christians are wondering if they might have been wrong all these years!

"Really, Martin." Ecken shook his head with the sadness of a father who was deeply disappointed in his wayward son. "How can you assume that you are the only one to understand the Scriptures? Will you elevate your own opinions above the judgments of so many famous men and claim that you know more than they? Hmm?"

Martin started to answer, thinking the legate had finished, but Ecken continued, more strongly now, pointing his finger at Martin and allowing his voice to rise.

"You have no right to question the most holy and orthodox faith. No right to hold up to public scrutiny the faith that was instituted by Christ, proclaimed by the apostles, sealed by the red blood of the martyrs, confirmed by the sacred councils, and defined by the Church. You have no right, Martin Luther, to attack the blessed Church in which our fathers believed until death and gave to us as an inheritance. And you have no right to dispute that which we are forbidden by the pope and the emperor to discuss lest there be no end of debate." He paused for a few seconds to catch his breath.

"Now," he said in a low tone, "I ask you, Martin—answer me candidly and without loops and holes—do you or do you not repudiate your books and the errors they contain?"

Here Luther looked directly at Charles and spoke without hesitation. "Your Majesty," he began. "Since you and your lordships"—he glanced around the room—"desire a simple answer, I will give one. Unless Scripture and plain reason convict me, I do not accept the authority of popes and councils, for they have contradicted each other. My conscience is captive to the Word of God. I cannot and I will not recant anything, for to go against conscience is neither right nor safe. Here I stand, I cannot do otherwise. God help me. Amen."

Sweat streamed down Martin's face. The room was still as death, the tension as thick as the black smoke that curled toward the ceiling from the hundreds of candles that flickered along the walls. Charles spoke quietly to Ecken, who then addressed Luther.

"His Majesty would hear your defense in Latin."

Luther blinked the sweat from his eyes and breathed a silent prayer of thanks to the Lord. He was grateful for the emperor's challenge. Having defended himself in the vernacular of the German people, the emperor was offering him an opportunity to make the same defense in the *lingua franca* of the Empire. A defense in Latin was a double-edged sword. It would seal his fate in the official language of the court, but it would also broaden the impact of his message.

He repeated his confession in Latin, then paused briefly and smiled at the emperor and at Aleander and then at Ecken. It was too much. Ecken exploded, his words flying like metal shards. Luther responded in a white-hot rage, matching the papal legate with a volley of stinging accusations, his words detonating on contact.

Finally the emperor rose from his chair and called an abrupt halt to the proceedings. Immediately Martin's enemies filled the room with hissing and jeers, some of the Spaniards shouting, "*Al fuego*—into the fire!" Luther turned and marched past his opponents and into the cheering crowd of his supporters, his arms raised high over his head—the gesture of a German foot soldier who had survived battle.

A little over fifty miles to the south in Pforzheim, Elizabeth was undergoing a trial of her own with one of Maggie's customers. Aside from being a well-respected midwife, Maggie had a talent for dyeing fabric, weaving, and sewing. And Elizabeth's good business sense had helped build a healthy and growing enterprise. It was Elizabeth's first time to run the small shop on her own. Maggie had gone to Stuttgart to purchase supplies and had left her in charge, assuring her that the day would go smoothly. Elizabeth started out a little nervous, though she had no reason to be. She had completed scores of transactions on her own. It was just that Maggie had always been there if she needed her. But despite her fears, everything had gone fine, right up to closing time. That was when an old customer, Kurt Radulf, wedged himself through the door, wanting to buy some of Maggie's most expensive cloth on his very shaky credit. For the last half-hour Elizabeth had remained tactful with the large, sweating man, but her patience was wearing thin. The other patrons had gone home, leaving Elizabeth to deal with Radulf by herself.

"Herr Radulf, I've tried to make it clear that we can't extend any more credit until you have paid what you owe. It wouldn't be fair to our other customers, and it wouldn't be fair to Maggie."

"But, I don't understand…," the man said, holding the deep red cloth he wished to purchase close to his chest.

"I'm sorry, that's as plain as I can make it," Elizabeth said, folding her arms.

"No, no, I mean, *you* don't understand. My wife, she saw this cloth in Stuttgart, and she must have it. The weaver there said he had bought it from you."

"He did, that's true. But if she saw it in Stuttgart, then why didn't you purchase the cloth for her there?"

Radulf cleared his throat and tugged nervously at his purse. "One moment," he said, fidgeting. "Let me count again, and see how much I have exactly." He turned away, unsnapped his coin purse and began to count, whispering the sums to himself as he clinked the silver coins one by one into his open palm.

Elizabeth felt sorry for him. Radulf was well dressed and successful in his business. But as everyone knew, he was a slave to his wife who had inherited a small fortune and was busy spending it as quickly as she could. Word was out that the money was almost gone, and Radulf was piling up debts right and left. He hadn't purchased the cloth in Stuttgart because his credit had run its limit there as well. Elizabeth was sure of it. She heard him snap his purse shut. He squared his shoulders and turned back to face her. His face was stern and his chin high.

"Please, Fräulein. I have been a good customer for many years."

"You have been…," Elizabeth started to correct him but stopped in midsentence. She uncrossed her arms and shook her head. "You have been," she said more gently, her inflection suggesting that he had in fact been a faithful client. "But Herr Radulf, surely your wife will under-stand that we cannot—"

"My dear girl," Radulf interrupted, leaning on the counter until it groaned under his weight. "You have no idea." He looked away and chuckled, shaking his head. "My wife…," he began, but he stopped and bit his lower lip. He sighed deeply and placed the cloth back on the counter. Elizabeth was about to speak, to offer a compromise, when he lifted his head. "Well then," he said. "It's been a pleasure. My regards to Maggie." He bowed slightly, turned and squeezed through the shop door then set off down the street toward the tavern.

The plenary session of the diet was over. Luther retired to his lodgings as did his prince, the elector Frederick. Georg Spalatin, who was both Martin's friend and the chief advisor to Frederick, met Frederick in his rooms.

"It was a brief session, Your Grace," Spalatin said, trying to open the door to a conversation. He wanted to know what his prince thought of the proceedings, but he had to be circumspect. Frederick was well aware that he held Martin's life—and with it, the future of the reformation—in his hands. As Martin's prince, he was sworn to protect him. But as the electoral prince of Saxony he was also bound by an oath to obey the emperor—an uneasy balance to sustain under the best of circumstances.

"Too brief," the elector said. A deep frown creased his face.

Spalatin decided to risk a direct comment on the proceedings. "Luther spoke well, I thought."

"No," Frederick said, shaking his head slowly and staring at the table. "Dr. Martin spoke brilliantly. And there's no doubt that everyone heard, but I'll tell you, my friend, he's too daring for me."

Spalatin didn't push. He knew the elector was still undecided, though now he seemed to be leaning toward siding with Luther's enemies.

"You were there, Georg," Frederick said as if the realization had just dawned on him. "What did you think?"

"I think Rome failed to make its case, sire," Spalatin said, in an effort to appeal to Frederick's German nationalism. The German prince tented his fingers and leaned forward, still staring at the table. He spoke in a low voice, mostly to himself.

"I wonder. Do the Scriptures convict him or do they not?" He shook his head as if to clear it. "I'll sleep on it, Georg," he said, looking up for the first time.

"Very good, sire." Spalatin took the cue from his prince and left him to wrestle with his decision. "You will be in my prayers, my lord."

When Georg saw Martin in his lodgings later that night, the doctor was in a feisty mood.

"I felt certain," Luther said to his good friend as he paced the room, "that the pope would damn Tetzel and bless me. Tetzel was nothing but a moneychanger—a filthy indulgence peddler who would have cheated the poor widow out of her last two mites. Rome should have driven the old moneygrubber and his indulgences out of the church with a whip. But no. Tetzel receives the blessing of the pope; and I get thunder and lightning. Fine. If it's a storm she wants, it's a storm she'll get. Rome will soon learn that James and John weren't the last sons of thunder!"

Early the next morning, acting on Aleander's orders, Jonathan visited each of the electors to find out where they stood on Luther. He returned to Aleander after noon with his report.

"They are all agreed, Your Eminence," he said, trying to mask his disappointment. "They believe the charges against Luther are too serious to dismiss." The alliance was tentative at best, and it stopped short of condemning Luther outright. But the balance was definitely shifting to the side of the emperor, and Aleander sensed it.

"Agreed? All six?" Aleander was incredulous. "Even Frederick?"

"All, sir."

"So…," Aleander mused. He smiled and began to walk away, lost in thought, then turned to address his assistant. "Well done, Jonathan. I will mention your service to His Excellency."

Jonathan said nothing but bowed low and whispered a prayer for forgiveness.

Later that afternoon, after hearing Aleander's report, the emperor called the electors and some of the princes together.

"What do you think, gentlemen?" Charles asked calmly.

Frederick rose to address the emperor. "We would ask for more time to consider, Excellency. The charges are grave, and Luther's response—"

"I will give you my opinion then," Charles interrupted. He pulled a paper from inside his cloak and began to read. It was in French, and he had composed it himself.

"I am descended from a long line of Christian emperors of this noble German nation, and of the Catholic kings of Spain, the archdukes of Austria, and the dukes of Burgundy. They were all faithful to the death to the Church of Rome, and they defended the Catholic faith and the honor of God. I have resolved to follow in their footsteps.

"A single friar who goes counter to all Christianity for a thousand years must be wrong. Therefore I am resolved to stake my lands, my friends, my body, my blood, my life, and my soul. Not only I but you of this noble German nation would be forever disgraced if by our negligence not only heresy but the very suspicion of heresy were to survive.

"After having heard yesterday Luther's obstinate defense of his lies, I regret that I have delayed so long in proceeding against him and his false teaching. I will have no more to do with him. He may return to Wittenberg under safe conduct. But he may not preach or create any turmoil among the people. I will proceed against him as a notorious heretic and ask you to declare yourselves as you promised me."

When Charles looked up, he saw not men but ghosts—pale shadows of Germany's nobility. No one said a word. No one breathed.

The emperor dismissed the gathering and wished them a good night's rest. Tomorrow they would decide Luther's fate.

Chapter 20

The electors convened on the following day, amid wild speculations that they had already decided to burn Luther on the spot. The emperor lost no time in asking for his electors' official support of his position contra Luther. Each man declared himself in agreement with the emperor, but only four of the six were willing to put their names in ink.

The two who refused were Ludwig of the Palatinate and Luther's protector, Frederick, the territorial prince of Saxony. Charles smiled. He had enough support to ban Luther from the empire as a convicted heretic, but he didn't want to alienate any elector and especially not the politically valuable Frederick. He was too influential with the other electors. He was too powerful in Saxony, which occupied a strategic part of the empire in Europe, and he contributed too much to the Roman coffers. Charles would tell Aleander to proceed with a final draft of the edict against Luther, but it would be a milder version, a draft that would not offend Frederick, and one Charles would personally endorse. Soon Luther would be a man without a country.

Word of the electors' decision spread quickly. Jonathan told Justus after he left Aleander, and Justus went immediately to Martin, whom he found reading his Bible. Justus sat on a chair beside the desk Martin was using and told him the news.

Martin leaned back and folded his hands across his stomach. "So," he said quietly. "It's done."

"Jon says there's still some hope," Justus said quietly. "Frederick and Ludwig refused to sign—"

Luther waved his hand. "Doesn't matter. Charles doesn't need a unanimous vote, only a majority. Besides, signing is only a formality. Frederick supports the decision in his heart. So does Ludwig. They won't oppose the emperor in this. No, it's over." He breathed deeply.

The two friends sat in silence, neither of them moving. Finally Luther spoke, though more to himself than to Justus. "Vindicate me, O Lord, for I have walked in my integrity."

"What?" Justus asked.

"Psalm 26. I was just reading it before you came in. Here," Martin said, sliding the text over to Justus. "Read verses nine through twelve."

Justus found the reference and began to read aloud, "Do not take my soul away along with sinners, nor my life with men of bloodshed, in whose hands is a wicked scheme, and whose right hand is full of bribes. But as for me, I shall walk in my integrity; redeem me, and be gracious to me. My foot stands on a level place; in the congregations I shall bless the Lord."

He looked up to see tears streaming down his old friend's cheeks.

"Our Lord," Martin whispered. "Our dear Lord is so kind to lead me to this verse in my darkest hour. He knew the electors' decision before it was made. He knew they had condemned me in their hearts before they ever cast a single vote. So he gave me this verse to comfort me."

"What will you do?" Justus asked.

Martin laughed and wiped away his tears. "Die, I imagine, if Charles has his way. And the sooner the better."

"Martin—"

"Justus, there's nothing to do. I told you before we ever left Wittenberg that it might very well come to this. Either I believe it enough to die for it, or I don't. There's nothing to add, and I refuse to take anything away from what I've written."

"Martin, I wish I could…," Justus started but couldn't finish.

"No, no, my friend," Martin said, shaking his head. "There's nothing you could or should do to try to stop this. It's in God's hands. Let it be."

"Aren't you afraid?" Justus asked.

Martin paused before answering. "Not of death. The perfect love of Christ has taken that fear away. But I would be lying if I said I wasn't afraid of the way to death—the cross itself. Or the fire. Or the ax. But, Justus, the Lord has reminded me in this wonderful psalm that my foot stands on a level place. When the time comes for me to suffer for his name's sake, I know now that I won't stumble, I won't fall. But by his grace, and in the strength of his Spirit"—Martin paused and placed his hand on the open Bible—"and on the authority of his holy word, I will stand."

Just past midnight the wind was blowing in gusts, stirring up dust devils, whining as it slipped through cracks in the walls of the shops. A small group of men left one of the many taverns in Worms on an errand. A tall man in a hooded robe stood in their midst and gave quick directions. The group of ten moved slowly across the street to a darkened alley. They carried no lamp, no candle. In their hands they held placards and small nails and hammers. They spread out through the city, running from door to door, flitting in and out of the shadows like leaves that had forsaken their branch.

In the deepest part of the night, Albert, Archbishop of Mainz, was having a nightmare. His bed was soaked in sweat as it had been so many nights before. He hated the city of Worms, he hated this assembly, and most of all, he hated Luther. His whole life had become a nightmare, and Luther was the cause. Albert owed an enormous sum of money to the Fugger Bank—well over fifty-two thousand ducats after interest, which he had borrowed in order to make a contribution to the building of the new Saint Peter's basilica in Rome. In return for his generosity, Pope Leo had agreed to allow Albert to hold more than one diocese. It was a clear violation of church law. At twenty-four Albert was too young to assume an episcopal office, and the church strictly forbade the accumulation of church offices. It was true that he *was* already archbishop of Magdeburg and administrator of the diocese of Halberstadt. But it was also true that the pope was the supreme authority in the church and would certainly do what was best—which obviously included issuing a special dispensation effectively making him cardinal and archbishop of Mainz, the largest archdiocese in Christendom.

It was a delightful office to hold, and worth every ducat he had to pay to get it. True, he was bored with theology, and he disliked preaching. But as archbishop of Mainz he was able to exercise his unique gift for collecting relics. So far, he had even outstripped Frederick the Wise, who owned thousands of relics in his own right. But Frederick's collection paled in comparison to Albert's. By viewing his collection at Halle, a Christian pilgrim could obtain thirty-nine million days indulgence— thirty-nine million days he wouldn't have to suffer the consequences of his sin in the fires of purgatory. Yes, Albert had been a blessing to the church.

There was, however, the nagging problem of repaying his debt to the Fugger Bank. He had made a deal with Pope Leo that allowed him to sell indulgences in order to expedite repayment of his loan from the Fuggers. Half of the proceeds from his sales would go to the building of Saint Peter's, and the other half would go to the Fugger Bank. All was proceeding nicely—tens of thousands of Christians were paying handsomely for indulgences—until Luther got in the way. He had condemned the sale of indulgences in his ninety-five theses. And now, largely because of Luther and his arrogant claims, the peasants had grown restless. Some were refusing to purchase indulgences. And there were rumors that some were planning a revolt. Without their money, Albert couldn't pay his loan to the Fugger Bank. It was as simple as that. It was all Luther's fault. The man had no ability whatsoever to heed the voices of compromise and common sense.

So Albert had voted against Luther—had voted to silence him and to ban his writings from the empire. He hoped the vote hadn't come too late to save him from his debtors. Albert had bought his church office. Now he wished he could buy a decent night's sleep, a respite from the nightmares. This one had been particularly disturbing. The bizarre image of a great fish hovered over the earth—its belly ripped open and a flood of pestilence and war spilling out of it. The earth was torn apart in the rush of death—peasants fighting, swinging their scythes, slicing through the roiling waves of destruction. Opposing them were the pope, his cardinals and princes, all crowded together, screaming for someone to save them.

Suddenly the peasants grew still. They parted to reveal a man standing in their midst. He wore the habit of a monk, and his eyes burned with a white fire. It was Luther. He held a Bible in his right hand. He raised his left hand slowly from his side, and the earth began to shake. The peasants began to chant the Pater. "Our Father, which art in heaven, hallowed be thy name…" As the volume of the chorus rose to a thunderous roar, the priest pointed his index finger at the pope and lightning burst from his fingertip. It forked through the air like an electric serpent, lacing itself in and out of the pope's ears and eyes, incinerating him and all those standing near.

Standing to the side, Albert heard a cracking in the sky. He looked up to see Michelangelo falling from his scaffold in the Sistine. The earth opened to receive him and closed back over him. Above Albert, the dome of heaven spread from horizon to horizon, but it was the painted roof of the Sistine chapel, fragmenting now in the cataclysm into thousands of pieces and crumbling and falling down on them all. Albert saw the great fish hovering again, still erupting. Bits of plaster and liquefied paint from the broken Sistine sky mixed with the flood from the fish's belly until the thickening sea began to envelop the imperial throne and Albert felt himself drowning. He sat bolt upright in bed, gasping for air, bathed in a cold sweat.

An April breeze rattled the shutters as he leaned over the side of the bed and took his candle from the nightstand. A night's worth of unattended burning—the archbishop had fallen asleep while reading—had reduced the candle to a yellow-white glob of wax with a charred wick poking through the center. A tiny blue button of light remained, making the thin edges of the candle glow—barely enough for Albert to make his way down the hallway without bumping into the furniture.

He decided he might as well visit the privy located at the rear of his lodgings. The only way to it, however, was through the front door, since there was some construction going on at the rear of his rooms that prevented a more discreet exit.

He opened the door and peered out into the darkness cautiously, glancing up at the night sky involuntarily to check for flying fish. It was strangely quiet, even for the deep night. Albert had just stepped off the raised threshold to enter the street in his nightclothes when a fluttering caught his eye. Someone had tacked a placard to the door. He held the flickering candle up to the piece of paper. What he saw there sent chills up his back. He started shivering uncontrollably as a thin veil of perspiration broke out on his brow. On the paper was stamped the *bundschuh,* the clog of the German working man, and crushed beneath it, the high boot of the German aristocracy.

The peasants had been seething, threatening to erupt for nearly a hundred years. The bundschuh was the symbol of their cause. Many of the poor couldn't read or write, but they could draw a picture of a simple German clog that screamed out a warning any prelate could hear: "Condemn Luther and suffer the consequences!"

Albert turned away from the poster to gaze down the street. There, nailed to every shop door, ragged pieces of paper fluttered in the night wind. He leaned back against the frame and tried to catch his breath. He started to tear the poster off the door but then thought better of it as he gazed back down the deserted street, trying to penetrate the shadows. He couldn't know—there might be one of them out there, one of the rabble—watching, waiting for him to do just that. All they needed was a little excuse. He went back inside. The privy could wait a bit. Until the sun came up anyway.

At dawn Albert summoned his courage and ripped the poster from the door. He took off in a mad dash to the emperor, who received him with a sleepy mixture of mild irritation and curiosity.

Albert offered the poster as evidence of the peasants' threat to the peace. Charles sat half asleep, but when Albert told him about his nightmare, he couldn't suppress a small burst of laughter.

"My dear Albert," he said waving his hand dismissively, "this is nothing. Please, go back to your lodging and get some sleep or have a good breakfast or do whatever it is archbishops do at this unholy hour. We will deal with Luther in the appropriate manner."

"Begging Your Majesty's pardon," Albert said, barely able to contain his frustration. "But I know these people. These placards are a warning."

"Oh?" Charles said, smiling. "And what will they do? Throw their clogs at us? Albert, please."

Albert didn't know what to say. His emperor actually thought him a coward for taking the threat seriously.

"Now," Charles continued, "if you will excuse me, I intend to order my breakfast and prepare for the day."

Albert left the room, knowing what he must do. He hadn't risen to the post of cardinal by giving up at the first sign of opposition. He walked quickly to his brother Joachim's rooms and told him of the placards, his dream, and the emperor's response.

"The fool," Joachim said of the king. He was an angry man and ruthless. He hated Luther, and he despised the arrogance of Charles.

"If we told him that the peasants are spreading a prophecy…," Albert began.

"He wouldn't listen. He doesn't believe in prophecies or dreams." He was pacing now. "All the peasants need is a little spark like this to set them off," he said, pulling up a chair to face his brother. "Here's what we have: There's a real possibility of an insurrection if Luther is condemned. The emperor obviously doesn't believe the threat is real because he is determined to condemn Luther. Our only option is to get Luther to back down, modify his position, something. Luther bends a little, the emperor saves face, we avoid a peasant insurrection."

Albert agreed, and a few minutes later he and his brother had formed a plan. They left the apartments quickly and approached each of the electors with an appeal to ask the emperor to call Luther back before the diet. The electors all agreed, and the brothers presented their signed petition to the emperor later that day. Charles was short with them, saying he would have nothing to do with it but that he would grant them three days to question Luther on their own.

Martin himself welcomed the meetings. He appreciated the fact that Frederick had managed to get Richard of Greiffenklau, the Archbishop of Trier, to arbitrate the meetings. Richard was perfect for the job. Luther, as well as his opponents, counted Richard to be fair and just. He was important for another reason as well. He was highly respected because he had obtained one of the most highly valued relics in all of Christendom: the seamless robe the soldiers had draped across the shoulders of Christ at his crucifixion.

Without the presence of the emperor and the volatile Ecken, the meetings between Luther and the electors were actually congenial, at least in the beginning. The estates received him warmly, applauding Luther's writings on good works and on the Ten Commandments. They declared he was justified in his opposition to the abuse of indulgences, and even went so far as to support his indictment of Roman corruption.

But when it came to his pamphlet *The Freedom of the Christian Man,* Richard of Greiffenklau became passionate.

"Your words, Doctor, threaten to split the church." Richard looked at Martin and he continued in a calm voice, "I beg you, all of us beg you, Martin. Do not rend the seamless robe of Christendom."

Martin responded quietly. "It was never my intent to split the church. I never counseled nor will I ever counsel anarchy. I will encourage the German people and Christians throughout the empire to submit to the authorities, even if they be as evil as Rome herself. As for the content of my message, before you judge me I would ask only that you wait and see if my teaching is from God or man."

Luther was alluding to Gamaliel's advice to the Sanhedrin in Acts 5. There the self-righteous council had opposed the apostle Peter's message. Aleander picked up on the subtle allusion. "Think of someone other than yourself for once, Luther," Aleander shouted bitterly. "If you are destroyed, what do you think will happen to your beloved Melanchthon and Bucer and the rest?"

Martin bowed his head. Aleander's barbed words had found a chink in the monk's armor. *I am taking not only my own life but the lives of my trusted friends in my hands. Must they pay with their lives for my obstinacy? Am I being obstinate? Unteachable?* Tears ran down Martin's cheeks.

"Who would you have as a judge then, Martin?" Aleander spat out the words, but he had waited a fraction of a second too long. He had given Martin time to think. He pushed on, imagining he still had the advantage. "Who could be worthy of discerning whether your teaching is from the devil or not? The pope? Would he be exalted enough, spiritual enough for you, most learned Doctor?"

At this, Luther raised his head and glared at the papal ambassador. "I would name a child of eight or nine as my judge, sir. And I would prefer that child over the pope in the wink of an eye. For the pope has shown himself to be no judge of matters pertaining to God's Word and faith."

Martin would not back down. Albert's heartfelt pleas for peace made no difference. Threats of excommunication from Aleander made no difference. A misguided attempt at flattery made things worse. Finally the meeting disbanded, and the committee returned to the emperor empty-handed.

"Luther is dead," Aleander announced as he strode into his apartments. His black robes billowed behind him, creating the illusion of an enormous bird of prey coming home to roost after feeding on carrion.

"Sir?" Jonathan asked, thinking he must have misunderstood. He had been sitting on an ornate chair under a window in the corner of the room reading à Kempis.

Aleander stood silently before the small wall mirror in the corner of the room, slowly caressing the embroidered sleeve of his purple cassock—the color signifying his status as bishop in the church hierarchy and his importance in God's eyes. His heavy-lidded eyes closed at the exquisite touch of velvet on his skin. He had told Jonathan that God had given his churchmen velvet as a foretaste of the rewards that awaited them in heaven. "You know," he said, ignoring Jonathan's query, and furrowing his brow, "I've grown weary of purple. It bores me. Red suits me much better, don't you think?"

Jonathan had grown weary of Aleander's often-repeated and too-obvious desire to attain the office and the vestments of cardinal. Still, he had to say something, and the first thing that came to mind was, "Of course, Your Eminence." But he was anxious to turn the conversation back to the subject of Luther's fate. "You said Luther is…" He waited for Aleander to complete the sentence.

"Dead. Yes. Oh, not physically," Aleander said, still appreciating his reflection in the mirror. His voice was quiet and relaxed. "Not yet anyway. But it won't be long. I've just been with Charles, and he has given me his personal word that he will sign the edict banishing Luther."

"I see…"

"The two cowards who wouldn't sign go home tomorrow," Aleander continued, referring to Frederick and Ludwig. "That will certainly make everything smoother. Charles is much wiser than I had allowed." He turned slightly and looked sideways to catch more of his profile in the mirror. "Yes. I should be wearing red before the year is out."

He sauntered across the room to the delicately carved glove box in the corner and pulled his gloves off slowly, tugging one finger at a time. He spoke, looking out the side window. "Luther will be banned throughout the empire by the church and by the state. He'll have a small yard to play in—there in his little corner of Saxony." He tossed his gloves dramatically into the velvet-lined box and shut its lid decisively as if the gloves were Luther and the box his coffin.

The movement made Jonathan sick to his stomach. The arrogance of the man. He actually despised Luther as much as he adored himself. Jonathan didn't know how to respond. He fumbled his words.

"Frederick…did he…"

"Frederick has his head in the sand as usual. He knows nothing of Charles's plan. Besides, it's none of his business," Aleander snapped. "Good riddance, too, if you ask me. Meddlesome old fool, only thinking of himself. And then he poisons Ludwig against the emperor. Inexcusable." He cursed, frustrated with the knotted cord at his throat. "Pay attention, boy, and help me with this cape."

Jonathan resisted the temptation to tighten the knot considerably and instead rose to help. He balanced the small volume of à Kempis on the arm of the chair and began to help his master, but his mind was spinning. *Why wait until Frederick and Ludwig go home to banish Luther? There was nothing they could do to stop it—unless Charles needed Luther's protector and his entourage out of the way for some darker reason.*

Jonathan's fingers felt thick and clumsy. As his knuckles pressed lightly into Aleander's neck, he felt his pulse, saw the blue-black vein throbbing under the thin veil of flesh, and was faintly surprised to think of the bishop as having a heart.

Aleander pushed him away roughly, cursing as he turned back to the mirror. Finally the knot surrendered to his prying fingers. Aleander let it drop unceremoniously to the floor and kicked it aside. He crossed the room to a wash basin and rolled up his sleeves. He waited as Jonathan poured fresh water from the pitcher over his outstretched hands, then bent over the basin to moisten his face.

He said something down into the water, but to Jonathan his voice sounded far away, as though he were speaking in a tunnel. "Luther is a Satan, and he has blinded the minds of those who listen to his drivel."

He straightened and dried his face with the small white towel Jonathan had folded so carefully that morning. "But he won't bother us much longer." His voice was as cold as a slab of rock, as final as a gravestone.

"Yes," Jonathan said absently, and suddenly he understood. *They were going to have Luther killed.* He spoke quickly. "But he could still make trouble in Saxony, couldn't he, Father? I mean, you yourself said he would be safe there." He tried to make it sound as if he was disappointed at the prospect of Luther living safely in his own land. His conscience pricked him. It was a lie of style if not of content, but he had to know for sure if Aleander was planning Luther's death.

"My dear boy," he said with another twisted grin. "He has to *get* to Saxony first."

Until that moment Jonathan had managed to sustain a thin hope that all would be well. No longer. Now he must find a way to save Luther.

The stars kept their distance that night. A half-moon hung suspended on invisible wires, like a lantern with the shade partially open and tipped toward the shadowed earth.

Jonathan hurried through the streets of Worms still crawling with beggars and whores. He kept close to the shop walls and tried to stay in the shadows. He turned a corner and stepped quickly into an alley off the Kämmererstrasse. He almost cried out as he stumbled over two drunks lying there in a stupor. Neither of them stirred. Jonathan dropped to one knee and caught his breath in short gasps that turned to sobs. His skin was slick with a clammy sweat. He shivered with a chill that rose half from the frosty night air and half from his fear of what he had just done.

He knew it was right. Still, he took a deep breath and prayed that Aleander wouldn't find out.

"Georg? Georg, get up. Georg?" Frederick called loudly in the hallway.

He could hear his chief advisor, Spalatin, stumble across the room and open the door suddenly, a stump of a candle glowing in his hands. Frederick jumped back, startled by his disheveled appearance.

"Oh, my liege!" Spalatin jumped as well, almost dropping the candle. "Is something wrong? Please, please come in out of the draft."

"I'm sorry to get you up at this hour, Georg." Frederick stepped across the threshold into the comparatively small room. He clasped his hands in front of him as he sat in the one large chair near the foot of the bed.

"No, no, please tell me—is something wrong? How can I help?" It didn't matter what kind of fix Frederick the Wise was in, Georg Spalatin would be there for him. Frederick knew that—they were much more than an employer and employee. They were dear friends and had been for more than thirteen years. Frederick valued not only his friendship but his counsel. He had even written to Spalatin once that "while many Germans called me 'wise,' few understand that what passes for my own wisdom is, more often than not, a reflection from a brighter, though inconspicuous sun."

"Georg, I've just had a visitor," Frederick said. "He asked me not to reveal his name." He paused and looked at Georg questioningly.

"I wouldn't think of asking, sire," Georg said.

"No, of course not. Certainly not," Frederick said, shaking his head and frowning. "Well, this, this person has it on good authority that Martin will be attacked on his way back to Wittenberg."

"Attacked? But he has the promise of safe conduct from the emperor himself."

"I'm not sure the emperor even knows about this," Frederick said. He stopped pacing and gazed into the empty fireplace, looking for an answer among the charred pieces of wood. "All I know is that Martin's life is in danger. And my hands are tied."

Chapter 21

Luther's cart rumbled lazily along the Eisenach road on its return journey to Wittenberg. The entourage of churchmen and university professors glanced nervously from side to side, watching and waiting, hoping that what they feared most had remained back in Worms. Luther was particularly quiet. He held on to the sides of the rough carriage to steady himself, but he kept his eyes closed.

"O Lord," he prayed. "I ask only that you might guide Charles to honor his promise of safe conduct. Not for my sake, Lord, but for these dear brothers who are traveling with me. Protect these servants of yours, Father, and bless them. Hinder the evil one as he seeks to destroy all that you—"

"What's that?" someone whispered in a frightened voice. Martin looked up from his prayers and listened. Then he heard it too. A low, rumbling thunder of horses' hooves on hard-packed road.

"What do we do?" one of the men asked fearfully.

"Run!" one of the men said. "Run into the trees and hide. Come on, Martin, we can—"

"No," Martin said. "These men aren't after you. They only want me, and I will not run. No matter what happens, do not try to defend me. That is my wish." He could tell the men surrounding him knew he was right. There was no place to run, no place to hide. Not one of them

203

had ever lifted a sword in combat, so the idea of fighting armed soldiers was ludicrous. And besides, the time for action had just run out.

The soldiers swept down on the small group of clerics and surrounded them quickly. "There he is," one of them said. "That's Luther. Come down, sir. Now." But Luther didn't budge. One of the horsemen galloped up alongside Martin's cart, dragged him from it and threw him to the ground.

Luther said nothing.

Suddenly and quite unexpectedly Georg Spalatin rose to stand on the cart's seat. He thrust out his chest and his chin, pointed his finger dramatically at the cursing thugs—then proceeded to berate them, "You vile pig-men," he shouted. "You infestation of vermin. How dare you accost this assembly of God's priests. We have been granted safe conduct by the emperor, Charles V. Do you presume to act in defiance of a promise granted from the lips of the Holy Roman Emperor? Well, do you?" he thundered.

The leader of the brigade raised his hand as if to silence Spalatin and said, "That's a fine sermon, but this business is between us and Herr Luther. The rest of you are free to go." He then ordered one of his men to hoist Martin onto an extra horse, which he did under another volley of invective from the courageous Spalatin. Once Martin was secure in his saddle, the captain and his fellow soldiers turned back down the road and disappeared into the forest with Spalatin's anathemas ringing in their ears.

Frederick's "abduction" of his favorite priest had come off without a hitch, leaving Luther with nothing worse than a couple of bumps and a bruised ego. On the other hand Georg Spalatin, who had been in on the ruse from the beginning, emerged as the most daring scholar in anyone's memory—a legend, the fires of which he would stoke for years to come.

Martin and his abductors rode for a whole day, taking different roads, doubling back over their tracks, striking out through the pathless woods. It was unseasonably warm for early May. Still, they didn't stop to rest, eating bits of bread and dried meat as they rode and gulping water from the skins tied to their saddles. Finally, near midnight, they emerged from a thick copse of holly into a clearing

"There it is, Father," the captain of the soldiers announced. "Your new home." Martin looked up. The massive walls of the ancient castle known as the Wartburg rose above him.

"A temporary shelter, captain, that's all," Martin said as he rode forward. "God forbid I should ever call this place 'home.'"

MAY 5, 1521
THE EMPEROR'S CHAMBERS

Charles rested his elbows on the table, his head in his hands. He had been awakened in the middle of the night with the news that Luther had been abducted by unidentified soldiers on his way back to Wittenberg the day before. One of the emperor's soldiers had met Luther's party near Wittenberg and learned the news, which he quickly brought back to Worms. Girolamo Aleander, angry and frustrated at having been rousted out of a sound sleep to answer for something he knew nothing about, stood now before the emperor, trying to hold his tongue.

"It's a simple question," Charles said for the third time, speaking down into the table. "Who took him? That's all I want to know."

"As I've said, Your Majesty—," Aleander began through clenched teeth.

"I know what you said!" Charles shouted, erupting from his chair and slamming his hand down on his desk. "'They aren't my men. I already know that! I don't want to hear, 'They aren't my men' again. I want to know whose men they are. And I want to know what they've done with Luther!"

Aleander cleared his throat and kept his voice calm. "I sent my assistant to inform Frederick of the abduction."

"Frederick? Why?" Charles asked.

Aleander continued, "I thought he should know quickly lest he think we had anything to do with Luther's disappearance,"

"Really?" Charles asked, his eyes half closed and his voice taking on the smirk that made Aleander's skin crawl.

"Well, yes, Your Majesty. He is Luther's protector. I thought—"

"No, see, that's the problem," Charles interrupted. "You didn't think at all!"

"Sire?" Aleander asked.

"You said it yourself, and you still don't see. Frederick is Luther's protector. You say you informed Frederick of Luther's disappearance? You may as well inform the fox that there's a sudden shortage of chickens."

The sudden realization of what had happened slammed into Aleander, leaving him stunned. "Frederick kidnapped his own man?" he asked dully.

"Of course he did. He played us all for fools."

"Oh," Aleander said, feeling nauseous. "May I sit down, Your Majesty?" he asked.

"There," Charles said motioning to a chair in the corner. Aleander sank into it gratefully and put his head in his hands. Charles continued, "But proving it is a different matter. And he knows I dare not accuse him of something so preposterous. I can't risk it. He's too powerful and he knows it. He probably hired some mercenaries to spirit Luther off somewhere." Charles took in a deep breath and stood with his back to Aleander, leaning against the mantel of the rock fireplace. "I should have seen this coming," he said to himself.

Aleander lifted his head. "I suppose there's always the chance they were Luther's enemies, sire?" he offered, trying to sound positive. "In which case our troubles would be over."

Charles shook his head. "No, if they wanted him dead, they would have killed him on the spot. They took him somewhere to hide him away, I'm sure of it." Turning back to face Aleander, he spoke more calmly now. "Well, then, it seems that Luther is under a double ban. I ban him to Saxony, and Frederick bans him to some hole in the ground where he'll rot away the rest of his miserable little life in hiding. This is perfect."

The keeper of the castle, an elderly knight whom Frederick had left in charge of the nearly empty edifice, appeared quickly at the enormous gate and welcomed them in.

Luther had never visited the Wartburg, though he had certainly heard of it. The castle was as much a part of German history and legend as the stories of Wotan. As Luther made his way to his chamber, he walked on paving stones that had been laid nearly five hundred years before. He crossed through halls that had once welcomed nobles and knights, with poets and musicians. Luther stepped over a curiously positioned stone pavement at the far end of the great hall. He paused just long enough to imagine what it must have been like for the king or the court performer to stand here and gaze out on the hundreds who could have packed the room. The refrain of Eschenbach's poem "Parzival" still hung in the air, its dynamic images suspended from the great arches like spectral tapestries too permanent ever to dissolve.

There were no artists like Eschenbach anymore, Luther thought. No one to match his soaring vision of the Divine or to search so honestly for the truth about man and his relationship to God, unafraid of what he might find. So it was up to poor theologians like him to sustain the quest.

He had always enjoyed the story of how Parzival progressed in his maturity and stature until he was granted the high honor of becoming the keeper of the Holy Grail. Martin smiled. Perhaps God would entrust *him* with keeping the Grail one day.

Then he thought, perhaps the duty was already his.

The flickering images faded, and suddenly, the hall was empty again. The castle was quiet now and the only tenants were the owls and bats that ruffled the darkness as they soared under the canopied arches.

Martin opened the door to his chamber and collapsed onto the bed, too tired to remove his outer cloak. That was when the sounds began—a popping, cracking noise, like nuts striking the ceiling. Then a sudden thunderous rumbling in the hall, like beer barrels tumbling down the stairs.

"So, Lucifer," Martin murmured to the devil, "you think a few bumps in the night will unsettle me? Ha!" He rolled over. He was tired. He needed sleep.

Yet he couldn't.

The high, thick walls of the Wartburg offered no protection from the enemy that Martin carried with him everywhere he went. But it wasn't Satan keeping Martin awake. It was his own inner voice that was haunting him, damning him. *Are you the only wise man, Martin?* came the insistent whisper. *Has the church been wrong for so many centuries? What if you are not the one, Martin? What if your father was right and the voice you heard in the thunder was the god of this world and not the God of heaven? What if the lightning addled your brain, as the woman with the book said? What if it addled your soul?* The rumbling in the halls stopped. *Martin. Martin. How many will you take with you to hell?*

May 6, 1521
The emperor's chambers, Worms

Aleander stood confidently before the emperor, who was reading the new version of the edict against Luther in Latin and then in German. Jonathan, still serving as Aleander's assistant, waited just outside the door of the emperor's private chambers. Charles smiled as he finished reading and picked up the quill to sign. Then he hesitated and put the pen down.

"No," he said. "This isn't right."

Aleander swallowed hard and closed his eyes.

"I must submit this to the diet." The emperor looked up from the table. "We will continue the other business of the diet and issue the decree at the proper time. That will be all, Aleander. Thank you for your good work."

"Your Majesty." Aleander bowed, took both copies of the edict, and left the apartments. He returned with Jonathan to his own rooms, saying nothing along the way.

Jonathan opened the door quickly, allowing Aleander to enter his lodgings without breaking stride. He didn't bother to knock, since he was sure Ecken wouldn't be there, which wasn't unusual. The chancellor spent as little time in Aleander's presence as possible. Aleander marched into his rooms and snapped his fingers—a signal for Jonathan to follow. He held out the documents dramatically for Jonathan to see.

"He didn't sign!" Aleander said in a tone that suggested it was all Jonathan's fault. "He didn't sign!" he said again. Then he shrugged and tossed the copies on a table. "Don't ask me," he said disconsolately. "After all he promised. Nothing." He rubbed his face angrily as if by rubbing he could erase his disappointment. "He was about to sign. He had the quill in his hand ready to sign, then he lays it down and says he has to submit the edict to the assembly!" He cursed and threw his cap angrily across the room as he plopped down in a chair. He lifted his right foot for Jonathan to remove his boot.

Jonathan said nothing as he crossed the room, thanking God silently that his service to this pompous prelate would soon be done and he could return to Wittenberg. But there was more than pride at work in Aleander. The man was a murderer—or would have been if Jonathan hadn't warned Frederick of the plot to kill Luther. Still, he felt a vague tug at his conscience for continuing to serve the man he had betrayed only a few nights before.

Aleander regarded Jonathan through narrowed, dark eyes. "What's your name, boy?" he asked as Jonathan removed the first boot.

Jonathan looked at him, pausing for a moment, hoping his disgust for this prig of a man wouldn't show through. "Jonathan, Father," he said, pulling off the second boot.

Aleander sneered. "Jonathan," he mumbled to himself, rolling the name on his tongue, considering it as a dung beetle might consider a work in progress. "Well, in light of the incredible good luck you have brought me, Father Jonathan, I think you will not be returning to Wittenberg."

"Sir?"

"Please, Father. You think I didn't see the way you looked at Luther? The way you smiled when he posed one of his ridiculous arguments?"

"Sir, I assure you—"

"Do you? I think not, Father. No, you bring me no assurance at all. What you bring me, Father Jonathan, is betrayal. What you bring me is embarrassment. I brought you here to Worms to help me put the Hussite Luther in his place. Obviously, I made a mistake. You and Luther both deserve banishment at the very least."

Jonathan said nothing. His face expressed no emotion.

"But I am too generous," Aleander continued. "Yes, far too generous even to those who abuse my kindnesses. It's the curse of being born with a forgiving spirit, Father. So there you have it." He sighed, raised his eyebrows in a bit of studied nonchalance, then tilted his head to one side and folded his hands resignedly in his lap. "Well, I've given this matter some thought, as you can see. I've decided that Wittenberg's no place for a young man of your considerable talents."

"Sir?" Jonathan asked. He could feel something coming. Someone would pay for this man's frustration.

Aleander smiled. "I told you on our first meeting that God rewards those who help the church, didn't I? I'm sure you came here expecting something wonderful. A new position, perhaps? Yes, I think so, and as it happens, I have just the place for you. Reichenau. You might have heard of it. It's on a small island on Lake Konstanz. There's a quaint little monastery there that should take full advantage of your gifts. Far better than the bustle of Wittenberg and quite a bit more than a stone's throw from Luther, whom I'm sure you detest as much as I. Reichenau's full of great men, too. Or at least men who dreamed of greatness, once long ago. Like you."

Jonathan's heart sank like a stone. Reichenau sat in the middle of Lake Konstanz in Southern Germany. Once, on a trip to visit relatives in the south, he had accompanied his mother across the mile-long causeway that connected the island monastery to the shore. He remembered the place primarily for how old and decrepit all the monks were. And how lonely the place felt.

Aleander rose and opened the door. "I'll have a letter of transfer drawn up after the diet. Well," he said, standing abruptly and feigning a yawn, "I'm tired. Good night, my son. And thank you for all your help."

Jonathan walked out into the hall without another word. He couldn't have spoken if he had wanted to. He kept his back to the door, not wanting Aleander to see the tears that streaked his face. As the door closed behind him with a soft finality, he leaned against the smoke-darkened wall and wept.

Aleander's fears that he had failed turned out to be groundless. He was thrilled at the fact that the diet proceeded without a ripple of protest after Frederick and his co-dissenter Ludwig had returned to their respective homes. Then, when there was only a remnant left to condemn Luther, Aleander beamed as Charles pulled out the Edict of Worms and presented it to those present. The paper concluded with these words:

"This devil in the habit of a monk has brought together ancient errors into one stinking pool and has invented new ones. He denies the power of the keys and encourages the laity to wash their hands in the blood of the clergy. His teaching fosters rebellion, division, war, murder, robbery, arson, and the collapse of Christendom. He lives the life of a beast. He has burned the decretals. He despises alike the ban and the sword. He does more harm to the civil than to the ecclesiastical power.

We have labored with him, but he recognizes only the authority of Scripture, which he interprets in his own way. We have given him twenty-one days, dating from April 15. We have now gathered the estates. All shall regard Luther as a convicted heretic. When the time is up, no one is to harbor him. His followers also are to be condemned. His books are to be eradicated from the memory of man."

It was a solemn occasion, though the emperor appeared light-hearted, and Aleander fought the temptation to laugh out loud. Charles looked up and smiled at Aleander after he signed the German version of the decree.

"You will be content now," he said in the tone of a father who was finally giving his anxious child a piece of candy.

"Yes, Majesty," Aleander cooed, receiving the decree from the emperor's hand. "And His Holiness will enjoy even greater content-ment, as will all Christendom." Aleander gazed at the signature, lost in the moment, as close to ecstasy as he would ever come. The ink on this paper meant the end of Luther and his diabolical heresies, and a return to catholic unity. And it almost certainly meant a blessing for himself and a higher appointment from His Holiness. He could barely contain himself.

Later that night he recorded in his journal, "I was going to recite a paean from Ovid when I recalled that this was a religious occasion. Therefore blessed be the Holy Trinity for his immense mercy."

Chapter 22

Thomas Munzer pulled the needle through the cotton material one last time, tugged the bright red thread to make sure the knot was secure, then bit it off.

Finished.

He rose from the long wooden bench where he had been working through the night and stretched the ache out of his tired muscles. He looked around the room, surveying his upstairs garret with pride. The rent was only five ducats a week, and the money, which he kept tucked away in a locked metal box, would last him for months more.

He had become the leader his people had been waiting for. Luther was a coward, afraid to take up the sword. Afraid to really lead. The Bible was a chain around the necks of the people; it needed to be broken to let the life-giving Spirit in.

The Spirit of God had been speaking to Thomas for months now. At first he wasn't sure. It took time for the Spirit to break through. Time. He had to cleanse himself of all the old ideas, the filth, the excrement his teachers had poured into him from the time he was a child. Words, ideas that confused him—angered him. He put it aside. Began to pray. To think. Ate only to stay alive so he could pray more. Not for pleasure. Nothing for pleasure.

Then he knew. Suddenly, though not unexpectedly. It happened all in a rush one late afternoon on one of his long walks through the Black Forest. He had found a spot. Ancient, dark, quiet as a tomb. So quiet…he heard the Spirit of God. Saw It!

Fire in the wind. Translucent tongues of flame, licking the air. Whispering in feather-soft voices. *You, Thomas, will lead my people out of bondage. They will love you even as they love me. The letter kills, Thomas. But the Spirit lives. The Spirit gives life. Lead my people out of the darkness, Thomas. Out of Babylon. Away from the Roman whore. The dogs will lick the blood of the harlot from the streets. You are my warrior, Thomas. You are my sword. What is your name?*

"Thomas."

Your real name?

Thomas paused, staring. The fire touched him. The tongues of flame rested on him. Wisdom filled him.

"Jesus."

Please me, my Son, my righteous Sword.

"Yes."

The people would support him. They would follow him. They would offer him a crown just as they had offered him a crown during his first incarnation as the carpenter. But this time he wouldn't refuse. He would receive their offering, then he could take his money and dump it out on his mother's grave, and he would say, "Woman, behold your Son." It would all start tomorrow.

He thought of all the peasants he would lead. He thought of his brothers, robbed of their pasture, robbed of the right to hunt and to fish on the land they had settled.

Many of his friends had been forced to tend the haymaking, harvesting, or wineries of their overlords even at the expense of their own crops. If deer or wild boar were destroying their crops, they dared not run them off, much less shoot them; it would upset the hunt should their overlord decide he wished to give chase. And if the lord's hunting dogs happened onto their chickens, they could do nothing to stop them from devouring as many as they wished. They were forced to offer livestock to the castle before selling it elsewhere. They chopped firewood for the castle, and cut timber and wood for the stake on execution days.

If they refused, they were imprisoned in the lord's dungeons where, if they were fortunate, they would only have their eyes gouged out. The princes had slaughtered thousands merely for being in the wrong place at the wrong time.

Thomas thought of the men who had come to him only weeks before, demanding that he lead them. He felt the hand of God heavy on him as he stared at the scroll tied with a red ribbon, which lay at the far end of the table. The single sheet contained sixteen articles, written in his own hand on behalf of the peasants. He had heard of other lists, some containing thirty-four, some sixty-two points of declaration, but he thought it best to come to the point quickly, so he had limited his list to sixteen demands. Sixteen righteous articles!

Let Luther correct them if he dared.

Thomas was sure he would not. Because he could not. The Scriptures were too weak, and so was Luther. Besides, God was on the side of the peasants. They had already begun to fight and to win. And what was more important, they had met virtually no resistance. God had blinded the enemy. Who would dare try to quench the fire the Spirit had ignited?

Thomas shifted his gaze to the curling sheets of paper he had pinned to the slanted roof walls. Page after page of pictures—images of people, inky limbs akimbo, tacked between two rafters. Woodcuts of Pisces suspended above the earth, disgorging itself in a flood of destruction. The pope and all his vassals cringing below. The peasantry taking up hammer and scythe, pitchfork and pike. *Yes, old fish. About ready to burst, aren't we? Saturn. The planets all in a line. Lead on, old god of the fields, god of the common man.*

Thomas stared at the tumble of cloth on the table in front of him, and he felt a weariness in his bones so deep he ached. He longed to lie down. To sleep. Sleep, then look at the work of his hands by the light of the sun. He breathed deeply and tried to relax. He hadn't slept in two days. Even Jesus had to sleep.

But there was so much to do. To get ready for the kingdom.

For the judgment.

Thomas blinked his eyes once. Three times in quick succession. The rush was coming back.

Suddenly he was impatient. Agitated. Sweating. So hot here in this upper room. Shaking. The Spirit was speaking. Moving in him. The Spirit had to see the finished product. Had to see it now.

He swept his sewing tools aside. The thread, scissors, and scrap material went flying off the table. He tossed the cup and plate he had used for dinner the night before across the room, almost turning over the candle in his burst of excitement. He grabbed for it and steadied it at the last minute, spilling a bit of the hot wax on the back of his hand. He took a deep breath as he brought the candle up to his eyes, the back of his hand to his bearded mouth. He licked at the hot wax, already turning white on his mottled skin. He liked the feel of the smoothness on his tongue.

The roof of the garret sloped at an odd angle on the west side of the house, allowing for a small shelf. Munzer had rigged a hook to hold a lantern. He inserted the candle into the lantern and suspended it from the hook, steadying it with trembling fingers.

The candle was burning low but shed enough light for him to appreciate his handiwork. He flapped out the length of rectangular cloth and spread it on the table, smoothing the edges. He stood back and studied it.

A rainbow spread before him. A new world would rise out of the ashes of the old. Noah's world had perished by flood. This one would crumble in an ash heap. But God's rainbow—*Thomas's* rainbow—would fly above the ruin. He loved all the colors, but the red was his favorite. He had torn it from the inside of the duke's carriage three nights before. Yards of it. Red velvet. He had spent the first hour back in his loft stroking the fabric with his hand, running it over his arms and his face.

Asking forgiveness for the pleasure.

There would be enough of the blood red fabric to fashion a cape and a hat.

God would smile.

The Spirit would be pleased.

ZWICKAU, SOUTHERN GERMANY

A long, jagged line of men and women snaked its way down the twisting road and across the stubbled fields toward Zwickau. The local pastor had proclaimed a "historic event" for this day—he had invited a fiery young preacher named Munzer to address the people in the town square. The entire population of Zwickau had turned out.

They had trampled the streets into a bog hours before, forcing the new arrivals to the relatively dry edges of the footpath. The dingy clouds seemed tacked to the ceiling of heaven, parts of it drooping in great bulbous lumps like the underside of a rumpled quilt. The icy breath of winter, bitter and sharp, raked across the faces of the crowd, stinging their eyes and numbing their hands, forcing them to keep their heads bowed.

Elias Sklaar stood still in that slow stream of humanity, his head up, his eyes scanning the crowd hungrily. He wasn't interested in listening to a Christian preacher. He was after something else. His gaunt face bore the stubble of several days' growth. The eyes were set deep in his skull like two dried and cracked pieces of amber. There was no moistness there. Only a cold and distant fire that shriveled him from the inside and withered his soul.

He hunched over a twisted walking stick and pushed himself along the path, leaning into an opposing wind colder than any this world could conjure—his soul in perpetual winter, his heart a shard of ice. A black bag hung from four tightly curled fingers of his right hand. A crumpled sack added a deformed hump to his already curved back. Two buttons had slipped the leash binding them to his long black coat, leaving the top gaping open. Even hunched over as he was, he noticed people staring. Having made his way to the end of the street, he stood for a moment, peering into the murky tavern, then stepped across the threshold.

Munzer's voice rose high and brittle as ice on that midwinter afternoon. "Bible, babble, bubble!" he shouted, lifting the sacred text high above his head and letting it fall with a loud crack on the platform at his feet.

The crowd gasped.

"What good is it?" he yelled, his eyes burning with the fire of a zealot. "What good is the letter of the law without the Spirit to interpret that letter? I tell you that between these boards," he said, placing his foot on the wooden boards that bound the Bible, "are words on paper. Ink scratched out by the hand of men—men who put down the pen to embrace a harlot with the same hand! This day we lift our hand—a hand of righteousness against them."

Franz von Sickingen nodded in agreement. The time for talk was over. Twenty knights were gathered round him on their horses about halfway back in the crowd that packed the city square. They sat mounted on chargers, ready for battle. Munzer was uniting the peasants for a war, and he was building on Luther's reforms to do it. So be it. Sickingen and his soldiers had traveled far and were exhausted. But this sermon galvanized them, strengthened them. Gave them hope.

"Luther is gone!" Munzer roared. "Luther is dead! Killed by the king's own men! Why, you ask? Why would God allow such a thing? Because, my friends, God judges those who put their hand to the plow, then look back to the comfort of their home fires. God strikes down the weak and the cowardly who tremble in the face of the painted Roman whore! Luther put his hand to the plow! God was ready to tear into the heart of the Roman field, but Luther looked back to his home fires! God called Luther out of the Roman Sodom, and he started to leave; we must give him that. Yes, he started to leave that wicked city, but Luther looked back! He looked back with a weak heart, and God struck him down as surely as he turned Lot's wife into a dead pillar of worthless salt!

"Now, my friends, it's up to us. It's up to you. It doesn't matter that most of the knights of Germany are too cowardly to take up the sword against Rome. God defeated a hundred thirty-five thousand Midianites with fewer men than we see here! How much more will he do for righteous Germany? How much more will he do for the *true* believers?"

This was a knight's dream. This was destiny. All the years of training, of longing for honor and glory. And freedom. Sickingen felt his throat tighten, his breathing grow shallow. He was a knight! Called by God Almighty to this place, this hour. To declare his allegiance, to raise his sword for the cause of Christ. Sickingen and his men thrust their swords into the air and shouted with the rest of the crowd, shouted until the tears came.

Munzer raised his arms to quiet the crowd. Several minutes later he continued over the low roar. "We must cleanse the fatherland of the Roman infection. Of all who would force upon you the letter of this killing law," Munzer shouted, pointing dramatically to the Bible under his foot. "We trust in the Spirit, who gives life, the Spirit who burns within each and every true believer. The Spirit who, by his mighty hand, will scorch this earth and cleanse it with his holy fire. Only then will the Kingdom of our God come. Only then will the Lord Jesus Christ return in power and glory to reign as King of kings! Now is the time to take up arms! Arise, ye knights and princes! Arise, ye kingdom of priests and bring forth the Kingdom of God on earth!"

Again, the crowd roared its approval. Sickingen had heard enough. The time for words was over at last. Germany's long night was about to give way to the dawn of God's Kingdom—a kingdom of peace that would be established, as all great kingdoms were established, on the horns of war. And he, Franz von Sickingen, would be leading the armies of the righteous to prepare the way of the Lord. He reined his horse sharply to one side and spurred it on, plowing through the crowd and lifting his hand in a signal for his men to follow.

Women and children jumped out of his path, narrowly escaping the hooves of the chargers as Sickingen and his men forced their way through the mob. More than once the mounted knights had to dodge the thrusts of pitchforks and staves as the peasants stabbed the air in response to Munzer's call to arms.

"Death! Death to the pope!" they shouted, oblivious now to Munzer's oration. The shouts had become a chant that rolled out across the frozen hills.

Sickingen rode past the last line of people on his way toward the Reichenbach road. He scanned the low line of shops for a tavern. He and his men would stop for a drink before they began the long ride back to the Ebernburg where Ulrich von Hutten awaited his report.

The tavern was only a few degrees warmer than the street and, in some corners, not as clean. A few of the rougher sort, fearful of any presence that represented the law, got up to leave when Sickingen and his twenty soldiers walked in. The rest of the patrons sat quietly, drinking their beer or gnawing on tough beef, glad to have shelter from the cold.

Sickingen paid for a tankard and some cheese, then looked for a place to sit. He walked to a small table near the back where a man in a black coat sat alone. "Share your table, sir?" he asked.

The man looked up. Candlelight reflected off his small oval glasses as he stared toward the entrance without making eye contact with Sickingen. His stein was half empty, and there was a piece of stale bread and some cheese with a knife stuck in it on the table in front of him. He broke off a piece of bread and dipped it into his beer for a sop. Sickingen took the gesture as permission. He put his beer down and sat to the man's right. He noticed the black bag on the floor near his chair.

"You're a medical doctor, sir?" Sickingen asked.

"I practice medicine, yes." Sklaar said in an oily voice, still not making eye contact.

"Franz von Sickingen," the knight said, removing his riding glove and holding out his right hand.

Sklaar regarded him with a sidelong glance through half-closed eyes. "Sklaar," he said, extending his pale hand. "Dr. Elias Sklaar." He wrapped his fingers around the knight's in a viselike grip.

Sklaar withdrew his hand, reached inside his black coat, and pulled a piece of paper from the left inside pocket. He placed the paper on the table and unfolded it for Sickingen to see. He smoothed the corners mechanically but with a studied grace as if he had done it a thousand times before in a thousand different towns. "You travel a lot," he said pleasantly. "Do you recall seeing this woman? In some other town, perhaps?"

Sklaar watched as Sickingen studied the drawing closely—studied it as he had studied it himself every night, as he had memorized every line of it. The artist had hurried the work along the edges, but he had stumbled upon a truth in his haste, a vision of such innocence and beauty that it had slowed his hand. It wasn't the kind of lifeless Gothic sketch currently in vogue. The girl in the picture welcomed her guests. Then held them. Then haunted them. It was as if she had tried to depart this life but the artist had captured her spirit on canvas before it could fly to heaven. Her eyes returned the gaze of her admirers. Her lips parted slightly, sensually.

Sklaar's eyes fluttered slightly behind his glasses. He licked his lips, allowing the virginal image on the paper to feed his hot fantasies even as Sickingen sat gawking at her, touching her. Sklaar hated him for it, hated him for wanting her. Every man looked at her the same way. They all wanted her. But it wasn't their fault. Sklaar knew that. It was her fault. He would teach her a lesson when he found her.

Teach her not to run.

Not to flirt.

He withdrew the portrait slightly, just out of the knight's reach. "Have you seen her, sir?"

Without lifting his eyes, Sickingen whispered, "No. I've never seen this girl. Is she your daughter, sir?"

Stupid man. Sklaar folded the paper abruptly and thrust it roughly into his coat pocket. "The drawing is old," he said abruptly. "We were to be married. But..." He paused and took a sip of beer. "She disappeared one night. Kidnapped. That was four years ago. I swore to God I would find her."

"Four years. Young like that and pretty with no one to watch over her? She's dead, sir. Dead or worse."

"She's not dead," Sklaar mumbled as he drank the last of his beer. "I would know."

Chapter 23

Light slipped through tenebrous clouds, wrapping the early morning in a cold, gray shawl. Martin's breath came out in frosty puffs as he walked down the road, reciting his prayers for prime. The prayers kept his mind off the cold, though it felt so good to be outside the walls of his castle hideaway that he barely noticed. He had been a virtual prisoner in the Wartburg since May 4—nearly seven months. It had been a productive time, filled with study and his translation of the New Testament into German.

However, mixed reports led Martin to waste much of that time fretting over the ripple effect of his reforms. The nation was on the verge of anarchy, and rebellion was imminent. For some reason that Martin couldn't fathom, his old friend Georg Spalatin was refusing to publish some of his recent tracts. Duke George, who had grown to hate Martin since the Leipzig debate, was threatening his protector, Prince Frederick, with war unless he handed Martin over for trial. Karlstadt, his teaching colleague back at Wittenberg and one of the chief champions for reform, was pushing too hard and too fast. And it was creating more problems than it was correcting.

Finally Martin had heard enough. He decided to risk leaving his hideaway in Wartburg Castle for a brief incognito visit to Wittenberg. With his long hair and bushy beard, he would pose as Junker Jorg, a knight in the service of Prince Frederick. He planned to enter the town, learn as much as he could about the true status of the reforms, and get out quickly, before anyone recognized him and started trouble.

DECEMBER 4
THE CASTLE CHURCH, WITTENBERG

The doors to the castle church in Wittenberg stood ajar. Stepping inside, Martin paused, giving his eyes time to adjust to the dim light of the chapel. The pockmarked walls had absorbed so many prayers, the floors had been washed with so many thousands of tears, the ancient chapel had almost become a living thing—an old friend welcoming him back. But something wasn't right.

Martin stepped quietly onto the paving stones that led to the altar. There were no candles burning. No sounds at all, except for an old man praying, hunched over and shaking, weeping. Martin approached slowly, not wanting to disturb the man. Then he saw—it was his old friend, Johannes von Staupitz. He hadn't spoken with him since the night in Augsburg when Staupitz had released him from his obligations to serve him.

He placed his hand gently on the priest's shoulder. "Father," he said.

Staupitz jumped and shouted, raising his arm to defend himself. "No, no! Please," he cried.

Martin took him by the hand and knelt to face him. "Father, it's me. Look at me. It's Martin." Martin saw the blood immediately. A gash across Staupitz's forehead was barely crusted over, and this new exertion had reopened the wound. Martin pulled a cloth from his belt and pressed it gently to his friend's brow.

"Martin?" the priest asked, unbelieving that this bearded knight could be his beloved student. He grasped Martin's arms. "Oh, God be praised. Martin?" His eyes filled with tears as he embraced his son in the faith.

"What happened to you, Father?" Martin asked. Glancing up, he noticed the missals were absent from the altar. "What happened here?"

Staupitz leaned forward, holding the cloth to his head. "Last night. The people went crazy. Not just here—all over Wittenberg. They came in...animals..."

"Who, Father? Who were they?"

"Students, people from town. So many, I don't know. They were all wearing cloaks. It was so cold, so I...I...didn't think..." He put his other hand to his head.

Martin felt hot, angry tears on his own cheeks. He would find out who had done this. After a minute, Staupitz was able to speak again.

"They all had knives. Under their cloaks. Knives in the church, Martin." He shook his head. "And they took the missals from the altar. Who knows where they are, or what they've done to them. And they drove us out, all the priests, drove us out of the church.

"They threw rocks at whoever was praying." Staupitz sniffed and stared at the paving stones. "Women, men, even the children." Martin could hear the anger rising in his mentor's voice now. "Whoever they thought might be praying to the Virgin."

Martin didn't know what to say. His mind was a jumble of thorny contradictions. Wherever he turned for an answer, a reason for this madness, his conscience pricked him. *It's your fault, Martin. Yours.* "I'm sorry, Father. I'm so sorry," he whispered. *You might as well have thrown the stone yourself,* he thought. *All this violence. Why? Because you, fool, you believe you have the answer.*

Staupitz breathed deeply and let his breath out in a shuddering sigh. "We all want reform, Martin," he said, the gentleness returning to his voice. "But not this. Not rebellion. This," he said pointing to his head wound, "this will heal. But the church may not. You must stop this,

Martin. You must do something. Not for my sake but for the sake of the church."

"I promise you, Father," Martin said through his own tears. "I will do something. This will not happen again."

WARTBURG CASTLE

After a brief stay and a visit with friends, Martin returned to the Wartburg, shocked and disheartened that the people—all of them, from students to bankers to merchants and farmers—were breeding hatred and rebellion. He penned a hasty warning from his hideaway, urging moderation:

"Remember," he wrote, "that Antichrist, as Daniel said, will be broken without the hand of man. Violence will only make him stronger. Preach, pray, but do not fight. Not that all constraint is ruled out, but it must be exercised by the constituted authorities."

He sealed it with a prayer, and with the faint hope that God would use the man who had started this violence to help stop it.

Chapter 24

Elizabeth had made her long business trip to the southern tip of Germany without consequence. Her expanding business opportunities had never carried her this far south before, and she had been nervous about making the journey alone. She entered the city of Konstanz early in the afternoon, the folded samples of her best wool tucked safely away in locked boxes built into the side of her cart.

Over the past four years with Maggie, Elizabeth had developed an eye for fabric and for dyeing that most didn't possess, and the demand for the beautifully dyed wool was growing. She had also learned to deal with lustful men who were too often out for more than she was willing to barter in exchange. She quickly discovered that Konstanz had more than its fair share of coarse tradesmen. They all reminded her—although in a negative way—of what she had lost in Jonathan.

The last transaction of the day had been with a prominent city councilman who proved the exception to the rule of rude merchants. He treated Elizabeth with respect, then placed a generous order that would keep Maggie busy for the next three months. She felt so good she decided to splurge and buy a new blue ribbon for her hat. She climbed into her wagon and urged her horse on toward the milliner's shop she had passed earlier in the day.

She touched the amethyst necklace hanging at her throat—the one

Jonathan had given her years ago. And remembered the softness of his kiss. She wondered if he had found another girl and married her. And started a family. And where in the wide world he might have settled down. Elizabeth wondered if he ever thought of her—or remembered her name.

Jonathan had just finished begging. The people of Konstanz were going home to their families, and the shops would be closing shortly. And he still had to make the long walk back to the Reichenau monastery.

It was unusual for him to have to leave Reichenau for any reason. The monastery there was virtually self-sufficient. Their garden provided the priests with all the vegetables and fruit they could want, and their clothing needs were simple. The few cattle and goats on the property provided more than enough milk. The priests, most of whom were aged and in need of care themselves, stayed behind the monastery walls and tended to their small domestic duties and to prayer. So Jonathan was surprised when the prior of the monastery asked him to go into Konstanz to beg for money. It was the duty of his office as an Augustinian monk that he most disliked but one that was needful both for the humiliation of the soul and to help meet the physical needs of his fellow priests.

But the reason offered by his prior added a bit of sting to the assignment. It seemed that, despite its isolation and poverty, the little monastery had come under the scrutiny of Rome. Contributions to the papal coffers had dwindled to nearly nothing over the past few years due to a declining population. The congregants either had died off or had migrated to the more conveniently located church in Konstanz. Now Rome was demanding that Reichenau make up for its poor showing.

Aleander was no doubt behind the official request for more money. It was Aleander, after all, who had effectively banished him to this remote outpost. He would know that Jonathan, being the youngest and by far the most able-bodied of the priests at Reichenau, would bear the greatest responsibility for raising the additional funds.

Still, none of that mattered now because Jonathan had just received word that Staupitz had ordered him back to Wittenberg. Odd as it would have seemed on his arrival at Reichenau, he felt ambivalent about leaving. He had come to appreciate the fellowship with the older priests. He no longer regarded them as castaways but enjoyed their company and had learned much from their wisdom. He wished he had earned more on this last journey into Konstanz—enough to purchase a small parting gift for the brothers.

He emptied his bag and counted out thirteen silver coins—a decent offering for the Lord's work. But only enough to buy the few supplies the prior had told him to purchase for his brothers at the monastery and still have most of the offering left over for Rome. That's what they would want at any rate. He had spotted a milliner's shop at the far end of town. If he hurried he would just have time to get some cloth and sewing thread before the shop closed for the night.

Elizabeth crossed the street and was just about to enter the milliner's shop when a movement caught her eye at the far end of the street. She glanced in that direction and then stopped dead still, staring.

It was Elias Sklaar. He was making his way up the opposite side of the street.

Over the last few years Elizabeth had almost managed to convince herself that he was dead, shriveled and rotting in his grave. She blinked and stared, her mouth open, unable to reconcile this charred fragment of an old nightmare with the life she was living now. But there was no denying it was Sklaar. He still wore the black coat and clasped the tattered medical bag tightly in his left hand. He kept his broad-brimmed hat pulled low over his eyes so it appeared to swallow his head. Even at this distance Elizabeth could see the long, bony fingers of his right hand as they curled around the top of a piece of parchment.

He was showing it to some tradesmen. She watched as the men shook their heads. Apparently, they weren't providing the information Sklaar wanted. He folded the paper quickly with one hand and continued on his way without another word. The soft afternoon light glinted off his small oval glasses, as he turned his head from side to side, sweeping the streets again, searching. What did he want? What was he doing here? She felt the old fear seizing her again, taking her breath away, making her want to run.

The milliner's shop was small and much longer than it was wide. One row of shelves occupied the center of the store. Signs were up everywhere, boasting special prices for this day only. Apparently, the advertising had done its job, because the store was packed. Customers, mostly women, squeezed past each other in the narrow space on either side of the shelves, digging through boxes upon boxes of buttons and ribbon and thread. Jonathan had just found the thread he needed and a bit of patch cloth when he heard the small bell over the front door ring. He hoped it was someone leaving rather than entering. He didn't see how one more person could fit inside the small shop.

Elizabeth ducked inside and closed the door behind her. Moving quickly to the window, she watched Sklaar walking up the street in her direction. She caught a glimpse of her own reflection and pulled back farther. Sklaar started to cross the street toward the shop but stopped, not forty feet away, and spoke to another small knot of men. He extracted the paper from his coat and unfolded it for them to see. Elizabeth was barely breathing, standing perfectly still, staring out the window. She had to do something.

Think. Move.

She had to find another exit. Had to get out. She glanced quickly to her left. Nothing but a solid wall lined with shelves floor to ceiling. She turned to her right. People packed two long aisles. A tall man—a priest—stood on the opposite side of one row of shelving looking right at her. There was something about him, something in his eyes that looked familiar. A customer of Maggie's, perhaps, someone she had met in Pforzheim. There was no time to think. He obviously recognized her, would be able to point her out to Sklaar. She turned and pushed her way to the counter at the back of the shop.

The owner moved down the counter toward her. "Are you all right, miss?" he asked.

Jonathan had been inching his way along the wall opposite the door, trying to make his way through the crowd to get to the counter, when he caught a glimpse of her, and immediately he knew.

Elizabeth.

Several women moved between them, blocking his view of her. But he was sure. He moved back to his right to try to get around the end of the long row of shelves to see her again. As he rounded the shelves he saw her. She had moved away and was standing at the counter at the back of the store. She glanced back in his direction, but he couldn't be sure she had seen him. The door opened between them, the bell jingled, and several more women pushed inside. Jonathan moved forward, drawing irritated looks from the matrons as he tried to pick his way through the crowd. He could just see Elizabeth leaning on the counter, talking to the owner of the store. He saw her point back in his direction.

Just then, an enormous woman in a bright blue bonnet lost her footing and toppled into him. The two fell backward, knocking over a small table filled with bric-a-brac and thimbles, which went spinning across the floor. By the time Jonathan helped the woman to her feet and apologized for being in the way, Elizabeth was gone.

It took him another minute to make it to the clerk who was helping a woman make a purchase.

"Please, sir," Jonathan said.

"Yes, Father, I'll be right with you," the owner said, returning to his customer.

"I'm sorry, but I need some help. There was a young woman, just a minute ago…"

"Father, please."

"Look, this is important. I'm sorry, but I must know. Where did she go?"

The store owner sighed and shrugged his shoulders. "Father, there are so many young women in my store, as you can see…" Here he winked at the middle-aged woman he had been waiting on.

"No, no. She was just here—about this tall," Jonathan said, holding out his hand to Elizabeth's head height. "Wearing a hat, brown dress…you just spoke with her!"

"No. You are mistaken, Father. I'm sorry."

"She told you not to talk to me," Jonathan said, his voice demanding.

The milliner turned back to his customer. Jonathan grabbed his shirt and pulled him close. The woman beside him screamed. "I must know," Jonathan shouted. "She told you not to talk to me, didn't she? Don't lie to me."

The man's eyes were wide.

Jonathan looked down at the counter and saw the necklace, the amethyst he had given her those years earlier. "Where did you get this?" Jonathan asked as he released his grip on the man's shirt.

"Someone…" The man was a horrible liar. He eyes faltered, and he went on, "She left it, to pay for my help. Said she'd bring cash to buy it back later."

"Is there another door? Back there?" Jonathan asked urgently. The man said nothing.

Jonathan turned quickly to go. Then he remembered he hadn't paid for the thread and patch cloth. "Here," he said, placing two copper pennies on the counter. "This should be enough, and some for your trouble." The store was perfectly quiet. The customers parted for him as he ran to the front door. He put the thread and cloth in his pouch as he ran to the edge of the street and looked from one end to the next. He ran to the corner and looked again, then to the end of the street, in and out of every shop. Nothing. She was gone. He walked back toward the milliner's shop, thinking. He stood in front of the door, wondering if he should speak with the owner again.

No, it was useless. He turned and crossed the street again and began to walk away, lost in thought. *Why would she run from me? What did I do that could frighten her so… She still had my necklace. Why would she keep it if she didn't still love me?*

He bumped into someone. "Oh, pardon sir," he said, then noticed he had stumbled into a small group of men. In the center of the group was a tall, lean man dressed in a black cloak and a broad-brimmed hat pulled low over his eyes. At his feet was a black bag. Jonathan knew him. His mind searched to connect the face with a name. In his hands, a piece of paper with a sketch of some kind.

"Good day, Father," one of the men said.

"Father Jonathan, isn't it?" another said.

"And it's uh…James. James Schmidt?"

"John. But no harm done. Good to see you, Father."

"And you, John."

"Perhaps your friend would be of some help?" the man in the black cloak said, stepping forward and unfolding the parchment—a drawing—for Jonathan to see.

Jonathan recoiled instinctively, lurching a step backward. The men standing behind Jonathan steadied him. Jonathan knew this man. The one who stood staring at him now had stood on a bridge four years ago and told him that Elizabeth was to be his wife. He was sure of it.

"It isn't your day for walking is it, Father?" John said, laughing.

"No. No, sorry. Clumsy of me…," Jonathan said. The man in black stood perfectly still, staring. It was obvious the man didn't recognize him. Jonathan kept his head bent toward the ground. "I'm sorry, sir," Jonathan said. "Your drawing?" he asked, reaching out for the sketch.

The image on the paper pierced him like a knife. It was indeed Elizabeth. Not as he had just seen her minutes before but as he had known her that summer in Rosheim. All he could do was stare, his mind racing with a thousand questions. But something told him to keep still.

The man in the black cloak stood straight, his hands folded in front of him.

"Perhaps you've seen my wife, sir?" he asked.

Jonathan looked up. "Your wife?"

The man closed his eyes and breathed in deeply. "The picture is not recent. She was kidnapped several years ago."

Jonathan looked down at the picture again. Kidnapped? Elizabeth? And married to...to this man?

Suddenly the man snatched the drawing out of his hand. He folded it quickly and tucked it inside his coat. "Well?" he asked.

"I meant no disrespect, sir," Jonathan said. "I should think a lovely young woman such as your wife wouldn't be hard to find."

"I've been looking four years," the man said.

"I'm sorry for your loss," Jonathan said.

The man rubbed his nose hard. "I'll find her," he said, and without another word he picked up his bag and walked across the street toward the milliner's shop. The men on the street disbanded and went their separate ways . Jonathan stayed, watching the man as he entered the shop across the street. He heard the little bell above the door as the man went inside.

So. It was true. The marriage had been arranged, and she had married him after all. But kidnapped? It didn't make any sense. Unless the man in black was lying and she was in fact running from him.

Then Jonathan noticed something. He had been staring at the large window beside the shop door since the man went inside. It was directly across the street from where he stood—the very spot where the man in black had been standing only minutes before, showing Elizabeth's picture to the townsmen.

She *had* been looking out that window...

Maybe she didn't recognize me, he thought. He had certainly changed more than she had in the last few years.

He had almost decided to start looking for Elizabeth, when the greater reality of the situation hit him. None of this really mattered. Whether she had seen him or not in that store was beside the point. He was a priest now, and she was a married woman. If she had seen him, she was right to run. If she hadn't seen him and was running from her lawful husband, then it was a mercy, because they could never be together now. God hadn't allowed it when they were younger. Obviously, God wasn't going to allow it now.

He felt the thread and the cloth in the bag at his side and turned up the street to start the long walk back to Reichenau.

Sklaar pushed his way to the back of the milliner's shop. The shopkeeper approached him quickly. Sklaar already had the parchment with Elizabeth's likeness out of his coat and was unfolding it. He placed it on the counter.

"I'm looking for my wife," he said. "The picture is a few years old."

The shopkeeper shook his head after glancing at the picture. "I'm sorry, sir. So many girls come into my store. But perhaps you could use some thread to take care of that tear in your coat?"

Sklaar cleared his throat and put his finger on the picture. "Look again."

The storeowner studied the picture for a few moments. His brow wrinkled and he touched the paper with the tips of his fingers.

"You've seen her?" Sklaar asked.

The man looked up at Sklaar but said nothing. His expression had changed. He handed the drawing back to Sklaar. "Like I said," the man said, his voice cold, "I get so many coming in here. Now I have customers to wait on, if you'll excuse me."

Sklaar looked down at the counter and saw the necklace. The amethyst glittered. He would have known it anywhere; he'd seen it in his dreams countless times, the vision of the last time he had seen Elizabeth in the flesh, lying on her bed. The shopkeeper was lying. Elizabeth must have given him the jewelry to buy his silence.

Sklaar folded the picture, placed it in his coat pocket, and rubbed his nose. He slowly lowered his head to the countertop, staring at the necklace, and sniffed like a dog seeking a scent. He stood slowly, smiling. "Elizabeth," he said to himself, "I've found you, my dear."

Elizabeth ran her horse at a full gallop for nearly two miles. She was afraid her little wagon was going to fall apart, but the worst of the rattling stopped when she slowed the horse to a trot. The road to Pforzheim stretched out in a long dusty ribbon before her. A gaggle of confusing thoughts tumbled through her mind: Sklaar, Maggie, the little shop she had helped make such a success, her friends and clients in Pforzheim.

Her mother…

Strange. She hadn't thought of her mother in ages. Not like this anyway. Not the way a daughter thought of her mother when she wanted to talk, when she needed advice. There had to be a way out. Her mother would know what to do. Elizabeth missed her so, wished she could sit on her bed and talk as they used to. Hot tears welled in her eyes.

No. She wouldn't do this. She would not cry. Would not let Sklaar control her. She had to stay focused. Think clearly.

Halfway home she knew what she had to do. Run—leave Maggie, the business, everything. And she would have to leave without Maggie knowing. Because Maggie would never run from a man like Sklaar. And who knew what he would do to her if he knew he was close and Maggie stood in his way. *I keep pulling innocent people in,* she thought. *Nice people, trying to help me. And they always get hurt. Like Jonathan.* Instinctively she reached to touch her necklace, but of course it wasn't there. She wiped her tears with trembling fingers, feeling as if she had left her heart on the milliner's counter and with it her last tie to her one true love. She would go back for it. Someday. When Sklaar wasn't there to find her.

The road forked, and Elizabeth took the left branch that led to Pforzheim. Even if Sklaar had found someone in Konstanz who recognized her from the old drawing, the chances of his choosing the same road she had taken were remote. If she pushed on through the day, stopping only to rest her mare, she should be able to make Pforzheim before morning.

It was well past midnight when she pulled her horse to a stop outside Maggie's house. Everything was still and dark inside. Maggie, ever the frugal one, hadn't put a candle out. Quietly, Elizabeth scrawled a hasty note telling Maggie that she had to leave, that she couldn't say why, and that she hoped to be able to return someday. She included instructions for filling the orders she had received for cloth in Konstanz, along with all the money from her trading except for the little it would take to help her get established in another town. She promised to pay Maggie back as soon as she was able.

Tears rolled down her cheeks as she folded the letter. Then she wondered why she had gone to the trouble. She unfolded it, smoothed the creases and left the letter on the table where Maggie would see it at first light. After packing a warm coat, a bit of food, and a few pieces of clothing in a travel bag, Elizabeth stepped out into the night. She made sure Maggie's horse was watered and fed, then she took a last long drink from the well. With a final backward glance at the old shop, she started walking down the moonlit road that turned north and east outside of Pforzheim.

The shadows slipped around her, glided over her as she quickened her pace. She imagined Sklaar hidden behind every tree, waiting around every bend in the road. It had been four years, but Elizabeth could still taste the medicine he had used to drug her. She could see his little black bag and hear the sharp *clink* of metal on metal when he set it down. She was determined to put as much distance as possible between herself and Sklaar. She smiled ruefully, feeling as if she had walked this same road before, on a night like this, running from the same man. She had prayed before that God would help her, and he had led her to Maggie.

She would pray again, she decided. And see what happened.

Chapter 25

She had been walking for days. Elizabeth pulled open one of the heavy wooden doors and entered the castle church in Wittenberg. It was packed with people, mostly women and children, and warm. She moved quietly to the last bench near the door, and sat with her back against the wall, careful not to attract attention. The priest in front had his back to the congregation as he elevated the Host.

It was a Christmas Eve Mass. The candles cast a saffron radiance around the room. Elizabeth settled back and took a deep breath. Her eyes were drawn upward to the high ceiling and its massive wooden beams that seemed to stop just short of the stars. She was astonished at the immensity of this sanctuary, though in other respects it was much the same as the small church she had attended during her stay with Maggie.

Elizabeth found Christians surprisingly like the Jewish friends she had played with as a girl. Back then, of course, she would have had nothing to do with Christians. She feared them more than she feared the wolves in her grandfather's bedtime stories. The wolves that pretended to be nice but then would gobble up the foolish children who had stopped to talk with them. Grandpa Scheerson had told her about the Christians too.

Elizabeth smiled. It was ironic for her, a good Jewish girl, to be

sitting now in a Christian church, feeling so safe. She had become familiar, at home, with Christians. Maggie had taught her much about what
Christians truly believed, and she had come to understand and grasp for
herself the gift that Christ offered by his death. The story of his resurrection had stunned her at first, but as she listened to Maggie, she slowly
came to see that the resurrection was the proof that Jesus truly was
Messiah—*her* Messiah.

She sat now with her head bowed, enjoying the warmth. The words
of the Mass mingled with the incense to envelop her.

The wind blew hard against the walls and roof of the old church.
She opened her eyes briefly to see the still flames of the fat candles, curling upward around invisible wicks, undisturbed by the winds outside.
She loved the chants, the male voices rising and falling together like
ships on a swelling sea. And the smell of the burning incense, and the
soft voice of the priest as he mumbled the Mass. She had come to love
the Nazarene whose name her father had not allowed to be spoken in
his house.

She had been hiding so long.

She sat, leaning against the back wall, and closed her eyes. Memories crept along the edges of her consciousness. She breathed deeply and
slipped into an uneasy sleep.

Something crashed, shattering the stillness of the sanctuary, jolting
Elizabeth out of her half sleep. A woman screamed as the doors burst
open and an angry mob poured in. The priest, a young man with close-
cropped blond hair, was finishing the benediction. Elizabeth had taken
no real note of him before, but as he turned to face the intruders, she
caught a glimpse of his face. It was the man she had seen in the milliner's
shop.

Her attention shifted as the mob surged down the aisle, overturn-
ing benches and shouting obscenities. The priest turned to face the
intruders. "This is God's house," he shouted in a strong voice that surprised Elizabeth. It wasn't the volume of his voice but its tone—not like

a priest at all. He sounded as if he was ready for a fight. "You have no right—"

Two of the largest men bullied their way forward and grabbed him roughly. "Shut your mouth, priest!" one of the men shouted as he swung a rough branch and struck him in the forehead. He fell hard onto the stone floor where several men pinned him with their boots.

One man at the rear of the crowd caught Elizabeth's eye. Sklaar. He hadn't seen her yet. She caught her breath and pulled the shawl over her head. He wasn't shouting like the rest but was scanning the crowded church. She started to run but stopped at the last second. She couldn't possibly outrun him if he saw her. She bent her back to appear smaller and hopefully older than she really was.

Sklaar continued to peer out from under the brim of his black hat. He looked up and down the rows of pews, trying to distinguish the faces of the frightened worshipers. He adjusted his small, cracked glasses and squinted, trying to bring some focus to the cloudy images. His deteriorating vision had forced him to hone his other senses over the years. Especially his sense of smell. It meant going more slowly. It meant stalking rather than chasing. But that was acceptable. It would make his reward that much sweeter. He moved slowly, methodically, through the crowd, not making a sound. He lifted his head, closed his eyes and sniffed the air, trying to pick up Elizabeth's scent.

One rough man, drunk and brandishing a walking staff, yelled over the tumult, "Yeah, bless you too, Father!" He stumbled to the front of the mob and made the sign of the cross with his staff. Then he whirled to face the priest, still lying on the floor, and smacked him in the head with the knobby end of his staff. "Bless you we do, with hellfire, Father. Bless you with pestilence!" The priest lay half-conscious on the floor, staring at the feet of the man who had struck him. The ruffian grew quiet for a moment, as if expecting the priest to shout back.

When he said nothing, the man with the staff exploded at him, furious, his eyes bulging, screaming like a wild animal, "You don't have anything to say? You and your kind have held us down long enough!" Then a stream of expletives flew from his mouth. He turned on his heel and shoved his way back through the now quiet crowd, out the chapel doors, and into the street where he joined another chanting mob.

Most of those who had followed him in followed him out. There were two who had held the priest to the floor. Seeing their leaders retreat, they were among the first to go. But a few remained. The chapel was quiet now. So quiet Elizabeth could hear the candles burning. Then a soft weeping began and several of those who had burst in so rudely approached the young priest and helped him to his feet. His head was bleeding, but he seemed to take no notice as the people approached and knelt before him, asking forgiveness for their sin.

Elizabeth's eyes were on Sklaar. He had stayed behind as well. He made his way slowly down the left aisle, looking into the faces of the parishioners. When his back was turned and he was walking away, Elizabeth slipped noiselessly out of her seat and out the door at the back of the church. She stood only for a moment. Scared. Trembling. She caught a movement out of the corner of her eye through the slightly open door. The priest. He was saying something. He had seen her, was moving toward her. Sklaar, at the far end of the church nearer the altar, stopped and turned. Elizabeth's nerve broke and she started running.

She ran across the bridge that led out of town, across an open field, and past a line of trees. Farther and farther, deeper into the tangle of thorn bushes. She was crying now, crying desperately. Knowing that if she stopped she was dead. Or worse.

Finally she broke through at the top of a small hill. She tried to stop, but her foot slipped on the wet grass and she tumbled down the bank and into a stream. Out of breath, she collapsed, plunging her hands into the icy water. Barely able to sustain her weight, she hung her head low and let her tears fall into the swift current. The cold stung her. The sound of the rushing water covered her crying.

She heard a noise behind her, footsteps high up on the bank and coming down.

The wild light of a lantern reflected off the stream. Without looking back, she pulled herself to her feet and started to run. Her foot slipped on one of the slick rocks, and she fell hard into the stream, striking her head against a stone. There was a bright flash of light, then darkness.

Chapter 26

Martin Luther's dear friend and colleague at Wittenberg, Andreas Karlstadt, stood in the open window of the bell tower, breathing deeply and allowing the music of the bells to fill him. It was a tradition of his, to ascend the tower just before sunrise on Christmas morning. He would close his eyes and imagine what the first Christmas morning must have been like—when the sun first rose and shone into the sleeping eyes of the One who had said, "Let there be light!"

What must it have been like in heaven? The air in that distant place would have been something like this air, cold and brittle, about to crack at the pealing of the bells that celebrated the birth of the Messiah. Oh, how he loved the sound of the bells! The treble tintinnabulation of silver danced around the sonorous tolling of the massive brass and iron bells, the music creating at once a bright symphony of chromatic laughter and a joyful cacophony, a surging river of sound.

This was as close to heaven as Andreas could get, and he longed to share it with all the wide earth below. Today he would get his chance. Most of Wittenberg's twenty-five hundred residents had already packed the castle church and were overflowing into the courtyard. Andreas drew one last deep breath and exhaled a prayer that what he was about to do would honor the Lord of Christmas. What he was about to do was bold, he knew. But it took a bold man to advance Luther's reforms, to put them, literally, into the hands of the people. It would enrage Rome. But it would glorify God. He was sure of it.

A surprised murmur ruffled through the crowd as Karlstadt took his place behind the pulpit. Several drew sharp breaths. Others turned away, embarrassed, but looked back just as quickly. It was what Karlstadt was wearing.

A plain black robe. Not a vestment in sight. Never had any priest dared to perform the Mass without vestments. Andreas smiled. His parishioners were probably as eager to see whether God would strike him dead as they were to hear what he had to say.

"This day," he began, his voice ringing off the stone walls, "is a day of celebration. We come together in faith to honor the birth of the Savior of the world. And together we will partake of his Holy Communion."

Another ripple of whispers.

"Do not be afraid," Karlstadt said above the voices. "But let all who are contrite in heart partake of this sacrament." He paused, gazing at the two thousand faces, all staring at him as if he were an angel. Karlstadt smiled again. This was not politics. This was freedom in Christ.

"All you need, you already have. You need only the faith that saves you. The longing of your heart to partake in the blessedness of Christ himself is evidence of that faith. See how our Lord makes you a sharer in his blessedness if you only believe. See how he has already cleansed you and set you apart through his promise. See how he stands here in our midst. How he lifts from your weary shoulders all your struggle and doubt, so you may know that through his word you are blessed."

After reciting a brief version of the Mass in Latin, he returned to German to consecrate the elements. He turned to the hushed crowd and looked into their faces, savoring the moment as a father would enjoy the anticipation in his children's eyes before handing them their presents on Christmas morning.

Then he spoke. Slowly. And for the first time in their lives, the two thousand people gathered in that room heard God's word in their own language. "This is the cup of my blood of the new and eternal testament, spirit and secret of the faith, shed for you for the remission of sins."

They hesitated at first, not knowing what to do. But Karlstadt held out his arms. He was inviting them to come forward. To take with their own fingers a morsel of bread from the plate, and a sip of wine from a common mug rather than from a chalice. Finally one man moved forward. Then another, then they came en masse, slowly, trembling, fearful of desecrating the body and blood of the Lord. And of damning their own souls to hell.

At first the children held back. According to custom they could not partake of the Holy Communion, but Karlstadt encouraged them to come. Christ had not denied the children of his own day fellowship with himself. Why deny them communion now if they professed a love for him and a sorrow for their sins? The children moved forward quietly, hand in hand with their mothers.

One man trembled so as he took the bread that it tumbled from his hand onto the floor. Those near to him pulled back, horrified. The man himself gaped wide-eyed at the bread on the floor, then at Karlstadt.

The priest nodded down to the floor. "Pick it up," he said softly.

But the man, shaking now and weeping over his carelessness, could not bring himself to touch it again. How could he? For in his mind, as in all their minds, there on the muddy floor of the castle church lay the Bread of Life, the body of his Savior.

Chapter 27

The small bell outside the convent gates clanged, disrupting the evening calm. The sun had set, but the clouds on the horizon glowed a dull red and purple as if a great bruising hand had left the sky swollen and sore. Jonathan stood impatiently beside his horse and small wagon outside the convent gate. He had tethered a second horse to the back of the wagon. Both beasts needed water and rest from the exhausting journey. Jonathan pulled the leather bell cord hard again, twice. No answer. The tethered horse nickered, impatient to keep going.

Jonathan returned to the side of the cart. Elizabeth lay unconscious on a thick bed of straw. Jonathan examined the bandage. The bleeding from the cut had stopped, but she was still in a deep sleep. He gazed at her, lying there, the moonlight caressing her cheeks, the pulse of life barely detectable along the graceful line of her throat. For the first time since he had rescued her from the stream, Jonathan allowed himself to think. To wonder what life would have been like had she not married the man in black. Had she come to him that day at the stone bridge. How he had longed for her. How he had loved her then—and still loved her.

He turned back to the gate and peered across the yard to the low, roofed buildings attached to the chapel. He rang the bell again—three sharp clangs. The door to the chapel across the yard swung halfway open and a portly sister poked her head out.

Jonathan waved. She put her hand to her lips for him to be quiet, then glanced back into the chapel.

"Come on, Agnes. Come on…," Jonathan whispered.

She closed the door behind her and set out at a brisk pace across the courtyard.

"What in the name of heaven?" she sputtered, coming to within two feet of the gate before Jonathan pulled back the hood of his cloak and smiled.

The sister stopped dead in her tracks and drew in a sharp breath. "Jonathan!"

"Hello, Agnes, and how are you this fine Christmas Day?" he said, laughing.

"Well! Merry Christmas to you too, you scalawag!" she shot back. She unlatched the gate and stepped outside and around the corner. In the time since his first visit, he'd made numerous trips to Nimbschen. The friends exchanged a brief hug. "So you're back in Wittenberg."

"Yes, thank God."

"We heard Father Staupitz had called you back from Reichenau. How long was it?"

Jonathan shrugged. "Just a few months. Not bad. I've been back less than a week. Apparently Aleander found out and kicked up some dust about my leaving, but in the end I don't think he wanted to go to the trouble of fighting Staupitz."

"Well, it's good to have you home, friend. And I see you brought back our wagon," she said, moving to the side of the cart. "The Mother Superior's been threatening to—" But Agnes stopped in midsentence, gazing down into the wagon bed.

"Who's this?" she asked.

"A visitor," Jonathan said softly.

"Jonathan…," Sister Agnes started.

"Her name is Elizabeth."

"Jonathan, another one? This isn't a good time," she said firmly. "And what's that on your head? You've been cut."

"It's nothing. Just a bump. Agnes, please. You're the girl's only hope."

"Mmm-hmm. I'm always the girl's only hope. And you're bleeding. Here," she said, handing him a cloth from her pocket.

"Thanks." Jonathan daubed the wound as he looked back to Elizabeth and wondered if he would ever again see anything as lovely. He felt his throat tighten. "Please, Agnes," he said, still gazing at Elizabeth. "There's a man she's running from. I can't explain now, but he must not find her."

"Is he close by?" Agnes asked.

"No. I saw him in Wittenberg last night. He was looking for Elizabeth." Agnes folded her arms. "Agnes, he won't come here. I'm sure of it."

"Jonathan, you can't start bringing them here again. What if the abbot finds out? Have you thought about that? It isn't like it used to be. You know how strict our new Mother Superior has been—"

They heard the door to the chapel open with a loud creak. Agnes looked back over her shoulder. Someone was crossing the courtyard.

"Please?" Jonathan asked.

Agnes sighed and closed her eyes. "I suppose…"

"You won't regret this, Agnes," he said as he turned with a fluid movement, gently lifted Elizabeth and her small bag out of the back of the cart, and placed them in Agnes's ample arms. "Can you manage?" Jonathan asked, as he untied his horse from the back of the cart.

"She's no more than a sack of flour. You go on. And watch yourself."

"You won't be sorry, Agnes, I promise." He swung into the saddle with the grace of an experienced rider, pulled at the horse's reins, then stopped. "Tell her…," he began.

"Sister Agnes?" the other nun called out as she neared the gate.

"Tell her my prayers are with her," Jonathan said quickly.

Agnes started to speak, but Jonathan turned his horse away quickly and took off at a gallop.

"Sister Agnes?" the other nun repeated as she approached. "Who was that?"

"Katherine! I'm glad it's you. Hold the gate open, will you?"

"What happened?"

"Another visitor, courtesy of Father Jonathan. Her name is Elizabeth," she said as she carried her through the open gate.

"She's hurt." Katherine said, noticing the bandage.

"You know as much as I do. We have an open room, don't we?"

Katherine looked up at her. "Mother Kiersten isn't going to like this."

"I know. Let's just get her to the room for now. I'll deal with Mother Kiersten."

Katherine shut and barred the gate, then led Agnes across the lawn and down an open corridor to the recently vacated room.

Elizabeth moaned as Agnes laid her gently on the bed. "There," Agnes said, examining the wound. "She's going to be fine. Just a nasty bump. Poor thing." She turned to Katherine. "Would you mind staying with her for a while? She'd be scared to death if she woke up in a strange place."

"Of course," Katherine said.

"Good. I'll tend to some other things, and I'll bring you a blanket and a pillow and a bit of food for Elizabeth when she wakes. Do you need anything else from your room?"

"I'll be fine. Thank you."

Agnes gave Katherine a quick hug, then left on her mission. "I'll be back shortly," she whispered as she closed the door softly behind her.

Katherine picked up Elizabeth's bag, thankful that it had fallen to her to stay with Elizabeth rather than having to attend to the "other things." It would be up to Agnes to explain to the abbess why they suddenly had another mouth to feed when the last outcast had left only the evening before, and the pantry was low. Agnes was one of the few sisters brave enough to risk a conversation with Mother Kiersten at the end of the day. It wouldn't be the warmest of welcomes for young Elizabeth. But at least it would be safer than the streets of Grimma.

The vacant cell was cold and dark with one high window facing west. The light from the candle glimmered off the roughly pebbled glass.

Elizabeth opened her eyes and tried to sit up. "What? Where am I?" She fell back onto the pillow with a moan.

"Shh," Katherine whispered, pulling her chair close to the bed. "Elizabeth, I'm Sister Katherine, and you've had an accident. You're in the Nimbschen Convent near Grimma."

Elizabeth put a hand to her head. "Oh, I must have hit my head on a rock."

"You fell?"

"Yes, in a stream. Someone was chasing…where did you say this is?"

"Nimbschen Convent, outside Grimma."

"How did I get here?"

Katherine put her finger to her lips "We must speak quietly," she said. "Someone found you in Wittenberg and brought you here. It's not really that far."

"Who? Who found me?" Elizabeth whispered.

"A priest. Father Jonathan is his name. I guess he saw that you were hurt and brought you here. Do you feel like eating something?" Katherine asked. "Sister Agnes should bring some food before long."

"Actually, I'm starving, yes," Elizabeth said, sitting up slowly. "But the priest…what did you say his name was?"

Someone knocked at the door—two quick, a pause, then another.

"Agnes," Katherine whispered to Elizabeth. She went to the door and slipped the latch.

"How is she?" Agnes asked looking in.

"We're fine," Katherine said. Agnes entered with a pillow and blanket for Katherine, and some fruit on a tray for Elizabeth. "Elizabeth," Katherine said, "this is Sister Agnes. She carried you in."

"Thank you. I'm sorry to be all this trouble," Elizabeth said, eyeing the food.

"Oh, it's nothing. Here," Agnes said, "you must be starving. Help yourself."

Elizabeth took an apple and bit into it hungrily. "How did you know my name?" she asked.

"I guess you must have told Father Jonathan before you passed out," Agnes said. "The important thing is that you're here and you're safe. Jonathan said a man was after you, trying to harm you. Was it your husband, dear?"

"Oh no," Elizabeth said. "He tried, wanted to marry me. But I would never, never marry that horrible man."

"You're safe now." Katherine patted her hands as she turned to Agnes. "Did you speak to Mother Kiersten?"

Agnes pursed her lips slightly, then spoke to Elizabeth. "I'm afraid we can only offer you shelter for the night, dear," she said.

"Only for one night?" Katherine said, rising from the bed. "You explained the situation?"

Agnes nodded. "We should count our blessings, Sister. Mother Kiersten has had a difficult day. We were doing well to get one night."

Katherine closed her eyes but said nothing.

"I'm grateful for the night. Thank you, Sister," Elizabeth said. She was smiling, and it made Katherine wish even more that she could stay.

Agnes shook her head. "Maybe Mother Kiersten will reconsider in the morning. Who knows? It's the time of year for miracles," she said with as much cheer as she could muster. "Now you, young lady," she said pointing to Elizabeth. "Get some rest. And don't worry about a thing. God's in this. Sister Katherine will get you whatever you need. Good rest to you. Oh, I almost forgot," she said, smiling. "Father Jonathan said to tell you his prayers are with you. Merry Christmas." She closed the door softly and padded away.

"Christmas," Elizabeth whispered. "I'd forgotten."

"Forgotten Christmas?" Katherine asked.

Elizabeth smiled but said nothing. She touched her bandaged forehead and winced at the pain. "You said the priest who found me was named Jonathan?"

Katherine smiled patiently and leaned back against the wall. "Yes," she said. "Why?"

"Oh, nothing. I knew a boy named Jonathan once years ago, and a long way from here," she said with a small laugh. She wiped away a tear. "I'm sorry. I'm just tired. Father Jonathan was so kind to bring me all this way. I wish I could have met him."

Katherine studied Elizabeth's face for a moment, then spoke. "Oh, I'm sure you will. Father Jonathan never stays away too long. He's a special man. If he finds people in need, he brings them here for help. Usually girls without a home. Doesn't matter where he finds them, he always brings them here. We do what we can. They stay a few days, sometimes longer. Two years ago, not long after I had met him, he brought Sister Agnes just as he brought you tonight."

"How many others has he brought here?"

"Ten," Katherine said.

Elizabeth's eyes opened wide. Katherine smiled and noticed the sparkle in Elizabeth's eyes, and the way her mouth quirked up into a smile. Katherine was nearly twenty-two, and she figured Elizabeth couldn't be much younger.

Elizabeth looked at her quizzically. "Are you…?" Elizabeth asked, allowing Katherine to finish the question.

"One of the ten? Oh no," Katherine laughed softly, then put her hand to her mouth, reminding herself to keep her voice down. "No, my father brought me when I was a child. Sister Agnes is the only one left of the ten. The rest stayed only a short while. Our new Mother Superior isn't overly fond of guests."

Elizabeth leaned over and whispered, "It must have been painful for her."

"Hmm?"

"To help so many only to have them walk away."

Katherine rose slowly from the bed and walked to the door. "When you find a bird with a broken wing, you take it in, you help it heal, and then you set it free. The last thing you want to do is put it in a cage. Try to get some sleep. And don't worry about where you will go," she said with a smile. "I have something up my sleeve."

The next morning, after prime, Katherine and Agnes brought Elizabeth some food. Each had secreted away most of her own breakfast, then added a couple of apples in a napkin, and carried the meal to her room. Elizabeth tucked the food in her bag and walked out through the front gate with the two sisters following close behind.

Agnes and Katherine hugged her good-bye one after the other. "We wish you all God's goodness, Elizabeth," Agnes said, then Katherine chimed in.

"Sister Agnes and I have prayed Saint Christopher to guard you on your journey."

"My journey?"

Katherine's eyes looked back over Elizabeth's shoulder. She waved and shouted, "Gustaf! Welcome!"

An old man in a long gray coat and driving a large wagon had just rounded the corner of the convent. He returned Katherine's wave and pulled his team to a halt in front of the gate.

"Good morning, Sister!" he said cheerily. "Is this our passenger?" he asked.

"It is indeed, Gustaf! Elizabeth, meet Gustaf Erricson, a dear friend and the best fisherman in Weinsburg!"

"How do you do?" Gustaf said with a warm smile. Elizabeth extended her hand, which the elderly gentleman shook firmly but gently.

"Come, come, we haven't much time," Agnes said. "They'll be calling us to prayers any minute." She helped Elizabeth up into the wagon beside Gustaf while Katherine tried to explain.

"Here," Katherine said, handing Elizabeth a letter. "I told you last night I had something up my sleeve. This is a letter to an old friend in Weinsburg. The Countess Ingrid von Helfenstein. Ingrid comes from a family my father befriended years ago. Well, as the Lord would have it," Katherine said, smiling, "Ingrid is with child and is in need of a nurse, someone to help care for the baby when it arrives."

The man nodded and smiled, "That she is, Sister."

"In short," Katherine continued, "I knew Gustaf was visiting a friend in Grimma. I went to see them last night and, well, Gustaf said he would be happy to give you a ride back to Weinsburg and would welcome the company." She was beaming with pride at her accomplishment.

"I'm most grateful, Sister. And I'll be glad to deliver your letter to the countess," Elizabeth said, placing the letter in her bag. "It's the least I can do after the kindness you've shown me."

Katherine laughed out loud. "Oh, Elizabeth, we wouldn't ask you to carry a letter all that way just for us. This is a letter recommending you to their service."

"But why should they hire me to care for their baby? They don't even know me. *You* don't know me."

Katherine smiled. "You just be yourself and give her my letter. Father Jonathan is a good judge of character, and so am I, for that matter. It doesn't take me long to see through people—to see if they are wearing masks or if they are real and true. You are both. I'm as sure of that as I am that God will take care of you. Everything will work out for the best, Elizabeth. Trust me."

A bell rang, calling the women to prayers. Agnes opened the gate, and Katherine followed her back inside.

"Ingrid's a wonderful Christian girl," Katherine said between the bars of the gate. "But the world has always been a temptation for her. You'll be a good influence. We'll pray for you, Elizabeth. You take good care of her, Gustaf!"

"No worries, Sister," Gustaf said as he pulled his horses around and back onto the road.

"God bless you, Elizabeth," Agnes said, as she and Katherine turned to go.

"God bless you," Elizabeth said quietly, as Gustaf urged his team on, and they took the first steps on the road that stretched away to the southwest and distant Weinsburg.

A week later the bell rang at the convent gate early in the morning. Jonathan could see Sister Agnes approaching. He dismounted and stood on the other side, his bridle in one hand, the other behind his back. Since the day he left her at the convent, Elizabeth had filled his every waking thought. He could actually feel his heart beating faster as he waited for Agnes to open the gate. He had made up his mind. Today he would declare his renewed love for his dear Elizabeth. God had reunited them, and Jonathan didn't intend to lose her again.

"Jonathan!" Agnes said, opening the gate.

"Agnes," he said, "I've come to see Elizabeth. Would you tell her I'm here?"

She sighed and folded her hands in front of her. "I was afraid this might happen," she said.

"What?" Jonathan asked, fearful that he wouldn't be able to see Elizabeth. Perhaps her condition had declined. Or worse. "Did her husband—?"

"She isn't married. She said she couldn't marry when she loved another."

Jonathan felt his heart breaking. He remembered the milliner's shop. The amethyst necklace. "Were those her words?" Jonathan asked softly.

"As nearly as I can recall. She left for Weinsburg the day after you brought her. To care for the Helfensteins' new baby. She said to thank you."

Jonathan nodded. He looked away for a moment, lost in thought, then back to Agnes. "You, dear Agnes," he said, "have been more than a friend to me. You have been God's messenger to me—to save me."

"Jonathan, what…?"

"You saved me from myself. I renounced this world. I took a vow to love Christ first, only, always."

Agnes put her hand on Jonathan's. "You loved Elizabeth," she said simply, her eyes shining.

"I'm a priest," Jonathan said, turning to go. "I love Christ."

He paused, then handed Agnes the rose he had had been holding behind his back and without another word, he mounted his horse and rode back toward the monastery in Wittenberg.

FEBRUARY 28, 1522
WARTBURG CASTLE

Justus Jonas stood shivering in Martin's unheated room in the old Wartburg Castle. The wind blew in frigid gusts through the un-shuttered casement. Martin stood with his fingertips resting on the splintered wood, looking out high above the forest as it slowly materialized, lumpy and gray, from the night shadows. He seemed oblivious to the icy wind as he stood staring toward Wittenberg. Unconscious of everything except the letter in his hand.

"This changes everything," Martin said still looking out the window. Justus didn't respond. Martin looked over his shoulder and glanced at his old friend. He smiled, then turned his gaze back out the window.

"I know what you're thinking, Justus," Luther said quietly.

"Oh, so now you're a conjurer," Justus said, half jokingly.

"Why bother with conjuring when it's written all over your face? You think I shouldn't return to Wittenberg because Frederick doesn't want me back. Because he fears for my safety. Am I right?"

Justus affected a bored shrug and turned to gaze out the window. The castle church, in fact the whole city, had invited Martin to return to Wittenberg. Martin held the invitation in his hand. In fact, Justus had delivered it himself. But he had delivered it with his own advice to reject the invitation.

Martin knew that Justus loved him like a brother, but he also knew that Justus's loving concern for his safety could blind him to the greater needs of the church and the reformation that God had set in motion.

Justus cleared his throat. "Martin, I said nothing about what Frederick wants or doesn't want. But you know in your heart what he desires and what's best. It sounds more like your conscience talking than me."

Martin dismissed the retort with a "Psshhh" and a half grunt. "My heart! How can my heart know what Frederick doesn't know himself? He's in a dither and he's scared."

"Martin, he has good reason to be cautious. If you return to Wittenberg—"

Luther interrupted, "If I return," he said, pacing the long end of the room, "the Diet of Nuremberg threatens to intervene. It's a powerful assembly, Justus. They might send in troops."

"Along with the emperor," Justus reminded him. "And who knows what our new pope will do."

Luther turned to face him. "Adrian Florensz. Yes, an interesting choice for pope. Philip told me when he came last week—said he's still in Spain."

"As far as we know. I wonder how Father Giulio is taking it," Justus said, referring to Father Giulio de' Medici, the cousin of the recently deceased Pope Leo X and a leading contender for the papal throne.

"Ha!" Martin laughed. "Giulio would have been pope now if it hadn't been for Florensz, and the Medicis would have been back in power. How do you *think* he's taking it? Thank God he couldn't control the votes in the conclave. I think he might have been worse than Leo, if that's possible."

Justus frowned, shaking his head. "I wonder what happened."

Martin leaned back against the wall and folded his arms. "I'll tell you exactly what happened," he said. "When Giulio saw he wasn't going to get the votes, he suggested Florensz. The old fox has his eyes on the henhouse, you can bet on it." He breathed in deeply and gazed at the ceiling.

"I suppose we'll have to wait and see," Justus offered.

Luther returned to the window. "It's hard to *see* anything from this blasted old castle." Martin unfolded the paper in his hand and looked at it again. "The city—my flock, Justus—they want me back," he said half to himself.

Justus chanced a direct assault. "It's a dangerous move, Martin. I don't think—"

Luther interrupted him again, holding up the document in his hand. "This, my friend, is the voice of God calling me home. I will not allow a bunch of old women to keep me holed up in this dungeon."

"Duke George and the Bishop of Meissen are hardly old women," Justus said. He took a few steps toward Luther and looked him squarely in the eyes. "They're serious, Martin. These men want you dead."

Martin took a deep breath and nodded slowly. "Very well," he said. "I'll agree to that. If I die in the service of the gospel of God's grace, so be it. This much I'll do for Frederick. I will wear a disguise going home. And I'll release him from any responsibility for my death. That should stay his trembling hand." His cheeks flushed with anger. "But they will have to kill a lot more than Martin Luther if they want to muzzle the truth. They will have to kill more than all the Germans who believe in salvation by faith. These hypocrites are going to have to kill the gospel itself, because others will rise up after us who will discover the same truth, and then they will have to kill them too. I am going home, Justus. And you should do the same!"

Chapter 28

Justus knocked softly at Martin's door. The morning skies hadn't lightened yet, and there wasn't a hint of warmth in the stone hallway. Justus could see his breath by the light of the candle he carried. He could just make out a thin wedge of yellow light tracing the bottom edge of the door. Lauds was still a good half-hour off, but Justus knew what his old friend was doing—getting an early start, as he was fond of saying.

"Martin?" he whispered loudly as he knocked. No response. He knocked again. He heard movement from the other side. The door opened slowly. Martin smiled patiently and stepped back into the small chamber, absently rubbing his belly with both hands.

"Bad stomach again?" Justus asked. Martin grunted and waved off his friend's concern. "I take it the warm milk didn't help?" Martin didn't answer at all this time. He was lost in thought.

Justus glanced around the messy room. A candle burned before the altar near the rumpled bed. Martin rarely made it and never washed the bed linens. His months in the solitude of Wartburg had served to deepen his habits of praying and writing late into the night. There he would work until he was unable to keep his eyes open any longer, then fall into bed, fully clothed, asleep before his head hit the pillow.

Justus noticed his writing tools, pens, papers, and Bible stacked on the desk across the room. He hadn't been writing. Then he glanced at the blanket, folded on the floor in front of the small altar. It bore two deep impressions.

"How long have you been at it?" Justus asked, knowing that his friend had probably been praying all night. He had been encouraging Martin to get more sleep. His stomach had been keeping him up.

"I think I have my answer," Martin said cryptically. Justus moved to the end of the bed and sat. Martin remained standing, pacing. His hands went back to his stomach again automatically. "These nuns are our sisters in the faith. They have come to a knowledge of the truth, and it's our responsibility to help them."

"Wait, wait," Justus said. "You mean the nuns in the convent at Nimbschen? The ones Father Jonathan couldn't stop talking about last Christmas?"

"Yes, apparently he's had some contact with the place over the last few years—helping the poor find lodging, that sort of thing. I recall he made any number of trips down to Nimbschen before Aleander shipped him off to Reichenau. At any rate, he got to know a few of the nuns there—well enough for them to confide in him anyway. They've requested help, and I think I have a way."

"How exactly do you intend to help these nuns, Martin?" Justus asked. "You mean teach them somehow? I suppose we could get them more of your pamphlets, perhaps some—"

"I mean help them escape," Martin said, interrupting his friend.

"Escape." Justus's mouth was hanging open. "Help nuns escape their own convent. Martin…" He was so flustered, he rose from the bed and walked to the door, muttering.

"Justus," Martin said, "you know what it's like for them."

"No worse than for us," Justus countered.

"Yes, worse," Martin said. "Because they want to leave, but there's no way of getting out. They've come to know God's grace, but they are chained to the convent by a vow they made under the law of Rome."

"It is still a vow!" Justus argued.

"An unholy one and therefore not binding."

"Martin, the mother superior will burn those women alive if she catches them trying to escape."

Martin nodded. "That's why they must not be caught."

Justus faced Martin squarely and tried to speak calmly. "I know you're not going to listen to what I have to say, but I have to say it anyway, or I'd never forgive myself when they come to haul you away." Martin began to speak, but Justus closed his eyes and held up his index finger, stopping him. He took a deep breath before continuing. "You know that kidnapping nuns is a capital offense. You also know who exacts the penalty for this offense—Duke George. Need I remind you that the duke will take supreme pleasure in watching you burn?"

"Justus, really—"

"Martin, hear me out. The man will use your books as tinder to light the first batch of twigs. And don't expect Frederick to stand in his way. So far you haven't broken any laws. None I can think of, anyway. But stealing nuns—think, Martin. If Frederick did support you, he would be inviting Duke George—his own cousin for heaven's sake—and the emperor himself to march in here and take us all to the stake."

Martin folded his arms and stared at the ceiling.

"Martin, think of your reforms. Gone. All of them. Because you want to play the hero and rush in to rescue a bunch of man-hungry nuns!"

"Justus!"

"Oh, well, correct me if I'm wrong, but I'm assuming that their newfound evangelical zeal has led them to the conviction that they should marry like all the others who have escaped, am I right?"

Martin was silent.

"I thought so. Martin, I beg you, don't do this. There's far too much at stake and far too little to gain."

Martin brought his gaze around to focus on Justus. "Are you finished? Because if you are, I need to go to the privy. Excuse me." He brushed by Justus and opened the door. "You've filled me up with your tripe. I've digested it and now I'll rid myself of it. Wait here." He closed the door solidly behind him and left Justus feeling as if he had just spoken naughtily to his father.

Martin returned fifteen minutes later, angrier than when he had left.

"This is how I see it. We have a chance to help these nuns escape, yes, but also to help them find Christ and his grace if that's what they want. Would you protect your own life at the cost of a single soul?"

"What if they want nothing more than marriage?" Justus persisted, but he knew he was losing ground.

"Then I will find them husbands. And if that's all they want it's still better than rotting away in a nunnery. At least they can produce children, and they may grow to join us if nothing else."

Justus sighed. The fight was over. "I suppose you have a plan," he said.

Martin laughed. He was a firebrand when he was angry, but once he had won the argument he was the first to reach out to embrace. "Have you ever known me *not* to have a plan, Justus?" He walked to the door and opened it. "It's time for lauds. We'll go to prayers, then you and I will take a walk and I'll tell you all about it. You, my friend, will be taking a little trip to Torgau this afternoon. There you will meet an old friend of mine—a fish merchant named Kopp."

APRIL 3, 1523
NIMBSCHEN CONVENT

At nine o'clock that evening, just after compline, Sister Katherine and the nuns of the Nimbschen Convent padded softly along the hallways to their tiny cells. Stars twinkled in a cloudless sky, bathing the courtyard in a soft, silvery light. A few stray beams peeked timidly through the convent's windows. The nights had whittled away at the moon until only a thin sliver was left dangling by an invisible thread above the eastern horizon. There were no crickets chirping, no darkling sounds at all.

It was the kind of stillness that made a person feel as if the night were holding its breath, waiting for something to happen.

Two hours later the door to Sister Katherine's room opened on silent hinges. Katherine stepped out onto the cold paving stones and closed the door just as quietly. She moved down the hallway, silent as a shadow, quiet as a prayer. She tapped lightly on Sister Ave's door. The two sisters made their way to the end of the hall and across the court-yard to the doors of ten other nuns. They all wore their dark habits and went barefoot, carrying only the shoes they wore to work in the gardens. Nothing else. They had to travel lightly, and they had to move fast. If they were caught trying to escape the convent, breaking the vows of poverty and of chastity they had all taken upon entering the convent, they could be hanged or burned at the stake. The abbess, Mother Superior Kiersten, wouldn't hesitate to enforce the strictest, the most painful punishment at her disposal, to set an example for the remaining nuns.

The women moved as a group along the perimeter of the courtyard, staying as far away from the mother house as possible. Mother Kiersten slept only three or four hours a night, and then fitfully due to her chronic stomach problems. Following compline, Sister Theresa, a novice nun from Thuringia, had slipped a pinch of brownish powder into Kiersten's warm milk—a sedative that they hoped would ensure a deep and restful sleep well into the next day.

Sister Ave, the prioress and second in command to the abbess, was among those taking their discreet leave of Nimbschen, though Sister Katherine was the natural leader of the group. She had carefully arranged their meeting and escape through Sister Agnes and contacts made by Father Jonathan. Katherine had tried to talk Agnes into going with them, but she said she had nowhere to go, and that Nimbschen was home. Besides, she said, she could do more good for the escaped nuns if she stayed behind.

Katherine had sensed that Agnes would be willing to lie for them, and she insisted that her old friend not commit a premeditated sin for the simple convenience of their escape.

"Lying won't be necessary," Agnes had said. "Since I don't know which way you are intending to go—at least not exactly—I'll tell the abbess that my best guess is that you will head south toward Zwickau where your radical ideas will be more welcome." Katherine smiled. They would be actually going in the opposite direction. North, toward Wittenberg.

As they crossed into the courtyard, a sudden flurry of whispered prayers fluttered up into the darkness. Sister Katherine stopped and whirled around. She made a quick movement with her hand to signal silence. They continued quickly out the gate without another sound.

Katherine closed the gate quietly and took one last look back toward the mother house. She scanned the low building slowly, looking for any sign of movement—still as a graveyard. No hint of candlelight. She hurried, leading the sisters along the wall and around the corner. There, waiting in the shadows of an enormous oak tree, was a wagon loaded with empty herring barrels and a tall man with a long gray beard.

"We're ready, Mr. Kopp," Katherine said, breathlessly. "Do you have room for all of us?"

Mr. Kopp smiled and chuckled quietly to himself. "Sister," he said, "Kopp always has room for one more fish. Come." Katherine counted quickly and noted that, indeed, he had brought thirteen barrels neatly arranged in rows. He had even thrown in some old charred logs. A nice touch, Katherine thought. The messier the wagon, the less suspicious their pursuers would be. The old fish merchant couldn't have inspired more confidence had he been wearing a sword and armor.

"I dried them out as best I could, Sister."

"I'm sure they'll be just fine, Mr. Kopp. Thank you." Katherine said as she helped the other sisters into their hiding places. The fish odor was still keen but bearable. After Katherine had climbed into her barrel, Kopp set the lids on loosely so they could have as much fresh air as possible.

"Very well then. Let's not dawdle, Mr. Kopp. But don't appear to be in a rush either. We don't want to attract any undue attention," Katherine said from inside her barrel.

"As you wish, Sister."

Just fifteen minutes after leaving the gate, they were on the long road north to Wittenberg. The wagon rumbled noisily along the road. It was late, but occasionally Katherine could hear a man call out a greeting to Mr. Kopp as they passed by. She didn't hear Kopp respond.

The barrels jostled against one another, and more than once Katherine banged her head against the side. She felt as if her cask was about to tip and dump her unceremoniously into the waiting arms of Mother Kiersten. Katherine understood from Father Justus that Kopp was a religious man, but she imagined his wagon had never been saturated in prayer as it was that night. Those prayers may have helped explain his calm, almost jovial attitude. She could hear him humming softly. Not out of fear like a boy whistling through the graveyard but like a father singing by the bedside of his frightened children. Singing to calm their fears, she thought. She prayed God's blessing on him again.

About twenty minutes later Katherine figured they must be at least a mile from the convent. The smell of fish had grown so strong she could hardly stand it, so she slowly slid the top of the barrel back until she could grab its edge with the tips of her fingers. She moved it farther back, raised herself up to her knees and inched her head out of the top of the barrel, until she could see over the rim. All the other nuns were already peering out as well and looking back along the road that led to Nimbschen. They had just entered the edge of the forest and were about to pull onto a side road that led along the bank of the Mulde River when they heard the convent bell. Sounding the alarm.

Chapter 29

"Mr. Kopp! Mr. Kopp!" Katherine whispered, peering out from under the lid of her barrel. The wagon hadn't picked up its slow pace, and Katherine was sure the search party was already on its way.

"I heard the bell, Sister," Kopp said without turning around.

"Well, don't you think we should try to hide or something?"

"Nope," Kopp said, then he addressed his horse. "Come on, Bella!" he called out as he guided the old mare into a clearing and tied the reins to the brake handle. "You sisters stay put, no matter what you hear." Kate watched as Kopp climbed down from the wagon, quickly unhitched Bella, and tied her to a tree. He gathered a few stones and placed them in a circle, then pulled the charred logs from the back of the wagon and piled them in the center of the fire ring. He spread a blanket on the ground and threw a small roll of old rags at one end for a pillow. Drawing another blanket from beneath the wagon seat, he lay down on the first blanket beside the fire ring, fluffed his "pillow" and waited.

There was nothing Katherine could do. She lowered the barrel lid and settled into a slightly less uncomfortable position, her legs tucked tightly beneath her. Soon she heard horses galloping up the road, coming from the direction of Nimbschen. The search party. Then a man's voice shouting, "Over there! Check the wagon!" She heard the rest depart while what sounded like two riders trotted over to their camp. "Old man! Hey!" one of them shouted. They were only a few feet from the wagon now. Katherine imagined she could hear them breathing. Every muscle in her body tensed as she held her breath involuntarily and prayed silently, "O Lord, O Lord, please protect us—please keep the other sisters quiet. Let us escape, Lord, please." Then she felt it. A cramp in her right calf muscle. But she couldn't move.

Kopp stirred and sat up.

"What? What do you want?" he asked, his voice challenging. "I have no money. I'm only a fish merchant, leave me be!"

"What? Kopp, is that you?" one of the men said.

Kopp rose to his feet. "Herman? Herman Geisel?"

"Yes. What are you doing out here this time of night?"

"I'm sleeping, or trying to. What's going on?"

"Escaped nuns. Ten or more," he said, yawning.

The other man rode over to the wagon. "What's in the barrels?" he asked.

"Kopp here's a fish merchant," Herman said. "Sold herring to my father ever since I was a boy."

The man was reaching over to touch the lid of one of the barrels. Kopp walked over to the wagon and held out his hand.

"The name's Kopp. Leonard Kopp."

"Erich Jurgen," the man said, shaking Kopp's hand.

"Well, Mr. Jurgen, like I always say, it may be late, but it's never too late to sell fish." Kopp mounted the side of the wagon and pulled the top off one of the barrels. He reached inside and pulled two salted herring from the barrel full of fish. "I have a few left if you'd care to take some with you."

The man reined his horse away with a disgusted look on his face. "Come on, Herman! We've got work to do!"

"Wait, I'll give you a good price!" Kopp said, waving the two fish over his head.

Herman laughed and turned his horse to follow his companion. "See you, Kopp," he said as the two galloped off down the road. "Love to Ursula!" And they were gone. Kopp walked over to the wagon and rapped on the side of Katherine's barrel.

"All's well," he whispered.

Katherine cracked the lid and peered out, then stood awkwardly, massaging her leg. "I'll give you a good price? Mr. Kopp!"

Kopp chuckled. "We'll wait until they pass back by, then we'll be on our way. It shouldn't be long." He made sure the other sisters were as comfortable as possible, then settled down to wait. An hour passed before the search party returned. They passed Kopp without a look, on their way back to Grimma. Kopp waited until he was sure all the riders had passed. Then he hitched up Bella and pulled the wagon back onto the winding road to Wittenberg.

The tops were off all the barrels now, and the nuns were peering out, gazing wide-eyed at their new surroundings, bathed in the sunlight of a beautiful afternoon. Their ride had been long and bumpy, and they all smelled of herring, but it was the aroma of freedom.

Kopp and the sisters crossed the river bridge and entered through the Elbe Gate on the southern side of Wittenberg. Katherine had expected more brick and less mud in this capital city of electoral Saxony. Years before, she had seen Erfurt with its beautiful university and tall buildings. Wittenberg, on the other hand, with its low, stall-like mud-and-wood houses seemed more a sprawling village than a prosperous city. She lifted her eyes to see the spires of the castle church near the center of the city and the castle itself farther to the west. The wagon rolled over a large stone, jostling the barrels and almost toppling Katherine from her perch. She grabbed Kopp's shoulders and righted herself.

"Sorry, ladies!" he shouted. "Only a bit more to the university. The road's better from here on." The filthy streets barely left enough room for the wagon. They often had to pause to let people squeeze past on foot. A half-hour later the wagon pulled into sight of the Black Cloister, the three-storied main building of the monastery that housed the university classrooms, the library, and the living quarters for most of the faculty. The door to the building swung open as if on cue. Katherine saw a man of medium height with a blocky face and small, dark eyes walking briskly toward them. She knew in an instant that this must be the famous Doctor Martin Luther, the man she had longed to meet for so many years. But there was something about him—perhaps the way he walked, almost a swagger—that she didn't like.

"Well, well, well!" he said, as he crossed the sparse grass courtyard. "Kopp! Good to see you! So you've brought us a fresh catch, then!"

"Aye, Father," Kopp said, smiling as he tied the reins around the wagon's brake handle.

Several of the faculty had gathered around the wagon by this time and were helping the nuns out of their barrels and down to the ground. Several of the younger nuns giggled at the sight of so many men.

Kopp dismounted the wagon and landed in the small space of ground between Katherine and Luther. "Father," he said, sounding a little awkward. "This here's, uh…I'm sorry, Sister," he said, turning to Katherine.

"That's all right, Mr. Kopp," she said, patting his arm. "A long ride like that will tire the mind as well as the body." She turned to address Luther. "My name is Katherine von Bora. And you are Doctor Luther."

Luther smiled and bowed. "I am, Sister. Welcome to Wittenberg."

Katherine started to speak, but Luther turned to Kopp and continued without giving her an opportunity to respond. "I trust God gave you safe journey, Kopp?"

"No troubles, Father," Kopp said. "Smooth as a baby's bottom, begging your pardon, Sister," he added, nodding to Katherine.

"Dr. Luther," Katherine said, a bit more stiffly than she had intended, "the sisters have had a long journey. I wonder if there might be a well nearby and perhaps a place for them to rest a bit."

Luther looked at her for a moment without speaking. A small fire kindled in his eyes. "Of course. Please, forgive me. I was so glad to see you had arrived safely, I forgot my manners," he said, and she thought she detected a slight edge to his voice which smoothed quickly. "We have places for you to stay—good families, fine people here in town. But you must be starving. We weren't sure when you would arrive, so we asked the cook to have some cheese and bread ready. There's beer if you'd like or cold water. Please, allow me. Sisters…" And he turned to escort the nuns to the university kitchen.

"Sister Katherine!" Jonathan called out, interrupting the procession. He had just rounded the corner of the Black Cloister and was running toward them.

"Father Jonathan! It's good to see you!" Katherine said as he stopped beside the wagon.

Jonathan turned to Martin, who was frowning at his sudden intrusion. "Excuse me for interrupting, Father. Sister Katherine and I are old friends."

"Yes," Luther said. "I'm aware. Father Justus told me…"

"Yes," Jonathan continued. "Well, Sister Katherine has been very kind to take in strangers who have no home."

"Sister Agnes sends her best," she said.

"She didn't come with you?" Jonathan asked.

"No, I tried to convince—," Katherine started, but Luther stepped forward.

"You two can stand out here and jabber all day if you want, but I have guests to attend," Luther said. "Follow me, ladies," and he turned and strode away with the other nuns in tow.

Katherine folded her arms. She and Jonathan stood still as the others filed past.

"Is he always that abrupt?" she asked Jonathan as she stared after the retreating crowd.

"Oh no," Jonathan said with a crooked smile. "Sometimes he curses as well. You'll get used to it."

Katherine continued to stare, her eyes flashing. "Hmm" was all she said.

Martin left the other nuns in the company of the cook and a few of the faculty who had been assigned to escort them to their hosts' homes. He and Justus turned to climb the stairs to the second floor where a handful of Luther's students were waiting for a private lesson in Psalms. Justus was on his way to the scriptorium. "Well," Justus said when they were well out of earshot of their new guests. "What do you think?"

Martin paused for a moment on the stairs. "Oh, they seem to be good women. I don't know, Justus. They're *women*, what can I say? But who can blame them if they're a bit giddy after what they've been through? Being trussed up for so long in that prison they called a convent down in Nimbschen would make anyone silly, I suppose."

"Yes, I suppose," Justus agreed. "You've already found husbands for some of them, haven't you?"

"There's no shortage of good men looking for pure women to take to wife. I'll find husbands for the others quickly, I'm sure. For the most part anyway."

"For the most part?"

Luther took a deep breath and puffed out his cheeks before continuing to climb the stairs. "I don't know about the one named Katherine," he said, shaking his head. "Whoever gets her for a wife is going to have his hands full."

August 1523
Wittenberg

It had been a particularly good day for Martin. He sat at the dinner table with several of his students and a few of the nuns who had escaped

Nimbschen Convent four months earlier. The women had settled comfortably into the homes Luther had found for them. Their days were filled with service in and around the monastery, and they enjoyed the fellowship of the university students and faculty.

Martin had just succeeded that afternoon in arranging a marriage for the third of his charges. He was celebrating with an extra mug of beer and a few jokes after dinner when Justus Jonas entered the dining hall with a letter. He handed it to Martin, then took an empty place at the far end of the table.

"It comes from Antwerp," Justus said. Martin could tell from the look on his face that the letter must contain terrible news. He opened it and began to read.

"What does it say, Father?" Sister Katherine asked brightly.

Martin sat staring at the missive in his hands. Though it was only a single page, he continued to look at it, reading it over and again silently. Tears were streaming down his cheeks now and his hands trembled. The script was in a messy scrawl, as if the writer had composed it in haste.

"Father?" Katherine asked gently.

Luther collected himself. His voice cracked slightly when he spoke. "God has been glorified, my friends. And his glory is not cheap. Two of our friars, Henry Voss and John Esch, have given their lives for the cause of the gospel."

Several at the table whispered protests of disbelief. They had known Voss and Esch personally. The two men had grown up in Eisleben, Martin's hometown. And they were all members of the same Augustinian order. Luther continued, "They were tried and found guilty. And then they were taken to the square in front of the town hall and put to death."

Another silence.

"What was their offense, Father?" Justus asked.

Luther looked down at the paper and found the passage, blinking several times to clear his vision. "The letter says they were condemned for teaching that men ought to trust only in God since men are liars and deceitful in word and deed and so are unworthy of trust." Here Martin chuckled and wiped away a tear. "I can hear Henry saying that, can't you, Justus?"

"I can hear him, Father," Justus said softly. "I'm sure they both died well."

"Died well. I suppose. As well as any two men could at the stake."

Sister Theresa, one of the younger nuns from Nimbschen who was sitting next to Katherine, leaned forward. "They burned them?" she asked.

Martin looked at her and responded gently to her innocence. "Yes, child," he said. "But we shouldn't despair. The letter says they went to their deaths singing and proclaiming that they were dying for the glory of God and for the gospel. It says they even—let me see…" Martin glanced down at the letter. "It says that on arriving at the place of execution they both joyfully embraced the stake to which they were to be bound. When they were tied in place and the fires were lit, one of them said, 'Roses! You cast roses at my feet!'"

Martin lowered the letter onto his lap and stared at the ceiling. "Roses," he repeated the word half to himself. "It was John who said that. No man tended a better garden or grew a sweeter rose than John Esch."

He spoke quietly, then looked slowly around the table. Finally his eyes came to rest on the woman at his side. "How old are you, Sister Katherine?"

"Twenty-four this year, sir."

"Look at this maid, ladies and gentlemen," Luther said. "A young woman, full of vinegar and of promise. Full of life." The former nun blushed. Luther put his hand to his mouth. "Henry was your age, Katherine." He looked at the rest of the group, some of whom were weeping now. "I tell you, God offers us no guarantees for a long life or an easy one. No promises except that Christ won't desert us if we are called on to make the same sacrifice as John Esch and Henry Voss."

He folded the letter and closed his eyes. Then he whispered, "I wished that I might be the first to die in his name for this cause. Oh, Lord, I wished it."

Chapter 30

"Kate, please. Be sensible." Luther stood just inside the archway of the pantry where Katherine, or "Kate," as Martin now called her, was peeling potatoes.

"Kaspar Glatz may be the rector of the university, but he is an ugly man with a vile disposition," she said flatly, tossing one potato into the pile at her feet and picking up another.

"Kate, the man's offering you his hand. Take it—"

"Take his hand? How can I when he keeps it balled up in a fist, holding tight to his money? Besides, his hand is connected to the rest of him, and I'll have nothing to do with *that!*"

"I see. You've made up your mind that you'll have nothing to do with any man that displeases you in the slightest way," Luther said, flinging the letter at her feet.

"That's not wholly true," she said, disregarding the letter and keeping her attention focused on the potatoes. "I have to deal with your lordship every day."

Luther took a deep breath and closed his eyes. He spoke in a measured tone, "Now, Kate, you are rejecting Glatz because you're still dreaming about that young fellow, Baumgartner from—where was it?"

"Nuremberg," she said without looking up.

"From Nuremberg. Now I know for a fact that Jerome

Baumgartner is an honorable man, and he did want to take you for his wife. I also know you were counting on it and that you had some considerable affection for him. I have no idea why his family objected. But the fact is they did, and that's that." He cleared his throat.

"Oh," Katherine said tightly, "I think we both know why they objected, Herr Doctor. They didn't want a former nun in the family. After all, a woman who would break her vows to the Lord might all the more easily break her vows to her husband."

Another potato hit the pile, this time with a bit more force.

"Lord, this is worse than debating Eck," Luther muttered.

"Well, I can put your mind at rest there, my lord," Katherine said.

"How's that?" Luther asked.

"Because there is no debate here. I've made up my mind, you said so yourself."

Luther covered his mouth and grunted three times in quick succession. "Kate, you'll never marry at this rate," he said, bending over with another grunt to snatch up the discarded letter. "What am I supposed to do with you?"

Katherine continued to peel potatoes.

Luther sat on a barrel just inside the archway, holding the crumpled request for Katherine's hand by his fingertips. "None of the other nuns caused me half this much trouble. Were you like this at Nimbschen?" It was an invitation to another sparring match, but Katherine stayed in her corner.

"I am as I have always been, Father, except now I see the truth, thanks to you, and that truth has set me free. And that means being free *not* to marry a man just because he's a man!"

"Enough!" Luther whirled around and stalked out, waving the letter of proposal over his head. "Heaven knows what I'm going to tell this one. I've used every excuse I know."

"Tell him 'thank you'!" Katherine shouted after him. She was sure she heard laughter as Luther turned to mount the stone stairs.

The night wind blew in chilly and damp through Martin's window. He rose to pull in the shutters. His stomach was growling at him again. Martin had written to the rector Kate had rejected that afternoon, and he was praying over the letter before he sent it. It was never a pleasant business, telling one of Katherine's suitors that she was not as available as the gentlemen always supposed.

As he reached outside the casement, he glanced up at the moon and took a deep breath of the cool night air, then pulled in the shutters and latched them with the small metal hook. He walked back to his desk, stretched and yawned. The late hour had cast his night prayers adrift among the stars. He shook his head and sought an anchor for his thoughts. He had one last bit of business to attend to before calling it a day. He had sent for Jonathan earlier in the evening, but his classes often ran late. Now Martin was tired and trying to focus on the mission he had in mind for Jonathan. But all he could think of was Kate.

He had convinced himself that he had nothing more than a priestly interest in her. No. He had never wanted any woman for a wife. The idea was ludicrous. Not that he lacked the natural desires of a man for a woman. Not that he didn't dream of having a family. But as a renegade priest and convicted heretic, he probably wouldn't live long enough to marry, much less raise children. No. It wouldn't be fair to marry a week before going to the stake. He wouldn't think about it, refused to dwell on...the keen mind and the sharp tongue that challenged his thinking.

Someone knocked at the door. "Come," Martin said, clearing his throat. Jonathan opened the door and peeked inside. He held the candle up near his face so Luther could see who had disturbed him at that hour. "You sent for me, Father?" he asked.

"Ah, at last. Come in, come in," Luther said. "Late class?"

"Yes, I'm sorry for the hour," Jonathan said, placing the candle on Luther's desk.

Luther grunted and waved his hand dismissively as he sat on the edge of his bed. "This won't take long. I have something—"

"Father," Jonathan interrupted. "There's something I've been wanting to tell you first, if I may. It's been on my mind for some time now and, well, when you sent for me tonight, I…"

"Jonathan, it's late. Out with it." Luther said, rubbing his face.

"It's, uh…it's…my mother. You knew her," he said.

Luther frowned. "Your mother? When? Where?"

"The night of the storm. The night you were struck by lightning. It was my house you came to."

Luther stared for a moment, his brow furrowed, saying nothing. Then his face relaxed. "And you were the boy." He smiled and shook his head. "Well, I'll say. You've been here, what? Two years? Three? Why didn't you tell me when you first arrived?" Luther asked.

"I…don't know," Jonathan said. "Scared, I guess. I don't know. Honestly. You saved our lives that night."

"Is that how you remember it?" Martin asked. "I remember your mother leaving a lasting impression on your father's head with a poker."

"He was my stepfather," Jonathan said. "Still, if you hadn't come when you did…"

"Yes, well, that's all water down the river," Martin said with a wave of his hand.

"She said I would find you."

"Find me?" Luther asked.

"She said I would find you, and…" Jonathan hesitated for a split second. "And that you would lead the German people to freedom, and that you would pick up the sword and fight for the poor. It was in a book she had. A prophecy in an old book."

"Jonathan—," Luther started.

Jonathan interrupted, his eyes shining. "I've been wondering something for a long time. Just before you left our home when I was a boy, you told me you had a promise to keep."

Luther looked at him through narrowed eyes. "And what? You think I made a promise to start a war? Is that what your mother told you? That I promised to lead the peasants to war?"

"To lead them to freedom."

Luther started to speak but checked himself, folded his hands and looked up at the ceiling. He took a deep breath, then looked at Jonathan and spoke in a measured voice. "Jonathan, listen to me. My promise was to Saint Anne. I made a vow to her that night, standing in the middle of a muddy road, that if she would save me, I would become a monk! That's all!"

"But if the people rise up, it would help our cause, wouldn't it? It would be in the name of justice that—"

Luther interrupted him, "If the people were fools enough to take up arms and fight against trained knights, they would be slaughtered, *and* they would be wrong."

"They would be wrong?" Jonathan heard his own voice rising. "To fight against tyranny, to try to stop—"

"You're not thinking, Jonathan." Luther's voice was terse. He rose from the bed and stood in his stocking feet, holding on to his bedpost. He drew in a deep breath and let out a long, tired sigh. "There's nothing new in this. You're too young to remember the 'Alliance of the Shoes' down in Spires. Or Breisgau—the priests themselves were in on that one. Or the 'League of Poor Conrad,' in Wurtemburg, back in '14. Look at Carinthia or Hungary just a few years ago if you want to see what real fighting will get you. Too many dead to count, that's what. All because they wanted their 'rights,' same as today. Well, God isn't interested in their rights." His voice had grown gentle, a teacher with a favorite student.

He took a couple of steps forward. "Nothing's changed, Jonathan. The people are the same as they have always been. They won't fight against 'injustice' or 'tyranny.' Those are words for kings and zealots like Thomas Munzer. The people will fight because they want more than they have. I'm not saying they haven't been mistreated. But that doesn't excuse the peasants for their treason.

"If they steal game from the land of their protectors, if they empty their fishponds and kill those who are sworn to protect them, then they are nothing but murderers and thieves. Greedy, lusting for riches. And, Jonathan, they will never be satisfied. They are just looking for an excuse to sin, to try to harvest comfort from a field of hardship."

He was preaching now to a congregation of one, though no less passionately than if he had been standing before the royal court itself.

"God didn't put us here to be comfortable. Our purpose is to spread the true gospel of God's grace and mercy. Only *that* gospel can free them to love those who oppress them. The rebels won't be Christians, mark me. They're all too ready to throw off the yoke of Rome, but ask them to take up the yoke of Christ and they will spit in your face. The rebels don't give a whit about the gospel. If they did, why would they take up their pikes? How many converts do you think we will win on the tines of a pitchfork, Jonathan? How much Christian love can you beat into a man with a club?"

"But the knights are joining us," Jonathan protested.

"Humph," Martin snorted as he returned to the bed and lay down on top of it. He put his hands behind his head. "Remember Franz von Sickingen? You couldn't find a braver knight. Or a more foolish one. He was on our side too, if you recall. But he listened to Munzer, then tried to bring in God's kingdom with his sword. That's why he wound up with his head on the block. Stupid. Our job is to bring peace, not the sword," he said, reaching over to the table near his bed. "That brings me to the reason I called you here in the first place." He shuffled through some papers and pulled a sealed letter from the bottom of the pile.

"There's going to be trouble in a town called Weinsburg. Prince Frederick returned yesterday from a trip there. The whole region is waiting to explode. He has it on good authority that the leaders of several of the peasant armies are looking for an excuse to attack Count Ludwig von Helfenstein. It won't take much of a spark to set them off. Helfenstein's supposed to be a reasonable man. He'd better be, or he's going to get himself and his family killed."

Martin held the letter out to Jonathan, and he took it. "This is a letter calling for Helfenstein to seek peace with the peasants before it's too late. I'm not ordering you to take it, Jonathan. I'm asking. It's a dangerous trip and long, and I have no right to demand it of you. It will take you the better part of a month, I should expect, what with the spring rains and all, and the fight may be over by the time you arrive, for all I know. Still, I think there's a chance of avoiding more bloodshed if we can convince the count to negotiate with the peasants."

Jonathan couldn't believe his ears. He was going to Weinsburg! To Elizabeth. Perhaps God had other plans for the two of them. "Father," he said, his voice firm, "it would be an honor. I'll leave at first light."

Back in his room Jonathan packed with trembling hands. But it wasn't the danger of the journey that had rattled him. Nor was it the responsibility with which Luther had entrusted him.

It was the thought of seeing Elizabeth again.

Almost four years had passed since she had left Nimbschen Convent to go to Weinsburg. In all that time, Jonathan hadn't written, or tried to find her, convinced that what God had torn apart no man should try to mend. If God had wanted him to be with Elizabeth, he wouldn't have let her leave Nimbschen. He wouldn't have let her go hundreds of miles away to Weinsburg before Jonathan even had the chance to speak to her. He had to believe that. But as the days lengthened into months and years, his resolve began to crumble under the steady assault of his love for her. And his belief that she loved him too. He'd even gone back to the milliner's shop to see if the owner might take something in trade for the amethyst necklace. At first the shopkeeper had insisted on hard coin only. But then Jonathan had placed something special on the counter—a rosary with a beautifully delicate pearl strung among the blue and red beads.

"I'm an honest man," the milliner had said. "This pearl is worth far more than the amethyst."

"Not to me," Jonathan had said, and he left holding the amethyst necklace tightly. It was foolish, he knew. But he couldn't help himself.

For years he had dreamed of Elizabeth. Night after night he pulled her, unconscious, from the stream. Then, in those sweet, quiet moments, holding her in his arms, he felt complete. He had desperately wanted to kiss her the night he had saved her—when no one would have seen. Even she would never have known. Sometimes, in his dreams, he did kiss her, tenderly, and it was so real, he could *feel* the softness of her lips. But then he woke, feeling lonely and empty beyond words. As though he had left part of himself behind in the shadows.

But now God was bringing them back together. The man in the black hat had disappeared—vanished the same night Jonathan had seen him in the castle church in Wittenberg. Surely, Jonathan reasoned, he had given up trying to find Elizabeth by now. But Jonathan would never give up. If she hadn't yet married, if she still loved him and would have him, he would never leave her again. If that meant leaving the priesthood, then so be it.

Jonathan stood beside his bed and drew a deep breath, grateful for the hard day's work that would allow him some sleep. His bag was packed. He was ready and would leave at dawn. He lay down on his bed, folded his hands across his chest, and stared out his window into the starlit night. The wish of his heart became a prayer.

He closed his eyes and took her hand.

Chapter 31

MARCH 15, 1525

OUTSIDE THE HOME OF THOMAS GEYER, NEAR WEINSBURG

Jaklein Rohrbach leaned against the tree, crossed his arms, and gazed into the eyes of the young woman who stood before him—and he couldn't think of a thing to say. He looked away, back toward the lighted window of Thomas Geyer's home, to collect his thoughts, but it did no good. The moonlight drew his attention back to the girl he would marry in a little over a week.

Moira Geyer was eighteen and possessed the confident spirit of a woman twice her age. But it wasn't her spirit that scrambled Jaklein's attempt at speech. He was nearly eight years her senior, but he was as tongue-tied as any schoolboy, as struck by her beauty as he had been the day he had met her in Bockingen three years before. And all he could do for the moment was stare and try to look thoughtful. Her golden hair fell in soft ringlets to her slender waist. The top of her head barely reached Jaklein's chin, but he wasn't foolish enough to imagine that his height afforded him any real advantage. She could, with an arch of her brow and a glance of her incredibly blue eyes, buckle his knees at will. He wondered how much more he could possibly love her after they were married. But he couldn't wait to find out.

At the moment he was trying to be firm with her regarding her father's stubborn refusal to come live with them in Bockingen after their marriage. Finally the words came. "He'll have to get used to it, that's all," Jaklein said with more conviction than he felt. He knew what was coming next. The game. A verbal chess match between the two of them, the rhythms refined over the last year of courtship. It was her move.

Moira put her hand on his arm. *Yes, this first, always the touch first.* She looked into his eyes. *Unfair advantage.* But there was nothing he could do. "Jaklein, you don't know Papa. He won't leave."

"Then that's his decision." Jaklein took a deep breath. *Bad timing, Jaklein. Rephrase.* "Moira, he loves this place, this land. I understand that. I also can see how a proud man like your father wouldn't want to go to work for his son-in-law, and especially in a tavern in Bockingen."

"But he said you could come…"

"And I'm not a farmer," Jaklein interrupted. "I wouldn't know the front end from the back end of a plow. Besides, I'm not going to spend the rest of my life working to fill Toffler's belly. The tavern will bring in more money in a week than your father has seen in the last ten years. And it will be our money. No one will take it from us."

"You know the money doesn't matter to me," Moira said. "But whatever you think best."

Jaklein smiled as she drew close to him. *What's this? He was winning. The game—this game at least—was within his grasp. Check.* She rested her head on his shoulder.

"It's just that I love him, Jaklein," she said softly, the words catching in her throat. *An unexpected move.* "He deserves some happiness after all that Toffler's done to him, and what with Mama's passing last year and all…"

"Shh, shh," Jaklein whispered, kissing the top of her head. "I know." He paused, holding her, and smiling to himself. She had him cornered. "Tell you what. Let's give it another week. Maybe I can come up with something that will appeal to him. No promises, but I'll try."

She looked up at him, tears streaming down her cheeks, and traced the contour of his face with her fingers. "Jaklein Rohrbach," she said, smiling, "you're a fine, good man, and I love you more than words can tell."

He pulled her back to him and brushed her tears away. "Do you think," he said quietly, touching her hair, "you might bake me one of your famous berry pies one of these fine days?"

She laughed and punched him playfully in the chest. Then she put her arms around his neck. "You'll have to come back next week and see," she whispered, and her lips brushed his.

MARCH 20, 1525
WEINSBURG, NEAR THE CASTLE OF LUDWIG VON
HELFENSTEIN

Sklaar adjusted his small, oval glasses, pushing them so far up his sharp nose that they almost touched his eyeballs. His eyes had been failing him for some time so that he had to squint continually now, even with his glasses. The right lens had cracked years ago, further distorting his world. And the nearly translucent amber of his left eye had clouded over with the milky film of multiple cataracts. All in all, it made spying difficult.

He rested as well as he could, spread out on the rough branch of an elm, blending silently into the green foliage like a serpent. The crenelated garden wall of the Helfenstein castle was at least thirty feet in front of him and twenty feet high. From his vantage point in the elm at the back of the castle, he could peer over the top of the wall into the terraced garden to see about a quarter of the grounds nearest the castle keep.

The sun had risen, and scores of birds chirped in the trees that ringed the garden. Occasionally, Helfenstein, his wife, and their son would take their breakfast in the garden near the fountain. Sklaar knew because he had been watching them for almost a week, and he had noted a few of their habits. He had circled the castle endlessly, mostly at dusk and during the night, noting the windows that allowed him to peer in on the second-story living quarters and bedrooms. The third window facing east, along the servants' wing, had captured his imagination. Because in that window he had seen Elizabeth. Or someone he imagined to be Elizabeth.

When he had arrived in Weinsburg a week and a half before, the wife of one of the local merchants had told him that the royal family had taken on a new servant girl, a stranger, four years before. Sklaar showed the woman and her husband the drawing of Elizabeth, but they didn't recognize her. They were sure they had heard a name, but they couldn't recall it, and "Elizabeth von Gershom" didn't sound right. They had only seen the girl once in town. Why was Sklaar looking for her? they wondered. He never answered. They were too curious, too prying.

Sklaar had stopped referring to Elizabeth as his wife months before, as it seemed to put people off. She was his lost daughter, he told them, dabbing at his eyes. A wandering band of gypsies had stolen her away years before, and he would never rest until he found her. He tried enhancing his story with a variety of broad gestures, gasps, and weeping, but the overall effect actually seemed to frighten some of his listeners. Several of the women had backed away, excusing themselves abruptly, and one had fainted in the middle of the street.

Soon after his arrival in Weinsburg he had set up camp in the woods, where he brooded and plotted how he might reach Elizabeth. Finally he had a plan he believed to be infallible. He had risen early that morning and had combed out his beard and thinning hair for the first time in months. Then he scoured his face and hands until they were raw. Not trying to get clean so much as trying to feel clean.

He examined himself in a shard of mirror he carried in one of the pockets of his coat. Most of the silver had worn off long ago and along with it the uncomfortable truth of the reflection. "Hmm," he mused, stroking his beard. "Good." He wrapped the mirror in its oily rag and placed it carefully back in his coat pocket.

He didn't really care how he looked to Elizabeth. He was going to kill her as soon as he got her out and away from her guardians. He had decided that weeks ago, after another of his dreams in which she had laughed at him again. Justice. That was what Elizabeth needed. But he had to get to her first, and to do that he had to be presentable. He straightened his longcoat and set out for the Helfenstein castle to convince the high and mighty count that he was Elizabeth's father.

He paid a single copper coin to a coachman to carry him to the castle gate. It would, he hoped, make a slightly better impression on the gatekeeper than arriving on foot. As the carriage rolled to a slow stop, Sklaar scanned the top of the wall. He could see the tops of the sentries' heads, marching along the parapet on the other side. He stepped out of the carriage onto the barbican, the entryway in front of the main gate of the castle, put his hand on his hat to keep it in place, and shouted up, "Dr. Elias Sklaar to see Count von Helfenstein," he called, squinting through his cracked lenses.

One of the sentries stopped, looked out at him. He called back to another soldier, who joined him. They stared at Sklaar, saying nothing.

Sklaar's heart thudded against his ribs. Elizabeth was on the other side of those gates. He was sure of it. He could smell her. "Dr. Elias Sklaar," he repeated, though this time his voice cracked into an unnatural squawk. He cleared his throat quickly and continued. "To see…"

But he stopped in midsentence. The guards were laughing at him.

"I beg your pardon, sirs," Sklaar said in a lower voice. "I wish to see Count von Helfenstein."

One of the guards responded, "Show us your invitation, old man."

Sklaar adjusted his glasses. "I'm a doctor. I've traveled a long way…to see him," he said, barely controlling his anger. "I won't take much of his time, I assure you. I simply want to ask him—"

"Hey! I guess you don't hear so good," the guard called, cupping his hands to his mouth and shouting. "I said, 'Show us an invitation, old man!'"

Still laughing, the two turned away as if they were turning from an idiot. As if he was unworthy of the time it took to give a man the courtesy of a simple reply. Sklaar's jaw tightened. Why would they reject him out of hand like that? Why would—? Elizabeth! Of course. He spat on the gate and walked away.

Elizabeth, the little shrew, had somehow gained favor in the royal household. She must have poisoned her new protectors against him. Oh, the lies she must have told about him! That was why the guards had laughed. Elizabeth had told them to spurn him, to turn him away like a mongrel dog. "Elizabeth," Sklaar mumbled to himself as he walked down the street away from the castle gates. "You have so much to learn about respect. And I will teach you, my dear. Oh yes. I will not spare the rod, my spoiled little girl. You will respect me!" Sklaar put his hand to his brow and paused in the middle of the street, talking to himself. His head felt as if it were about to burst. "Must think," he muttered, his eyes closed tightly, trying to push back the pain. "Must think, must plan."

He opened his eyes to narrow slits, then walked to the side of the street where he could escape the light of the sun. Then down another shaded street and back to the far side of the castle wall. He looked carefully around to make sure no one was watching, then climbed his secret elm, where he sat, watching. The pain in his head melted slowly away as he lay prone on the branch in the cool, dark shade. Waiting. Listening. Able to think again of how he would take her. And how he would punish the house of Helfenstein for mocking him. So many people had hurt him unjustly. So many needed to be punished.

Late that afternoon Sklaar went for a walk. Away from the castle, out beyond the gates of Weinsburg. He walked slowly, taking in the fresh air, trying to clear his head, trying to calm the fever burning in his brain.

He had gone about a mile from the town in the direction of Bockingen when, in crossing a small bridge, he noticed a path beside the stream winding away into the woods. He stepped off the end of the bridge and inched his way carefully down the gently sloping bank to the edge of the path. The sun was three-quarters of the way down the sky, so he wouldn't have long, but the new scenery invigorated him. Perhaps the excursion might help him think of a way to get to Elizabeth.

Sklaar knew the land probably belonged to one of Helfenstein's nobles. Helfenstein owned Weinsburg, but several of his knights had purchased or simply taken much of the surrounding property from the peasants who had lived there all their lives. The new landlords either killed the peasants, threw them out of their homes, or charged them to continue farming. In the few days Sklaar had been there, he had heard of a few of the more brutal men. He wasn't sure which of them owned this particular piece of land. He should be safe though. It was legal for him to walk here as long as he didn't hunt or fish or take anything from the land.

The stream gurgled over rocks and the large limbs of fallen trees. It widened gradually until it joined a river about three-quarters of a mile from the bridge. Sklaar looked up the river and decided to continue for a few more minutes. He climbed the bank slowly. In the course of his trek, the land surrounding the stream had risen gradually until the bank was now nearly twenty feet above him. He struggled a bit on the leaf-strewn path, slipped once and struck his knee sharply on a rock. He got up, muttering curses. As he topped the bank, he saw that the woods extended only about thirty yards in front of him.

The sunlight was golden on the field beyond the line of trees where he saw someone moving. He crept along the bank's upper edge, keeping trees between himself and the stranger as he moved to get a better view. Not twenty yards to the tree line. He inched up to a thick trunk and peered around it. The peasant in the field was directly in front of him.

A woman. Young. Golden hair. Bending down to get something, then rising quickly, nervously. Looking around, then bending again—like a timid deer watching for the hunter. She was facing away from the woods toward the open field but staying close to the tree line, Sklaar guessed, in case she needed to hide quickly. She was scared.

Which gave him the idea.

He strode quickly out into the field, no longer trying to mask his sound. The girl whirled around wide-eyed and faced him coming at her out of the sun.

"You!" he barked. "What are you doing on my land?"

The blood drained from the girl's face. She half collapsed, half knelt as Sklaar approached. Trespassing was punishable by death. She dropped her basket, spilling wild strawberries onto the ground. Sklaar squinted at the object and adjusted his spectacles.

"Sir, please forgive me. I meant no harm. There are so many—"

"What's your name?" he asked, his voice brittle.

"Moira, lord," she said, trembling.

"You know it's against the law to steal from your master," Sklaar said coldly.

She began to sob. "I was only going to make a pie. Just a pie, lord."

"A pie from *my* strawberries," Sklaar said, glancing around to make sure the actual owner wasn't in sight.

"It wasn't for me, lord," the girl said, still kneeling. "I was making it for my husband. Or the man to be my husband. For our wedding. Oh, please forgive me." She bent her face to the cool ground and wet the earth with her tears. The thought of being cast into prison or worse for stealing the wild fruit obviously horrified her.

Sklaar's mind coiled around a new thought.

"You know who I am, girl? You know whose land you're stealing from?" he asked, keeping his thin voice as even as he could.

"I haven't forgotten, Lord Toffler," she said. "I beg your mercy, sir."

Toffler! The most feared knight in von Helfenstein's service. A vile man, from all accounts—a man who would exact a severe punishment for thievery—and especially on a pretty, young virgin. Just the spark the peasants needed to ignite the rebellion in Weinsburg. Just the punishment von Helfenstein deserved. Sklaar said nothing. He was enjoying the moment too much to spoil it with words. The girl remained silent with her forehead pressed to the ground.

"What's the boy's name?" Sklaar asked, his rasp less noticeable now.

"Boy, sir?"

"The boy you will marry. What's his name?"

"Jaklein, sir. Rohrbach."

"Is he an honorable lad?"

She sniffed several times, then spoke. "The best, sir. He's the inn-keeper in Bockingen, lord."

"Yes," Sklaar said. "I've been there. He's got a hot head, your Jaklein. I saw him break a man's brains open."

"He's a good man, lord. We're to marry."

"Yes, so you said. When?"

"Five days hence, lord."

"And you have permission?" Sklaar asked.

The girl hesitated, then began to cry again. "Oh, please, sir. Forgive me, sir. It's just a few berries. Please don't, please don't take them."

Sklaar smiled to himself. "Of course not. I wouldn't dream of it. In fact, I've a wedding gift for you."

"Sir?"

"Tomorrow. You may pick berries again. In fact, I command it. Here. At the same time."

"Lord?"

"Well, you can't make much of a pie with this paltry bunch, can you?" he said, kicking the basket lightly. His voice almost sounded friendly. "Tomorrow then?"

"You won't judge me, lord?" she asked, her voice quivering with hope.

"I can't condemn someone I haven't seen, can I?" he said, looking down at the girl. "I can't really say that I have seen you—at least not well enough to identify you in my courts."

The girl hesitated again, then reached out and grasped the heel of Sklaar's shoe and kissed his foot. "Thank you, Lord Toffler. Thank you. God bless you, sir. I'll never steal from you again, sir. Never. I promise."

Sklaar bent down and picked a handful of strawberries. "Of course you won't," he said, biting the stem off and spitting it out. "Do not rise until I have left. I have no wish to see you. Once I have gone, you may leave."

"As you wish, lord." She stayed stretched on the ground and covered her head with her hands as if to protect herself from any stray glimpse of the gracious man before her.

Sklaar turned and walked away into the woods and down to the path by the river, eating strawberries, so happy he almost smiled.

The Inn at Weinsburg welcomed a diverse clientele: peasants and nobles, counts, knights, priests, and town burghers. While most of the patrons entered the door with a keen sense of their place in society, class distinctions tended to dissolve as the hours passed under the influence of the Weinsburg's dark ale. Men who would never acknowledge each other in the street swapped lies together as if they were old comrades. In short, it was the kind of egalitarian atmosphere Sklaar needed if his plan had a chance to work.

He arrived at the inn shortly after dark, when it was already more than half-full with its nightly assortment of bedraggled humanity. The air in the tavern already hung thick with the pearl gray smoke that rose from the cherry bowls of twenty or more long pipes, all puffing like miniature chimneys. Conversations rolled out over thick lips, low and thrumming, assuming the soft rhythms of familiar dialogue made fresh by the day's gossip.

From his post just inside the doorway, Sklaar squinted through the irritating smoke. He shuffled between the tables, looking into each face, searching for one man in particular. He turned toward the table where a group of knights was sitting.

"What do you want, Jew?" a voice behind him asked.

Sklaar turned to face the innkeeper, a brawny man who stood at least a half-foot taller than himself.

"I am Doctor Elias Sklaar," he said, lifting his black physician's bag slightly as proof of his identity. "I've come on business. I'm looking for Lord Toffler. I thought I might find him here."

One of the knights turned his gaze on Sklaar. He was a thin man, with a slab of scarred granite for a face. An immense black mustache grew like a wild bush along his upper lip and down the sides of his mouth. His heavy eyebrows met just above the bridge of his straight nose at the vertex of an exaggerated V, giving him a perpetual frown. His eyes were deep brown with overlarge pupils that allowed him to penetrate the shadows where every man was his enemy. If the man had ever tasted kindness or gentleness, it obviously hadn't agreed with him.

"Now," he said, in a voice that sounded like dust, "what business would I have with a Jew doctor? I don't believe in circumcision, if that's what you're after." The rest of the men laughed and looked to the doctor for his response.

"I have news. Disturbing news, I'm afraid, of a personal nature. If I could have a word in private, sir," Sklaar added with as much humility as he could muster.

Toffler was curious. But he wasn't disturbed. Or anxious. Sklaar understood why. Of the seventy knights in the ranks of Count Helfenstein, Toffler was the most brutal, leading raids and slaughtering peasants at will. He had no family, and no one would dare disturb his manor while he was away. He had been careful to enhance his reputation over the years as a vicious bully and a philanderer in all the villages in the region. It didn't matter where he and his cohorts found violators—in groups, alone, or walking through the forest. Toffler regarded them as vermin to be exterminated. He would kill without provocation and without the slightest compunction. Peasants avoided his land as if it were cursed, which, in fact, it had been many times over.

"Over here," he said, rising from the chair. He led the way in long lanky strides to the empty fireplace and stood with his foot resting on the hearth, posing, even in this semiprivate moment. He was almost exactly the same height as the doctor, but he managed to look down at him. "Talk."

"I know of a peasant who is stealing from you."

Toffler looked into Sklaar's eyes. His voice was barely audible. "Tell me what you know before I lose my patience."

"I saw a woman. Stealing food from your land east of the Old Town Bridge. Picking strawberries from a patch by the river."

"I know the place. Well off the main road. How did you come on her?"

Sklaar had anticipated his question. "I was walking, lord. Taking an afternoon stroll. I heard her laughter, and thinking there might be something amiss I climbed the bank and hid nearby to listen."

Toffler's eyes narrowed. Sklaar couldn't afford more questions, since he had technically been trespassing himself when he stepped onto the count's land. He hurried on with his story.

"She was with her thieving friends, bragging that she had been stealing your food for days and that she would come tomorrow again even if they were too scared. She said you would never catch her. That you were too, well..." Sklaar hesitated, appearing to be embarrassed at the revelation he was intent on making. He lowered his voice to just above a whisper. "She was disdainful of your lordship's manliness."

Toffler stopped breathing. His eyes fixed, unblinking, on Sklaar. When he spoke, it was in a monotone, and it wasn't what Sklaar had expected. "Why are you telling me this, old man? You want money?"

Sklaar managed to look wounded and put off at the same time, as if he were incapable of stooping to such a level. "No. No, your lordship," he said plainly. "I simply despise the parasites that infect our land." He lowered his eyes and spoke in a quivering voice. "Peasants cut up my child and wife in the wars down south. Animals." He looked at Toffler again. "I have a debt to pay, sir." Toffler didn't change his expression. Sklaar couldn't tell if the count believed him or not. But the next move was his.

"You say the wench is coming back tomorrow?"

"Tomorrow at dusk."

"I will be there."

Sklaar nodded. He smiled as he started to speak, but Toffler continued, "And so will you. If this is a trap, or if the girl doesn't show, I'll do to you what I was going to do to her. Only I'll use this." He patted the hilt of his sword.

Sklaar's smile faded. The knight's face broke into an unnatural grin. "Meet me at midafternoon by the bridge. If you don't show, I won't even bother looking for the girl. I'll come for you. And I'll find you, Doctor." He walked away to rejoin his friends.

Sklaar turned and left the inn. One hand clasping his medical bag, the other balled into a tight fist. He had to stop shaking.

Next evening

White, low clouds drifted lazily just out of reach of the tallest trees that ringed the quiet meadow. The birds held their song as a light evening breeze, silken soft, whispered through the tall grass, ruffling the black capes of the men who stood staring beside their black mounts. Staring. The girl on her back wasn't making the annoying cries for help anymore. Her broken head was turned to the side, her bloodied eyes focused on the wicker basket that lay on the grass next to her, on the strawberries that had spilled out onto the soft black earth. Sklaar patted the neck of the horse nearest him as he watched his companions brutalize her. Watched as she turned her head slowly, her eyes searching then finding something in the sky. Sklaar glanced up but saw only the low drifting clouds, silent, just out of reach.

Chapter 32

The sun clung to the earth like a red blister, staining the wisps of cloud in feathery purple plumes. The air moved, heavy, leaden, warm.

It was time for Jaklein Rohrbach to light the first candles of the night. He replaced two that had burned out in the rim of the great red wheel he had lowered from the tall ceiling. He lit the wicks with a flame from a piece of burning tinder, tossed the stick into a waiting bucket of water, then pulled on the hoisting rope until the heavy wheel hung eight feet above his head. There was another eight feet beyond that to the peak of the roof. He had devised a small innovation on the roof of his inn just above the great wheel: a small chimney that allowed the candle and pipe smoke in the room to climb into the night sky but which could be capped in the event of foul weather. It had been the talk of Bockingen for weeks.

He went to the door and peered down the empty street. His Red Wheel Inn should have been crowded by now. He turned to go back inside, glad for the unexpected time he would have to put together some final plans for his wedding in two days.

Then, just as he was crossing the threshold, he heard it. A low rumble at first, but soon it became apparent that the approaching thunder came from the streets and not from the sky. He gazed up the dirt lane that wound away from his tavern. Between the buildings at the

296

far end of the street, he caught a glimpse of wild black hair in the fading light and heard the sound of tramping feet.

Men. At least two hundred strong, lurching, half running toward him. They rounded the corner of the last building and marched straight for the inn. At their head strode the woman feared more than any man in the region. A hooded black cloak billowed around her lank frame as she walked. She fixed her dark eyes on Jaklein. The tasseled ends of a bright red sash, tied loosely at the waist, fluttered at her side. Slightly behind her a tall man in a dark longcoat and a broad-brimmed hat struggled to keep up.

"Jaklein!" she shouted above the tramping crowd, and her voice went through him sharp as the dagger she carried in her red girdle. He wanted to turn back inside the inn, but he could not. She held him, as she had for years, with a power that he was at once unable to explain and unwilling to renounce.

The Black Hoffman.

He had known her all his life. Something had happened to her Gypsy mother when she was a child. And she had been left alone to grow up alongside Jaklein, though she remained in the shadows of the village, watching. As an adolescent she had tried briefly to make a respectable living, tending cattle for a local landowner, but it hadn't lasted long. She turned to fortunetelling and, some said, black magic. Over the years, she grew increasingly mysterious and eccentric, never answering to any name, and always dressing in black.

The members of the community had taken to calling her the Black Hoffman, though the reason for the name had faded from memory. Perhaps it was an early guess at her paternity. Years before there had been a layabout named Hoffman whose sole contribution to the township had been to provide grist for the rumor mill.

Jaklein's father, on the other hand, was a town burgher and would have publicly branded the gypsy girl a witch had it not been for the intercession of his son on her behalf. Jaklein himself didn't fully understand why he had defended her. She meant nothing to him. And yet there was something about her that captivated him. A fire in her eyes that held him, burning, even now as she drew near. He could read her mind.

Come on, Jaklein. You know what to do.

"Jaklein!" she shouted. She was seething. "Inside!" she said, walking past him and into the inn. The man in the dark coat followed just behind.

"What's this? Black Hoffman?" Jaklein asked, trying to sound good-natured, though his stomach was already churning.

About sixty people crowded into the inn, leaving the majority of the crowd to mill about in the street. Everyone inside was tense and quiet, watching the Black Hoffman hover over Jaklein, who was sitting now at one of the round tables.

"What?" Jaklein asked.

She circled him, watching him, then stopped to loom directly in front of him. Her hood was still in place, her untamed hair protruding wildly from the front, framing her face in a mass of oily curls. The man in the dark coat stood nearby, his hands folded in front of him.

"Moira. It's Moira, isn't it?" Jaklein asked in a hoarse whisper.

The Black Hoffman pulled back her hood. "Be still and listen. The girl is alive and in her father's care. But she's lost to you, Jaklein," the gypsy muttered in a voice as thick as it was low. There was no compassion. Only hatred. Jaklein could say nothing.

"A fine Christian man spoiled your woman, Jaklein. Took your bride like an animal." The Black Hoffman continued to speak as she swung her arm in a slow arc over her head, keeping it straight and extending her index finger to a sharp, rigid point. Slowly, the arm descended, completing the circle as she spoke until the point of her ragged nail rested on Jaklein's forehead. He was frozen. She continued, "Beat her. Used her. Threw her away. Your woman, Jaklein."

"You've seen her?" he managed to mumble.

"This one did," the Black Hoffman said, pulling the dark-clad man forward. "Talk," she said to him. "Tell him."

"Who are you?" Jaklein asked.

"Sklaar. Doctor Elias Sklaar, sir."

"Tell me what happened," Jaklein said.

Sklaar adjusted his cracked glasses and began to speak, "I was visiting friends in Weinsburg when I saw the girl's father—Thomas, they called him. He found her out in the field. I offered to help, but there was nothing I could do to help the poor thing."

"Who did this?"

"Two men, maybe three," Sklaar said. "From what I could gather, the one who raped her was one of Count von Helfenstein's noblemen. A man named Toffler."

"Toffler!" he spat out the word. The memory of his father's murder at Toffler's hand brought bile to his throat. "You said there were others. Who else?" Jaklein asked without looking up.

"Helfenstein himself, according to her father. There might have been a third, but we aren't sure."

Jaklein stood and put his face within an inch of Sklaar's. "But Helfenstein? Count von Helfenstein watched Toffler do this to Moira? That's what you're telling me?"

Sklaar stood his ground. "Helfenstein held Toffler's horse is what I heard. He watched."

Jaklein stared at him, searching his milky yellow eyes for the truth. "Why? What had Moira done?"

"I understand the dear girl was picking strawberries," Sklaar said sympathetically.

"What?" he choked the word out.

"That's all," the Hoffman said. "Just picking strawberries. For your wedding. Of course they said she was stealing them off Toffler's land." The room had grown deathly still. "It's time, Jaklein. Now's the time to throw off the chains. Now is the time to take vengeance for poor Moira. No one else will, Jaklein. It's up to you. It's up to us."

Her eyes burned. He knew she despised the aristocracy. The aristocrats were destined to fall. It was in the stars. In the book. She had seen.

As a child she had seen through to the other side. Jaklein would be her tool to destroy the rich, the powerful, those who had killed her mother.

"I'll kill them," he said in a voice just above a whisper. "I'll kill the men who did this."

Sklaar adjusted his glasses and melted back into the crowd.

"They are only two," Hoffman said, moving closer to Jaklein. "But we must kill them all or be killed ourselves. We must cleanse our land. How many more of our people must die, Jaklein?"

Jaklein nodded slowly. "Yes," he said in a voice just above a whisper. "Yes, it's time." Then, as if waking from a dream, "Moira." Pushing his way through the crowd, he ran from the inn and down the road toward Weinsburg.

Chapter 33

Elizabeth sat on a white iron chair in the middle of Count Ludwig von Helfenstein's castle garden, wrapping a ball of colorful yarn. The Helfensteins' four-year-old son played at her feet in the shade of an enormous oak. The count and his wife, Ingrid, were taking their afternoon tea and had invited Elizabeth to leave her household duties and bring John out to the garden to join them. They were as natural and unaffected with her now after her four years of service as if she were a member of the family.

The count put down the book he was reading and looked at his son. "Come here, John," he called in a playful voice. The tot immediately ran to his father's outstretched arms. "My, you're getting so big. So big. He's growing too fast, don't you think, Elizabeth?"

Elizabeth nodded. "Have to put a rock on his head, sir, to slow him down."

"Oh, good heavens," the count's wife, Ingrid, said looking up briefly from her painting. "That's the silliest thing I ever heard."

Elizabeth glanced at Ingrid von Helfenstein, who was already absorbed again in her art. She was a vain creature, totally unaware of the world outside her castle walls, but she had a kind heart, as well as a real interest in God. She would speak of the deity in the oddest moments—while watching the leaves drift from the trees in autumn. Or during dinner conversation. Or at tea. Her husband, the count, seemed to take little notice and rarely responded to her observations and questions. That duty fell to Elizabeth, and she had come to look forward to their impromptu visits on the nature of God and the universe. It seemed perfectly natural to Ingrid to speak of her creator in the most casual way. As if she were well acquainted with him. It was an attitude that delighted Elizabeth and reminded her of Maggie and her conversational prayers.

Ingrid daubed her paintbrush in the swirl of raw umber and struck a bold line on the canvas she had been mauling for the past hour. Without looking up, and sounding bored and distracted, she said, "Johnny is a precocious child, darling. And it's well known that brilliant children grow at a quicker pace. He's already taller than..."

But her own canvas seized her attention again, and she grew quiet. Elizabeth smiled to herself. The countess had formed the habit of interrupting herself. Her thoughts, like a string of imitation pearls, were easily unstrung and scattered. Several seconds passed before she gathered them again. "What do you think, Ludwig? Is the light right on this side?"

She tilted her torso away from the canvas so her husband could see. He studied it for a few seconds.

"Hmm. A dash more pink in the clouds..."

"Here?"

"Down more. Yes. A bit more pink there, I think."

"Johnny, my dove, what do you think?" She dipped her brush in turpentine and wiped it on a rag. "More pink?" she said, scooping up the four-year-old and giving him a quick squeeze before setting him back down again. He scampered away to play with a toy horse. Ingrid stepped back a pace or two and studied the painting.

Elizabeth could see it perfectly from her chair beneath the oak. The countess had chosen a pastoral scene. In it, Ludwig was leaning against an ancient oak, smoking a long-stemmed pipe while Ingrid sat on a black-and-red blanket in its shade, playing with little Johnny. It struck

Elizabeth that the picture was at once romantic as well as a realistic depiction of their happy life behind the walls. Ingrid loved her husband desperately—that much was obvious. And he loved her, at least when he was behind the walls, Elizabeth thought. And they both adored their only child.

Elizabeth glanced over at the count. Something about his manner with his wife and child didn't ring true. She had suspected for some time now that the count might be a different man once he left the side of his wife and small son. It was a combination of things: the mildly suggestive language when he was alone with her, his frequently touching her shoulder and back and hand. The way she caught him looking at her when Ingrid was preoccupied.

And then there were the rumors. On her rare trips into town to buy supplies, Elizabeth had grown increasingly aware of the peasants' deep-seated fear of Helfenstein. The ivy-covered walls of the castle had shielded Ingrid from the reports Elizabeth now heard with disturbing frequency. Reports of atrocities, rumors of callous and frequent butchery of men and women and children. Yet, inside the castle walls, whenever they were in Ingrid's presence, Elizabeth noticed, Ludwig and his knights made sure their boots and their swords were wiped clean—the model of gentility. Their courtliness only gave Ingrid further excuse to disregard the "unsophisticated rabble," as she called them, outside the walls, who required so much of her husband's civilizing influence.

Ludwig placed his blue-rimmed china cup on the iron table gently so that it made no sound. Ingrid's gaze turned toward the downward movement of the cup. The corners of her mouth lifted in a delicate smile. Another small victory of style and grace over the barbarity of Weinsburg. "Well," Ludwig said, standing and dabbing the corners of his mouth with his napkin, "I've a meeting with Toffler and Felix in town. I should be back before dark."

"Elizabeth," Ingrid said, "Would you see to Johnny for me? I think he's had enough sun for this afternoon."

Elizabeth put down her ball of yarn and rose from her chair.

"Johnny, boy," she said in her let's-play-a-game voice. "Come to 'Lizabeth." The four-year-old jumped up and down with delight. He squirmed out of his mother's arms and hit the ground running full tilt across the flagstones into Elizabeth's outstretched arms. She picked him up and swung him around in a dizzy arc.

"Oh, Elizabeth," Ingrid called as she turned to go back inside, "have you finished that shawl? I'm dying to see it."

"It's almost ready, ma'am," Elizabeth said. "I hope you'll like it. I have some ideas for other patterns, if you'd like to see."

"Of course. Let's have a look tonight after dinner."

Elizabeth curtsied and left with Johnny. She was happier than she had been since she left her home in Pforzheim.

Sister Katherine had been right. Ingrid had needed help with little Johnny, and as it turned out, Elizabeth had arrived just in time to help with his birth. The months following were bright and happy—and mixed with longing. There were times, especially in spring, when she would ride out beyond the gates of Weinsburg and into her private cathedral. That was how she had come to regard the glade in the forest that reminded her so of the meadow back in Rosheim where Jonathan had first told her he loved her. She would sit alone near a sparkling stream and imagine that Jonathan was there beside her. She could almost hear his whispers in the murmuring breeze. "And I love you," she whispered in return. She prayed that God would watch over him and bring him joy. And bless the one he loved, whoever it might be. There Elizabeth found peace. And the assurance in her heart that the Lord would answer her selfless prayers.

Chapter 34

APRIL 5, 1525
WITTENBERG

Katherine turned from the western window back into the soft shadows of her room. She had just watched the sun slip over the rim of the world. The softness of the evening invited reflection. The Reichenbachs had been kind to take her in after her arrival in Wittenberg. The ample garden behind the house offered the perfect setting for sorting out the tumble of ideas that had been coursing through her brain. Actually, she was near to settling on the decision she had been considering for weeks.

"Lord," she thought as she picked up her shawl, "help me decide today, or I'll go mad. Send me some guidance, some sign, if you would, to lead me the last bit of the way."

Early evening was her favorite time of the day. As she opened the door, a cool breeze rushed through the room, carrying with it the breath of honeysuckle and the promise of spring roses.

She closed the heavy oak door behind her and began her winding circuit of the garden path, taking her time, studying the different plants that grew there. Smelling the freshly tilled earth that held scores of vegetable seeds, trying to classify the kind of smooth, angular stone that passed beneath her bare feet. Meister Reichenbach was a jurist and a city scribe, and so he could afford this beautiful garden, which his wife tended with loving care. Everything in this small world invited discovery:

the plants, the soil, even the stones, each of them softer and somehow more accepting of analysis in the evening light.

She came at last to the back of the garden and her favorite spot at a carved bench, poised on a small hill that offered a lovely southern view. She sat and stared dreamily into the distant shadows. Not so far away, beyond the twisting black ribbon of the Elbe, at the end of dusty forest paths, lay the village of Grimma and her old convent of Nimbschen. Her home. She had thought often of the sisters she had left there and how they had fared under the iron hand of Mother Superior Kiersten. She thought of Sister Agnes, her best friend. And how she missed her

Mrs. Reichenbach had welcomed Martin and ushered him to the back door. She was about to open it and call out to Katherine when Martin asked if they could be alone for a moment. She agreed, though she had a puzzled look on her face as she returned to her housework. Martin stood silent before the oak door. He needed just a few more seconds to think through the best way of broaching the tender subject of Kate's future.

He took a deep breath and tried to relax. "Lord, help her decide today, or I'll go mad," he prayed quickly, then he opened the door and stepped out into the garden.

"Sister Kate?"

She looked back over her shoulder. "Father," she said, smiling.

"May I join you?" Martin asked.

"Please." She moved to give him room to sit.

"I thought I might find you here," he said casually. He sat on the edge of the stone seat. Katherine kept her eyes focused on the distant trees. They were silent for a minute or so, though Martin felt as if an hour had passed before he could think of something to say. "Thinking of Nimbschen?" he asked.

"I miss it sometimes," she said, frowning slightly, her eyes still on the horizon.

"You miss the company of your friends, Kate," Martin said. He had told himself this was not going to be a lecture, but he was already slipping. He had already corrected her. He must soften his approach.

"Of course," he said, his voice now warm and fatherly. "It's understandable. Anyone would feel lonely living with a family she hardly knows. But we're trying to correct that, aren't we?" Now he was sounding condescending. Why was it that whenever he spoke two sentences to this woman, one of them was bound to carve a furrow in her brow? Katherine kept looking out across the hills. Her expression hadn't changed, although the frown might have deepened slightly.

Martin bit his tongue, sighed and started over. He would be straightforward. It was the only way. "Kate, I've been through the lists. I've written to every eligible bachelor I know and some I know only by reputation, and you have rejected them all." She didn't say a word, but Luther thought he saw the corner of her mouth turn up slightly, then relax. He didn't know what to make of this. He never knew. Women.

"I've done my best, Kate. I know it's taken a long time to find you a good husband, but with the peasants and the nobles at each other's throats and all, I haven't, uh…

"I assure you, Kate," he pushed ahead, "I didn't intend any offense in suggesting Herr Reibenstein as a husband. But now I understand that you find him, uh…"

"Insufferable. *Enormously* insufferable."

"Yes, that. And I admit he's a bit, shall we say, bulky for his height, but he is one of the most respected burghers in Eisenach. And let's face it, Kate, you're twenty-six…" He knew he shouldn't have said it as soon as the words left his mouth. She shifted slightly away from him.

"Kate?"

Nothing.

"Kate, you must help me here. I've done all I know to do."

She blinked.

He decided to try a firmer approach. "You're going to have to decide, Kate." He lowered his voice to achieve the rumble that struck fear in the hearts of his students. Unfortunately, it seemed to have no effect on Sister Katherine other than to make the corners of her mouth rise again. Martin was about to speak when she interrupted him.

"But I have decided, Father." She looked at him. It wasn't a hard look, or reproachful. It wasn't an angry look. Martin had spent years deciphering the facial expressions of his students and those he debated, but he had never encountered a look like this one. He wasn't sure what it meant.

"Uh, well, then. Good." He was stunned at her sudden turn. He shouldn't have been, of course. Katherine, he had learned, was a woman of conviction and decision. She had a strong mind, especially for a woman. "Very good. I trust I wasn't too harsh."

"No, no. Not at all," she said. "I thank you for your courtesy."

She smiled softly, and Martin felt color come to his cheeks. The back of his neck prickled slightly and he rubbed it. "If you would simply, uh, let me know," he stammered. "At your convenience, of course, though we mustn't wait too long." He frowned and shook his head slowly, gazing off toward the forest. "I do hope it isn't the margrave you've decided on. He has made other arrangements with Count Lowenstein's daughter. But at any rate, whatever I can do for you, Katherine—"

"I'm surprised Dr. Amsdorf didn't tell you."

"I beg your pardon?"

Amsdorf was an old friend who had agreed to serve as a liaison in the negotiations between Kate and Luther. He had, in fact, told Martin that Katherine, not wishing to be unreasonable, would be willing to take either himself or Martin as a husband. Luther had laughed it off as an absurdity. She was, of course, being most unreasonable. Both men were well beyond their marrying years. Luther himself was forty-two, and half the world wanted his head on a plate.

"Well, no matter," Katherine continued with seeming indifference. "You can marry me, Father."

Martin paused, waiting for her to complete her thought. When she didn't continue, he stepped in helpfully. "I'll be glad to marry you, my dear child, but to whom? Amsdorf? Well, he's a good man, a fine Christian—a good choice all in all. Yes, good choice. A bit mossy, perhaps, but…"

Katherine blinked.

"For a lady as young as yourself, I mean," he added.

Katherine looked at him with such an incredulous expression that, had Martin not been so thoroughly confused, he would have laughed out loud.

Katherine shook her head slightly and pursed her lips.

When she spoke, her words were matter-of-fact, but they could hardly have made a greater impact on Luther had they been boulders hurled from heaven itself. "I would marry your gracious self, lord," she said simply.

Martin paused. She was looking right at him. With the same look she had given him earlier: the suppressed smile, the amused nonchalance. He swallowed. She wouldn't look away.

Eck had been more merciful than this.

He felt himself sinking—his logical mind desperately clutching at arguments like a drowning man grasping at straws—sinking into those eyes. All that his brain could assimilate—and this came with sudden and startling clarity—was that he now understood the meaning of her look.

Chapter 35

Jaklein Rohrbach could still see the stars, though the eastern horizon was lightening. The bell of the Weinsburg church tolled in the distance, calling the faithful to early Mass. Jaklein stood with his back against a great oak, his arms folded in a tight knot, his eyes red from lack of sleep. He looked out over thousands of tents and lean-tos that made up the peasant army. A few men and women were rising, making their way to the brook to relieve themselves or to gather water for washing and cooking.

Jaklein studied them. Some of them, perhaps most of them, wouldn't be alive by the end of the day. But they had to take a stand. They all had to fight—for the thousands of women and children who had been burned out, robbed, beaten, and raped. Every man had a hundred reasons for fighting that day. Jaklein needed only one. This day he would fight for Moira. This was his day of vengeance.

Jonathan stretched the weariness out of his tired muscles and stared off in the direction of Weinsburg. He had been walking for weeks since leaving Wittenberg, stopping only to eat and to preach peace in the villages where trouble seemed most imminent. He had slept little over the last forty-eight hours, knowing that Weinsburg—and Elizabeth—were only a few miles farther on. There! He could see the

310

city walls, less than half a mile ahead. Tired as he was, he quickened his pace. As he neared the south entrance to the city, he noticed the gates were closed. The sun was well up, and they should have been opened by now.

"State your business, Father," a voice called out from the top of the wall.

Jonathan looked up to see an armed soldier silhouetted against the pale blue sky.

"Father Jonathan," he shouted. "I bear a message for Count von Helfenstein from Dr. Martin Luther in Wittenberg."

There was a pause before the sentinel issued the command, "Open the gate." Then he turned back to Jonathan, his voice tense and commanding. "Enter quickly, Father."

The streets of Weinsburg were empty. The church bell that Jonathan had heard as he approached had stopped ringing. He glanced around. Apparently all the gates were shut and barred. He could see sentinels standing armed and ready all along the southern wall, and he imagined they were also stationed at the other corners of the city wall and above the gates. He could see those nearest him scanning the hills and the line of trees that ringed the city for any sign of movement. They were obviously expecting an attack at any moment. As he ran down the empty street toward Helfenstein's castle at the center of the city, he prayed he hadn't arrived too late.

"What is it, Ludwig? Where are you going?" Countess Ingrid asked sleepily. The heavy drapes were pulled tight to keep the morning light out of their cavernous sleeping chambers. It was still dark as midnight in the room. Helfenstein had been awake for a couple of hours already and was dressed for battle with his sword at his side. He removed his chain-mail glove and leaned over to kiss Ingrid on the cheek, running his fingers through her hair.

"Go back to sleep," he whispered as he turned to go. "I have some business to attend. I'll see you at Mass." He started to go.

"You will be there, won't you, love? It is Easter, after all," she said, yawning. She was asleep again before the door closed behind him.

At the bottom of the stair, Albert Toffler, dressed for battle as well, waited for him. The two men walked out of the small antechamber into the hallway that led to the south wing of the castle. Their mail shirts made a dull metallic shifting sound as they moved. The doors to the dining hall stood open. Toffler entered behind his liege lord and took his place on the right side of the table. Thirty other knights rose to their feet. Forty more turned from their conversations, armor clinking softly, faces hard as the steel that wrapped them, eyes fixed on the young count.

"Any word from Stuttgart or the Palatinate?" Ludwig asked quietly of the man on his left.

"None, sire," the man replied darkly. The count's hope for reinforcements evaporated in those two words. "But there is an emissary from Wittenberg."

At this, a monk stood forward. "Father Jonathan, lord. With a message from Dr. Martin Luther."

He held out the sealed letter to Helfenstein. The count opened it and began to read as Jonathan spoke, "I have delivered this message to many of your fellow knights in Saxony and throughout Thuringia, sire. They have all indicated they are willing to abide by—"

"He wants me to capitulate?" Helfenstein interrupted, glancing up from the document.

"Not capitulate, sire," Jonathan said. "Negotiate. Some of the peasants' claims are small and would cost you little, but you stand to gain much in the bargain. We implore you, do not take up the sword against your own people. Otherwise there will be no end to the bloodshed."

"My people? Have you seen them, Father? Have you?" Helfenstein turned to one of the younger knights who stood near the door. "How many would you estimate, Ivan?"

"Near four thousand, sire. They keep coming."

Helfenstein turned back to Jonathan. "Four thousand, Father. And what do these men want to do? They want to kill us all. These men aren't my people, most of them don't even come from my lands. And they don't come looking for peace. They want to rule in our place." He crumpled the letter and tossed it on the floor. "You go back to your good Dr. Luther and tell him what you've seen here. You tell him that we fight to protect our women and children and the faithful citizens of Weinsburg. If he wants to help us, he will join us in the fight." He started to turn away.

"Let me pray for you," Jonathan said.

"What?"

Jonathan stepped forward. "There's no time to go back, and Father Martin wouldn't come anyway. If I stay, at least I can pray for you and your family."

Helfenstein thought for a moment, then turned to the boy at the door. "Clarence," he said. "Take Father Jonathan to the church." Jonathan nodded and followed the servant out.

Helfenstein turned to Toffler. "Guns in place?" he asked.

"Three at each of the gates, five at the breach in the north wall."

"How's the ammunition?"

"Not that good, sire. Maybe ten rounds per man and barely enough powder for that."

"Cannon?"

"Two. A stone-ball breechload on the north gate, an iron ball on the south."

Helfenstein nodded and studied his men. Most were armed with simple swords. About twenty carried old matchlock harquebuses, heavy guns that had belonged to their grandfathers. A handful, no more than five, had acquired expensive new wheel locks that were strapped tightly in holsters at their waists. These men he would leave in charge of defending the castle and all his possessions.

"To your posts. And God save us," he said, though he knew in his heart that God would be no help at all.

The Black Hoffman stood on a high slab of rock. Thousands of peasant soldiers knelt before her, their heads bowed. Receiving her benediction.

"Blessed be the avenging blade!" she screamed. Her voice rose in a high-pitched wail, her words sailed like barbed arrows on the wind.

"Blessed be the hands that shed the blood of Helfenstein."

Most of the peasants in the United Contingent were holding not swords and spears but pikes and pitchforks and wooden staves. Anything sharp they could carry to the fight.

Jaklein Rohrbach closed his eyes, grasped the hilt of his father's sword, and leaned on it, piercing the earth with the tip of his blade. Sweat rolled down his cheeks and into his open mouth. He could feel it—the steel point of his father's sword slowly piercing the armor and then the heart of Count Ludwig von Helfenstein.

One of Helfenstein's mercenary soldiers peered out over the top of the city wall toward the hills that held the United Contingent of the Peasant Army. He saw two of their men, still far away, approaching across the plain.

He lifted his grandfather's matchlock into place and balanced it in a notch just beside the parapet. "Match," he said to his page. Immediately the boy leapt down two steps and ran to retrieve the smoldering wick that would ignite the priming powder.

The first of the two men who drew near carried a hat on a tall pole, a sign that the peasants wanted to talk. Behind those two, a swarming mass of humanity mounted the top of a long hill on the north side of the city. Occasionally, shouts drifted across the valley and over the city walls. "Open the gates," cried the one with the long pole. "You will open the town to the United Contingent!"

Helfenstein's soldier rested the stock of the hand cannon against his chest and flipped open the hinged cover to the flashpan. With his right hand he reached down to retrieve the powder horn at his side. He lifted it to his teeth and uncorked the end. Then waiting for a lull in the wind, he poured a small mound of priming powder into the pan and closed the lid.

"If you do not open the gates," the man with the hat pole shouted, "then release your wives and children."

The boy returned with the match and handed it to the knight. The frazzled tip of the wick glowed red, just right for a sure, fast light. He inserted the match, smoldering end down, into its holding arm, and adjusted the small jaws at the end of the arm to hold the match in place. He had already tamped the single ball into the barrel. The harquebus was ready to fire. The knight hugged the stock to his chest and sighted down the top center of the barrel. The muzzle was pointed, as nearly as possible, at the man doing all the talking. The knight felt along the smooth wood until his finger slipped inside the carved hole in the gunstock and wrapped around the metal trigger.

"Listen to me," the man cried. "All who remain in this town must be put to the sword! Send your women and children out now, or they will die with you!"

The knight squeezed the trigger. The mechanical linkage opened the flashpan cover, and the match descended into the shallow mound of black powder. "This is your last—" But the final word was lost in the explosion from the top of the city wall.

Before the sound reached his ears, the iron ball slammed into his upper chest. He fell into his companion, blood splashing on his leggings and onto the wooden pole that lay at his feet.

The man at his side screamed and ran away from the city gate into the near woods, away from the gathered armies. The wounded emissary rolled onto his stomach and summoned the strength to rise to one knee and then to stand and limp toward the now quiet army waiting on the other side of the hill.

On the echo of the shot, the Black Hoffman stopped her incantations. She waited, gazing with the peasant army toward the town, but unable to see the field that led to the base of the city walls. A full minute passed before she lifted her arm and pointed toward the city. "Behold, Jaklein!" she screamed. "The bloody answer to your herald!" The wounded man crawled over the low hill that rose between the peasants and the town. He tumbled into the shallow dale, twisting his red-soaked shirt in his hand. He lay sprawled on his back as several men ran from the edge of the crowd to help him.

They hauled him back to the center of the camp where the leaders and the gypsy witch stood waiting. They lowered him to the ground softly. He was dying as Jaklein cradled his head in his lap. He looked up into the eyes of his leader, and the fog of death cleared for a moment. He drew in one last shuddering breath and screamed at the top of his lungs, "Vengeance!"

Jaklein rose to his feet and lifted his sword high, the blood of his fallen comrade staining his own shirt. "Vengeance!" he shouted, and a thousand pitchforks pierced the sky, a thousand staves pointed heavenward, scores of swords sliced the wind, and four thousand voices answered, "Vengeance!"

Jaklein's blood raced through his veins. He looked to his left. Two of the commanders were already mounted and riding toward their troops.

To his right, Sir Florian Geyer, leader of the famed Black Troop of peasant soldiers, raised his sword. "Black Troop, forward," he shouted, and fully half of the United Contingent surged down the hill.

Jaklein ran up the hill and mounted a large rock overlooking the valley that separated them from the city. Just as Geyer reached the walls, Jaklein leapt down from his perch and began the charge down the hill toward the gates. The peasants ran pell-mell, trampling the ground and each other, howling and cursing and stabbing the air.

He could hear the Black Hoffman at his back, screaming from her rocky promontory, "Down, down with the dogs! Strike them all dead!

No fear! I, I the Black Hoffman, bless your weapons! God wills you to strike! God wills it! God wills it!"

Several minutes earlier Helfenstein and several of his knights had left the marketplace of Weinsburg where they had tried to convince the frightened citizens gathered there to remain loyal to him. Help would come, he had said. He was sure help would come by day's end, if they could just hold out until then.

Then he turned with the rest of his guard and entered the church inside the castle walls to hear the Easter Mass and to take the sacrament. He had reserved the church for the royal family, their attendants, and guests. The early Easter Mass was a tradition in Weinsburg and allowed the count and his coterie to celebrate the Resurrection without the distraction of the lower classes. On this Easter, it also offered sanctuary in case the peasant army breached the castle walls.

Helfenstein took his seat beside his wife and their son, then turned and looked for the priest whom he'd sent ahead. The countess, little John, and Elizabeth stared wide-eyed as more than seventy knights, all in shining battle armor, took their places alongside their own families on the benches.

Helfenstein removed his mail glove and took his wife's hand. "It is Easter, after all," he said and smiled, desperately hoping that if God saw him in church on Easter with his family, he might spare them.

One of the priests approached him and leaned over to whisper.

"A Father Jonathan came in just before your family arrived, sire."

"Yes, I sent him...to pray."

Helfenstein nodded as the cleric walked away.

Elizabeth leaned across Ingrid and touched the count on the arm. "Excuse me, my lord?"

He jerked at her touch and turned nervously to face her. "What is it, Elizabeth?" he asked impatiently.

"Begging your pardon, lord," she whispered, "but did the Father mention a priest named Jonathan?"

"Yes. He came from Wittenberg with a message from Luther. I told him to leave, but he insisted on staying to pray for us. He's—"

A sudden cry from one of the sentinels froze everyone in the church. In the next instant, the soldiers bolted from their seats and out into the courtyard. Two men stationed themselves inside as guards. They would bar the doors as soon as the other knights had left. No one was to leave, and no one was allowed in unless Helfenstein himself gave the order.

He turned quickly to his wife. "You'll be safe here," he said. "They won't come inside the church. Take care of John." Ingrid nodded but said nothing. Helfenstein turned to Elizabeth. "Elizabeth, you see to it."

"Yes," was all she could manage before he was gone.

Helfenstein ran out the doors, and they swung closed behind him. He raced across the courtyard and up the stairs to the top of the walls surrounding his own castle. There he gazed across the marketplace to the city walls. He stared, rubbed his eyes and stared again. He couldn't believe, couldn't accept, what he was seeing. Two of the peasants' tricolor banners already waved from the battlements. How? There had been no warning. Then it struck him. Traitors! Traitors had let the peasants into Weinsburg.

At the same time, he heard a distant crash. He looked to his left where he could just see the top third of the arch of the massive north gates splinter and fall, allowing the peasant troops to swarm into the city unimpeded. His knees buckled slightly as he turned and ran back to the church.

Inside the church, Jonathan had been praying for God to intervene and stop the battle before it began, and if not, then to protect the innocent. He tried to pray equally for both sides, but ever since Luther had commissioned him to carry his letter to Helfenstein, his heart had been torn. On the one hand, he despised those to whom he was appealing for peace. Arrogant despots like Helfenstein had abused his mother and the other peasants their whole lives. If Jonathan had been given the luxury of choosing, he would have taken up the sword in a heartbeat and fought with the peasants against the very man for whom he was now asking God's mercy. Praying for one's enemies was much easier to preach than to do.

On the other hand, Elizabeth was a part of this man's household, and so he found himself praying fervently for her protection. And for his own. He had come so far. Waited so many years. And now he was sure she was here, somewhere in the castle church with Helfenstein's family, waiting, praying for deliverance, and unaware of his presence. The irony of it choked his prayers. Now that he was within a few yards of her, a battle threatened. And he wondered if he would live long enough to find her and tell her that he still loved her.

He heard Helfenstein banging on the church doors, ordering them open. He exited the prayer closet and was moving quickly toward the front of the church, when he caught a glimpse of Elizabeth on the far side of the sanctuary. He was turning to call out to her when the doors swung open and Helfenstein ran into the vestibule, nearly bowling him over. The count grabbed Jonathan's robe, spun him around, and shouted in his face, "Get up on the castle wall, Father. Call for peace. Go! Now!"

Without a word, Jonathan sprinted out the door. Helfenstein was right behind him, shouting orders to shut and bar the castle gates. They had to act quickly. They pulled the heavy gates shut and barred them, but they knew it was an empty exercise. If the peasant army had broken down the enormous city gates, the castle gates would be no match for them. And the walls weren't high or thick enough to sustain a serious attack. It was just a matter of time, unless the priest could convince them to turn back.

Jonathan crossed the courtyard to the stairs and mounted the castle wall. He hadn't been able to see if Elizabeth had turned to look before he ran out. At least now he knew where she was, and he could come back for her.

He stood upon the parapet, took a deep breath, and waited for the peasant army to reach the broad street that led up to the castle walls.

Jaklein led his troops into the city through a breach in the northern wall. They filled the streets, running and shouting to the citizens, "Back, back to your houses, and stay there unless you want to die with your filthy lords and nobles. All who take up the sword will die! All will die by the sword!"

Jaklein looked up. All along the city walls the free lances and some of the nobles were deserting their posts. He saw them leaping down flights of stairs, some of them twisting or breaking ankles and legs in the process. Then the peasant soldiers simply ran them through where they lay. Those who survived joined the rest running down back alleys and side streets, either toward the castle church for sanctuary or toward the city walls to escape to the outside.

After he found one man hiding in a baker's oven, Jaklein ordered his men to search the homes of the shopkeepers and tradesmen. He walked out the back door, down a narrow street, and past an abandoned courtyard. As he passed a breach in the wall, he looked out across a plowed field. What he saw stopped him in his tracks: an enormous "lady" sporting a bonnet and shawl, a dress several sizes too small, and heavy boots, lumbering away from the city toward a line of near trees.

Jonathan saw them surging in a thick wave down the main street toward the castle. He lifted his arms and shouted, but he soon found he couldn't even hear himself above the screams of the peasant army. They ran up to the base of the wall and began scaling the short ladders. The soldiers to Jonathan's right and left were already shooting guns and arrows into the mob. "Peace!" Jonathan cried. "Peace, be still!" But his words were lost in the maelstrom of gunfire and screams.

Jonathan heard the high-pitched whine of an arrow just before it struck him a glancing blow on his left temple. He spun to his left and tumbled onto the landing several feet below the parapet. He hit hard on his right side, lost his breath, and slammed his head into the jagged stone. A sparking, fire-rimmed blackness enveloped him, and he lay still.

Chapter 36

Helfenstein stood in the courtyard, watching. When he saw Jonathan fall, he and the few knights that surrounded him turned to run back into the church. He left a small contingent of free lances and rangers to guard the castle precincts, then took his remaining nobles and entered the sanctuary. As soon as they had secured the doors, they heard the splintering crash of the castle gate, a victory shout, and the low rumble of a thousand tramping feet. A few seconds later the mob started hammering against the doors of the church, but they were thick and heavy, and the crossbeam that barred the doors was stout.

Helfenstein ran down the left aisle, past his wife and child and Elizabeth, to a deep recess in the back corner of the church. He slid back a hidden latch and a small portion of the wall swung back to reveal a narrow staircase.

"Come on," he said, his voice a harsh whisper. "It leads to the tower. We'll be safe there." As the eighteen nobles bolted up the winding stairs, Helfenstein ran to his wife.

"They won't hurt you," he said frantically. "Stay here. Understand?" He started to back away. "Understand?" he asked again, but they didn't answer. Ingrid looked shocked and Johnny clutched his mother's arm, his eyes wide and frightened. Finally he turned and ran back to the corner, entered the stairwell and pulled the door to. He secured the latch with a soft *clack*. The narrow chamber was pitch black. "Shh. Quiet!" he ordered, but their labored breathing and coughing echoed off the stone walls.

"We can't stay here!" Elizabeth said, recovering. There were only a few wives and children left in the sanctuary, the rest having fled after the nobles had run out. "They're going to kill us if we stay," Elizabeth said insistently. Ingrid sat frozen, gripping the edge of the bench. Elizabeth grabbed little John's hand and started to pull him away, but his mother reached out and pulled him back. "No!" she screamed. "Ludwig said to stay here. We're not leaving!"

"They'll kill us, my lady. They don't care that this is a church. It means nothing to them. Come on!"

Jaklein's troops had stormed the church courtyard, easily overpowering the small group of fighting men that remained there. He estimated more than thirty bodies strewn across the courtyard and along the walls of the castle.

Jaklein lifted his sword with both hands. "Helfenstein!" he screamed, beating the church doors with the hilt of his sword. "Coward! Come out and meet your death like a man!" He turned to the soldiers nearest him. "Break it down," he ordered. He dispatched several others to the side and rear exits to make sure Helfenstein wouldn't try to escape by those routes. Once the axes had done their work, Jaklein walked ahead into the church.

They met Elizabeth with John in tow coming up the aisle. Ingrid was close behind. Jaklein stepped into her path.

"So! The countess and her bastard son!" He reached out to grab the boy. Elizabeth screamed and lunged violently at Jaklein. Her fingernails cut into his cheeks, stunning him and sending him reeling to one side.

He recovered quickly and stepped forward, slamming the hilt of his sword into the side of Elizabeth's head. She collapsed onto the floor between two benches, blood streaming from her wound, and didn't move. "Keep an eye on this one," Jaklein said, indicating Ingrid, who stood with a crying John in her arms. "I have plans for her."

One of the peasants, a filthy little man with foul breath, grabbed Ingrid by the arm and held her fast.

The nineteen men in the darkened stairwell were now eighteen. Dietrich von Veiler had clambered past Helfenstein at the top of the stairs and scrambled out onto the gallery of the church tower. The count could see his old friend clearly from his position inside the stairwell. Veiler stood on the edge of the high gallery in full view of the peasants. He held up his arms in an effort to still them.

"Hear me!" he bawled. "I have in my accounts thirty thousand gulden. I offer it in exchange for the lives of these men."

"Ha!" Helfenstein heard one man shout. "Make it a barrel full o' gold, your lordship, you're all still going to die!"

Then he heard another voice—the voice of a woman, screaming. "Vengeance!" she cried. "Vengeance for the blood of our fallen brothers!" And with that, a shot from a harquebus. Blood spattered Helfenstein's face as Veiler crumpled and tumbled out of the tower, his armored body making a dull clank on the pavement below. The crowd roared.

Jaklein turned the latch suddenly and opened the door to the secret stairwell. He could see only the feet of those on the lowest of the spiraling steps.

"Helfenstein!" he screamed up the stairwell. No answer. He turned to the mob that had burst into the sanctuary. "They're in here! All of them!" he shouted. "Strike them all dead, but bring me Helfenstein alive!" He turned and stalked out to the courtyard as the maddened crowd rushed the stairwell.

He could hear the nobles trampling each other, some of them whimpering like children, trying to clamber up the few remaining stairs.

Jaklein positioned himself directly below the gallery of the church tower. Five of Helfenstein's nobles remained in the cupola, begging those in the courtyard for mercy, the flimsy wooden door to the stairwell latched uselessly behind them. "Throw down your weapons!" Jaklein shouted to them. "And we may receive you yet!" Swords were drawn and tossed immediately. They clanged on the paving stones in the churchyard. One stuck in a crack between the stones and wobbled back and forth.

"Pick them up, my friends," Jaklein ordered the peasants, and they retrieved the shining swords immediately. "Forward, lancers," he ordered, and fifteen men with spears and lances came to the front of the crowd. "Arrange yourselves here," Jaklein said, indicating where he wanted them to take their positions. "Fix your lances, stave end on stone." Fifteen rusty points thrust heavenward as the lancers placed the butt end of their spears on the pavement. "Spread out a bit. There. Hold your swords high, my friends! Now," he said, speaking up to the men in the tower. "We are ready to receive you, my lords. You have a choice. You may try to fly on your own, or we shall push you out of your nest."

A roar of laughter erupted from the courtyard and spread beyond the castle walls.

None of the nobles moved. None of them spoke. Several knelt and crossed themselves and began to pray. Toffler remained standing.

"Ah," Jaklein sighed dramatically. "Just as I thought. Cowards to the end. We will be up directly." He turned to the man on his left. "Take ten men with you and force them to jump. Don't throw them. Make them jump. But bring me Helfenstein." The man chose his companions, and they ran into the church.

They soon returned, dragging Helfenstein, his wife, and child out of the church. They pushed them into the center of the yard, where Jaklein regarded them, hands on hips.

"Good of you to join us, Helfen-swein," Jaklein shouted, laughing along with a few of the mob at his wordplay. "You have friends in high places, I believe." He grabbed Helfenstein by the hair and yanked his battered face up to view the tower. Ingrid screamed and clutched her crying child in her arms, turning his face and her own away.

Jaklein focused on the count. "You like to watch people suffer, huh? I'm sorry, we don't have any helpless women to entertain you today. Your men at arms will have to suffice."

There was a brief scuffle as the ten peasants burst through the flimsy door to the tower and subdued the nobles.

Toffler was the first to stand on the balcony, his hands bound behind his back. He stepped into place calmly. The toes of his boots hung out over the edge of the gallery ledge. His eyes burned with a black fire. Pure hatred. He looked down at the crowd—considered the sharp pointed pikes, the shining sword that had been his grandfather's, then his father's, and finally his own, now in the hands of a grinning fool. A bitter gall filled his throat, and he almost vomited. He closed his eyes and concentrated. He would not humiliate himself.

He opened his eyes and saw Helfenstein, his face turned up. The countess and her son stood locked in an embrace, staring down.

And there, just behind the countess on the edge of the crowd, a lean man in a black cloak, clutching a black bag—the doctor. The doctor he had met in Weinsburg. The man who had told him about the girl stealing his strawberries. He had goaded him into raping the girl that afternoon, then stood back to watch along with Helfenstein. Now he stood silently mocking him. The sun glinted off the doctor's small spectacles. He was smiling up at him and nodding. Toffler allowed his gaze to shift. He saw the mob shouting, lifting their pitchforks, throwing stones at him as if they were trying to knock an offensive bird out of a tree.

But he heard no voices. Only a low, rushing sound, like water in a subterranean tunnel. There was Jaklein Rohrbach, the innkeeper from Bockingen who had stirred up all the trouble. The strawberry girl had called out his name. Now Rohrbach stood, waving his arms, shouting something from so far below, so far away.

Toffler spat on the crowd. And leapt.

Elizabeth heard distant voices and the pounding of the wind against roof and walls. Her head throbbed with a dull, persistent ache. The smell of hay tickled her nostrils. She moved slightly and felt a hand pressing against her mouth, felt a warm breath on her cheek. Sklaar! She opened her eyes, then closed them immediately as the pain screamed through her head like a jagged knife. She had caught only the faintest glimpse of a man's head and shoulder, but even in that instant she knew it couldn't have been the doctor. She heard him whispering, "Shh, shh. Elizabeth. It's Jonathan."

He moved his hand away from her mouth. She was quiet for a moment. She reached up and touched his face with trembling fingers and formed the word "How?" with her lips.

He smiled as he put his forefinger to his own lips and leaned down to her. "I'll explain later," he whispered. Then she started to cry. Her head felt as if it would burst, but she couldn't help it. The battering wind covered the sound of her weeping as she leaned her head on Jonathan's chest. She was shaking. But it wasn't because she was afraid. Elizabeth was shaking because in that defining moment, she knew that he still loved her. And that she loved him.

Jonathan wrapped her in his arms and comforted her until her tears subsided. Then she noticed his monk's habit. She looked up into his eyes. "Jonathan, you're a priest?" she asked. He smiled and tipped his head as he put his lips close to her ear and whispered so softly she could barely hear him. "I'll explain later. We're in danger. Need to be quiet."

She nodded. "We're in a barn just outside the city," Jonathan whispered. There was a sound, a grunt from someone on the other side of the haystack where they were hiding. Elizabeth's eyes widened. Jonathan pointed in the direction of the sound. "Rohrbach's men," he said, even more quietly. "All drunk. Asleep." He made a motion for her to follow him. Together they crawled on their stomachs until they could just see around the edge of the haystack and out into the barn. "There are only four that I can see," Jonathan whispered. "I think we can—" But just then, not thirty feet away, a small clot of peasant warriors entered the barn, all of whom had obviously celebrated beyond their capacity. Two of those sleeping in the barn woke on their entry and sat up, rubbing their faces. The last man inside pulled the great door closed with a bang that woke the others. The soldiers were in a dark mood despite their recent victory over the nobles. The fierce wind gripped the sides and roof of the barn, shaking it like a child shaking a toy. Elizabeth strained to hear what they were saying over the roar of the wind.

"What'll we do with 'em then?" asked one.

"Give 'em over is all," said another. "Hold 'em as prisoners in the mill."

Another, more drunk than the rest and directly in front of her, whispered loudly, "Prisoners, ha! Ya hear me? Ha! I say!"

"Oh yeah! And who are you, Geyer, to stand up to the likes of Jaklein Rohrbach? Huh! Like to see that! Your head would roll like a punkin'."

"Thomas Geyer, that's who, you sot!" the first said, and for a moment Elizabeth thought they might start fighting. "It's my land he took. My home. It's my daughter was raped. My little Moira...give those thugs over...not likely..."

"Shut up, Thomas. You want Jaklein on us? He's back anytime now."

Thomas grunted and plopped down to sit with his back to a pole. "Jaklein Rohrbach was going to marry my little girl," he muttered. He rolled his eyes back and took another pull from the clay pot. Elizabeth could hear the liquid slosh in the jug as the men passed it around. "You mark me, Joe," Thomas said. "Jaklein wants Helfenstein dead worse'n me. Look at what he done to Toffler. Yeah, he wants 'em dead. All of 'em. I tell you—he's just waitin' for the right time, the right way. All I want's to run the pig through myself. Make 'im pay."

A half-hour later the troop had fallen into a drunken sleep, and the worst of the storm had passed. Jonathan waited another couple of minutes, then rose slowly from the hay and helped Elizabeth to her feet. She was in pain, and her crying had drained her of even more strength, but they had to move. They edged around the haystack but stopped immediately.

Three men lay sprawled before them. One had his back to the post that held the lantern. The other two were curled in fetal positions nearby. But there must have been fifty others scattered around the great barn that they weren't even aware of until now. Hunched in corners, lying on makeshift mats, leaning against posts, all asleep.

And no sign of Rohrbach.

Elizabeth felt Jonathan's hand close tightly around her own. "Do you think you can make it to the road?" he whispered.

She nodded and took hold of his arm for support. They tiptoed around and over the drunken men, across the floor, and to the barn door. He lifted the latch and opened it slowly. Enough for the two of them to slip through.

It was nearly two in the morning. The full moon was halfway down the western sky, and the stars helped bathe the country in a pearl gray light. The wind blew in gusts now, but the storm had spent itself, and there had been little rain. The fresh air helped clear Elizabeth's head, though it made the pain sharper.

The field barn belonged to one of Helfenstein's nobles. It sat on a country lane near the road that led into Weinsburg, only a quarter mile from the city walls. The path curved in a lazy S under the shadows of tall oaks. Elizabeth stared out into the darkness with Jonathan, trying to see any sign of Rohrbach approaching. About a half-mile away to their left, just outside the city wall, they could see the dark shape of an old mill. A slight movement there caught Elizabeth's eye. She pointed it out to Jonathan.

Halfway across the field and about fifty yards on the far side of some trees that separated them from the mill, several shadowy figures were making their way toward them. They cut a whispery path, the tall grass parting quietly for them. Their voices carried on the night wind. One of them belonged to a woman. Loud. Angry. Demanding.

They were still far enough away and absorbed in their own conversation so that Jonathan and Elizabeth could risk a sprint to the opposite side of the barn and then across the field to the town road.

"Ready?" Jonathan whispered. "Now." They moved quickly to the edge of the wall and around the long side toward the rear. They leaned against the back of the barn and scanned the line of trees that separated them from the road.

Elizabeth sank to her knees. "Wait," she whispered. "Wait."

Jonathan knelt beside her. The voices were getting louder, drawing nearer. He whispered, "If we can make it to the road, I can get you to Heilbronn. It's barely five miles. I have a friend in the convent there. Then I'll go on to Wittenberg and try to get Luther to come talk sense into Rohrbach. Maybe he can convince some of the other captains to lay down their weapons before it's too late."

"Jonathan—"

"Elizabeth, listen to me," he said, interrupting, trying to keep his voice calm. "Rohrbach's got the count and some others in the old mill. If he kills these men…" He stopped, trying to find the right words. "The emperor will send soldiers, trained soldiers, and they won't stop until thousands of men and women and children are dead. Someone has to stop the fighting. Luther is our best hope. I have to go."

"But why go to Wittenberg? You don't even know if Luther will be there."

"The emperor put a price on his head. If he's smart, he's there where it's safe. And if he isn't, then he's probably dead already, and none of this matters anyway. I know it isn't much of a chance, but I have to try."

They heard the barn door open with a loud creak. "Come on." Jonathan helped Elizabeth to her feet, and they ran to the trees. A half-hour later, after making sure Rohrbach hadn't posted guards to watch the road, they set out for Heilbronn.

Inside the barn Jaklein Rohrbach, the Black Hoffman, and several of Jaklein's lieutenants gathered in a corner. They had just returned from viewing the prisoners. They hadn't touched a drop of wine. The celebration would come later. Despite the hour, they still had work to do. Jaklein hadn't voiced his concern about what the other commanders might say if he killed Helfenstein. But he knew they wanted him to hold the men as prisoners to gain bargaining power, and they were trusting him to do just that.

The Black Hoffman came up behind him like a dark wind. "They won't lay a finger on you, Jaklein. I've seen to it. The spell of the Black Hoffman is on them. Our time is near. Our time to rise up. Take your vengeance. For Moira's sake. Kill them all."

Chapter 37

The door of the old mill creaked open. Only four-year-old John Helfenstein slept among the eighteen prisoners. The rest were praying or talking in hushed tones in the dark. The sound of the bar being removed startled them. They were all bound hand and foot. A few of Rohrbach's men entered and loosed the cords that held their feet. They jerked the prisoners roughly upright and forced them out the narrow door and onto the path that led into the town.

Rohrbach, the Black Hoffman, and around thirty peasants surrounded them, each carrying a pike, a pitchfork, or a sword. Jaklein stayed with Helfenstein as they moved down the path, the other nobles following.

"What? What's this? Where are you taking us?" the count demanded.

Jaklein whirled and struck him hard with the back of his hand. The countess, farther back in the line and carrying the still-sleeping child, screamed. The count stumbled backward but stayed on his feet. "No talk," Jaklein said, and pushed the count before him. After they had walked a few yards, Jaklein took Helfenstein by the arm and turned him toward a meadow. "That way," he said, pointing out into the broad field that lay between the mill and the barn. The young count looked at him for a moment and nodded.

They plodded slowly into the field and stopped near the center.

Little John had awakened at his mother's scream and was crying.

"Get yourselves in a half circle. Here," one of Jaklein's lieutenants ordered the group. The men moved slowly to form the arc and stood silently shoulder to shoulder. Jaklein took his place before them. The night was clear now and quiet except for the crying of little John.

"For crimes against your people, for abusing your power, for raping our women, for destroying our crops, for starving our children, you stand accused, and you are each and every one found guilty by this court of law."

"This is no court," one of the knights muttered.

"This is a court of divine justice, my lord," Jaklein screamed, turning on the man. "But I wouldn't expect you to recognize it, you've so little acquaintance with justice of any sort." He turned back to face the others. His voice lowered. "Well, you're about to get a taste of justice, gentlemen. You have dishonored your offices. You have brought shame on your families. You have disgraced the name of our God. And so you will die without honor. It is the judgment of this court that each of you run the gauntlet!"

Jaklein raised his sword and the men behind him formed two lines facing each other. They lowered their spears and pikes to form a double row of steel pointing toward the narrow space that separated them. The gauntlet.

The morning was cool and the breeze light, but Count Ludwig von Helfenstein was bathed in sweat as he stared at the shadowed valley between the rows of spears.

"Count Helfenstein!" Jaklein was shouting now. He paused. A steady stream of people was flowing out the city gate and down the gentle slope into the open meadow. They assembled behind Jaklein, away from the gauntlet, facing the prisoners. They were quiet now but tense as Jaklein shouted louder at the nobleman. "It's your turn, sir, to open the dance!" He swept his arm dramatically toward the double row of spears. The crowd grew restless but didn't cheer, didn't shout.

Several men moving toward them from the barn shouted suddenly, breaking the unnatural calm that had settled on the crowd. Thomas Geyer, Moira's father, was leading them. He broke through the outer circle of the crowd.

"Helfenstein!" he shouted, and lunged at the count. He slammed into him, knocking him to the ground and falling on top of him. "You! You raped my little Moira! You ruined her, you pig! You die! Die!" He broke into sobs as he flailed away at the nobleman, whose hands were still tied behind him. Jaklein and several others pulled him off and warned him to keep back.

"He's been condemned already, Thomas," Jaklein said. "Now you take your place along the gauntlet there. You'll have your chance. Go on."

Thomas grabbed his sharpened spear from one of his companions and, muttering curses, went to take his place, first in line.

Ingrid Helfenstein broke from the grip of the peasant at her side. Carrying her child, she threw herself on the ground at Jaklein's feet. "Mercy!" she cried, rolling over to clutch the screaming child. "God save us!" She managed to tear a piece of cloth from her dress to bandage little John's arm.

Jaklein lifted his face toward heaven and closed his eyes, savoring the moment, then looked down at her, his eyes shining, not blinking in the lead-dull light of the approaching morning. Words slipped out like daggers. "You pray for mercy, woman! You pray for your husband! Your ladyship cries out like a helpless girl! No! I will not spare him!" he screamed, seizing her by the arm and throwing her backward. He leapt on top of her, uncontrollable now, pressing his knees into her breast, holding his sword high above his head. Little John sat on the ground near his mother's shoulder, wailing.

"Vengeance!" screamed the Black Hoffman.

And as soon as the word left her lips, the mob answered, "Vengeance!" Excitement, like a bolt of electricity, surged through the mass of people. The mob pressed forward, hungry for a show.

One man on the outer edge of the circle stepped forward, about thirty feet from Jaklein. He carried a short, sharp knife in his right hand. "Countess Helfenstein!" he shouted, pointing the knife at her. "Your horsemen, your dogs, and your rangers destroyed my fields. When my boys tried to stop them, your men butchered 'em like pigs. Vengeance on you, woman, for the lives of my sons!" He raised the knife suddenly and threw it hard as he could at the countess.

Jaklein leapt to the side. The knife sailed high and wide of the mark, and struck little John in the arm. Blood spurted from the wound onto his mother's face.

"Mercy!" she cried, rolling over to clutch the screaming child. "God save us!"

Jaklein rose, laughing.

Another man from behind Jaklein stepped forward. He looked at the count, who remained motionless. "Helfenstein," shouted the man. "You threw my brother in prison because he didn't bare his head as you rode by! Did you ever once think of what that did to his family?" He unleashed a string of profanities as others stepped forward, shouting.

"My father," screamed one woman. "My father brought home food one day. We were starving, and my father brought home food. A hare he had killed in his own field. His own field! And you had his hands chopped off! God judge you, Helfenstein. God send you to hell!" she screamed, hot tears streaming down her face. They all began to shout then at once, and the roar grew. They would tear him apart themselves.

"Please!" the count finally cried out. "Please! Rohrbach, listen to me. I offer you my fortune. All of it."

Jaklein turned to the crowd and laughed. They all joined him so that Helfenstein had to shout to be heard. "And sixty thousand gulden from Emperor Charles himself. I swear it. I…" He sank to his knees, weeping. "On the heads of my wife and son, I swear it," he said, his eyes wide with panic.

Jaklein winked at his men and knelt to look Helfenstein in the eye. He placed the tip of his sword under the count's chin and lifted his head to face him. "My dear Count von Helfenstein," he said coolly. "Not for sixty thousand barrels of pearls would I spare you this moment. You are already on your knees, Helfenstein. It'll save you having to kneel to confess, for as I am Jaklein Rohrbach, I promise you will not live to see the sun!"

A priest stepped forward and received the count's confession as a piper started to play. At the priest's "amen," the people began to clap and several of Jaklein's men pushed the count toward the double row of spears. Jaklein lifted Ingrid to her feet roughly so that she might see her husband's death more clearly. Little John was still crying at her breast.

The Black Hoffman clapped her hands over her head, grinning as the young count approached the gauntlet. He stopped, five feet in front of the double rows of spears and glanced back toward Ingrid and little John. Then he turned suddenly and ran, screaming at the top of his lungs. He got no more that five steps before he fell, pierced through with a dozen sharp-pointed pikes.

Jaklein released Ingrid and took a few steps toward the body. He whispered low, to himself, "Vengeance. For Moira." Then he turned back to deal with those who remained in the death line.

At the end of a half-hour, the other knights, fifteen in all, had met the same fate. As the sun broke above the horizon only the countess and Little John remained. The bodies of her husband and the knights who had sworn to protect her lay strewn on the blood-soaked ground as if they had fallen into a sudden and careless sleep. Jaklein approached her. He spoke loudly again, so that he might draw the attention of the people. "You came to Weinsburg in a golden chariot. You leave it in a dung cart!" He reached into a cart that had been wheeled up and picked up a handful of horse manure and held it under the countess's nose. "Take this message to your Emperor Charles!" Jaklein tossed the manure back into the cart and signaled his men to come forward, but the countess spoke first. She held her son close and turned her eyes toward the sun. She wished it were Easter instead of the morning after. Her words were low and quiet.

"I have sinned greatly, and I deserve my lot," she said. The crowd hushed. The men, who had taken only a few steps toward her, stopped. Her voice rose slightly and she turned to face the crowd. "Christ our Savior also entered Jerusalem to the shouts of his people, yet he left that city before long, bearing his cross, mocked and spat upon by those he came to serve. He is my consolation. I am only a poor sinner, and I forgive you gladly."

Jaklein barked out an order and three of his men advanced on the woman, stripping her and then tossing her the rags of a peasant woman. The Black Hoffman laughed loudly, shouting curses on the countess and spitting on her and her child. Ingrid clutched Johnny to her breast as two of the peasant soldiers took her by her arms and threw her onto the dung cart. One of them flicked his whip at the pulling ox. The beast bellowed and strained in its yoke. The man whipped it again. The cart lurched forward out of its rut and started on its slow journey to Heilbronn with its load of dung, the Countess Ingrid von Helfenstein, and her son.

Chapter 38

Jonathan stumbled as he passed through the gates of Wittenberg. He turned to his left and knelt beside the city wall, placing his hand against the rough stone that formed the base for one side of the heavy wooden gate. Through trembling lips he prayed, thanking God for a safe journey and for Elizabeth's well-being. He had left her in the care of the sisters in the convent in Heilbronn and had spent the last four days slogging through the mud toward Wittenberg. His habit was torn and muddy, his golden hair caked with the grime of the journey.

He made his way quickly to the monastery and found Justus Jonas. But Luther wasn't there.

"He left for Dessau a few days ago," Justus said.

"He's traveling?" Jonathan asked. "If Charles's men catch him, we've lost everything. He was supposed to be *here!*" Jonathan shouted, pounding his fist into the wall.

His friend's anger surprised him, but Justus responded calmly. "Jonathan, you know Martin. He wouldn't sit still if he thought he could—"

"The peasant army has captured Count von Helfenstein and his family down in Weinsburg," Jonathan interrupted. "They are lost unless we find Father Martin quickly."

Justus turned away to think for a moment. "I know he was planning on going on to Halle after Dessau to try to make peace there," he said, half to himself. Then, to Jonathan, "It isn't far. Maybe we can catch him there."

After a quick meal and a change of clothes, Jonathan and Justus left Wittenberg in the early afternoon, headed southwest. By the time they arrived in Halle, the crisis was over, and Luther had already departed for another hot spot. The two priests spent days tracking Luther down, sometimes missing him by only a few hours. Finally, having walked scores of miles, they happened on another traveler who said he had heard Luther preaching in Eisleben, only a few miles from Wittenberg.

The two arrived late the night of Thursday, May 11. They found Luther eating at a back table in the Red Dragon, a smoky tavern on the edge of town. He rose to greet them, took one last gulp of wine to wash down a mouthful of bread and cheese, and held out his arms, grateful to see them. Tears stained his cheeks as he embraced them in a bear hug.

They had expected to find Luther worn and haggard but were surprised to see him in such apparently good health. The hard travel and constant threats on his life seemed to agree with him. He had put on weight, and his face had taken on a roundness. Still, it was obvious that he was upset over something and trying to cover it up.

Luther wiped away the traces of his tears. "Well," he said, almost smiling. "Good to see you both. It's been months. Come, sit, sit." He moved to the side to allow the young men a place at the table.

Jonathan looked at Justus, who shrugged a silent "I don't know." He turned to Luther. "Father…," he began, but Luther interrupted.

"I heard about Weinsburg," he said. "Terrible. Stupid, stupid. Here," he said, putting the plate of food between the two young men. "Some cheese, bread." He turned to fetch two cups behind the rough bar.

Justus took the bone handle of the knife and withdrew the blade from the block of cheese. He cut off a chunk and handed it to Jonathan, then took a piece himself as Luther poured wine for both of them. Jonathan saw Justus look at him across the table and slowly shake his head as if to say, "Let Martin do the talking."

Jonathan wrapped his fingers around the stem of his goblet and stared into it as if it might hold the answer to a riddle he had been pondering. Then he raised his eyes to Luther. "What's wrong?" he asked.

Martin gave him a look of resignation and sank slowly into his chair. He pulled a letter from his coat pocket and took a deep, shuddering breath. "Everything was going so well," he said. "Until this evening. One of the boys from Wittenberg brought this," he said, tossing the letter onto the table. "Frederick is dead."

The two younger men sat in stunned silence. As the Elector of Saxony, Frederick was the most powerful political ally they had. Without Frederick to protect Luther, Emperor Charles could march into Saxony, take Luther, and leave the reforms a literal heap of ashes. But the future of the reformation wasn't on Luther's mind. "He'd been ill for some time," Martin continued, wiping the tears away from his eyes. "He died a few days ago."

"Father, we're so sorry," Justus offered.

"I know. We're all sorry, Justus. He was a good man. A brave man. He did more than protect me—he protected the gospel."

Jonathan looked down at his bread and cheese. He had been at Worms when Frederick had wavered in his support of Luther—when he had, in fact, been on the verge of voting to proclaim him a Hussite and a heretic.

"And you know he stood strong at Worms," Luther continued, as if he had been reading Jonathan's thoughts. "Try as he might, Emperor Charles couldn't force him to sign the edict condemning me. No, Frederick stood fast. A good man. God bless him." He took a sudden breath as if to clear his mind, to refocus. "So, about Weinsburg. I came across one of the free lances who escaped. He said the United Contingent took the town and killed Helfenstein and all his knights. He didn't know about Helfenstein's wife, and I think there was a child."

Luther looked from Justus to Jonathan, who was staring at the bread in his hand. "I suppose you got there too late with my letter, Jonathan."

He said nothing.

"What?" Luther pressed. "Were you there during the fighting?"

Jonathan took a long drink from his cup.

"Father Jonathan." Luther said, an edge of impatience creeping into his voice.

Jonathan took a deep breath and, still looking at the bread in his hand, began the story of his trip to Weinsburg, omitting the parts about Elizabeth. He ended with the most recent news. Just yesterday he and Justus had met a knight on his way to join the army of Philip of Hesse. Philip and his armed troops were uniting with the armies of various nobles to quash the rebellion among the peasants. They were all moving south to reinforce the nobles of Wurzburg where the peasants had entered the city to the cheers of its citizens only a few days before. The princes and nobles and their forces had quickly retreated to the ancient fortress of the Marienburg and prepared for a siege as they waited for reinforcements.

Jonathan leaned forward, placing his elbows on the table. His voice was calm but with a strong undertone of command. "We've come to ask you to intercede in Wurzburg. There will be a great bloodletting if you don't."

Luther didn't hesitate. "Frederick's death forces me back to Wittenberg."

"Father, please—"

"I cannot be everywhere at once, Jonathan."

Jonathan rose and put his hands, palm down, on the table, his voice shaking. "Father, the peasants believe in you, in your words. They will listen."

"Jonathan, with Frederick gone, anything could happen. All that we've accomplished, all of our reforms hang in the balance. God wants me in Wittenberg, and that's where I'm going," Luther said flatly.

Jonathan sat down slowly and leaned back in his chair, staring at Luther.

Luther pressed his point home. "No single man can stop all the fighting. Only God can do that by changing the hearts and minds of the peasantry *and* their princes. We are not alone in this." His eyes were burning as he looked at the priest. "God is with us. I've seen him work, with my own eyes."

Jonathan sat, saying nothing. Hundreds had died at Weinsburg. But if Wurzburg fell to the peasants, thousands would perish. How could the reformation survive, baptized as it was in the blood of Christians?

Luther folded his hands. His voice was calmer now, reasoning. "You remember Brentz and Myconius," he said, looking at both young men. "Good men, faithful to the Lord and his call. I left Brentz at Halle. Six hundred citizens heard him preach, and those people stood up for the gospel. They stood up, Jonathan, against four thousand peasants, and the peasants ran. At Ichterhausen, a mob was about to destroy several castles and put their lords to death. Myconius went out and preached to them. And by God's grace those people turned around and went home. Brentz wasn't alone, Jonathan. Neither was Myconius. Nor are we. God has called me to Wittenberg to stand in the gap in Frederick's absence. I must go, or there'll be even more bloodletting." Luther folded his hands and leaned back against the wall. "Still, perhaps there is something I can do."

"But how—"

Luther interrupted him, rising from the table as he spoke. "You give them something to eat."

Justus smiled, but Jonathan only frowned. It was time for action, for taking up the sword, not for word games.

"I'll provide the loaves and fish," Luther said, enjoying the young priest's frustration. "You distribute them and we'll see if God blesses. Come on." He led the way to his room, where he wrote several letters. The first three were for Justus to carry to the commanders in Wurzburg. Martin wasn't sure who would be in charge when Justus arrived. He wanted to make sure he had one letter addressed to each of the prideful men by name.

The other letter he composed for Jonathan to deliver to Thomas Munzer. He knew the fiery preacher would be somewhere near Muhlhausen, but it would be up to Jonathan to find him. "I know what you're thinking," Martin said as he finished writing. "You're thinking you've already delivered one letter to Helfenstein, and look at the good it did." He sealed the letter and handed it to Jonathan. "We can't make men obey, Jonathan, any more than we can make them believe the truth. But we can show them the way."

It would take a miracle for the people to listen.

Both men left immediately, but Justus returned to Wittenberg only a few days later, tired and discouraged that his journey to Wurzburg had done no good at all. The peasant army had been defeated in a bloody battle, and her captains had fled by the time he arrived. On his way back to Wittenberg, he discovered a new tract that Luther had written and dispersed to the nobles in the few days he had been gone. He had picked one up and was now sitting across from an angry and sullen Luther trying to understand why he had written it.

"Martin, you know this is only going to get more people killed."

"Then so be it!" Luther said. "That's what happens when you defy the God-ordained law of the land. Or haven't you read Romans 13 recently?"

Luther had been in a foul mood ever since his return to Wittenberg for Frederick's funeral. He had gone out of his way to visit a few more towns and villages on his way home only to have the peasants greet him with insults and bounce crumpled copies of the Twelve Articles off his head. By the time he reached Wittenberg his patience was gone, and he sat down to pen the treatise that Justus held in his hand now. It was entitled, "Against the Murderous and Robbing Hordes of Peasants."

Justus took a deep breath. He knew if he angered Martin any further, he would only dig in deeper. He had to proceed cautiously. "Martin, is it possible you wrote this in anger?" he asked, trying his best not to sound condescending.

But Luther exploded. "You're not my schoolmaster, Justus! Of course I wrote it in anger. I'm still angry, and with good reason." He grabbed the pamphlet out of Justus's hand and opened it to the first page. "Listen," he said, and began to read his own words: "The peasants commit three horrible sins against God and man, and thus deserve the death of body and soul. First, they revolt against their magistrates, to whom they have sworn their allegiance; next, they rob and plunder convents and castles; and lastly, they veil their crimes with the cloak of the gospel." He creased the paper and put it down on the table as if that sealed the discussion.

"I've read the words, Martin," Justus said. "But they sound more like Aleander than like Luther. Listen for yourself." He picked up the pamphlet and continued where Martin had left off: "Crush them, strangle them and pierce them, in secret places and in sight of men. Nothing can be more poisonous, hurtful, or devilish than a rebel. It's like killing a mad dog—if you don't strike him, he will strike you, and the whole land with you. Furthermore, anyone who has the authority then hesitates to use that authority to rid the land of insurgents sins against God. If you die in fighting the rabble, then you die a happy man. A more blessed death can never overtake you, for you die in obedience to the Divine word and the command of Romans 13:1. You die in the service of love, to save your neighbor from the bonds of hell and the devil." Justus put the pamphlet down on the table. "First you supported the peasants, then you turn on them, now you call for their murder by supporting the aristocracy? The aristocracy that bends the knee to Rome?"

Martin's face was the color of an overripe plum about to burst. "I never supported the peasants!" he shouted. "They read their own selfish desires into my words and used them as an excuse to plunder and kill their rightful masters. I fight for the gospel, Justus, and I bless those who uphold the gospel, no matter who they might be. If old Beelzebub himself preaches the peace of Christ through the gospel, then I'll bless him too!"

"But these aren't words of peace, Martin. These aren't the words of the gospel."

"My judgment is God's judgment, Justus. Prove to me from Scriptures that I'm wrong. Show me!"

It was impossible, and Justus knew it. Not because he couldn't make an argument from the Bible but because anger had blinded Martin, and nothing, not even a call for Christlike compassion, would alter his course.

Chapter 39

Elizabeth had developed a fever on entering the convent at Heilbronn almost three weeks before. She drifted in and out of a fitful sleep for the better part of two weeks. The fever broke during the latter half of the second week, though headaches persisted and her improvement was slow. During the third week she began regaining her strength slowly, but her worries only increased. Jonathan should have been back days ago. She tried not to think about it, but that only made it worse. And she feared the worst for Countess Ingrid and little John. Still, she continued to improve, the severity of the headaches diminished, and she was able to eat a bit more each day.

Late one afternoon she was feeling restless and decided it was time to get out of bed. The fresh air smelled wonderful after weeks shut up in her tiny room. She was breathing in the scent of the flowers from the garden, when she saw someone who looked familiar sitting alone on a stone bench at the far end of the garden. She drew closer. It was indeed Ingrid von Helfenstein!

"Countess?" Elizabeth said softly.

Ingrid turned to face her. Elizabeth ran to her side.

"Oh, Elizabeth, Elizabeth," Ingrid said through her tears. The two women embraced and wept together for several minutes before either of them could speak. Then Ingrid told Elizabeth all that had happened to her since the horrible morning of the attack. Little John's wound was healing well, she said. But even more miraculous than that, she said, God was doing a wonderful work of healing in her own life.

"It's difficult to explain. I don't think I really understand what's happening myself. What happened in Weinsburg—God used all that to show me my own sinfulness."

"But you did nothing to deserve that. Count von Helfenstein—"

"Elizabeth," Ingrid interrupted, "all the times we talked back at the castle in Weinsburg—all that time, I was searching for something. I had everything a woman could possibly want, but I still felt empty inside. You know that feeling? I was looking for something to fill up that emptiness. And the strangest thing—with all my reading and with all my questions, I never found it until I stood out in that field and lost everything in the world that had ever meant anything to me, except little John. God let me keep little John. But he showed me that morning how poor and wretched and naked I really was, and how much I need Christ to clothe me in his righteousness."

Ingrid breathed deeply and took Elizabeth's hands in hers. "So I've been doing a lot of thinking. A lot of praying since I came here. I've spoken with the sisters, and all I know is God is changing my heart." Her eyes were shining, as if she had just accepted a marriage proposal to the king himself. "I want the rest of my life to count for something, Elizabeth. I want to help those who are suffering, the way the Lord has helped me in my suffering."

Elizabeth was stunned. She had known the countess as a fragile woman, selfish and vain, consumed with social position and material possessions. It was true that during their years together in Weinsburg Castle she had talked often about God, and in particular about the Nazarene. But Elizabeth had regarded her interest as little more than superficial curiosity. She couldn't imagine Ingrid surviving the horror of seeing her husband and friends butchered. And yet here she was, strong, resilient, talking about her faith in Christ and wanting to help others.

"But, those men killed your husband," Elizabeth said. "And they would have killed you and little John."

A deep pain born of great sorrow rose to Ingrid's eyes. "I know," she whispered. She looked at the ground as tears coursed down her cheeks. "I know. And this is the strangest part of all, Elizabeth. God has let me forgive them."

"Forgive them!" The words were out before Elizabeth could stop them.

"Yes," Ingrid said, smiling through her tears. "Oh, don't get me wrong, I must forgive them anew every day. But he has forgiven me so much more. I am determined."

"But…" The words stuck in Elizabeth's throat. *Forgive them!* She could understand strength and determination. Those were noble qualities, marks of character. She would have understood the desire for vengeance, a passion she had harbored for years against Sklaar. But *forgiveness* meant giving up all hope of justice, all hope of repaying those who had hurt her. Maybe that was what Ingrid had done. Just given up. But giving up was weak, and Elizabeth sensed a great strength in Ingrid's forgiveness. Perhaps it really was Christ in her, helping her to forgive, granting her his peace. Blessing her.

Elizabeth turned the conversation, and the two passed the next hour talking of all the rest that had happened, and finally, of Jonathan and his plans to come back for Elizabeth.

"I'm afraid something has happened," Elizabeth said. "Jonathan should have been here days ago. I must find him."

Ingrid took Elizabeth's hands in her own and spoke quietly. "Elizabeth, if something has happened, there's nothing you can do. He would want you to—"

"I don't know that," Elizabeth interrupted. "I don't know that there's nothing I could do. If he's been hurt or taken prisoner, then I need to know. I need to try at least. I didn't try at all last time to find him. Not really. I'm not going to lose him again."

"Elizabeth, Jonathan brought you here to keep you safe."

"No ma'am. He brought me here to get me well. I was wounded, but now I'm well. I need to find him."

Ingrid sighed and smiled. "It's going to be dangerous, especially now. A rider came through yesterday, and he told us that George Truchsess and his Swabian army have come all the way up from the south and have taken Boblingen. They'll march on Weinsburg next."

"But why march on Weinsburg?"

"There's only one reason I can think of," Ingrid said. "I believe he wants to punish the people for their part in what they did to my husband and our friends."

The words hit like a hammer. Elizabeth sat still for a moment, trying to think clearly. "Maybe that's why Jonathan hasn't come yet," she said half to herself. "Luther might have sent him to try to stop Truchsess. I must go." She started to pull away, but Ingrid put her hand on her shoulder.

"Then I'm going with you," she said.

"What?"

"If I go, and Truchsess is there, he might listen to me. My husband and I have known him for years. He's a rough man, but I think he will listen to reason if I can get to him and beg his mercy on Weinsburg."

Elizabeth shook her head. "Countess, little John needs you here. If anything were to happen to you…" She could tell from Ingrid's face her argument had hit home. "If I find Truchsess, I'll present myself as your attendant and ask him to come to you here."

Ingrid nodded. "I'll write a brief note commending you to Truchsess. You'll need a horse. My husband had some business with a man here in Heilbronn. He's a town burgher and owns a blacksmith shop. I'll introduce you. I'm sure he'll lend you one of his own horses as a favor to me."

They went inside the convent where Ingrid penned a note to George Truchsess, commending Elizabeth, Luther, and Jonathan to his confidence. She folded it and placed it in the inside pocket of a long black cloak.

"Here," she said, handing the cloak to Elizabeth. "It belonged to my husband. I want you to have it."

"Oh, I couldn't…," Elizabeth said.

"I have no need of it here, and it will give you at least some protection from the weather. Go on now, before it gets any later. God bless you and keep you safe, Elizabeth."

"And you, my lady."

It was already late afternoon when Elizabeth mounted the borrowed black mare and spurred her on toward Weinsburg.

The sun was setting, and Elizabeth was still three miles away when she saw the smoke of the city spiraling up into a bright orange sky. Half a mile off, she slowed her horse to a trot.

Then she stopped and stared. Weinsburg was in flames, though most of the main buildings and many of the homes were little more than piles of ash and glowing coals. Elizabeth could see shadows darting in and out between the fire and smoke—a few on foot, some mounted—the surviving inhabitants of Weinsburg, and the men who had been left behind to hunt them down.

She could hear the soldiers calling to one another but couldn't tell what they were saying. Occasionally she could hear a woman scream, or a man, and then silence. The men had exterminated an entire town. She worried about Jonathan. What if he had been here during this terror? A new fear grew in her heart, but she calmed herself. She had no proof that Jonathan had returned to Weinsburg, so she would go on the assumption—the hope—that he was safe. It was all she had.

Elizabeth arrived in the next village just as the sun was beginning to rise. When she didn't find Jonathan there, she rode on to another village farther north, and then another and another the next day, searching, denying herself sleep and food. She followed paths through the forests whenever possible, and for good reason. The main roads and the trees lining the roads of the Baden-Wurtemburg region were littered with the rotting corpses of those Truchsess had mercilessly cut down and cast aside.

On the evening of the following day she entered yet another village and came upon forty or fifty of Truchsess's men who had just arrived. She recognized a few of them. She had seen them standing in the inner circle nearest the fire in Weinsburg. She dismounted near the town store and slipped behind some boxes. She overheard two of them talking to one of the burghers. They were looking for Rohrbach.

She turned to go inside for some food, only to meet the shop owner coming out the door, carrying a pitchfork in one hand and a sack of what looked like potatoes in the other. He put the potatoes down and fumbled with the keys on the ring at his belt.

"Sir," Elizabeth said. "I wonder if you might—"

"Sorry, miss," he said, still trying to find the right key. "We're closed for the night."

"It's just that I haven't eaten in two days. I have money, I just—"

"Here!" the man said, thrusting his hand into the bag and pulling out a small, hard potato. "Take it, take it, take it! No charge!" He found the key and jammed it into the lock and twisted it. Then, without another word, he hurried off down the street, carrying his pitchfork and potato sack. Elizabeth took one of the three copper pennies she had left out of her boot and slipped it under the door.

As she turned to her horse, a light caught her eye at the far end of the street. A crowd moved out of the shadows, and leading them was Jaklein Rohrbach. She recognized him immediately. This was the man who had knocked her unconscious in the church at Weinsburg and left her for dead. Then raped her town. Then murdered her master. This was the man Ingrid had forgiven.

Men and women with torches surrounded him, talking loudly and calling out for others to follow. They carried pikes and scythes. Near the middle of the crowd, Elizabeth saw the storeowner with his pitchfork and bag.

Truchsess's men had disappeared, but Elizabeth was sure they were close by. Rohrbach couldn't have known about them, or he wouldn't have been so bold. She mounted her horse and followed the crowd as they made their way down a broad street toward one of the city wells. She stopped on the edge of the crowd, which had swelled to more than a hundred, and watched. Rohrbach mounted a low wall near the well and turned to address the crowd. She saw his face in the light of their flaming cressets. She looked back to see if any of Truchsess's men had followed them. No one. She rode forward a few paces to get a better look.

Suddenly something leapt at her out of the shadows. A woman. Black hair. Strong hands pulled her from her horse and threw her to the ground.

"My Jaklein needs this animal more than you, sweetheart!" she screamed.

"Black Hoffman! Bring her to me!" Rohrbach cried above the roar of the crowd.

A few of his men grabbed Elizabeth away from the woman and pushed her roughly toward Rohrbach.

"What's your name, woman?" he asked. He had obviously been drinking.

The woman he had called Black Hoffman forced her way inside the circle of men. She just stood there, breathing hard, staring at Elizabeth.

"My name is Elizabeth," she began, but someone came up from behind her, grabbed her hair, and yanked her head back. The man pulled a torch down close to Elizabeth's face and she saw…his yellow eyes. Sklaar!

His face was so close to hers, she could smell his breath.

"E-liz-a-beth," he moaned, dragging out the name as if it were a curse. He grabbed her by her collar with one hand and held her hair in the other and roared, "Witch! You stinking, vile devil!" And he slapped her as hard as he could with the back of his hand. Elizabeth fell to the ground as Rohrbach grabbed Sklaar and held him back.

"She's a devil, Rohrbach, and she'll take you and your men to hell with her if you don't kill her now!"

Rohrbach pushed him away, and Sklaar fell back at the feet of the Black Hoffman.

Then, out of nowhere, it seemed, horsemen came thundering down the street, shouting and brandishing swords. They surrounded the crowd quickly. "Throw down your weapons!" one of them cried. "Now!"

"Who are you, and what right do you have to give orders?" Rohrbach demanded.

"I'm the captain of the third brigade under Sir George Truchsess, and you, sir, are my prisoner."

Rohrbach put his hands on his hips and spat at the captain. "You show me George Truchsess, *captain,* and maybe I'll believe you."

"You'll see him soon enough, Rohrbach," the knight said. Then addressing the crowd, "At Frankenhausen. You people hand this man over to us and go back to your homes and we will leave you in peace."

The crowd hesitated.

"Hand him over now, or die where you stand!"

Rohrbach started to say something, but when the horsemen drew their swords, the people panicked. A few of those farther back picked up stones and began pelting the soldiers, while those in front were trying to get out of harm's way. Quickly the resistance broke down, and the crowd became frantic, screaming and trampling each other in their flight.

Sklaar grabbed a dagger from the waistband of the Black Hoffman. She shouted something at him, but Elizabeth couldn't make out the words in the blur of sound and motion. As the horsemen moved to take Rohrbach, Sklaar lunged at Elizabeth, but someone tripped and fell between them, knocking Sklaar off his feet and dumping a sack full of potatoes on the street. Sklaar jumped up quickly, but as soon as he did, he stepped on one of the rock-hard potatoes, and he was on his back again just as fast. By that time Elizabeth was up and running, pushing her way through the howling mob.

She could hear Sklaar screaming for her to stop, screaming orders for someone to stop the witch, but she couldn't see him. The soldiers spurred their horses into the crowd, bashing skulls with their sword pommels, trying to clear a path to Rohrbach who was still shouting his own orders from atop the short wall. His cries were useless. No one was listening. Horses reared in the confusion, biting and striking out with sharp hooves. Some lost their balance in the melee and tumbled over, crushing those who had fallen in the street.

Elizabeth saw Rohrbach jump from the wall, then she lost sight of him as she saw a soldier near him lift his blade and bring it down hard. She fought against the sea of people, trying to make her way back to her horse. She scrambled to her feet, squeezed between the soldiers' horses, and broke just outside the perimeter of the crowd. There she stumbled onto her own mount where the Black Hoffman had tied him to a post. The animal was wild-eyed and rearing, but Elizabeth loosed the reins from the hitch and calmed him enough to mount.

"Nooo!" the scream rose above the din, and Elizabeth knew the woman in black had discovered the body of Rohrbach. She glanced over her shoulder and saw the Black Hoffman leaping at the mounted soldier who had struck Rohrbach down. She scrambled up the horse's side before the soldier could react.

"You murdering, bloody filth!" she screamed as she scratched at his eyes with her fingers. "You killed him! You killed my Jaklein!"

The second soldier spurred his horse forward a few paces, drew back his sword, and with a mighty thrust, ran his blade through the heart of the Black Hoffman. She arched her back and clutched at the man she had been attacking. Her eyes rolled back in her head, and a rattling sigh escaped her mouth as the soldier pried her fingers from his cloak and pushed her off. She fell back onto the ground, the sword still lodged in her back, and lay beside the corpse of Jaklein.

The mob surged, shouting, screaming at the soldiers. Elizabeth's horse reared again. As she grabbed for the mane to keep her balance, someone jerked hard on her cloak, yanking her backward, almost toppling her. The cord loosened around her neck and the cloak tore free, but in the same instant, she felt a sharp, stinging pain in the middle of her lower back. Instinctively, she twisted away from her attacker. Turning, she saw his face. Sklaar! She kicked as hard as she could and caught him square in the face. He stumbled and fell to the ground with a cry, the black cloak tangled around one arm, the other beneath him— and he didn't move. The horse bolted, and Elizabeth hung on as her mount raced into the night.

Chapter 40

The tattered little town of Frankenhausen squatted under a rumpled sky. Pointed rooftops thrust upward at odd angles, threatening to tear the rain-heavy clouds that hung in deep, wet folds above the town. Gusting winds swept bits of debris from the empty streets, spackling the walls with scraps of paper mixed with dried leaves and strands of frayed cloth. The citizens of Frankenhausen huddled behind bolted doors, whispering. The same was true for the nearly eight thousand peasants encamped on a hill outside the city gates. They were listening, waiting for something to happen.

Jonathan pulled his horse up behind the cavalry. Thousands upon thousands of soldiers stood in ranks before him, waiting for their negotiator, Maternus von Geholfen, to approach the rebel Munzer with an ultimatum: surrender and save the lives of thousands of his followers, or resist and suffer the consequences.

Either way, Munzer would perish, the back of the resistance would be broken, and the ruling class would reassert itself. Jonathan had arrived just before the young envoy was due to cross the tense ribbon of land that lay between the nobles and the peasant army. He found Geholfen quickly. The negotiator had withdrawn to pray when Jonathan approached him with the letter from Luther.

355

"I will gladly present the letter to Munzer myself, my lord," Jonathan said. "It was my charge from Dr. Luther."

Geholfen unfolded the paper and scanned it quickly. "I can't imagine what Luther must have thought writing this. Surely he knows that half of these soldiers would like to see his head on a pike next to Munzer's. Still…" He read more carefully, this time all the way through. His attitude changed even as he read. "Hmm. Maybe this is the answer to my prayers. To all our prayers," he whispered as he finished. He looked at Jonathan and smiled. "It was your charge to deliver the letter to Munzer, Father, and so you have. I am merely your emissary, and that is my charge. Pray for me, Father," he said, tucking the letter inside his cloak. "Pray that Munzer will listen to reason."

Jonathan tried to pray but soon gave up. He had spent too much time berating Luther in his mind for refusing to pick up the sword on behalf of the peasants. He desperately wanted them to win, wanted Geholfen and the princes and their knights to lay down their arms and go home and treat the peasants fairly instead of bullying them and cheating them and taxing them until they hadn't enough to buy food for their families.

But he knew it would never happen. Not as long as priests such as he were offering up prayers for peace with their lips while they were lifting up swords in their hearts. God didn't listen to hypocrites. Survival was all that counted now, and the only way to survive was for the peasants to surrender. There was no hope left. Not for a righteous end. Not for true reform and justice.

Jonathan looked around and took in the scene. The combined forces of several armies were divided into camps, each flying the standard of the prince of that region. Jonathan recognized the ensigns of the Landgrave of Hesse, Duke Henry of Brunswick, and Duke John, the late elector Frederick's brother. Rank upon rank—thousands upon thousands of professional soldiers—filled the field alongside hundreds of guns and cannon. All of them trained on the rickety rampart of over-turned wagons the peasants had erected the night before.

Most of the peasant army stood in plain view behind the broken circle of wood and weathered harness. But as large as the professional armies were, the peasant army had a definite advantage in numbers. Perhaps as many as two thousand more. They might be able to win if they attacked now. If they could utilize the element of surprise.

Then, almost imperceptibly at first but growing unmistakably real, Jonathan and the gathered thousands felt the ground shudder, tremble beneath their feet, as though the earth itself feared what was coming.

Not far away, the deep thunder rumbled close overhead, dimpled the pools of water at the bottom of stone wells sunk deep in the earth. Thrumming, drumming soldiers' feet, broad blades striking hard leather-covered shields. Teutonic blood in the vein pounded out the slow, ancient rhythm of war. An approaching storm of steel and lightning—quick thrusts.

The peasant army needed a sign quickly.

Thomas Munzer walked along the peasant side of the wagon barricade, looking over his army. Thousands of men and women and a few hundred children sat in family groups, clustered according to village and tribe. Most of them spoke only with those in their own clan. Though all were German, the solidarity of the local clan was still stronger than the slowly emerging sense of regional identity. Only a few years before, their patriotism had extended only to the borders of the clan in which they were born. They shared little in common except a desire to have what had been denied them. Most of them had grown up in the villages of their ancestors, and few had ever ventured from the woods that provided the timber for their homes, the wood for their fire and the game for their table.

They followed men of action. Men like Munzer, who were willing to throw off the old ways, even if that meant throwing away the Bible to take up the sword of Christ for a cause they believed in. For months now, he had fired their imaginations in battle after battle with promises of food and wine. They would retake their lands, he told them. And they *were* winning, as he had promised, overwhelming the surprised knights and their small forces by sheer force of numbers.

It was only the beginning, Munzer told them. If they followed him, he would deliver them out of Roman bondage once and for all. They would win back for all Germany the freedom Rome had stolen and given to the princes who abused them so. And they need never doubt whom God had chosen to lead them. Their heavenly Father would give them signs, he said. Just as he had given signs to Moses, and to Jesus. Signs from heaven that Munzer was their true deliverer.

Munzer knew he must produce such a sign quickly or risk losing everything he had fought to gain. The faction that still supported him had fresh blood on their hands. The day before, he had ordered that a nobleman and a priest who had opposed him be beheaded. A show of brutal force. Necessary. Justifiable. To unify the people. Where was his lieutenant, Pfeiffer? Still at Muhlhausen? Why did he wait? Munzer had been wondering for the last two days.

Then Munzer felt it. There…that beating in the earth like a strong heartbeat. Yes. Pfeiffer. Hem them in, old boy. Yes. Flank them! Munzer's eyes blazed. There was hope after all. Victory, and glory. "Watch, young sir," he said to the envoy at his side. "You are about to see the hand of the Lord." The two men stood halfway up the hill facing south. The armies of the princes turned to face the hill behind them. But they didn't lift their arms for battle.

Thrumming, drumming, rumbling earth.

The army of Duke George of Saxony crested the hill on the far side of Frankenhausen, the flags of the forward guard fluttering in the wind. Hundreds of armed men marched, stomping the earth, pummeling the ground, striking sword on shield. A woman on the peasant's hill screamed. Wave after wave of soldiers—soldiers wielding ax and mace, lance and halberd—poured over the hill and across the plain to join the nobles, the princes, and their thousands. Blade, beak, and barb glowed silver bright even in the muddled light.

Now it was man to man, an even match. Munzer stared out at what he estimated to be at least eight thousand professional soldiers, arrayed in gleaming battle gear against his eight thousand peasants whose entire arsenal consisted of pitchforks, wooden staves, two guns, several cannon. And no ammunition. Munzer had neglected that small detail.

Maternus von Geholfen, the young man at Munzer's side, and envoy on behalf of the princes, turned nervously to face Munzer. "I remind you, sir, that I have come to you under the flag of truce, and so appreciate your protection under the code of honor that binds all soldiers."

"A pretty speech, sir," Munzer said distractedly, keeping his eyes on the swelling ranks across the way. "Now get on with your business."

Maternus reached into his cloak again for a letter handed to him only an hour before and bearing the signature of Dr. Martin Luther. Munzer had at first refused to look at it.

"Dr. Luther writes to you personally, sir," he began.

"What?" Munzer sneered as he drew close to the envoy, his leathery face only inches from the youthful face. "Dr. Easychair? Dr. Pussyfoot? Dr. Sycophant addresses Thomas Munzer personally? Ha! I would like to smell him roasted. He has such a tender jackass's flesh! Here's to Dr. Filth!" He grabbed the letter and tore it into bits and threw it into the rising wind. The pieces flew across the rampart and onto the field that separated the armies.

Geholfen's face hardened. "You understand the terms, sir," he said. "Surrender now, and you may still find mercy." By which Munzer took him to mean beheading rather than death on the rack, or worse.

It was all the goad Munzer needed. He must do something quickly, something to ensure the peasants would fight and not run. Munzer turned and strode away, up the hill. He passed one of the standard bearers as the wind picked up, agitating the peasant flags with the rainbow stitched into their fabric. "Seize that man and gag him," he told his bodyguard, indicating Geholfen. Three of them turned immediately, and walked back down the hill toward the envoy. Two of them grabbed him roughly by his arms. He struggled, but it was too late. The two held him while a third stuffed a rag in his mouth and tied another around the back of his head to keep the first rag in place.

Munzer mounted a low rock and turned to face his army of rustics. His voice rolled like thunder out across the valley. Here was David assailing Goliath. Here was mighty Gideon about to overwhelm the Midianites. "This day we shall behold the arm of the Lord," he said, "and all our enemies shall be destroyed."

An enormous gust of wind swept across the hill, nearly unsettling Munzer. His red cloak billowed around him, but he stood fast, his arms outstretched, about to call down lightning to consume the armies of the wicked. The people looking up at him saw the clouds part.

"Look!" several cried, pointing to the sky. A brilliant rainbow arced across the sky. "It's a sign! A miracle!" they cried. Munzer gazed at it, awestruck himself. But for only a few seconds. Turning back to the people, he pointed dramatically to the rainbow. "Fear nothing," he shouted to the peasants. "The Lord our God is with us. Let them fire their guns. I will catch all their balls in my sleeve." Here he pointed at Geholfen. "I tell you this, the enemies of the Lord will fall today, beginning with you."

On his signal one of the bodyguards drew his sword, while the other spun the envoy around. The blade went in at the base of the skull and up into the brain. Death was instantaneous, and there was little blood. "Throw him out onto the field. Let the dead gather up their own dead." They carried the body halfway across the field that separated the two armies and dumped it unceremoniously onto the ground.

Jonathan watched from behind the lines as the horsemen of the landgrave Philip of Hesse retrieved the young man's body and returned to the camp. Philip sat on his horse, facing his men and the collected armies of Duke John, Duke George of Saxony, and Duke Henry of

Brunswick. Behind him the thousands of peasants began to sing an old hymn: "Now Beseech We the Holy Ghost."

Philip's voice rose strong and carried across the field. Jonathan could hear it perfectly sixty yards away. "I know that we princes are often at fault, for we are but men. But we are not wrong in this. God commands all men to honor the powers that be. And by his design, whether according to his grace or his justice, I know not, we assembled here on this field constitute that power. If we don't stop them here, if we don't stop them now, then God have mercy on our wives and children, because these murderers will not. The Lord will give us the victory, for he has said, 'Whosoever resists the power, resists the commandment of God.'"

Philip raised his sword and thrust it toward the peasant line—the signal for attack. Immediately cannon thundered, splitting the air, shattering the clumsy wooden rampart, splintering the faith of the peasants. The screams of the wounded and dying were drowned in the war cry of the attacking armies. The people glanced to the rock, looking for Munzer, expecting thunderbolts to spring from the fingertips of their deliverer.

But he was gone.

Philip lifted his arm a second time. A buzzing like swarms of bees filled the air as hundreds of arrows found easy marks in the bodies of men and women and children whose only shield was their palms. The people crushed each other, trying to find shelter behind the barricade of wagons, but the cannon destroyed them along with their only protection.

Philip led his troops forward as the peasant army broke and ran, trampling each other in a mad rush, screaming in their confusion and pain, desperate for a hiding place but finding none.

Jonathan tossed a last handful of dirt onto the young envoy's grave mound. He turned then to help comfort those who were still in the agonies of death. He stared out at the thousands of dead who lay scattered about the fields and tossed in casual heaps. He hadn't stopped the slaughter, had done little or no good at all. And Luther's letter—after all that, the letter may have gotten the young envoy killed along with the rest. Who could have known with a madman like Munzer? What to do now… Bind up some wounds. Help the injured. Bury the dead. The smoke from a hundred smoldering fires burned his eyes and stung his nostrils. The heavy sweet smell of charred flesh and scorched hair curled slowly up from the burning dead and hung suspended in the gray-brown air. It looked and smelled as if hell had vomited up a bit of its excess.

Jonathan hadn't slept in the two days it had taken him to reach the battlefield. Now he was so exhausted, he fell asleep while praying with the dying. Time after time, he would begin the prayer, only to wake suddenly to find himself holding the hand of a corpse. The dead eyes stared past him. Through him. He knew they couldn't see, wouldn't blame him, hold him accountable. And yet he felt unmasked by eyes that saw more in death than in life.

He stumbled over another body and landed on his hands and knees beside the body of a young woman. Lifting his head, he tried to focus but could not. He drifted. Other images, half-waking dreams, flitted across his field of vision. Jonathan shook his head to clear the fog and forced himself to look at the girl. Her hair fell in a tangled, bloody mass across her face. He placed his fingertips against her pale, cold throat, searching for a pulse. He blinked, closed his eyes, felt himself sinking again… The dead skull turned in his hands, turned of its own accord, and spoke, though the lips didn't move. "Luther," it said, eyes fixed on the sky, clouds, stars, hell. The voice folded and cracked like old leather, a dry, whispery piece of death. A patch of matted hair, already stiff with dried blood fell away, revealing the face.

Jonathan froze. *Elizabeth!*

The voice continued, the cracked lips still as paint on a doll. "Liar, hater, lover, fool…," followed by an interminable sigh that drifted up into the smoke and away across the spired rooftops of Frankenhausen. Jonathan wept. He bent low over the corpse, stroking the face, touching the lips. Suddenly the face changed. Skin wrinkled, hair turned white. He blinked, cleared his eyes, and looked again. His tears fell on an old woman's face. A stranger.

It was then the thought came to him, shattered him like lightning, this idea, clear as God. He would leave the priesthood forever. He would go to Elizabeth, make her his bride.

A movement caught his eye. A horse and its rider crested the near horizon and raced down the gentle slope. A dark cape billowed as the black horse galloped across the broad plain, its hooves tearing the blood-stained turf, drumming the ground. Racing toward him.

Herman von Goetz, a mercenary soldier fighting for Duke George, took a deep breath and closed the door behind him, slouching with his back against the rough wooden planks. The killing earlier in the day had worn him to the bone, but the search for the peasant leaders who had escaped in the melee had been even more tiring. Somehow Munzer had managed to slip through their fingers along with a handful of other leaders and was probably halfway to Geneva by now.

Herman knew there would be a handsome reward for the man who brought Munzer back alive, and he could use the money. So he had searched for him with every ounce of his strength. Breaking through the doors of village homes. Rousting out families. Killing those foolish enough to resist. It had been a distasteful business, even for a professional soldier. Herman was, however, a soldier under orders to his lord, and his livelihood depended on following those orders. But the day was done now, and he had failed in his ultimate quest. He consoled himself with the knowledge that most of the rebels were dead. All he wanted now was a straw mattress and a night free from bedbugs.

This billeted home provided the bed, but he had seen several mice already and had heard the skittering of tiny clawed feet—a guarantee that the bed would be infested with a variety of gnawing vermin. At the end of the loft, the setting sun slanted through the long cracks between the planks that made the western wall. The mattress rested atop a wood-framed bed with rope slats. A pile of woolen cloth lay in a disheveled heap in the center of the bed. Herman took a step forward and heard a moan. The pile of rags moved.

Instinctively, Herman reached for his sword. "Who are you? Show yourself, or I'll run you through where you lie!"

"Oh, please, sir," the voice moaned again. The form shifted, but the man's face remained turned toward the wall. "I'm sick. Please..." The man sounded delirious.

Herman glanced into the shadows in the corners under the rafters. He drew in a shallow breath. He was painfully aware that he had precious little in the way of protection in case this was a trap. He had removed most of his heavy armor before climbing to the loft, and so was left wearing his chain-mail shirt, the tace and tasset around his hips, and his leg pieces. He consciously loosened his clenched fist as he knelt at the side of the bed, slipped the point of his sword under the fold of the man's sack and flipped it back. "Who are you?" Herman demanded.

"Please...fever." The man's head was bandaged, and he remained facing away from Herman, not moving.

Herman reached down and rummaged through the sack, looking for money. A folded pouch tied with string bulged with paper. He snipped the string and dumped the papers, all letters, onto the floorboards. "What's this?"

The invalid lay perfectly still. He seemed to have stopped breathing.

Herman picked up a handful of letters, all addressed to the same person, presumably the man on the bed. He walked around the end of the bed, turning his back to the wall. The floorboards groaned under his weight. *Oh, you're a stealthy one, you are.*

He glanced at the man on the bed. Strips of yellow sun cut across his body at odd angles. The head bandage was dry, though the man was sweating. His eyes were closed, and his lips moved slightly as though he was praying. Herman held the tip of his sword at the man's neck as he moved the pages from side to side, trying to make out the salutations. A strip of light fell across the black scrawl at the head of one letter. Herman had never been much of a reader, but he could recognize names if given time. Slowly, silently, he formed the name at the top of the page with his lips.

Then again, lowering the letter, gazing hungrily at the man on the bed, he said the name. A name that only hours before had been weighty enough to move an army of thousands but which now hung in the air insubstantial as the particles of dust in the slanting light: "Munzer."

Chapter 41

Jonathan lifted the towel from the basin and sat on the edge of the bed. Tears streamed down his cheeks as he wrung the excess water back into the bowl. He folded the cloth and gently pressed its coolness against Elizabeth's brow as she lay insensible on the straw bed.

It was she who had raced to his side. Their eyes had met, but before either of them could speak, she had fallen from her mount, unconscious. Jonathan had wrapped his arms around her and pulled her limp body to him, instinctively sheltering her from the fall. He had felt something warm and wet between his fingers as they pressed against her back. He pulled his hands away to see them stained crimson. Carrying her quickly across the battlefield, he stepped around the dead and dying, caring now only for the one in his arms.

He burst into the first house inside the city gates and called out for help. The home was empty. He found the family bed quickly and lowered his charge onto it. He rummaged through the house and found bits of cloth to clean and dress the wound. Taking a pitcher with him, he rushed outside and down the street, in search of the town well. He found it quickly and returned with the pitcher full of clear water.

He peeled back Elizabeth's torn shirt, revealing an ugly gash. The blood had thickened around the wound, so the bleeding had stopped, but her breathing was shallow and uneven. He dressed the tear in her flesh as gently as he could. Then he waited. She slept for most of that day, and through the night. Then just before dawn the next morning, Jonathan lifted his head from his arms. He had been asleep on a stool beside the bed, but he was sure he had felt her hand touch his hair—there, her fingers curled softly. She touched his hair with her fingertips and whispered his name. Then her eyes fluttered open.

"Jonathan! Ah!" she whispered, throwing her arms around his neck and clinging to him but wincing at the sharp pain in her back.

"Shh, easy, easy," he said softly, easing her back down onto the rough blanket but still holding her. He felt her body tense as her back touched the bed. "Oh, Elizabeth, I thought I'd lost you. You must lie still, or the bleeding will start again."

She wept into his shoulder, great sobs wracking her small frame. He held her for the first few minutes of a lifetime. "Seems every time we meet I'm putting you back together again," he said, laughing and crying at the same time.

She laughed but caught her breath quickly.

"I'm sorry," Jonathan said. "No more jokes, I promise. Here, drink this." He lifted a cup to her mouth. She took only a little sip, then settled back on the bed. "Who did this?" he asked, looking into her eyes. His voice was tender, but his eyes were blazing.

She squeezed his hand and turned her face away, tears filling her eyes again. "Sklaar," she whispered.

Though Jonathan had never heard the man's name before, he knew who Sklaar was. The man who'd lied to him on the bridge, who'd kept them apart all these years.

"Elizabeth, I swear the man will—"

"No!" she said suddenly. She shut her eyes tightly against the pain. "No," again, more softly. "Promise me you won't."

"He almost killed you. I…"

"Promise," she insisted, squeezing his hand and looking at him with unblinking eyes.

Jonathan didn't say anything but took a deep breath and covered her other hand with his own. "Heart of my heart," he said, smiling softly. "Do you love me as I love you?"

She stared at him still, wonder filling her eyes.

"My only hope, my only prayer, is that you love me as I love you," she whispered.

"Then," he said, "you must know that the one who wounds you wounds my own heart. Would you have me suffer so?" Without waiting for an answer, he asked her to tell him what had happened if she felt strong enough. She nodded and drank deeply from the cup he offered her.

She pulled his hand to her cheek and, turning her head slightly, kissed the fingers that curled around her own. She began in a soft voice, relating all that had happened to her from the time he'd left her at the convent in Heilbronn until the night she barely escaped Sklaar.

"I was just trying to hold on," she said "Then someone tried to drag me from my horse, pulled my cloak off—oh…" Her eyes filled with tears.

"What? What is it?" Jonathan asked.

Elizabeth shook her head and dried her tears. "I was carrying a note from the Countess von Helfenstein to George Truchsess, asking for mercy for Weinsburg. It was in a pocket of the cloak. I was too late. Then Sklaar was there, pulling at my cloak. As soon as it came free, I felt the knife in my back. I looked back and just caught a glimpse of him. I kicked at him, then fell across my horse's neck. I guess he bolted and ran. I don't remember much else after that. Just bits and pieces. Somehow I held on. Until I found you."

Jonathan was breathing hard. He nodded slowly, making a private, solemn resolution. "As God lives, I will never lose you again," he said.

Elizabeth looked away. "Jonathan," she said softly. "I came to warn you. But we cannot—"

"Elizabeth," he said, interrupting, "look at me. Look at me."

She turned her head to face him.

"What do you see?"

"I see a priest," she said quietly. The meaning in her words was clear.

"Then your eyes deceive you," he said. "You see this cowl, and you see a priest. But God looks on the heart, and he sees a man in love with the dearest, the bravest of women. From this night forward, I am no priest. But I would be your husband, if you would have me."

Her lips trembled as she touched his face gently with her fingers. "When you look at me, what do you see?" she whispered.

"My love. My life."

"Then your eyes deceive you. For you cannot love what I am."

Jonathan smiled uncertainly. "What could...?"

"Jonathan," she said, her voice soft but firm. "I am a Jew."

Chapter 42

Emperor Charles looked up from his writing desk. Girolamo Aleander approached with a quick, sure step. Charles had learned to read Aleander over the years—a confident approach invariably meant a favorable report.

"What news?" Charles asked.

Aleander stood before the emperor, his hands folded, obviously containing his excitement. "Luther will marry the nun in two weeks, sire."

Charles leaned back in his chair and stared at Aleander. A slow smile creased his face. "You're serious," he said.

Aleander nodded.

"Ha!" the laugh exploded from Charles and rang off the walls. "This, this is what we've been waiting for."

"Precisely, sire," Aleander said calmly.

Charles rose and began to pace behind his desk, speaking as much to himself as to Aleander. "My armies can't touch him in Saxony without starting an all-out war. Every trap fails. He's too wily for that. But a woman! A nun! Who needs an army when you've got lust to fight your battles for you?" He laughed again and shook his head.

"Rid yourself of him now, my lord," Aleander said. "John Frederick can't possibly continue to protect Luther in this blasphemous marriage."

Charles sat down slowly. "No, Father. You move too quickly. John Frederick may be new to his office, but he is his father's son. If anything,

370

he's more committed to protecting Luther than his father was. We will wait for the marriage. God may well do our work for us and strike Luther and his whore dead on the spot."

Aleander shifted uncomfortably. "My lord, we have already seen that God's patience is long with this heretic. The arm of the Lord must strike and strike soon—"

Charles held up his hand. "God's patience was long with Pharaoh too, Father. Until he struck his firstborn dead." He paused and leaned back in his chair. "What happens to children born to a nun and a priest?"

"If the thing lives, it would be evil. A son of the devil."

"Deformed?"

Aleander tilted his head and looked at the emperor as though he had never seen him before. Then he smiled. "Undoubtedly."

Charles steepled his fingers. "God is a politician, Father. He knows the common people are ignorant. They need a sign to convince them that Luther is the devil in a cowl. The nun is probably already pregnant, wouldn't you say?"

"There are rumors to that effect, sire."

"Then, whether she miscarries or gives birth to a monster, either way…"

"Luther is judged," Aleander said, completing the emperor's thought. "And the people will abandon him."

"And the people will abandon him," Charles repeated. "Now if you will excuse me, Father, I still have some work to do. Good night."

Aleander bowed and started to leave but turned back at the door. "But if God doesn't judge him? If he doesn't strike Luther or the child?"

"Then," Charles said, "*we* become the arm of the Lord."

JUNE 13, 1525
THE BLACK CLOISTER, WITTENBERG

Luther stood with his hands folded in front of him. He had asked for a private audience with his soon-to-be bride just before the vows. On the other side of the door, along with the few guests who had come at Luther's invitation, Pastor Bugenhagen waited patiently to perform the ceremony.

Martin cleared his throat. "Kate," he said, his voice steady.

"Herr Doctor."

Luther frowned. He recognized the look she was giving him now. He had come to think of it as "the garden stare"—the same gaze she had cast on him in Frau Reichenbach's garden the day she had agreed to marry him without his having asked. It tended to turn his mind to jelly.

"You know there's a price on my head."

"I do, my lord," Katherine said. There was no worry or fear in her voice. It was just a statement of fact.

"I want to make sure that you grasp this, Kate. I have no earthly goods to my name, and I may not live long enough to make you much of a husband. You understand that?"

"I understand, through my lord's gracious instruction in the holy Scriptures, that God is sovereign, and that I needn't worry about 'earthly goods' since they are all in the providence of our heavenly Father. Is there more that I should know?"

"No. No, no. Nothing more. I just wanted to make sure you understood, that I, uh…"

"Have no money and may not live long," Katherine said, completing his thought for him. "I do, Herr Doctor, thank you."

"Certainly. You're welcome. Uh, there is one more thing. Small thing. I know we haven't had much time to talk," he said. "To work things through…"

"My heart is calm, my lord," Katherine said. "And it is yours, as you will."

"Kate, Katie," Martin said, touching her on the arm to stop her. He had grown to appreciate his young bride's intellect, but her quick tongue was another matter. "Let me finish. I know that what I said earlier about my reasons for marrying you must have come to your ears, and I—"

"Oh yes, my lord. You marry me not because you love me but 'to spite the pope and the devil,' I believe were your words," Katherine said simply.

Luther winced and nodded.

"You see, I will make a good wife, Herr Doctor," she said with a hint of a smile. "I listen carefully."

"Yes, well. I just want to get this cleared up before—"

"We get married."

"Kate, please. I'm forty-two years old. I need to say this before I die."

"I'm sorry, my lord."

Luther took a deep breath. "I wanted to apologize for my words. They weren't intended for your ears. In fact, those words, to be perfectly honest—and I always want us to be honest with each other, Kate. That's very important. Always, always honest. Am I understood?"

"So far, my lord," Katherine said.

"Very good. Well then, those words, as I was saying, are no longer true. I do love you, Kate. Not as a husband should, I'm sure. Not yet as our Lord loves his church, as I'm commanded to do in the Scriptures. But I confess. I confess I do love you, Kate." He cleared his throat again. "So. There it is."

Her eyes were softer now, compassionate. As if she had just heard a little boy admit that he stolen some candy that was too sweet to resist, unaware that the candy had been intended for him all along.

She reached up and touched his face tenderly with her fingertips, and smiled.

Martin took her hand and kissed it, then placed it on his forearm.

"Are we ready, then, Katie?"

"We are, sir," she said. And as they stepped across the threshold and into the chapel, a small tremor rippled through the earth all the way down to Rome.

JUNE 27, 1525

11:05 P.M.

WITTENBERG

"Good night, good night!" Luther called out to the magistrate. The last guest had finally gone home. Martin had married Kate two weeks before, but they had postponed the public ceremony until this day—a day that had begun with parades in the streets of Wittenberg and ended with a reception in the Black Cloister, which was to be their home. The exhausted groom closed the door to the cloister and leaned against it as he stared at Katherine.

"We would have had to make breakfast before long, wife," he said, smiling.

Katherine walked up to him and straightened his collar. "You see, Doctor! It's good the beer ran out after all. And you were so upset. All that blustering, and God meant it for good."

Martin laughed. "You'll be teaching my classes before long, Katie."

"I wouldn't be much of a teacher," she said smiling. "I could only teach what you have taught me."

"Oh, ho! How should I take that? That you lack originality or that you lack a good teacher? I'm going to keep my eye on you, yes…" He embraced his young wife, kissing her gently on the forehead, and then, almost without thinking, on the lips. Martin pulled back slowly from their embrace, studying her face. There was more to this woman than he had calculated.

He had begun to discover that there were more than political or doctrinal advantages—not to marriage in general but to marrying *this* woman. She was his equal in many ways, and his love for her was blossoming. It was so unexpected at his age, and so delightful.

But it was still a confusing business. In his rush to establish a precedent for all clergy in marrying, Martin found himself tripping over a quite singular joy, and he wasn't sure how to regain his balance. Martin looked around, suddenly aware that he was staring at Katherine. Or rather that he was watching her staring at him.

"It's a big house, Kate," he said without knowing why.

"Then we must keep it full," she replied, a tease in her voice.

He held her close for a few seconds, then they turned to go upstairs.

Just before they entered their bedroom, there was a knock on the door.

"Someone must have left something," Katherine said.

"I'll get it. You go on in."

He waited until his wife had entered their bedroom and closed the door before he opened the door to the outside. "Friend, couldn't this wait—?" he began, but the words died on his lips. There, kneeling before him on the steps of the Black Cloister, was a man in simple peasants' clothing. Martin stooped to lift him by his arms. The man rose slowly but kept his head bowed. Martin put his hands on the man's shoulders, peering with disbelieving eyes first at his bleeding feet, then at the drawn face. "Andreas?" he whispered. It was indeed his old friend and recent enemy Andreas Karlstadt. The man who had served with him at Wittenberg and later railed against him in Jena, calling down God's curses on him and practically running him out of town.

The man nearly collapsed into his arms. "I beg you, Father Martin," he said. "Grant me shelter. I know I have no right to expect it, and I have abused your good name in word and deed, but I have nowhere else to go. They'll kill me if they catch me, and I can't run anymore."

He had the audacity to seek sanctuary under Luther's own roof! On the night of his wedding feast!

Karlstadt lifted his head slowly. "Please?" he asked, his eyes full of tears.

"Come in. Here, we have some soup left." The voice belonged to Katherine. She came up behind Martin, took Karlstadt by the arm, and helped him inside.

Martin was surprised at her sudden, quiet appearance and more than a little flustered. "Ah, yes. My wife. Andreas, you remember Kate—Sister Katherine von Bora. We were just married…this morning, in fact."

"Come, Doctor Karlstadt," Katherine said, "come into our home. You are welcome here."

Karlstadt mumbled something, then made a feeble attempt at a bow, though he could do little with his arm around Katherine's shoulder. She started to help him inside.

"Uh, Kate…" Martin started to say something, though he wasn't sure what.

She cut him off with a smile as she led Andreas into the kitchen. Luther sighed and shook his head. Katherine winked at him over her shoulder. "I believe we have a bed to spare," she said to her guest. "Oh, and there's a little of that good Torgau beer left, husband, if you would be so kind."

"Ah," he said, trying not to show his surprise. "I thought it was all gone."

"I kept some back for you to have tomorrow," Katherine said. "But it seems the Lord had me save it for one with a greater need." The news seemed to strengthen Father Andreas, and he stood under his own power.

"So that's the way of it," Luther mumbled to himself once she was gone. "Lord, who is this woman you've sent me? She serves Torgau beer to my enemies and invites them to share our wedding night." Luther scratched his head and yawned as he made his way to the kitchen. "Lord Jesus," he said half aloud, "I only wish my Kate had been keeping the inn on the night you were born."

Chapter 43

"You're crazy," Justus said, fighting a yawn. "Martin would never approve it."

Jonathan was wide awake, as he had been most of the night. "He doesn't need to know," he whispered.

Lightning flashed, illuminating the blue-black shadows of the chapel. Thunder pounded the walls as a sudden rush of rain and wind lashed the white stone, blowing through one of the high, open windows in wet gusts. Stubby votive candles flickered in uneven rows, casting long, nervous shadows on the walls at the front of the sanctuary.

For the moment, Jonathan held the decided advantage in his conversation with Justus, and he was intent on keeping it. He had to convince his friend to help him, and there wasn't much time.

Justus was still half-asleep. Jonathan had roused him from a sound sleep just a few minutes before, asking Justus to follow him to the chapel. He would explain later.

Justus got dressed quickly and followed Jonathan across the courtyard to the chapel. Now, sitting on one of the forward benches, he rubbed the sleep from his eyes and tried to focus his thoughts. "He'll find out, and you know it. He always finds out," he said through an enormous yawn.

"How? How could he? We're the only ones who will know."

"Jonathan…"

"No, Justus. Listen to me. You can do this. Luther just got married himself. Even if he does find out, how could he object?"

"Luther didn't marry a Jew."

"No, he married a nun. Please, Justus."

"An ex-nun, if you want to press the point."

Jonathan had anticipated his objection. "Not in God's eyes, she wasn't. Not according to the church. The woman had taken a vow, and she was still a nun when he married her. He was still a priest."

"You have taken a vow too."

Jonathan was quiet for a moment. He knew that his decision to marry Elizabeth meant he was breaking a promise he had made to God. But he should never have made the promise in the first place. Jonathan felt that God would forgive him. He was equally sure Luther would not. The one thing he knew with certainty was that Elizabeth was part of God's purpose for his life. Nothing could shake their love for each other. Nothing could change his resolve to marry her. If Justus wouldn't marry them, he would find someone somewhere who would. "You won't do it then?" he asked, impatiently.

"I didn't say that."

Jonathan threw up his hands.

Justus took a deep breath. "Jonathan, Elizabeth isn't a Christian. She's a Jew. Even if I said the words, you wouldn't be married in the eyes of the church."

"She is a Christian—she's professed faith. Being Jewish doesn't mean she can't believe. She can experience God's saving grace just as much as you and I. "

Jonathan leaned in close and spoke quietly. "I love her, Justus, and I know she loves me. And by God's grace she'll grow in the Lord, just as I will."

Justus looked at him for a long moment without saying anything. "I don't feel good about this—she's still a Jew."

"You're afraid of what Luther will do if you marry us?"

"No. I'm afraid of what *you* will do if I don't."

JULY 2, 1525
WITTENBERG

"Here, this way," Jonathan said as he led Elizabeth by the hand through the dark streets of Wittenberg. The moon was full, but the narrow alleyways were cloaked in deep shadow. "Justus said he would meet us near the trees down by the river." The streets were still busy, though it was already well past midnight.

Elizabeth stopped suddenly. "Jonathan!" she whispered. She was looking behind them. "There…someone…"

"What?" Jonathan asked.

"Someone following, I thought…"

Jonathan put his arm around her. "No one knows. I made sure. Only Justus, and he promised not to tell. Come on. We have to stop by the cloister for one last thing, then we'll meet him down by the river."

They made their way quickly to the Black Cloister. Jonathan ran inside to his cell and retrieved a small package, then back to Elizabeth. They walked across town, through the Elster Gate, and down a gentle slope toward a line of trees near the river. They could see the glow of a fire reflecting off the lower branches of a few trees.

"There," Jonathan said, and they cut through the trees toward the light.

They walked into a small clearing just up the bank from the Elbe. A fire crackled, burning brightly in a small circle of rough stones.

"Justus?" Jonathan called, but no one answered.

Suddenly Elizabeth took Jonathan's arm, holding it tightly. He turned to see that she was looking past the fire, into the shadows. Something moved, shifted. A rustle of cloth.

"Justus?" No answer. "It was nothing," he whispered to Elizabeth. "He'll be here soon."

"He won't, you know." The voice came out of the darkness—somewhere back in the shadows on the opposite side of the fire.

Elizabeth shrieked.

"Sklaar!" Jonathan exclaimed.

There was a long sigh, as though the trees themselves were exhaling the darkness. "You really should be more careful with the letters you carry, my dear," the voice said. "They could fall into the wrong hands so easily."

"Where's Justus?" Jonathan shouted. "What have you done to him?"

"He won't be bothering us," Sklaar whispered. "But then there's no need for a priest. The witch is already married to me."

"Come out where I can see you," Jonathan said. He wanted to run into the shadows, to get his hands on the man who had caused him and Elizabeth so much pain, but he couldn't leave Elizabeth unprotected.

And he wouldn't run. This had to end here. Now.

"Leave the witch, priest," the voice hissed. "She's mine. My wife. My witch..." The voice floated in and out through the shadows, making it impossible to pinpoint.

"Coward!" Jonathan shouted. "Come out and fight!"

Jonathan heard something move off to his left, saw a glint of a blade in the firelight as it came hurtling through the air toward him. He raised his arm just in time. The knife cut deep into the flesh of his forearm. In the next instant a black shape emerged from the shadows, howling, racing across the clearing toward Jonathan and Elizabeth, black cloak billowing behind, another knife raised to strike.

Jonathan reacted instinctively. He lunged at Sklaar's legs, hitting him squarely below the knees. Sklaar toppled head over heels, the knife skittering across the hard dirt, and he landed on his face with a thud.

Jonathan leaped toward him, in an effort to pin him to the ground, but Sklaar rolled to the side, and Jonathan landed hard where Sklaar had been, knocking the breath out of his lungs. The doctor was on his feet again in a flash.

Silhouetted against the fire, he retrieved the knife and held it in both hands, as he raised his arms for the final blow, then another shout! From the far side of the fire, Justus came flying across the clearing and slammed into Sklaar, knocking him into the flames. The long black coat ignited immediately. Sklaar rose quickly, screaming and cursing. He yanked at the cord that tied the cloak around his neck, but it wouldn't come loose. Justus picked himself up and ran to try and douse the flames, but Sklaar was a human torch now and neither Justus nor Jonathan could get close. He lurched from side to side, the cloak a billowing sheet of flame.

He began to run toward the bridge. He took only a few steps and stumbled over something in the dark. Rising slowly, his arms flailing like a wounded bird, an incandescent phoenix, he whirled in a fiery arabesque, stumbling to the center of the old bridge. As he turned, Jonathan caught a glimpse of his spectacles, the thin wire frames glowing bright orange now, curling, melting into flame.

Sklaar wasn't screaming anymore. The only sound now was of the fire that engulfed him, consuming cloth, hair, skin as he bent slowly over the bridge's railing and fell. Justus raced to the bridge, but Sklaar had disappeared beneath the current of the swift-flowing Elbe. The sickly sweet smell of burning flesh hung heavy on the night air.

Justus turned to walk back to Jonathan and Elizabeth. On the near side of the fire, he kicked something in the darkness. It clinked. Sklaar's black doctor's bag. He reached down to pick it up but found that it was surprisingly heavy. He carried it with both hands across the clearing to where Elizabeth was tending Jonathan's wound.

"Is it bad?" Justus asked.

"It could have been worse. What's this?" Jonathan asked.

"The old man's bag," Justus said, dropping it to the ground with a thud and the dull sound of metal on metal. "He must have stumbled over it while he was trying to run. I can't believe how heavy the thing is. Here, let's see." He unclasped the three leather straps that secured the top of the bag and pulled apart the hinged top.

It was full. Of gold coins.

ONE WEEK LATER
THE GARDEN OUTSIDE THE BLACK CLOISTER

Justus stood in the center of the garden, facing Jonathan and Elizabeth. Katherine Luther, married less than a month herself, was serving as witness and lookout. The ceremony was almost over.

"Father Justus, if you please," Katherine said, glancing over her shoulder. "We only have a few minutes."

Justus cleared his throat. "Very well then. Jonathan, do you promise to love and honor Elizabeth in all the conditions of life for as long as you both shall live?"

"I do."

"Elizabeth, do you promise to love and honor Jonathan in all the conditions of life as long as you both shall live?"

"I do."

Justus took a deep breath. "Then as an ordained priest of the church, I—"

"Wait," Jonathan said, holding up his hand. "Wait, Justus."

"Jonathan, please, there isn't time."

"No, I won't rush this." He turned to face his bride and withdrew the amethyst necklace he'd given her those years before. Then, placing it around her neck, he took her hands in his. "Elizabeth von Gershom, I love you. No man will ever love you more. No man will ever love you better than I love you now, in this moment. I ask only that you grant me the favor of loving you tomorrow and every day for the rest of our lives."

She reached up and touched his cheek. "On one condition," she whispered. "that you grant the same favor to me."

"He's coming!" Katherine whispered, and ran down to take Jonathan's arm.

"I pronounce you husband and wife," Justus said as he quickly made the sign of the cross. "What God has joined together let no man put asunder, amen."

Katherine was shuffling the wedding party around even as he spoke. "As we planned now—Elizabeth, you over beside Father Justus. Jonathan, you here on the left. Now we're walking, we're walking."

The four had just turned and started up the path when they heard Martin clear his throat before opening the garden gate. He looked up, obviously surprised to see his wife and friends enjoying a walk together in the late afternoon.

"Well, well! Good day to you, wife!" he said, laughing. "Good day to you all."

"Doctor," Katherine said, smiling along with the others. "We were just enjoying each other's company." She took in a short breath. "The roses are finally out."

"Yes, so I see," Luther said looking around. "Seems the blush of the rose has found its way to your cheeks, Kate."

"Really?" she said, putting her had to her face. "I must have picked up some sun."

"Mmm," Luther nodded, looking around at the other members of the group, who were all trying to appear nonchalant. "Seems you've all picked up some sun. Well," he said, clapping his hands together and cracking his knuckles. "Don't let me keep you. I was just coming out for a breath of air." There was a collective sigh as they parted and Luther started down the path. They had almost made it to the garden gate when Luther turned for a final word. "You know," he said. The group stopped and turned to face him as one. Luther was rubbing his chin thoughtfully. "It strikes me this garden could be put to some use."

"Some use, my lord?" Katherine asked.

"Mmm-hmm," Luther nodded sagely, surveying the grounds. "Use your imagination, Kate. It would make a fine setting for any number of special occasions." He turned slowly, still looking at the beautiful flowers, and started to walk away. "Especially weddings."

He placed his hands behind his back as he walked into the heart of the garden, whistling merrily.

Chapter 44

June 7, 1526
Wittenberg

The door opened slowly. The crowd of priests, soldiers, students, and faculty that packed the hallway outside Luther's bedroom in the Black Cloister had for the last few hours been engaged in lively conversation that several times had erupted into shouting, but they all quieted immediately on seeing the young woman emerge from the shadow of the doorway.

Luther, standing nearest the door, spoke. "Elizabeth—is all well?"

She stepped forward into the light, and his question was answered. Her face was radiant, though tears streamed down her cheeks. "It's a boy!" she said. "A *perfect* little boy, and Katherine is fine!"

A tremendous shout rang in the hall, drowning out Elizabeth's words. Elizabeth shushed them quickly. "She wants to…"

One of Duke George's soldiers pushed his way to the front of the crowd, interrupting Elizabeth again. He had been sent by the pope to confirm that the child was of the devil. "I must see the child."

Luther turned to him. "You may see my son when I *say* you may see my son."

"Father," the soldier said quietly, "I must take these men as witnesses to see the child."

Justus put his hand on Martin's shoulder. "There's wisdom in this. If they see the child in the presence of witnesses, there can be no claim of switching a demon child for, say, the healthy child of a peasant who had too many mouths to feed."

Martin nodded. "Very well," he said, turning his attention to the gathered soldiers, "you will see the child. In our company. And we will all bear witness that he is perfectly normal and healthy. The fruit of a marriage blessed by Almighty God. Elizabeth, see to it, if you please. Ask if we may enter for a brief moment. Tell Kate it's for the sake of peace and as a favor to me."

"She wishes to see you alone, sir."

"Really?" Luther asked as he followed Elizabeth back into the room and shut the door.

A quiet debate erupted on the other side of the door, but for Martin and Kate Luther it may as well have been on the other side of the world. Katherine had drifted into a brief sleep. Elizabeth took the babe gently from her side and handed him, wrapped in a clean, white blanket, to his father.

His hair was thick and black, and he smelled clean and fresh and new and alive. Martin had never held a newborn child before. The aroma of his son filled him with a deep and unexpected joy. He touched his son's tiny fingers one by one with his thick index finger. Then he counted his toes and breathed a grateful sigh when he reached ten. The boy kicked against his father's touch. Luther smiled. "Kick, little one," he whispered. "That's what I did to the pope, but I got loose."

Katherine stirred, and Martin laid his son beside her. He immediately began nuzzling his mother's breast, hungry for his first meal.

Martin knelt at her side, holding her hand. "Kate, you are a wonder. God bless you, my sweet wife. You've given me a son. We have a wonderful son."

"Hans," Katherine whispered. "Isn't that what you said you wanted to name your first son?"

"Hans, yes!" Luther said, smiling through his tears. "For Johannes Bugenhagen who married us and brought me such joy. Johannes Luther. It's a good name. A strong name." He tried to adopt a more dignified tone for what he was about to say. But as he said, "Kate, you must know," his composure failed him. He simply broke down, laughing and crying at the same time. "I've never been so happy in my life. Thank you, Kate. Thank you for the greatest gift you could ever give me."

Someone knocked lightly on the door.

Martin looked into his wife's eyes. "Duke George has sent a welcoming committee. Do you feel up to it, Kate?" he asked. "I know it's an imposition and a bother, but it would keep rumors at bay, at least a little."

The baby had finished nursing and was sleeping. Katherine covered herself and propped herself up in the bed. "Hand me my brush there, please, Elizabeth. I can't have the duke's soldiers seeing me like this." She brushed her hair and then tied it back with a kerchief. She wrapped her son in a small blanket, and Martin stood by her side. "Ask them in," she said to Elizabeth.

As the door opened and the soldiers of the pope and of Duke George entered, Martin caught a glimpse of Pastor Bugenhagen, the priest who had married Katherine and himself. Martin called out to him. "Father! Father Bugenhagen!" The priest poked his head into the room.

"Martin, I'm so happy for you. God bless you and Katherine," and he started to withdraw, but Luther stopped him.

"No, no, please come in. I want you to meet your namesake—and to ask you a favor."

"My namesake? Martin, I…," Bugenhagen stammered.

Martin, the professor, the orchestrator of events, continued, "And please bring Justus and Jonathan with you there. Yes." The three entered, and Luther introduced them. "These gentlemen, as I'm sure you are aware, come from our old friend Duke George. It seems that Rome has asked him to confirm that our child is, in every way, human and not demonic. Your witness will put a seal to the matter. Please, good Father, examine little Johannes in the presence of these men and let us hear your verdict."

Bugenhagen smiled warmly as he passed Martin. He examined the child quickly, then gladly affirmed that Martin's son was indeed human and quite healthy.

Luther turned to address the soldiers of Duke George. "This child, fully human in every respect, will be raised in the fear and admonition of the living God, until he comes to repentance by God's grace and is born to new life in Christ Jesus. You tell His Lordship I will pray that God might unstop his ears—so that, even in Rome, he might hear the cry of this wonderful child—this fruit of a holy union, blessed by God and man alike."

"You dare to speak to His Holiness in this—"

"I am no Moses lacking for words," Luther interrupted. "But the pope would pretend to be Pharaoh. We have become too many for him here in Germany. So he orders the children of our union destroyed. Not out of any real dread that this would be some two-headed monster but out of a deeper fear that perhaps this child will grow up to lead God's people to freedom from Roman bondage and so deplete his coffers. But look!" Luther said, pointing to Elizabeth. "Here we have a Jewish midwife! Even this girl is not afraid of Pharaoh Clement! No, we don't need to wait for this child to grow to escape the grip of Rome. His birth is simply the confirmation of God's blessing on his holy reformation. The great exodus has already begun. We have crossed the great sea turned red by the blood of peasants and nobles alike. We are a free people, and we will not go back to Egypt. In fact," he said, his eyes twinkling. "It's time for this little Moses to pass through the Red Sea! George!" Martin called out to an his old friend George Rorer. "I know we were planning on doing this a bit later, in the church, but now's the time, and you get the honors. Please, baptize my son."

Rorer stepped forward from the back of the crowd and bowed toward Martin and Katherine. Then, without a word, he moved to the side of the bed and gently lifted the tiny infant into his arms. He smiled down at little Johannes as he dipped his hand in the basin by the bed, raising a small pool of pure water in his palm. He held it just a few inches above the baby's head and tipped the water out in a slow, practiced stream. "Johannes Luther," he said, "I baptize you in the name of the Father and of the Son and of the Holy Spirit. Amen." And he kissed the child gently on his forehead.

Luther stepped forward and took his son and held him up for all the soldiers of the duke to see. He kept his eyes on them as he spoke to his son. "Johannes," he said, "you have just won your first disputation, and you aren't even an hour old. Though I will admit the quality of your opposition was wanting." With that, he handed the child back to Katherine and, without further resistance from the soldiers, ushered everyone from the room.

Jonathan was the last out the door. He held Elizabeth's hand. Martin stopped them just shy of the door and pulled them back inside. Jonathan started to speak, "Father, Elizabeth and I..."

"I know," Luther said. "Justus said you would be leaving for Pforzheim, then on to Rosheim to see Elizabeth's parents. I understand you have to return some missing coins."

"We do, Father," Jonathan said, smiling.

"Mmm," Luther nodded. "Elizabeth's dowry was in that lot as well, wasn't it?"

"Yes, but her father could decide to keep it under the circumstances, me being a Gentile and all."

Luther shrugged. "Perhaps. But I doubt it," he said with a smile. He took a deep breath as he turned to face Elizabeth. When he spoke, his voice nearly broke. "I owe you a debt of thanks, Elizabeth. Kate and I both." He cleared his throat. "Now hear me, young lady," he said. "This isn't an easy trip you are about to make. Your father isn't going to take this well. You know that. But his joy in seeing you again will go far to ease the pain he will feel for your taking a Gentile for a husband. The money should help too, I would think. And Josel von Gershom has a reputation as a just and a good man. Still, this will be a difficult bridge for him to cross."

"As it was for you, Father," Jonathan said softly.

"As it *is* for me, Jonathan," Luther said, opening the door. "One last word. Seeing as how you didn't think it prudent to ask me to marry you, you needn't think you avoided my commission. Now I understand that you are twenty-seven years of age, correct?"

"Twenty-eight, sir. After next month," Jonathan said.

"Ah! Even better. The age of twenty-eight is, of course, the age of promises."

Jonathan smiled, recalling the first time he had heard those words.

Luther continued, "Therefore, I, Martin Luther, commission you, Jonathan Reuchlin, as the spiritual head of your home, to keep the following promise: to love your wife as Christ loves the church. Love her tomorrow, and every day after for the rest of your life or until the Lord comes back. Agreed?"

Jonathan nodded and bowed. "Agreed, sir," he said.

Martin put his arm around him and spoke softly. "You're a good man, Jonathan. And you'll make a fine husband and father, I know. Now go. Kate and I will pray for you."

They embraced one last time. Elizabeth kissed Katherine and little Hans good-bye, and they walked out the door of the bedroom, then out the main door of the Black Cloister to the stables where Jonathan had asked the hostler to prepare the wagon. Jonathan and Elizabeth piled everything they had into one corner of the wagon, including the heavy black bag. Jonathan said a short prayer for their safety, then he slapped the reins on Molly's back, and they were off for a new life.

The downpour the night before had washed the air clean and fresh. A white sun brightened the clear summer skies, and a gentle breeze whispered across the plain. It wasn't the end of storms, but there was in this brief respite, in this slow-paced wagon, the promise of brighter days to come.

Epilogue

"Father?" Alaric, a student in his second year at Erfurt, tapped on the prior's door again. No response. "Father Winand?" He started to knock again and noticed the door was slightly ajar. He pushed and it swung back with a loud creak. Father Winand was sound asleep, his head tilted back and a letter in his hand. Alaric was disappointed. Winand had promised to unlock the ancient manuscript case in the scriptorium to let him study a first-generation copy of one of Aristotle's works. Alaric had earned the privilege through a lot of hard work and countless hours of Greek studies. Unfortunately, he had to sweep the dining hall that night, and it had taken him far longer than he had intended. He would simply have to come again some other night. He started to close the door when he noticed Winand's keys lying on the desk.

Alaric was sure he wouldn't mind if he borrowed them to study the manuscript. With only the slightest twinge of guilt, he picked them up quietly, slipped out of the room, then padded slowly down the darkened halls to the scriptorium. He pushed the door open and entered the room, then stepped past two shelves of manuscripts to the solid oak manuscript case that always remained locked.

Placing the candleholder on the floor, he found the smallest key on the iron ring and inserted it into the lock. The doors swung open on silent hinges to reveal a collection of ancient manuscripts so precious, so delicate, that only the most revered scholars and certain select students were allowed to handle them. It was an honor just to view them.

Alaric held the candle close and scanned the titles until he found the bound edition of Aristotle's *De Caelum*. He knelt and carefully began to pull the volume from its place. Then he noticed the book resting next to it. The large, loosely bound manuscript had tattered pages, its edges torn and burned. He pushed the Aristotle volume back and gently lifted the other much heftier manuscript out to view.

The scriptorium was stuffy, so he carried it to a side table, near a window that he opened to let in the fresh night breeze. The moon was full and shining brightly. A lovely night for discovering something new in something old. He placed the candle to one side, and sat on the wooden stool. Then, by the light of the full moon, he opened the book.

And he began to read…

Author's Notes

For the rest of his life, Luther was at the center of controversy, though the bloodiest part of the Reformation conflict ended with the peasants' rebellion in 1525. Serious illness started to plague him the same year Johannes was born (1526) and would remain a painful reminder of his all-too-human frailty for the rest of his life.

Five more children were born to Martin and Katherine. Elizabeth (December 10, 1527), Magdalena (December 17, 1529), Martin (November 9, 1531), Paul (January 28, 1533), and Margaretha (December 17, 1534). Little Elizabeth, born the next year, died at only eight months. While Martin loved all his children with a tenderness that, at first blush, would seem foreign to those who knew him only by his books and pamphlets, he held a special place in his heart for his daughter Magdalena. Her untimely death September 20, 1542—just three months shy of her thirteenth birthday—left both Martin and Katherine grieving and deeply depressed.

Still, given the abominable hygiene and primitive medical care available at the time, Luther and his children lived to fairly remarkable ages. Consider: During this slice of history fully half the European population died before they were thirty; a man in his early fifties often had the white hair and stooped shoulders of an eighty-year-old today; a young girl's life expectancy was only twenty-four. It is remarkable indeed that all of Martin's and Katherine's children, with the exceptions of Elizabeth and Magdalena, lived past thirty. Johannes lived to be almost forty-nine. Martin Jr. was thirty-two when he died. Paul was nearly sixty, and death claimed Margaretha at thirty-five.

After the dust had settled from the Peasants' War, the battles moved largely to the churches and halls of academia and were pitched with words, rather than with bullets and sabers. Luther's cannon was the printing press. His words and the words of the Bible, which he translated into the German vernacular, reached the laity in a volley of ideas so revolutionary, and so well aimed, that they shattered the chains that had bound them in ignorance and superstition. Of course, the nobles and ecclesiastics whose abuse of power had resulted in generations of spiritual bondage decried Luther's appeal to the common people. To that charge, one of Luther's pamphleteers replied,

> You subtle fools. I tell you there are now at Nuremberg, Augsburg, Ulm, in Switzerland, and in Saxony wives, maidens, and nobles, and princes such as the Elector of Saxony, who know more about the Bible than all the schools of Paris and Cologne and all the papists in the world.[1]

The Reformation swept through Saxony so that by 1527 electoral Saxony (where Luther lived) could be considered evangelical. Luther continued to fight for the truth as he understood it in Scripture. He believed passionately in the real presence of the body and blood of the Savior in the Eucharist. His small and large catechisms, designed for the church but also as guides for fathers to use in the home, appeared in 1529, and the first edition of his translation of the whole Bible in 1534.

The famed Augsburg Confession, drafted in June of 1530 by Philip Melanchthon and enthusiastically endorsed by Luther, marked the finest and the most moderate statement of Protestant evangelical faith to that point. The Confession served to draw the formal lines of difference between Roman Catholicism and Lutheran theology in unmistak-

---

[1] Otto Clemen, *Flugschriften aus den ersten Jahren der Reformation*, II, 172.

ably clear terms. Emperor Charles V didn't like the Lutheran Confession. He threatened to purge Europe of its Lutheran influence (he wouldn't hesitate to use the sword against clerics as well as nobles) unless they submitted to the historical confession of the Roman See. Luther, who had been hiding in the Coburg Castle during the Diet of Augsburg, appealed to the moderate faction of the Roman leadership. He asked his old opponent, Albert, Archbishop of Mainz, to counsel the Diet to pursue peace. Thankfully, the Diet took Albert's advice and spared Europe another bloodbath.

While serving as dean of the theological faculty at Wittenberg (1535-1546), Luther continued to dispute fellow theologians on the nature of man, on justification (1536), on the meaning of biblical law (1537-1540), and on the nature of the sacraments (1544). Through it all, his mercurial temperament would produce a family pulsating with life and laughter, and a theology that incited and then defined a reformation of doctrine unprecedented in the history of the church. Not the least of Luther's bequests was a catalogue of hymns, many of which he wrote with a casual eloquence that left other composers aching for his unique blend of theological sophistication and memorable music.

Luther's reformation of the liturgy was more than merely a logical by-product of his theology. It was a studied and passionate response to his beloved Latin Mass. Martin wanted the liturgy to reflect the beauty of God in music that would involve the congregation as participants rather than spectators. His influence on the liturgy was greatest in his reform of congregational song. His emphasis on the priesthood of all believers found practical expression in the local assembly where everyone in the congregation sang. Under Luther's guidance the monotone of the Gregorian chant assumed the multifaceted colors of Netherlandish polyphonic chorale. That he would take such pains with what many regarded as tangential (at best) to the *real* enterprise of worship (preaching, of course) only served to enhance his image in the minds of the congregation.

His exploits achieved a mythical status that would have been relegated to the dusty shelves of folklore were it not for the volumes of notes, quotes, sermons, tracts, pamphlets, treatises, and letters. Many of these flowed not only from Luther's pen but from a variety of unimpeachable sources that lend credence to this remarkable man's life and work. Images of Luther have survived in the black-and-white pamphlets of the day, the pictures depicting in their stark contrasts the differences between Luther's emerging theology and the centuries-old theology of the Roman See. Here were scenes embossed with the exaggerated lines of a sixteenth-century woodcutter, scenes so overwrought with celestial conflict that there can be no doubt of the impact of Lutheran thought on the world of the sixteenth century.

Here, the reader of Luther may well imagine him as the Saxon reincarnation of the ancient British King of Summer. Luther Pendragon must have been Martin's real name. He did, after all, extract the sword of the Living Word from the Roman stone where it had remained embedded for centuries. And he used that sword to set men free. The image of Luther as hero is a venerable part of the Protestant tradition. He will continue to occupy a place of honor in the gallery of those courageous souls who entered the arena ready to die fighting for the truth.

But Luther is not unassailable. The romanticized enameled portrait reveals cracks under the glare of critical lights. His soaring intellect was often more than equally matched by the depth of his baser passions. He had a volatile temper and an acerbic wit which, when laced with scatological language (even in a public forum), often offended more than it inspired. Few could match his grasp of theological issues, and fewer still could withstand the mature Luther in the pitched battle of public debate.

In his later years there emerged, alongside his prowess in the pulpit and at the lectern, a meanness of spirit, especially in his treatment of the Jews. The last sermon he preached took place in Eisleben on February 14 and was entitled "Against the Jews." Certainly his constant bouts with physical ailment and depression, not to mention the continual threat on his life from his enemies, played a large part in his irritability.

But those irritants infected his spirit so that some of his decisions lacked the wisdom and compassion that should have marked his final years.

One example will illustrate how far his passions had gained ascendancy over his nobler spirit. In 1536 Elector John Frederick issued a decree banning Jews from his territory, forbidding even their passage through Electoral Saxony. Luther should have taken a principled stand as he had on so many previous occasions.

He allowed his personal frustration with his own failed efforts at Jewish evangelism to dictate his response. In 1537 he rejected Josel von Gershom's plea that he intervene to avert the slaughter and displacement of thousands of Jews. Luther's intervention in this regional dispute would have built the bridge to the Jewish community throughout all Europe—a bridge he had wanted for many years. But his mind was made up. Once Luther had decided someone was God's enemy, that man was Luther's enemy for life. At least that was his public position. In fact, the inverse of that argument was probably at least as true: once Luther had decided someone was *his* enemy, then that made that person *God's* enemy as well. Either way, he rationalized his hatred and mistreatment of the Jews and of anyone else who opposed him.

But even in the light of these obvious flaws, what emerges in the end is a man of incredibly diverse talents and discipline. A man who practiced his faith as well as he knew how. The great Luther biographer, Roland Bainton, sums up the overall impact of the work of his later years:

> If in his polemical tracts he was at times savage and
> coarse, in the works which constitute the real marrow of
> his life's endeavor he grew constantly in maturity and
> artistic creativity. The biblical translation was improved
> to the very end. The sermons and the biblical commen-
> taries reached superb heights.[2]

---

[2] Roland Bainton, *Here I Stand: A Life of Martin Luther* (New York: Penguin Books, 1995), 300.

In February 1546, Martin made a trip (his third) to Eisleben to mediate a quarrel between two brothers who were counts in Mansfeld. The negotiations took two weeks and resulted in a brief reconciliation in which Luther rejoiced. He had looked forward to returning to Wittenberg, but it wasn't to be. He retired on the evening of February 17, feeling badly, and about three o'clock on the following morning, Martin Luther died at the age of sixty-two years and one hundred days.

His longtime friend Justus Jonas carefully recorded his last hours. The news of his death reached Wittenberg the next day, catching the town and Philip Melanchthon totally unprepared. Melanchthon was busy teaching his early morning class on Romans when the messenger entered with the news. Melanchthon was overcome with grief as he spoke to his class in a trembling voice, "Alas, *obiit auriga et currus* Israel." ("Alas, the charioteer of Israel has fallen!")

After Luther's death there was no reason to suspect that the Reformation he had engendered had any hope of survival. The Roman Catholic Church had, on the wave of the papal Council of Trent in 1545, launched a decisive Counter Reformation that would regather much of Europe into the papal fold. Just a few months after Luther's death, Emperor Charles V dealt a near deathblow to the Protestant Schmalkaldic League, a military alliance of Protestant states under the leadership of Elector John Frederick of Saxony. Charles installed Duke Maurice, the man who had betrayed the Protestant cause and almost single-handedly delivered the League into the hands of the emperor, as the new Elector of Saxony.

Maurice, however, was to prove the strange savior of the Reformation. He double-crossed the emperor just a few years later (1552, which also happened to be the same year Katherine Luther died), forcing him to flee Innsbruck. The result was the emperor's signing a treaty at the Diet of Augsburg in 1555, effectively guaranteeing the right of each sovereign to decide the religion of his subjects.

So Luther and his doctrines weathered the storm, and we wonder at how one man could be so strong, so courageous as to stand against an implacable enemy of such incalculable proportions. The answer is ultimately as complex as Luther himself and the forces that combined to fashion him. But at his core was a simple truth: He was a man of prayer. Like the tree in Psalm 1, the Lord had planted Martin Luther beside a spiritual river from which he drew sustenance. We wish we knew more of the particular character of his private devotions. But he managed to safeguard this singularly spiritual discipline from the intrusion of those who recorded virtually every other movement he made. The intimacy he enjoyed with his heavenly Father, as well as the terrors he endured during those storied battles on his knees, will remain secretly tucked away in that shadowed niche of his life.

The rest is there for us to examine—to appreciate his strengths, to acknowledge his weaknesses, and to emulate his unshakable faith in the Lord Jesus Christ, our anchor in the storm.

Glossary

abbot—The superior or governor of an abbey or monastery

archbishop—A bishop of the highest rank, heading an archdiocese or a province

breviary—A book containing the hymns, offices, and prayers for the canonical hours

brother—A member of a men's religious order who is not in holy orders but engages in the work of the order

canonical hours—The times of day at which canon law prescribes certain prayers to be said. These times are matins with lauds, prime, tierce, sext, nones, vespers, and compline.

cardinal—A high church official, ranking just below the pope, who has been appointed by a pope to membership in the College of Cardinals

compline—The last of the seven canonical hours, recited or sung just before retiring

convent—1. A community, especially of nuns, bound by vows to a religious life under a superior. 2. The building or buildings occupied by such a community

decretal—A decree, especially a papal letter giving a decision on a point or question of canon law

diet—A formal general assembly of the princes or estates of the Holy Roman Empire

elector—One of the German princes of the Holy Roman Empire entitled to elect the emperor

ex cathedra—With the authority derived from one's office or position; from Latin *ex* ("from") and *cathedra* ("chair")

Host—The bread of the Eucharist

indulgence—The remission of temporal punishment still due for a sin that has been sacramentally absolved

lauds—The service of prayers following the matins and constituting with them the first of the seven canonical hours

matins—The first of the seven canonical hours, traditionally beginning at midnight or 2 A.M. but often begun at sunrise

monastery—A community of persons, especially monks, bound by vows to a religious life and often living in partial or complete seclusion

monk—A man who is a member of a brotherhood living in a monastery and devoted to a discipline prescribed by his order

nones—The fifth of the seven canonical hours, usually begun the ninth hour after sunrise; no longer in liturgical use

nun—A woman who belongs to a religious order or congregation devoted to active service or meditation, living under vows of poverty, chastity, and obedience

paten—A plate, usually of gold or silver, that is used to hold the Host during the celebration of the Eucharist

pope—The bishop of Rome and head of the Roman Catholic Church on earth

prelate—A high-ranking member of the clergy, especially a bishop

prime—The second of the seven canonical hours, begun the first hour of the day or 6 A.M.; no longer in ecclesiastical use

prior—A monastic officer in charge of a priory or ranking next below the abbot of an abbey

purgatory—A state in which the souls of those who have died in grace must expiate their sins

rump—A legislature having only a small part of its original membership and therefore being unrepresentative or lacking in authority

scriptorium—A room in a monastery set aside for the copying, writing, or illuminating of manuscripts and records

sext—The fourth of the seven canonical hours, usually the sixth hour, or noon

sister—A member of a religious order of women; a nun

tierce—The third of the seven canonical hours, usually the third hour after sunrise; no longer in liturgical use

vespers—The sixth of the seven canonical hours

ABOUT THE AUTHOR

REG GRANT is professor of pastor ministries at Dallas Theological Seminary, where he teaches courses in preaching, drama, voice, creative writing, and radio production. He serves on the advisory boards for Nest Entertainment, the Dallas Ft. Worth Heritage, and Visual Entertainment, Inc. He has authored and coauthored several books and articles and has written, produced, and acted for radio, television, theater, and film. Several of his films have won major film festival awards; two have been voted "Top Educational Film in America" by *Booklist;* three have been nominated for Emmy awards; and two have won an Emmy. Grant currently hosts several national and international radio programs. He and his wife, Lauren, are the parents of three children and live in Dallas, Texas.

To learn more about Reg and his books, look for his Web site: www.RegGrant.com.